I0736083

FORGED by Sacrifice

LJ EVANS

Published by LJ Evans Books

www.ljevansbooks.com

Cover Design: © LJ Evans Books
Cover Images: © Unsplash kiwihug and Deposit Photos ninanaina / MaslovaLarisa / Olga_Bonitas / Marta_Lemaris
Developmental & Line Editing: Evans Editing
Copy Editing: Jenn Lockwood Editing Services
Proofing: Karen Hrdlicka

Library of Congress Cataloging-in-Publications in process.
ISBN: 978-1-962499-03-3

Printed in the United States

Playlist

Listen now on Spotify: https://spoti.fi/2LxdmUO

FORGED
by sacrifice

LJ EVANS

Hopeless Romantic - Meghan Trainor
Broken & Beautiful - Kelly Clarkson
A Good Night - John Legend & BloodPop
Can I Have a Kiss - Kelly Clarkson
Simple Man - Lynyrd Skynyrd
Church - Aly & AJ
Change - Christina Aguilera
You Say - Lauren Daigle
High Hopes - Panic! At the Disco
What If I Never Get Over You - Lady Antebellum
Why Georgia - John Mayer
Walk Me Home - P!nk
Don't Go Changing - Aly & AJ
Hurt - Lady Antebellum
More Than Friends - Jason Mraz w/ Meghan Trainor
Make Me Like You - Gwen Stefani
New Day - Robbie Seay Band
Butterflies - Kasey Musgraves
If Our Love Is Wrong - Calum Scott
Dress - Taylor Swift
Save Room - John Legend
Hurts 2B Human - P!nk w/ Khalid
Lay It All on Me - Rudimental w/ Ed Sheeran
Love Me Anyway - P!nk w/ Chris Stapleton
If You're Gone - Matchbox Twenty
Trying Not to Love You - Nickelback
Hold Me While You Wait - Lewis Capalid
Lay Me Down - Sam Smith w/ John Legend
Bruises - Lewis Capaldi
Like I'm Gonna Lose You - Meghan Trainor
You Are the Reason - Calum Scott w/ Leona Lewis

Message from the Author

Thank you for taking the time to read my story. "Bruises" by Lewis Capaldi inspired this story. Writing realistic characters and their path to their happily ever after is what writing is all about for me.

As in all my books, Mac and Georgie have to learn how to live their lives resiliently. They find a way to get through life's challenges with grace, humility, strength, and—most importantly—LOVE. I hope you feel it in my words.

I'm supposed to give you a long list of my social media sites, places to leave reviews, and a laundry list of my other books at this point, but the truth is, I don't want to give you those things… not yet.

I'd rather you get to reading. I'd rather you fall in love with my characters, their world, and the love, laughter, and *family* that is held within these pages.

I'll touch base with you again AFTER you've read the story…

Happy Reading!
L J Evans

Dedication

To Steve for living this challenging last year with me, and for never letting me give up on myself or this writer journey.

To all the members of LJ's Music & Stories who make me feel like a rock star every day.

To all the readers who have read and shared their love of my books with the world.

Thank you.

Chapter One

Mac

HOPELESS ROMANTIC
Performed by Meghan Trainor

The sun was afterburner hot when I tied off and locked up my boat before stepping onto the dock in Rockport. The humidity hit me hard after being on the water for a few weeks. It made me question whether I really wanted to spend time on land or not. But the solitude of my boat had reached its limit for me.

Besides, I hadn't been able to see both my best friends at the same time in a couple of years. I squinted at the road, waiting for Eli's black pickup to come barreling down, while I thought about how long it had actually been since we'd all been together. I'd seen Eli, and I'd seen Truck, and they'd seen each other, but it hadn't been the three of us since Ava, Eli's fiancée, had graduated from Juilliard. That was over two years ago, so this time together was both rare and much needed.

Since Eli had left the military, I'd been able to see him the most. With Truck in the Coast Guard and me in the Navy, we'd been at the beck and call of our leaders and the imbeciles who were running the country. I mentally checked myself. I had to lose that kind of talk about our leaders if I was really going to be one of them in the near future.

Turning on my phone, it blew up with texts and messages received since I'd last had a signal.

NASH: Macauley?!

ME: Just got into port. What's up?

NASH: Who the fuck did you leave in charge?

*ME: ** laughing emoji ** Are you making friends already?*

NASH: Seriously, the intel reports we're getting are crap.

Leaving the Navy and my work at the Department of Defense behind had been harder than I'd thought it would be. I was leaving a family. Some of them were actual blood, like my dad, and some of them were men who'd become brothers through bloodshed, like Nash and Darren. People who had depended on me to make sure no one came home in a body bag.

ME: I can talk to Dad, see what's going on.

NASH: Or just come back.

But Nash knew I couldn't. Not if I was going to be true to everything I'd worked for since childhood. I didn't know what else to say to him, so I opened the next round of messages from my sister, Dani.

Dani and I were a mere twelve months apart. I didn't even want to think about what that meant for how often my parents had been having sex in order for that to happen. But because of the small age gap, Dani and I were the closest of our siblings. Unfortunately, she was older and liked to remind me of it every single time we met, as if the twelve months had somehow endowed her with a lifetime more of experiences. I'd wanted her to come on vacation with me, but she'd said there was too much to do before Congress was out of session for the summer break.

BRAT: When are you starting again?

ME: Rag, rag, rag. Hello to you too, Gooberpants.

*BRAT: ** one fingered emoji ** I'm drowning in reports that I need you to look at.*

ME: I'll be back by the end of the month.

BRAT: I swear if you're later than that, I'll send an assassin after you.

ME: I think Nash is ready to do that for free.

BRAT: He's still pissed you left?

I didn't respond because I didn't need to. Dani knew everything, including how I felt.

BRAT: You have a right to go after your

dreams.

ME: I know. I just wish I didn't feel like I was letting people down by doing it.

*BRAT: ** Whining GIF ***

ME: Just for that, I may be late getting back to D.C.

BRAT: Did you miss the part about the hit man?

I was saved from further discussion about both my past and my future as Eli's pickup turned onto the street.

ME: Gotta go. Eli's here.

BRAT: Well, have fun for the both of us, and give Ava, Eli, and Truck hugs for me.

ME: Will do.

When Eli pulled up to the curb, I flung my bag into the bed before climbing into the air-conditioned cab.

"Mac!" Eli greeted, reaching across the console to give me a half-hug.

We were men. Military men. But we'd never been afraid to hug each other. We both had known, for a lot of years, that it could be the last time we were ever able to do it. Now that we had both lost our military titles—mine by choice, his by bad luck—we weren't going to be changing how we greeted each other.

"Thought you'd never get here. F—forking

humidity is enough to roll me over," I said.

Eli smirked. "Forking?"

"Really trying hard to get this political lingo down."

He laughed. I liked that he laughed so much these days. Since Eli and Ava had gotten together, he was almost jovial. It wasn't the only change. He was still as muscled as he'd been in the Coast Guard, but he'd lost the buzz cut. Instead, his hair was almost always long enough to see the dark color that was just a shade lighter than mine.

Mine was all black. It made my blue eyes stand out, and that was okay by me. My looks had always helped me with the ladies. Not as many as most people thought I'd scored, but I'd definitely sown my wild oats. I was tired of sowing oats.

Eli put the truck in gear and headed out of town to the beach house he and Ava had been living in since they'd come back to Texas.

"When's Truck getting here?" I asked.

"Friday," Eli answered.

"Did he say whether he was signing his re-enlistment contract or not?"

"What's with the twenty questions about Truck? You two not speaking or something?" Eli asked.

I chuckled. "No, asswipe. I've been on a boat in the middle of the ocean for two weeks. No signal."

"The senator from Delaware was accused of using the word asswipe when speaking to his aide," he said in a fake TV newscaster voice.

I flipped him off.

"I don't think Truck will ever leave the Coast Guard as long as he has a choice," Eli said.

That had been Eli's plan, too. Never to leave. Until a harbor seal had crashed into him and his knee and changed everything he'd ever wanted. I crossed my fingers and begged my mom's God that nothing like that ever crashed into my plans. I didn't know what I'd do if I got sideswiped from my course of action.

"You all set to work for your grandfather?" Eli asked.

I nodded. Between Granddad and Dani, I had a job working in Senator Guy Matherton's office. He was from my home state, and Granddad was his chief of staff. Dani had been working there since her own college days. It was going to be a challenge to prove it wasn't pure nepotism that had gotten me the job.

"I haven't signed on the dotted line yet because I'm waiting for the Navy paperwork to go through, but Granddad's already got a desk for me next to Dani's."

Eli grinned. "That oughtta be fun."

We pulled into the beach house. It was still the teal color we'd painted it six years ago. On the wraparound porch, stood a woman way too tall to be Ava. Not that Ava was short, but this woman was close to six-foot, easy. My heart leaped into my throat at the sight of her. Georgie. I'd had a hell of a time getting her out of my head after we'd met in New York City two years ago. It had taken me almost a year not to compare every woman I met to her. You would have thought that she and I had had earth-shattering sex with the way my body had seemed to pine after her.

But none of that was true. Georgie had barely given

me a second glance when I'd met her, and it wasn't the cold shoulder that had had me yearning for her. It had just been her. Tall. Stunning. Confident. She'd hit me like a meteor falling from the sky. The first time we'd met, she'd had short hair with purple spikes and eyes that were pale and lavender-tinted. The second time we'd met, her eyes had been such a deep blue that they'd almost been the twilight, and her hair had been longer and as dark as a black cat. She was as lean and coiled as a cat, too. I'd been starstruck and stuttered like a teen with a wet dream. It had been embarrassing.

On the deck, she stood tall and slim like before with her dark hair blowing in the breeze. I instantly wanted to know what color she was sporting in her eyes. My entire body leaned forward as if just waiting to feel the tension and desire that I'd felt each time I'd met her.

"What's she doing here?" I asked, trying to mask the longing I felt with nonchalance—and failing.

Eli looked at me over the top of his dark sunglasses. "Be nice."

"I'm always nice."

"Not that kind of nice, douchebag. She's one of Ava's best friends. We don't need you messing with her."

"I won't mess with her. I'm just surprised she's here. I didn't expect it."

"We didn't either. She called a couple weeks ago and then showed up all waiflike, needing a place to stay while she got some things sorted."

"Waiflike?" I teased.

"Don't start with me."

I opened the door and got out. When I risked looking back at the porch, Georgie was gone, and I felt oddly disappointed even though I knew she'd still be inside when we got to the top of the stairs.

I grabbed my bag and followed Eli into the house. I'd barely taken two steps through the door when Ava practically assaulted me with a hug that felt like a gorilla jumping into your arms. Eli had told me once that she'd hardly ever been hugged as a kid. Nowadays, it was like she was making up for it. I squeezed her back.

"Mac!" Her husky voice was always a surprise, even after all the years I'd known her. You expected a vibrant woman like Ava to have a littler voice, almost giddy like her energy levels.

"How the hel—heck are you?" I asked.

"I'm really good. Glad that everyone is going to be here for the Fourth of July."

"Are we partying here or at the bar?"

After she'd graduated from Juilliard, Ava had bought a bar in downtown Rockport called The Salty Dog. It had taken the last of her inheritance, from what I gathered from Eli. But with the money she had coming in from her royalty checks for the songs she wrote for the chart-topping sensation Brady O'Neil, I didn't think she needed to work at all. She just liked to keep busy. I couldn't imagine Ava ever standing still for too long.

"We're still working it all out. We've got time," Ava said and stepped back. Eli's hand went immediately to hers, like they had been apart for days instead of the minutes it had taken him to come get me at the marina.

"I can't believe you sailed all the way from D.C. by yourself. Isn't that some huge nautical no-no?" Ava asked, pulling Eli with her into the kitchen where they'd obviously been working on some kind of Mexican dish. A pitcher of margaritas stood, sparkling with condensation.

I set my bag down and risked looking around the open living space. No Georgie. My stomach lurched again. I sat down at the counter and poured myself a glass, hoping it would do something to calm the insane patter of my heart. Ridiculous. In the war room, I'd been in situations that would have made most people keel over, and yet here I was, wanting to hurl at the thought of seeing one woman again.

"Sailing by yourself isn't very smart," I replied with a shrug. "If something happens to you, who the hel—heck is going to pull you from the dink? But Dani didn't want to leave D.C. for three weeks, and all my other sailing partners were otherwise engaged." I waved the glass toward Eli.

"Wait. You asked Eli to join you?" Ava asked, knife halting midway through her murdering of a tomato.

"I did."

Ava turned to him, knife coming dangerously close to his shoulder. "You didn't tell me Mac asked you to come with him."

"Seemed ridiculous for me to fly to D.C. only to sail back to my own damn house."

"That isn't what he told me." I winked at Ava.

"What did he tell you?"

"He was darn sure not going to use up weeks of vacation time without you."

"Eli!"

Eli grabbed the knife from her, set it down on the counter, and wrapped her in a hug.

"I'm saving it for our honeymoon." He kissed her, and she melted. I normally would have harassed them both to no end, but these days, I always seemed to be eyeing the happy couples in my life with a level of longing that I'd never felt before.

"We're not getting married until October," Ava said.

"And I have honeymoon plans."

"You do? Don't you think I should know these things? I'll have to arrange for Andy and Lacey to cover the bar."

"Already done," he told her.

"You're impossible," she snipped back, but it was with a smile on her face.

Movement at the corner of my eye brought me to my feet. Georgie. My breath got stuck somewhere between my lungs and my throat as I got a better look at her. Her hair was dark, but more espresso-colored than black, and she had a single white streak about the width of my pinkie finger going through it. Her hair hung down around her shoulders in a beach-tousled look. Her eyes were green today, like a green-apple kind of green. It matched the flowered, off-the-shoulder, floaty dress she wore, showcasing sun-kissed skin and baring cleavage that made it hard for me to look away.

I loved that I didn't have to almost bend myself in half to look down at her. I was six-four. And most of the time, the girls I was with were almost a foot shorter than me, which complicated anything that happened between our bodies. Georgie was—at the most—five inches shorter, standing there barefoot.

I was staring. I knew I was staring, but I couldn't help it. I'd had this reaction every damn time I'd met her. Silent. Stalker-like. It was ridiculous.

"Mac, do you remember my friend Georgie from New York?" Ava asked.

"I do," I managed to breathe out, holding out my hand. "It's a pleasure to see you again."

Georgie smiled, and I swear to God, there were thunderclouds rolling somewhere when she did it, because that smile was one you were unable to ignore, just like a thunderstorm. The smile lit up her face that was all graceful lines. Smooth. Silky.

"You're the one that I wasn't supposed to be the same again after meeting, right?" Georgie's voice was light. Graceful, just like her, but infused with a confidence that spoke of life and experience. What hit me harder than her voice was the fact that she remembered our initial meeting, almost word for word, as much as I did.

She put her long-fingered hand into mine, and I shook it, trying desperately not to run my fingers along the smooth palm and embarrass myself. If her voice had been a thundercloud, her touch was lightning. The kind that left your heart stopped and your skin tingling.

"And have you?" I asked.

She frowned. "Have I?"

"Been the same?"

She laughed, running a hand through her hair, but didn't answer. I wanted to think that it was a good sign. That somewhere behind those color-changing eyes, she was as stunned and as glad to see me as I was to see her.

Chapter Two

Georgie

BROKEN & BEAUTIFUL
Performed by Kelly Clarkson

Seeing Mac-Macauley after two years of not seeing him, hit me hard. Almost as hard as when I'd seen him the first two times back in New York City. He was a tall, dark-haired beauty. The kind of gorgeousness that would have fit right in with my boyfriend—or rather, ex-boyfriend—Jared, and all his male model friends. It would also have fit right in with the hotshot finance guys who also frequented my salon and were harder to shake off than the ego-filled models.

Mac was several inches taller than Jared and much broader.

His blue eyes flashed at me, and all I could see were warning signs. Signs that said to stay away even though my body almost vibrated with energy when he shook my hand. I'd learned a long time ago not to trust my senses. Bodies were notorious for leading you astray. And I didn't need astray right now.

I sat down at the bar, turning away from him. He

joined me on the barstool next to mine, our shoulders almost touching. The air flitting between our bodies was like when I'd done an electrical current project in high school. You could almost see the zaps of light. Zaps that I'd never had to deal with when I'd been with Jared. Jared had been smooth, sexy, calming. This was energy that spoke of riling things up versus calming them down.

"Can I help with something?" I asked Ava.

She and Eli both shook their heads. "No, we got it. The one drawback of this house is that the kitchen isn't as large as it could be. Two cooks are about all it can take."

"Are you sure you can qualify as a cook?" Mac asked Ava, and I wanted to be offended for my friend, but she just smiled at the virtual magnetic field sitting next to me.

"I can cook," she said.

"But you're slaughtering those poor tomatoes."

Ava laughed—something she did so much more now than when I'd known her in New York. Eli had brought joy to her life. Filled her. It made me happy at the same time I knew I was never going to want that—a man filling my world. A partner like Jared had been perfect for me, moving side by side when needed, going it alone when needed, too. Even though we'd ended things, it hadn't broken either of us.

"I'm dicing them," Ava said.

"Is that what you call it?" Mac asked her.

She handed him the knife across the counter. He put down the margarita he'd been drinking, took the knife, and pulled the cutting board she'd been using closer to him. He started cutting the tomatoes with a much gentler hand than I'd expected, and the cuts he made were almost TV-cooking-show perfect.

It surprised me that he had such a gentle touch.

I reached for the margarita pitcher because I certainly needed a drink.

"So, Georgie, what brings you to Texas?" Mac asked, his gaze flitting toward me and away, as if he was as unsure about me as I was of him.

"I'll tell if you tell," I said, winking at him.

He smiled. "I'm here on vacation. Between gigs."

"Me, too."

He stopped his slicing to look over at me, surprise on his face. "What happened to the salon?"

"Sold it," I responded, and even though selling the shop was what I'd wanted, my chest pulled tight, and tears hit my eyes. It had been incredibly difficult to leave behind my grandmother's legacy. Leave behind everything I'd known with her. The people. The shop. Our home. She would have wanted it for me as much as I wanted it for myself, but it didn't make it easier.

"Wow. I don't know what to say to that." Mac's words drew me back from New York City and my old life to the present. He smiled and said, "I mean, I could ask a gazillion invasive questions, but I have a feeling Ava or Eli might gut me in my sleep if I did."

I laughed like he'd expected me to, and when I did, his smile increased, making thoughts of Jared and the salon trail into the sunset.

"Just ignore him. He has no idea what personal boundaries are," Eli said from where he was finishing up the spices on the meat he was going to grill for the carne asada tacos they were making.

"Look. You grow up with a father in the Navy, a grandfather in politics, and three older sisters, and you realize there is no such thing as personal boundaries," Mac responded with a shrug that caused his shoulder to brush against mine, increasing the awareness that filtered through me.

Mac was not only tall, but he was also a wall of muscle—like a pro football player. Muscles on top of muscles, but not in a way that made you think Blowfish. Instead, it was tantalizing. His tight T-shirt did nothing to hide any of the contours of his body.

With the tomatoes done, he pushed the cutting board back toward Ava and got up to wash his hands at the sink. Eli headed for the porch and the barbecue pit, and Mac tagged along with him. I took a gulp of the margarita as I watched the two men banter back and forth on the patio.

Ava joined me, taking up the barstool Mac had vacated.

"He's gorgeous but all swag-and-bag," Ava said.

I felt my cheeks heat slightly at being caught gazing at them and turned to her. "Thanks for the warning, but I'm not really into anything more than swag-and-bag."

Ava smiled at me. "Well then, swag away." She waved a hand toward the patio.

"No," I chuckled. "That isn't what I meant. I mean…he'd probably totally be worth a few nights of hot, sweaty, vacation sex, but I'm definitely not looking for even that right now. Besides, I wouldn't sleep with your and Eli's friend. It would be…"

"Awkward," Ava said just as I finished with, "Ill-advised."

"I plan on being around for your wedding, and I definitely don't want any weirdness to occur between him and me that would leach into that."

"So, sweaty sex was definitely on your mind, though." Ava grinned at me.

"Well, just look at him."

"You've been around a lot of sexy men with Jared and all those fashion gurus in New York. I'm sure Mac's like, what, a seven or eight, out of all those men?"

We both stared out at the guys on the patio. They looked in and caught us staring. Eli smiled at Ava. Mac just stared period.

"I'd say he's pretty close to a ten."

"Really?" Ava sounded surprised. "I feel like Eli is a twenty, and there's nothing to compare to that."

"That's only because you can't be objective with all that love potion flowing through you."

"Okay, what would you rate, Eli?"

"An eight or a nine."

"That was fast. You've thought of my soon-to-be husband in this regard before, I see." She wasn't mad at all. She continued, "But I don't agree."

"I know. Again. Not objective."

"But you really think that Mac is a higher rating than Eli?"

"Taller. More muscles. He's got the eye thing going for him."

"Eye thing?"

"Those blue eyes that I bet look even bluer depending on what he wears. And you know me, I'm a sucker for beautiful eye colors." I smiled at her, and she pushed my arm.

"I like your green ones today," Ava said. The timer let out a shrill noise, and she jumped up to stir the rice that smelled like heaven to me. Chorizo and onions and a scent I wasn't sure I could name. Ava said it was a secret recipe that Lacey from the bar had given her. I understood. I had a few of my grandma's recipes that weren't going to leave our family…or me…anytime soon.

The air conditioner kicked in, pushing my hair into my lip gloss. I pulled the dark strands away from my face. Leaving the salon behind me, I'd decided to just let my hair go back to its normal color and stopped attempting to hide the white streak I'd had since I was little. It would be too much work to keep it up without the salon. And, truth be told, I was more than a little tired of doing hair—mine or anyone else's. It had never been my dream. It had been a necessity.

Letting my hair go au naturel was one thing; my eyes were another. My contact addiction wasn't going anywhere. For me, it was like putting on the right jewelry with an outfit. I just didn't feel quite ready until I had the right colored lenses in. I had almost every color they made—and some they didn't— thanks to my friends in the fashion world. Like the black ones I rarely wore, and the ones that were almost black but were really a dark, dark blue. The bright green ones I'd put in today were one of my favorites. They were close to my real color but with an extra oomph to them.

I helped Ava bring the food out to the patio, and we placed the bug nets over it all. Even though it was hot and muggy, it still felt good to be out in the summer sunshine with the smell of sea grasses and the sound of the ocean pounding near us. It wasn't the first time I'd vacationed with Ava and Eli since she had graduated and come back to Texas, but it was the first time I'd vacationed without a desperate need to get back to New York and the salon.

As we ate out on the deck, the margaritas kept the banter easy and the mood light. Friends catching up after time apart. It was so different from the meals with my friends in the city. The beauticians who had worked for me, and Jared and my fashion friends, had always hung out at high-profile restaurants and bars where the atmosphere was as close to a high pitch as you could get—as if, one more notch higher, and you'd have to duck your head, shielding your ears. I'd loved it: the pace, the noise, the friendships. But I was also ready for a new pace. A new feel.

After dinner, Ava had to head downtown to the bar she owned. I'd been going with her almost every night since I'd been there, but tonight, I just needed quiet instead of chaos, so I declined. Eli and Mac went with her, and I had the house and the beach to myself.

I brought a blanket, a book, and the last of the margaritas down to the edge of Ava's property where she and Eli had built a firepit in the middle of an octagon-shaped wooden deck that hosted a smattering of Adirondack chairs and lounges. The deck was right at the end of the crushed-shell path, tucked in the sea grass just before it broke into the sand. It was a bit of paradise in Texas.

I read until the stars started to sprinkle the sky like fairy lights being turned on, and then I just sat, staring at the expanse. You never got to see the sky like this in the city. I missed it, and yet, I didn't. Just like I missed my friends in New York, and I didn't. The price to keep the salon and that life would have been too high. Not only the price of the new lease the landlord wanted me to sign, but the price of my own dreams that I had this one last chance to make come true.

As if reading my mood from a continent away, my half-sister, Raisa, texted me.

> *RAISA: Are you at the beach yet?*

> *ME: I've been here for two days.*

> *RAISA: What happened to going to D.C. to check out an apartment?*

> *ME: I just stayed the one night. The place I got is almost too good to be true.*

I hadn't planned on flying to D.C. before coming to Texas, but I'd discovered an ad for a loft in an apartment with two other people that I hadn't wanted to pass up. It was close enough to campus that I could walk, and it wasn't going to break the bank.

I'd met with one of the roommates, Daniella, and felt an instant connection. She was sassy and professional all at the same time. The apartment, with its views of the Capitol building, had still seemed too good to be true, but Daniella had said her family liked to rent the loft as a way of helping college students. I liked her and the loft, so I took it for what it was: a gift. I placed a down payment, got a key, and hoped the other roommate, Daniella's brother, wouldn't be a total schmuck when I finally got to meet him.

> *RAISA: I am a little jealous. I will be stuck in the dorms for a year.*

It wasn't going to be a hardship. She'd been accepted to Stanford University and was going to be staying in the best dorms they had. My stepdad, Petya, wouldn't have any less for his daughter.

> *ME: While I know you'll have a blast living in the dorms, the thought of me having to experience it again makes me want to vomit.*

> *RAISA: We will both be college students.*

It was hard to reconcile the fact that I was going to be in college again. Getting back into law school after the years away had been simultaneously easier and harder than I thought. I was ready to restart the dream I'd put on hold for five years. I was just hoping law school would be different from my first years of college life.

> *ME: Not the same. You'll have everyone drooling over your Russian accent and pretty blonde hair, whereas I'll be the slightly older woman with her nose in a book.*

> *RAISA: I have almost no accent. My English is impeccable.*

ME: Out of all that, you chose to focus on what I said about your accent? What happened to making me feel better about going back to school after all these years?

RAISA: It is you who said age is not a number, it is an attitude.

ME: I wasn't the first person to say it, but it's true.

RAISA: Then, do not worry about other students. Just have lots of attitude.

*ME: ** Hair flip GIF ***

RAISA: I have to go. Malik is using me as interference with Father again. What will he do when I am in the U.S.?

ME: Learn to stand up for himself.

RAISA: Love you, moy dorogoy.

ME: Love you, too, malyshka.

Raisa and I were ten years apart and lived on different continents, but we were closer than my half-brother and I. Probably because she'd spent the last few summers with me. Malik didn't want anything to do with my tiny apartment above the salon. I was going to miss being with Raisa this summer as we both started new lives.

Shoes crunching on the shell path had me twisting my head. I almost felt the looming shape of Mac before it appeared over the dunes, as if my body had known all along that he'd find me, even after he'd gone downtown with Ava and Eli.

He sank down in the chair next to mine, that force-of-nature pull he had on me instantaneously coming back.

"Were all the single ladies at the bar too smart for your charm?" I asked.

He snorted, leaning his head on the back of the chair, gazing up into the night sky like I had been. His large body filled the space, and with his legs sprawling out toward the unlit firepit, it caused his knees to career into mine. I pulled away, but he didn't seem to notice.

"It was too exhausting tonight," he responded.

"Must be pretty bad if you're too exhausted to schmooze the fairer sex."

A soft chuckle escaped his chest. "I've just spent two weeks in pretty much solitude on a boat. It takes a little to ease back into the real world."

His voice was deep. Barrel deep? Was that the right description?

"Isn't it dangerous to sail by yourself?"

He finally turned his head to look at me, and even in the dim light from the stars and the moon that had finally started to trek across the sky, I could see the flash of humor and more in those eyes.

"Did Ava tell you to harp on me about it? I swear she's practicing being a parent before they're even pregnant."

"No. Ava and I don't talk about you."

"So, I'm not a ten?"

"Wh-what?"

"A ten. Isn't that what you said?"

"You were spying on us out on the deck." I tried to be offended but couldn't really be with him smiling like that.

He grinned. "You weren't trying to be quiet."

I liked how his grin crinkled the corners of his eyes. I liked too much about him. The fact that we would soon be living in the same city was enough to give me heart palpitations, even if the likelihood of our lives overlapping was slim to none.

"Spying definitely lowers all of your scores by, like, half. So, now you're barely a five," I told him.

He laughed—a full laugh this time—no half-laughs or snorts. And it seemed to fill the night around us. It felt like it could echo in a cavern with the boom of dragons. It felt like it could echo into my hidden away places if I wasn't careful.

Chapter Three

Mac

A GOOD NIGHT

Performed by John Legend with Bloodpop

When Georgie hadn't been in the house or on the porch, I'd found my way down the shell path to the firepit that I'd helped Eli and Ava build the summer before. I'd found her sitting in one of the Adirondacks, a blanket she didn't need wrapped around her knees and a book unopened on her lap. Her hair blended with the shadows. Dark. Mysterious. Dreamy.

"Spying can hardly drop me to a five. It's what I do for a living."

I shouldn't have harassed her about saying I was a ten. Hel—heck, she was a ten, ten times over. A hundred. A gazillion. There wasn't a rating system that went high enough. But it felt good to tease. To get under her skin just a little. She was crawling all over and under my skin.

"You aren't a spy," she guffawed.

True. I wasn't exactly a spy. But I dealt with all the data that came back from them. I dealt with field reports, and black ops, and things that the average citizen would never want to know about. "Let's just say I'm in the know."

"Because you spy on conversations that have nothing to do with you." She wasn't mad. She wasn't even embarrassed; she was just giving me sh—a hard time.

"I think that conversation was entirely about me and my best friend."

She just ignored me, pushing off the chair, leaving her blanket behind, and heading out toward the sand and the water that pulsed against it.

"Where are you going?"

She glanced back. "Why do you care?"

I didn't respond. I just pulled myself out of my chair and followed her.

She headed toward the water, dragging her feet in the sand and writing something in the dampness. I watched as she wrote with her toes. Long toes on dancer-like feet that made it hard to look away from as they moved through the dark silt.

When she reached the end of her sentence, she kept walking away from the house and down the beach. I eased up on what she'd written. It was a cliché. "Follow your dreams."

I tagged after her, jogging the first couple steps to catch up. Georgie had never seemed like a cliché kind of person, and this made me even more curious about her than I already was.

"What dreams are you chasing?" I asked her.

She looked over at me as if she'd known all along that I'd follow.

"Why did you sail all the way from D.C. by

yourself?" she parried.

"I already said. Vacation. Between gigs."

"You didn't have to sail here. You could have flown. So…why sail here by yourself?"

I liked that she didn't really let me get away with anything. Pushed.

"I like sailing. No one could come with me that I could stand being on a boat with for two weeks." It was the truth. Plus, as much as I liked being around people, I'd felt a need to reacquaint myself with the me I was trying to be. Reimagine my goals.

"I'm sure there were plenty of your lady friends who would have accompanied you."

There it was. The question I'd been hoping and dreading would eventually come up between us. The fact that I was single. I wanted to know if she was single, or if she'd left some boyfriend behind. When I'd asked Ava while I was at the bar, she'd told me she didn't know. That Georgie had had a boyfriend the last time they'd talked, but she wasn't sure anymore, because it seemed like Georgie had put behind a lot more than just the salon and the city.

"Truth is, the longest I've ever had a girlfriend was for a month. I've never been a keeper," I finally responded to her question.

"You've never been a keeper as in the girls don't want to keep you, or you've never been a keeper as in you don't want a relationship?"

I looked down into her face, loving again the fact that she was barely shorter than me. That the look down into her face was barely a glance. Knowing that our bodies would fit together in a way not many people had ever fit me. Her eyes were shadowed. I couldn't see much more than a hint of a reflection in the moonlight, but I could still feel the curiosity wafting off of her.

"Maybe a little bit of both."

"And why have you never wanted to keep anyone?"

I couldn't help the small laugh that escaped me. "I wish Ava was here now to see you asking all these personal questions. No boundaries."

"You're right. I'm sorry. You don't have to answer that."

She pulled away from me to ease her feet into the water more, and my body missed the heat and tantalizing pull, like the ebb of the tide her body had had on mine.

"It's okay. I don't mind. When I was younger, it felt 'cool' to have ladies falling all over me," I told her. "Then, when I knew I was enlisting, I didn't want to leave someone behind. I knew how hard it was on my mom and us kids to have Dad gone for months. I didn't really want to do that to anyone, especially to someone who should have been out dating and partying and just being a twenty-something. Being free, you know?"

She nodded, kicking up the water and watching as the water droplets joined their brothers and sisters back in the waves.

"But you've been stationed in D.C. most of the time, right?"

She knew a lot about me. More than I expected her to know. More than I knew about her. It seemed unfair that the scales were so heavily tipped in her knowledge of me versus the other way around.

"Yep. Mostly D.C. But I spent some time on the USS *George Washington* and in Florida. Truth is, though, when you're in the military, you never know where they're going to send you next."

She turned and headed back the way we'd come, still playing in the water as we went.

"Your boyfriend care that you've come on vacation to this strip of paradise without him?"

Her turn to laugh—the light laugh that she'd had earlier. "You could have just asked, 'Do you have a boyfriend?'"

I waited for a few seconds, and when she didn't answer, I shrugged and asked, "Do you?"

"Nope. Sold him at the same time I sold the salon."

I snorted. "Sold him?"

She smiled up at me but was trying not to. Now that we'd turned toward the moonlight, instead of away from it, I could see her face better, and her white teeth had come down on her full lower lip to try to stop the smile. Sexy. Like all of her.

"Traded him in?" she offered, as if I would like that term better.

"Dumped him. You dumped him. Poor guy."

"Let's just say it was a mutual decision."

"Stupid. How come us males are so stupid?"

"Says the guy who just admitted to never having dated someone for longer than a month."

"True. But when I do decide to go all in, I'll be just that—all in."

"You'll go from never having dated to dating one woman and marrying her?"

"I didn't exactly say marry, but what's wrong with that?"

"How will you know she's the right one? If you've never tested out a relationship, how would you know the one you pick is the one for forever?" she asked.

"Instinct."

She gave a little disbelieving shake of her head.

"Don't you trust your own instincts?" I asked. "For example, what made you decide the boyfriend needed to be dumped and not kept?"

"Instincts are just another one of the senses. And senses can often lead you awry."

"Says who?"

"Says me and Descartes."

"This Descartes was not a military man, I take it?"

"Philosopher and scientist," she told me. "But what has that to do with anything?"

"When you serve…probably if your life is on the line in any job—police, military, whatever—you have to listen to your gut. It can save your life."

"That's training, not instinct."

"I kind of believe it's both. But this Descartes guy…why didn't he believe in using your senses?"

Her hand went to her ponytail, smoothing the wind-blown tendrils away from her face.

"Dreaming proves we can't trust our senses to determine truth from imagination. In our dreams, things feel incredibly real even when they aren't. So, we should, at the very least, be wary of our senses until we can test their veracity."

Her little speech quieted me. It spoke to a level of education that I'd been judgmental enough not to have expected in a hairdresser. Sure, she had to have been savvy to run a successful salon in New York City, but I hadn't expected a degree in philosophy. Not that I knew what her degree was in, but I hadn't expected this kind of discussion.

I was ashamed. Because I was routinely frustrated by people judging me for my brawn versus my brains. For seeing a uniform and thinking that it meant I was just some meathead with a gun who screamed, "Don't go quietly into the night." Yet, I'd done the same with her. Judged her by her occupation and the spiked purple hair she'd had when I first met her. Judged her by the row of earrings that went up her earlobe.

I was quiet for so long that I'd almost forgotten that she was still beside me.

"Too deep?" she asked with a slight curl of humor in her voice.

We'd made it back to the firepit. She picked up her blanket, book, and an empty glass before we continued along the path to the house.

"No. Not at all. I just was surprised. And ashamed."

She stopped and turned so suddenly that I almost ran into her. "Ashamed?"

"For judging the book by its cover when I hate that people do it with me," I told her.

"Oh."

We stared into the darkness of each other's faces for a moment. I wished that it was daylight, and I could have seen better what was going on inside her eyes. I was hoping they were full of desire. That she felt the way our bodies were talking to each other just as much as I did.

She turned and kept going.

"What did you major in?" I asked.

"Pre-law."

She kept dealing me more surprises. A three-of-a-kind hand that had come out of nowhere.

"What made you decide to go to cosmetology school instead of finishing the law degree?"

We'd reached the porch and climbed the stairs.

When she turned on the light in the beach house, it made me squint and hold a hand to my eyes as if the sun had come out from behind the clouds. She was standing there in the summer dress she'd had on earlier, feet bare, ponytail tousled by the breeze and the salty water. She was spectacular. Unforgettable. Like Audrey Hepburn and Gal Gadot rolled into one.

"I think we'll have to save some of those questions for another night."

I smiled at her. "Sorry. Nature of the job again. All questions, all the time."

She took me in from head to toe and then back again. "I'm sorry," she said.

"For what?"

"For judging you just like you judged me."

"Well, to be fair, I am a ten." I smiled at her, lightening our mood and the air that heaved between us as deep as the sea.

She snorted. "Goodnight, Mac-Macauley."

And she left me, going into the bedroom I normally slept in. The one that had my bag in it. But I knew I wouldn't be asking for it tonight. Tonight, I'd sleep in my skivvies and dream of a woman with eyes that were never the same color and hair as dark as night—and all the questions I still had to ask.

When I got back to my room, I saw that there were messages on my phone.

> *BRAT: Hey, before I forget again, I found us a roommate.*

> *BRAT: Are you ignoring me?*

> *BRAT: SQUIRTER!*

I shuddered at the family nickname, but payback was hell.

> *ME: Jeez, Gooberpants, hold your panties in place. I didn't have my phone with me at the beach.*

> *BRAT: Likely story. Who was she?*

Who was she? A stunning brunette with a white streak in her hair that I wanted to know all about.

> *ME: There's no "she." Please tell me the roommate isn't another tree-hugger.*

> *BRAT: That is absolutely not a politically correct statement. We have so much work to do if you really want to run for office.*

ME: God. You're right. Please tell me it's not another person who won't let us use the good kind of toilet paper without a ten-day lecture on sewer systems.

BRAT: Done. Definitely not that. She seems smart. Wore brown leather that made her dark hair and brown eyes stand out. You know our "environmentalist" would never have worn real leather. Or even pleather.

ME: When does she move in?

BRAT: Up in the air. Maybe end of July.

I wasn't sure I had the energy to deal with another new roommate. I liked people, liked interacting with them, but sometimes it was nice to have a place you could go back to without having a stranger hanging over your shoulder.

Although, to be fair, some of our roommates had become part of our family.

I wondered what my family would think of Georgie. Of her energy and sass. My sisters would love that she called me out on sh—stuff. My mom would love that I brought anyone home. My dad would probably run a background check on her. Or maybe that would be Granddad. I guess I needed to think that way these days myself. If I wanted to make a run for office, it would mean having a partner who was an asset, not a deficit. That seemed like such a cold way of choosing the right someone to be at my side, especially when I really believed what I'd told Georgie on the beach. I wanted to find the person who my heart and soul told me was the one. My heart was skittering around my chest tonight, wondering if maybe the one had come careening back into my life now for a reason.

Chapter Four

Georgie

CAN I HAVE A KISS?
Performed by Kelly Clarkson

I smelled bacon and cinnamon when I woke the next morning. I wasn't sure how Ava and Eli kept up the hours they did with both of them working days and nights. Ava was at the bar around the clock, and Eli joined her there every night after his job with the emergency preparedness consulting firm. The bar was closed on Wednesdays during the off-season, but during the summer, when the tourists were bringing in the core of their business, it was open seven days a week.

It wasn't a life I wanted. Even at the salon, which had been open six days, I'd only worked five. I needed time away. Ava said that it was because it wasn't my passion, and she was probably right. The salon had simply been a must. A way of surviving.

What I was passionate about was the law. Facts. Justice.

When Grandma had taken me in after Dad had gone to jail, she'd encouraged my goals the only way she could have: with love and work at the salon. She'd shown me that getting my cosmetology license and working through high school and college was a way I could get my degree without being buried in a lifetime of debt. And it had worked while I got my bachelor's. It had worked until Grandma died, and I was suddenly shouldered with a lease I couldn't break. I'd had to put off my dreams until the lease was up.

Until now.

But I'd never regret it because my grandmother had given me everything. A childhood filled with hide-and-seek between hair-washing stations and tickles between clients. A childhood filled with love and laughter. My dad loved me—just not as much as he loved money. My mom loved me, but she had a life in Russia without me. Both my parents loved me in their own way, but it was from afar. Grandma had loved me up close.

My phone vibrated, bringing me out of my memories of Grandma. I groaned internally at my stepbrother's text.

> *MALIK: Raisa says you found an apartment in D.C.*

> *ME: Yep.*

> *MALIK: And?*

> *ME: And what?*

> *MALIK: You're impossible to text with.*

> *ME: This is not news.*

MALIK: And where is it? Will we get an address so we know how to get a hold of you? Can I come visit?

ME: It's near the college. Raisa already has the address. And you won't want to stay there any more than you wanted to stay at my apartment in NYC.

MALIK: Fine.

Of my two siblings, Malik was always easy to rile up and the first one to pout. Raisa was fiery like our mother, whereas Malik was more of a spoiled, rich-kid heir.

ME: Don't be sore.

MALIK: Sore?

ME: Hurt.

MALIK: I just want to see you.

ME: Then come to D.C. and put a hotel on your Black American Express Card.

MALIK: Now you are sore.

*ME: **laughing emoji***

MALIK: Why is this funny?

ME: I don't want the price that would come with having one of your dad's credit cards.

Malik didn't respond.

ME: Hey. I was teasing.

No response. Typical Malik. If he didn't get his way, or felt slighted, you wouldn't hear from him for weeks. Now I'd have to send Raisa a message and get her to smooth things over.

Raisa and I got each other better than Malik and I ever had. Maybe because I understood wanting a dream the way Raisa wanted hers. She was majoring in bio and chemical engineering at Stanford so she could find a way to solve the world's energy problems. She had bigger goals than I ever had. I wasn't sure what Malik's goals were besides spending money. I wasn't sure why he wanted to stay with me instead of a fancy hotel with fancy foods and fancy people, anyway. It was more his style.

I hauled myself out of the bed in the room I'd chosen because it had a view of the ocean from the window and pulled on a pair of shorts and a T-shirt before making my way to the kitchen. I was surprised it was just Eli and Mac.

"Morning. Where's Ava?"

Eli and Mac both turned to me, Mac's hand twitching and splattering the bacon he was holding back into the pan of grease. He swore. Eli smiled.

"Morning. She was really dragging when we got home last night, so I didn't want to wake her."

"Will I be in your way if I grab coffee?" I asked, eyeing the Keurig with desire.

Both men shook their heads. I tried to squeeze around them the best I could, but Mac—who was closer to the pot—and I kept bumping into each other. Our bodies talking.

"Aren't you supposed to be at work?" I asked Eli once I'd backed out of the kitchen.

"I told them I'd be in late today."

The two men worked quietly together in the kitchen. I watched, admiring their sureness with each other. Their comfort. As if they'd done this many times before. Just as the food was ready, Ava emerged from the bedroom with dark circles under her eyes and a face so pale it looked eerie.

She put her finger to her nose. "What on earth did you cook?"

Eli's face broke out into a smile, and he came around the counter to give her a tender kiss, as if he hadn't just spent the night tucked up next to her.

"You look sick. Are you sick?"

"That smell is about ready to do me in. What did you cook?" she repeated.

"It's bacon and French toast. You love bacon."

She backed away toward the fresh air coming in through the French doors. "That doesn't smell anything like bacon or French toast."

We all looked at her funny.

Eli followed her out onto the deck. Their voices were quiet, but we could still hear them, which made me realize how Mac had been able to hear us the day before when Ava and I had talked about the two men. It made me flush a little in embarrassment. I looked up at Mac, and he winked at me. I was tempted to roll my eyes but didn't.

Eli was saying, "Go back to bed. I'll call in."

"We have guests. I'm not going back to bed. And you don't have to call in. I'll be fine. It must have been the beans last night."

"We all ate the beans, Ava. It wasn't the beans." I could hear the worry in his voice.

"She really should go back to bed," Mac said as he dished up a plate and handed it to me. "More bacon?"

I shook my head. "Thank you. You know Ava. She won't if we're here. I'll tell her I planned on spending the day downtown at the shops."

"She'll just want to go with you. That'll be even worse. All that walking."

He poured enough syrup on his French toast that it could have floated out to sea by itself. He saw me watching and smiled. "I have a sweet tooth."

I grinned. "That definitely does not fit with your image." I waved a hand at his fit frame.

"I know," he said before diving into his food.

Ava and Eli continued their conversation on the deck. Ava had her forehead pressed against his chest. He had his arms around her as if he could hold her and the whole world up at the same time.

"What do you say about taking a sail with me?" Mac asked.

"What?"

"It'll get us out of her hair and allow Eli to go to work. No one will feel obligated to entertain us."

It was a good idea. But that just meant a good chunk of the day in his company.

Ava pushed Eli away and went running toward their bathroom. Eli followed, almost forgetting we were there. "Do you really think he'll leave with her feeling this way?" I asked.

Mac shrugged. "I don't know, but I don't want him worrying about me and her at the same time."

I blew out a breath. "Okay."

"Really?"

"Yep. But I have to warn you. I've never been on a boat before."

"Wait. Like never?"

"Well, I've been on a ferry—the ones around New York—but never a small boat. And never a sailing boat."

He smiled. "I'm a good teacher."

"Somehow, I doubt that."

"Have you ever gotten seasick?"

"Not on the ferries."

We finished our breakfast in silence, left a plate in the oven on warm for Eli, and cleaned up the kitchen together.

"Should I change?" I asked him.

He looked me over in a lazy way that had all my senses firing. But like I told Mac the night before, I rarely trusted my senses. They usually had me running in the opposite direction. I ran a hand over my hair.

"You look perfect to me," he said finally.

It made me want to roll my eyes again, but I'd given up rolling my eyes when I was a teen. Grandma had made me do extra chores at the shop every time I'd rolled them at her. The memory struck me hard for some reason today. The hurt still there even after all these years without her.

"Let me be more specific, Mac-Macauley. Do I need to wear something different to go sailing?"

"Maybe bring a bathing suit? And if you have some non-slippery soled shoes. But barefoot works as well."

We headed down the hall to the bedrooms, and I was surprised when he followed me into the bedroom I'd taken up residence in. "Um. Excuse me?"

He smiled again. A smile that pulled at the shadow of a beard that had coursed over his face as he'd slept. A smile that made his eyes—which were a sparkling blue today—crinkle in response. My belly flopped over.

"Sorry," he said, but it didn't sound like he was sorry. "This is usually the room I'm in. I left my bag in here yesterday." He pointed at the military duffel I hadn't even noticed on the floor by the bookshelf that was full of Eli's comic books.

"Oh. I'm sorry. Do you want me to move into the other room?"

"God, no. You're settled here. It was just habit."

He grabbed the bag, hooked it over his shoulder, and then headed for the door that led to the shared bathroom. "You need in here, or is it okay if I jump in the shower?"

My mouth felt like a stale saltine cracker had been shoved into it. The thought of Mac getting naked in the bathroom that we would be sharing for the next few days. I tried to dump the image from my brain. Tried to imagine Jared. Tried to feel an ache for the man I'd just left in New York, but I couldn't. Jared and I had been done for a lot longer than we'd admitted.

I moved toward the closet.

"Nope. I'm all good." I was happy my voice didn't betray me or my thoughts. It had been developed over years of practice, just like my poker face.

I heard the door shut and the shower start before I turned back around to the mirror over the dresser. My face was flushed even though I hadn't let it show in my voice. Mac-Macauley was going to be hard to resist.

I opened the drawer of the dresser, pulled out a bathing suit, and threw it, a beach towel, and a bottle of sunscreen into a beach bag. Then, I pulled my hair up into a high ponytail that was becoming my signature hairdo now that I'd left behind salon life. It would, at least, stay out of my face in the breeze on the boat this way.

When I left the room, Eli was on the phone. I pulled a couple waters from the fridge, adding them to the stack of things in my bag. By the time Eli hung up, Mac had come out of his room, hair wet, shorts and a T-shirt on with his boat shoes.

"I'm going to take Georgie out on the boat," Mac said.

"You don't have to leave," Eli said.

"You know Ava. She won't rest if she knows we're here. She'll feel like she has to entertain," I jumped in with Mac.

Eli couldn't argue. He knew it was true, but he looked from me to Mac as if he was unsure. "God, Dad, I'm not going to steal her clothes and her virtue. We're just going out for a sail," Mac teased.

Eli squinted his eyes and then turned to me. "You

sure you're okay with this?"

I smiled. "I can handle myself. I learned self-defense at the hands of a cop who liked my grandma. If Mac-Macauley tries anything, I'll push him overboard and radio the Coast Guard for help. You'll hear all about it from your buddies."

Eli tried to hide his smile. "Fair enough, but wait longer than you think before you call for help. He's a Navy man, so he can tread water for a long time."

"Dude. That's just mean," Mac said, playfully punching his shoulder.

Eli fished a pair of keys out of the blue glass bowl on the table near the door. "Here, take Ava's car. She won't need it today."

He tossed the keys to me, not Mac. I caught them with a smile, and Mac grunted a protest before following me toward the door.

I turned back to Eli. "Make sure you tell Ava to just rest and feel better."

He nodded, and we left.

♫ ♫ ♫

We seemed to leave the mugginess behind us as Mac sailed out into the Gulf. We soon lost sight of land, and it was both discomfiting and exhilarating at the same time. Mac taught me some basic lingo, told me where to sit and stand so that I would be out of his way, and also what to do if he asked for help, but he basically managed the boat on his own. It wasn't surprising, as he'd been sailing for weeks on his own, but it was impressive in a way I hadn't expected to be impressed.

He was serious as he pulled the rigging and ropes. His muscles rippled as he worked, showing themselves under his white T-shirt and plaid shorts that seemed more fashion model than Navy man.

We were quiet while we sailed, the breeze rushing over me, the sun soaking into my bones like the syrup I'd had this morning on my breakfast. It was peaceful in a way that—like a lot of things about Mac himself—I hadn't expected.

Eventually, he turned the boat back toward the coast more, and when he put the anchor down, I could see land, but it wasn't close enough to make out exactly where we were. It was mostly just water, and sun, and ocean breeze around us. He disappeared below deck. When we'd first boarded the boat, he'd taken me down to show me around. It was small. There was a bed that was a pile of messy sheets up toward the bow, a small kitchen, and a built-in table. In addition, there was a bathroom that I wasn't sure how Mac fit into. The whole boat had the look of being well-used but was clean and neat other than the messy sheets.

When Mac came back up on deck, he had two beers and a plate of sandwiches. He placed them on the seat next to me and then sat on the other side of the food. Space between us.

"This is the second meal you've made me today. Are you sure you've never had a girlfriend?"

His eyes crinkled as he smiled slightly, and for a moment, I felt like I'd seen the smile before, but I couldn't place it and just pushed it aside.

"This is just common courtesy," he said. "I'd do it

for whoever was on the boat or in the house. I have three older sisters. If I'd made food and not made enough for them, I would have been tied to one of their bedposts with scarves, dressed in a tutu, and covered in makeup."

I laughed. The image of Mac in a tutu and makeup was so preposterous that it was more than comical. It was ludicrous. "I'd pay good money to see that."

"There are pictures."

We ate in comfortable silence.

"Do you have siblings?" he asked.

I nodded. "A half-brother and sister. They live in Russia with my mom and stepdad."

He took that in for a moment before saying, "I kind of suspected there was some Russian in you."

"Really?"

"It's in the cheeks and the nose."

I found my hand going instantly to those body parts. "I do look a lot like my mom, except she has blonde hair like my sister."

"Must be hard being so far from them."

"It is. And my mom isn't allowed back in the country, so if I want to see her, then I have to go there."

He looked a little dumbfounded. "Why isn't she allowed in the country?"

I wasn't embarrassed about my family. It was their actions, not mine, that had landed them where they were. I'd just been a little kid. But I'd had a lot of people look at me differently once they'd heard the story, and this huge balloon grew in my stomach at the thought of Mac being one of them. I took a swallow of the beer he'd brought up. I wasn't overly fond of the stuff—more of a mixed drink kind of person—but I drank it in order to ease the dryness that had suddenly taken over my mouth.

"My dad is Ian Astrella." When that didn't get any reaction, I continued. "You know, the guy who stole millions from people in Ponzi look-alike schemes?"

He sort of choked on his beer. "Holy crap."

I laughed. "Yep. And my mom was a Russian model who'd gone all in with him. The feds could never prove how much she was actually involved, but they definitely revoked her visa and sent her back with a 'You are not welcome back' sign stamped in her passport."

"Why didn't you go with her?"

"I did at first, but Dad still had enough pull that, when she filed for divorce, he won that battle."

"Isn't he in jail?"

"Oh yeah. He'll be in jail for at least another ten years, and then it's highly doubtful any parole board is going to feel enough sympathy to let him out of his multiple sentences."

Mac frowned. "I don't get it. Why wouldn't he want you with your mom?"

I shrugged. "I was only six when it all started to unravel. But they used to have these knockdown, drag-out fights that I still remember. They never hit each other, but the objects in our house were never safe. My mom would throw anything she could get her hands on. And now, looking back, I realize she had a coke habit. She doesn't now, but she did then. I remember being told the white powder was 'Mommy's special adult medicine' and that it wasn't for me. I'm sure Dad used the drug habit against her to make sure she didn't get custody."

"Who raised you, then?"

"My grandma. It was her salon I sold."

"Doesn't Grandma want it anymore?"

That pain hurt worse than any of the stories of my mom or my dad. Because she'd been my real parent. The person who had loved me the most in the world. "She died about five years ago."

Mac was quiet again. Taking it all in. I was surprised I'd told him all that. Mac had a way of making you open up when you didn't even realize you were doing it. Like I had last night. It made me realize he was probably really good at whatever information collecting he did for the government.

"I'm going to take a swim," he said, standing up, pulling off his T-shirt, and revealing a chest and abs that were beautifully defined, but it was in a way that talked of genuine hard work instead of weights and trainers. It was sexy. He had hair smattered all across it that neither Jared nor his model friends would have allowed. Their chests were always shaved, waxed, or lasered. Mac was all-natural male and maybe more gorgeous because of it.

"You going to come in?" he asked as he looked back at me from the edge of the boat, feet posed on the side, ready to dive into the brilliant blue water in his plaid shorts that I now realized were swim trunks.

"Sure. Okay to change down there?"

He nodded and then dove in. I barely heard the

splash as he hit the water. I stepped below deck, shaking myself out of the lazy feeling that had encompassed all of my interactions with Mac. Like a dream that was meandering its way through your conscious with no purpose other than just to dream.

Descartes would have been having a field day with my analogies.

I changed into the one-piece I'd brought for days when I thought I'd actually be in the water instead of sunbathing on Ava's beach, the cut reminding me of the forties and fifties and all the glamorous actresses my grandma had so admired.

When I came up on deck, I could see that Mac had swum quite a few yards away from the boat. That made me a little nervous. Were there sharks out here? Other sea creatures that might nibble at my toes? I sat on the step at the back of the boat—the stern was what Mac had called it.

I'd left my sunglasses on the seat, and it made it hard to see with the reflection of the sun on the crystal-like water. It added to the dreamlike quality of our day, the heat searing my skin even through the layers of sunscreen I'd added.

I placed my hand over my eyes and looked out at Mac. He turned, head bobbing in the gentle waves. "You gonna come in? I think there are sea turtles out here," he hollered back at me.

Were sea turtles friendly? I wasn't a naturally fearful person, but unknowns weren't my favorite thing. I liked to read and research things before I did them. I liked knowing what I was getting into.

Mac started swimming toward the boat, his muscled arms cutting through the waves easily until he was treading water a foot or so away from where my legs were curled up on the step with me.

"There's a whole bale of them. Come on, before they move off," he said.

I shook my head very slightly as uncertainty coursed through my veins again.

He smiled then, catching my wariness. "Are you afraid of sea turtles?"

"Afraid is a very strong word," I told him.

His smile widened, and he stuck out his hand. "Come on. I promise to keep you safe."

"What do they eat?" I asked, ignoring his hand. He swam closer, his body so close that his wet chest bumped my knees in my cross-legged position. He put a hand on one of them. Rubbing. Soothing, and yet, not soothing because my body liked it way too much. Reactions that were not fully trustworthy.

"They don't eat humans," he chuckled, pulling on my knee and sending my right leg careening into the water and colliding with his side.

"What about a toe if they think it's a fish?"

"I've never had my toes nibbled on by anything but actual fish."

"What about sharks? Have you been nibbled on by sharks?"

He laughed. "You watch too many scary movies or something? No sharks."

"I've seen *Soul Surfer*. That's not a scary movie. That's a cautionary tale."

"That's a tale about bravery and courage."

"Wait. How do you know that movie?"

"Did you miss the part where I said I grew up with three sisters?"

He pulled my other leg, and I went toppling into the water and into his arms. I let out a squeal that was nothing I normally did. I wasn't a squeal kind of person, just like I wasn't normally fearful.

I was being held against a chest that was warm while the water was cool, the sensations of heat and cold coursing through my veins. My heart beat wildly, not only because of his closeness, but because I was in the water and not sure I wanted to be there.

"See. No toes being bitten off." He continued to smile down at me, and I relaxed a little, pushing myself out of his arms.

"Not yet. But if I lose a body part, Ava and Eli will both come after you with machetes."

More booming laughter. Just like last night, it filled the air around us. If there had been birds nearby, it would have startled them out of their trees.

He swam out the way he'd come, looking back every so often to make sure I was following him. I did, with my brain screaming at me that I was not supposed to be trusting my instincts and that I hadn't fully researched anything that was about to happen to me.

When we got out several yards from the boat, Mac stopped and motioned for me to do the same. We did the minimum that was necessary to float, and pretty soon, I could see the turtles moving down below in the clear water. Most were about the size of a toddler, but some were smaller. Some were cruising around the bottom. Some swimming. It shouldn't have felt like a life-changing experience, and yet it almost was. Like the Earth had rotated into a new position around me. Like I'd learned something spectacular when I'd actually learned nothing.

We watched for a while, and then Mac flipped over onto his back, floating, looking up at the clear sky. I joined him. The blue of the sky was faded and pale compared to the sea around us—almost white— making me miss my contacts that were almost this same pale shade. We'd left so quickly this morning that I hadn't put any of them in.

Eventually, the coolness of the water started to take over the heat of my body, and I shivered. I flipped over and headed back toward the boat. When I pulled myself out of the water, Mac was right behind me. I grabbed my towel, rubbing away some of the water. I looked up to see he was watching me; the way my hands and the towel traced over my body, and I froze in the midst of an action that I hadn't intended to be a sexual one, but yet, he was suddenly making me feel was that and much more.

He came up close, and I dropped the towel as his body touched mine, the heat searing its way back into my cool one. His hand went to my arm, his fingers and palm dancing over my skin and up to my shoulder, before journeying to my neck, where it stilled.

"I'd really like to kiss you," he said quietly.

I looked into his eyes that were the color of the sky and the sea all rolled into one. His face was so gorgeous, with its day-old stubble and square planes, that it was like looking at a piece of art you'd never expected to see up close in person.

"I'd really like you to kiss me, too. But let's face it, it isn't a good idea," I answered back, unable to deny the attraction that existed between the two of us from the moment we'd met in my salon two years ago, regardless of the relationship I'd just left behind.

His head inclined in silent agreement. It wasn't a good idea. Disappointment curled through me even as I knew it was better this way.

His hand moved to caress my cheek. Gently. Soothing.

"Can I ask why you think it's a bad idea?" he inquired.

His voice had turned a notch deeper in blatant desire, making my heart pound against my chest in a heavy beat that denied my words. I ached to kiss him. To feel those almost too-perfect lips against my own. To feel the strength that poured from him, in muscle and character, reaching out to touch my soul.

"Ava and Eli," I said quietly. "Awkwardness later."

He nodded again, that new and unfamiliar feeling of disappointment reaching up into my throat at his action. My body didn't want him to nod, but my brain was still ruling my movements.

"One kiss," he muttered, a finger traveled to my lips, caressing the bottom one with a gentle touch like the one he'd used on the tomatoes the day before. Surprising. Sexy. My breath escaped in a gasp that sounded almost like a moan.

And then his lips were on mine, just like the touch, gentle and yet full of heat, longing filling us both, desire escaping from us and mingling in an excursion that felt like heartbreak and loneliness and promises that would never be. The gentleness gave way to a fierceness that was as unexpected as the tenderness had been. His hand went to my lower back, pulling me toward him tighter so that our bodies and curves joined in a way that felt like opposite ends of magnets finally clicking together. Parallel forces drawn, as if by physics itself.

My hands went to his shoulders, finding their way to the wet hair at the nape of his neck, twisting so that our lips were pushed closer, tighter, harder together. It was the best kiss I'd ever received in my life. I'd had many kisses—fewer partners—but lots of exploratory kisses. None matched the intensity of this one kiss, not even Jared's sexy smoothness. None that made my soul want to completely disregard the screaming in my brain.

The lack of air forced our lips apart, our lungs giving way to that need to breathe and involuntarily separating us in a way our souls wouldn't have done.

We both breathed in heavily. He looked down into my eyes, his sea-colored ones full of the desire that was still coursing through us both. Our bodies were still tucked together. Only our lips had moved away. It felt as if I was looking for something in Mac that I'd never looked for in any of my male partners. I wanted something more than desire to be there.

It was ridiculous. And that had me pulling away completely, not trusting anything my senses were telling me. He let me pull away, but his eyes went from my lips, to my chest that was still beating wildly, back to my lips, and then up to my eyes, lingering there.

"I like your real color," he said.

Then, he left me, going down below with a

muttered comment about changing. My heart slowly settled from its wild beat, but my emotions were still high. They were wrapped in the dream of the kiss and our day. Emotions that were untested. Unproven. Unreal.

I picked up the towel from where I'd dropped it and went up onto the bow to lie down, letting the sun soak into my already overheated body. The body that had lost the shiver from the cold waters with a kiss. It wasn't until I'd lain there for a few moments that I realized Mac had never told me why he thought kissing me was a mistake. And that one thought jolted me back to reality more than any other thing could.

Chapter Five

Mac

SIMPLE MAN
Performed by Lynyrd Skynyrd

The Salty Dog was filled with locals and tourists in the height of the holiday week as I poured beers from the tap for Eli. I wasn't able to make the mixed drinks, but I could still help while Ava felt like cr—crud. Andy and Lacey—the prior owners of the bar—were usually the ones who filled in when Eli and Ava needed it, but they wouldn't be back into town until the next day.

Eli was all business as a couple of female tourists flirted relentlessly with him. He wasn't being rude, but I wondered if he even recognized that they were flirting with him. His love for Ava often had him in a cloud of No-man's-land when it came to things like that. I moseyed up to the women and flashed them my best Mac smile.

"Ladies."

They turned their eyes on me, and the blonde's smile widened. "Hey."

"I'm not sure if you know this or not, but my man, Eli…he's pretty much got a ring on his finger." That turned both their smiles down a notch as they both glanced to his hand that didn't hold a ring yet. "I know, to a lot of people, that might not mean all that much—a ring—but I can tell you for a fact that his getting a ring isn't just some societal mark to him. It's part of his soul, so getting his attention in that way is pretty much going to be like removing a Kraken from the sea, if you get my drift."

"What's a Kraken?" the brunette asked.

I fought back a snide comment and just smiled wider. The blonde returned the smile, her eyes darting to my left hand, which was ring free. I didn't intend it to be ring free forever, but it was at the moment. That had my brain and my body going back to the kiss with Georgie that afternoon, and my body's reaction to that memory pretty much halted any other thought going in or out of my brain.

I didn't hear a word the blonde said. Eli had to actually nudge me out of the way to put their drinks down. I just turned and walked back to the other end of the bar and the tap. It was the rudest I'd been to a woman in my whole life. Eli followed.

"What the hell was that about?" Eli asked. "You don't normally walk away from that kind of flirting unless you have to report to duty."

My brain was still trying to kick my body out of the kiss.

The life-altering, seared-on-my-mind-for-the-rest-of-my-life kiss. The kiss that I had promised would be just one. Except, now that I'd had the one, my body and soul were calling for more. Many more. Lifetimes worth of more. Because I had known, just like I knew I would, that Georgie could be the rest-of-my-days kind of woman.

But she couldn't be. Not at all for the reason she'd given about Ava and Eli and the potential awkwardness if things went south between us, but because she'd opened up and told me something about herself that was a death sentence to any political career I'd ever want. She'd said the words Russia and prison in almost the same sentence. I hadn't spent my entire life keeping my nose clean for nothing. I'd partied with alcohol and no drugs. I'd never driven drunk. I'd kept my dick covered every single time I'd had sex.

I'd done everything for one purpose: to make a run for a political office. To change our world for the better in a way I couldn't have done, even in the office at the DoD where I had proposed and nixed black ops. But to have a chance at a political career, you didn't marry a woman with Russian ties by choice. No way in hell.

"Mac?" Eli nudged me again, bringing me back from kisses, and careers, and heartbreak that hadn't even had a chance to happen.

"Yeah, yeah. I'm good."

Eli laughed. "I didn't ask if you were good, asswipe. What gives?"

But I wasn't able to say any of what had been in my head to Eli, to the man who—even if his knee hadn't forced it on him—would have given up his career in a heartbeat to spend the rest of his life with Ava.

I tried to reason with myself that I didn't know for sure what could happen with Georgie and me. That what I felt could have been wrong. But getting out before I was in too deep was the better choice so I wouldn't have to decide between love or my career. It made me feel like a chickenshit, and that made me do two things I'd never done. It made me lie to my best friend, and it made me run.

"I have to head back to D.C. earlier than I thought. Dani is up in my rear end about the workload she's shouldering while I'm here gallivanting with you."

"Gallivanting? I doubt Dani ever used that word. Besides, Dani loves me."

"Not enough to allow me to stay as long as I'd hoped."

He took me in, as if assessing my level of honesty. I didn't budge. I had a good poker face. Not only because my family ate you alive at poker if you didn't have one, but also because I had to have one at the DoD. It was good training for a political career where you sure as sin didn't show what you had in your hand.

"You're still waiting to see Truck, though, right?" he finally asked.

I nodded. No way I was taking off before the three of us got to clink beer bottles together. It had been way too long as it was. Thank God Truck was getting his sorry ass into town the next day. I'd stay through the Fourth and then head out. That was just a couple of days. I could handle a couple days.

After helping Eli close up the bar and driving back to the beach house, I lay awake in my bed, thinking about the woman in the bedroom next door who seemed to fit in every perfect way with me except one. That had me tossing and turning and waking with the sea gulls.

I went for a run on the beach, trying to chase away the haze of sleeplessness, beating my body up and down the sand before the heat hit the day. When I came back in, Ava was at the kitchen counter, still looking gray.

"You still look like he—heck," I told her as I pulled a water bottle from the fridge. When I looked back at her, she was eyeing me in the way Eli had the night before.

"You don't look so great yourself. One night at the bar do you in that bad? I thought you were Mister Party-man?" she teased, but it was with only about half her normal snark.

"Time to throw aside the wild oats and settle down," I told her, sitting on the barstool at the other end of the counter. "You going back to bed?"

She shook her head. "No, I need to go into the bar and make sure we're stocked up for tomorrow. Brady called this morning and said he's coming to do a surprise performance on the Fourth before flying on to Phoenix."

That would be a huge moneymaker for the bar. Brady O'Neil had had four number one hits in the last two years singing Ava's songs. His showing up would draw a much bigger crowd than their normal tourist Fourth of July drew. I wasn't sure the tiny bar could handle it.

"Let me shower; I'll go with you. I can be your brawn while Eli is at work."

She put her head on her arms on the counter. "Thanks."

Her eyes were closed in a way that was so not Ava

that I watched her with concern as I drank the water. She didn't even open them when a door creaked down the hall, followed by Georgie appearing in the kitchen.

Georgie's hair was all mussed, and her eyes were still sleep-filled. She wore a tank top that showed more than it hid and a tiny pair of sleep shorts that showcased her long legs like her swimsuit had the day before. My entire body was more awake from the vision of her than it was from the run on the beach.

She ruffled Ava's hair, saying, "Morning."

Ava groaned at her, making my concern ratchet back up. Georgie seemed troubled as well, because she frowned slightly as she made her way to the Keurig.

She'd gotten all the way to the coffee machine before she risked a glance at me.

My body ached to kiss her again. To see if, this morning, she still tasted like the cherry blossoms blooming. Like my favorite season and my favorite fruit all in one. Her eyes drifted to my lips before she turned back to the coffeepot.

Ava peeked out from her arms to eyeball us. "What gives?"

"What?" Georgie and I both said at the same time.

Ava sat up. "Please tell me you did not swag-and-bag one of my best friends, Mac."

"No!" Georgie and I both said again, which was not helping our case at all.

The coffeepot started whirring, and the smell hit the air. Ava instantly put a hand to her nose, jumped down, and headed for the bathroom, passing Eli in the hall. He turned around and followed her.

I stood, taking Georgie in from behind. Her shoulders were back, standing tall, as if she could take whatever life threw at her. Like she already had. I wanted to know more about all of that—every single bump in her road that had made her the elegant, confident woman she was now.

"I'm going to shower," I said instead, pulling myself away from her and the way her skin was calling to me. Running didn't seem like such a chickenshit thing anymore. Running felt right.

I practically smacked into Eli as he came out of the master.

"Ava said you were going to go to the bar with her?"

I nodded.

"Thanks, man. I need to put in an appearance at the office today before I take tomorrow off."

"What time is Truck getting here?"

"I think his flight lands at around eleven. He should be here by two. I'll let him know to head to the bar if no one is here."

I nodded and headed for the bathroom so I could be sure to be ready when Ava was.

♫ ♫ ♫

It was early afternoon by the time we were done taking stock at the bar and filling every possible crevice we could fill before tomorrow came. Ava had spent the day, white as a sheet, going back and forth between the storeroom and the office while she checked in on the stock and the extra staff and security needed with Brady showing up.

Georgie had come with us, and she and I had done whatever Ava pointed at us to do. We brushed past each other without a word, but it felt like my body was building up enough electricity from the contact to be its own electrical storm. A storm that was waiting to be unleashed on something, anything, but especially her.

Ava finally sat down, and I could see she was shaking.

"Have you eaten anything?" Georgie asked, also noticing her friend's condition.

Ava shook her head. "Don't say food. The smells in here are bad enough."

"Should I take you to the doctor?" Georgie asked.

Ava shook her head again. "No, but I think I'm going to run to the drugstore and see if I can find something that will calm the waves down."

"'Kay. I'll go with you," Georgie said.

Ava went and grabbed her purse from the back, and they headed for the door. "Don't worry about me, ladies. I'll be fine right here until Truck arrives."

They both turned as if they'd forgotten me. I knew for a damn fact that Georgie hadn't. She'd been avoiding my gaze all day, just like I'd been avoiding hers. Just like she'd been avoiding me since I'd dropped her at the house yesterday after our sail and our kiss.

Ava gave me a tired smile that made me regret my attitude. "Thanks, Mac."

Then, she disappeared—so not the Ava we all

knew and loved. The one who could barely sit still for more than two seconds. The one who gave as good as she got. The one who pranced around stages with an attitude the size of Texas.

I sat at the bar while the daytime bartender continued the prep work behind the counter. I shot off a text to Eli.

ME: Your fiancée is about ready to pass out. Maybe you should come get her?

CAPTAIN: Shit. I'm on my way.

ME: She left with Gorgeous to the drugstore, so you have time.

CAPTAIN: Gorgeous?

I looked up at my prior text, and I had typed Gorgeous instead of Georgie. Worst Freudian slip ever. Eli would never let me live it down.

ME: Georgie. She left with Georgie.

CAPTAIN: You've got it bad, my friend.

ME: Nah. But she is gorgeous.

CAPTAIN: You can't fool me. I've known you too long. I'm just leaving Corpus Christi. I'll be there in about thirty.

ME: Yes, sir. I'll hold down the fort till you get here, sir.

*CAPTAIN: **middle finger emoji***

The door of the bar opened, and I looked up to see my other best friend, Travis Dayton, a.k.a. Truck, walk through. He looked both better and older than the last time I'd seen him when I'd gone to Hawaii on leave. His normally pale hair looked almost white it was so bleached by the sun. It had always been one shade away from white anyway, but now that he'd let it grow out, it looked like he could be ninety instead of twenty-eight.

"Douche!" I got up and almost jogged to the door I was so excited to see him. I hugged him tightly.

"Dickwad," he greeted back, squeezing me as hard as I was squeezing him.

"How's Hawaii?" I asked as we let go and made our way back to the bar. The bartender already had a pint on the counter for him.

"Good, but I'm itching to get out of there."

"Really?"

"Yep. Few more months."

"You're not going to reenlist?" I asked in surprise.

He laughed. "Shit, yeah, I'm going to reenlist, but I'm going to ask to get the hell out of Hawaii."

"Beaches, ladies, and umbrella drinks not everything they're cracked up to be?"

"Cost of living, crowds, and humidity that never stops is more like it."

I nodded.

"So, you came to more humidity?"

He grinned. "To see you two asswipes, of course."

"Lucky us."

"Damn straight," he teased. "So, how does it feel being a civilian again?"

"Honestly? It hasn't really settled in yet. Nash has been giving me shit nonstop."

Truck knew my S.E.A.L buddies from meeting up with all of us on leave. Nash wasn't the easiest man to get along with, but Truck had gotten on his good side in that way that Truck did with everyone.

"Here's to hoping you can be a better politician than you were a wingman." He held up his beer, and I refused to tap it with my own.

"I'm a damn good wingman."

"Until you set your sights on some unexpected lady yourself, then you abandon ship."

I was abandoning ship now, too, but it wasn't *for* a woman it was *from* a woman.

"If it takes you too long to close your own deal, and I get propositioned, you can't expect me to say no," I retorted, grinning over my beer.

"Hence, not being a good wingman."

"I take it you won't be voting for me come election day then?"

"That's years in the future. And you'd have to be in the same state as I am."

It sucked being spread all over the country from my closest friends, but it helped that I was tight with my family. Being away from my friends allowed me to focus on work in a way that I might not have been able to do if I was trying to balance all the portions of my life. The unexpected melancholy I felt at leaving the Navy hit me again, along with the agony of not being able to have a certain pair of pale-green eyes to call my own, and I ordered another beer to wash it away.

Chapter Six

Georgie

CHURCH

Performed by Aly & AJ

We ended up back at the house earlier than expected after Truck and Eli arrived at the bar, because Eli called in reinforcements. Andy and Lacey came in, took one look at Ava, and shooed her right out. She objected, and they stared her down like any good parent could. Lacey and Andy had their own sons somewhere, but they'd inherited Ava when she'd needed them most. I was pretty sure they were more like parents to her than her dad had ever been.

It still said a lot about how rotten she felt that Ava gave in. It said even more about it that, when we got back to the house, she went to her room and didn't come out until morning. But once she was awake, she announced to us all that we were spending the day on the beach with a picnic, and none of us argued. It was the perfect way to spend part of Fourth of July.

I loved the Fourth almost as much as Christmas. They were both usually full of lazy days, food, and lights. The Fourth's lights were in the sky, whereas Christmas's lights were in the trees and on the houses.

Plus, there was good music to go with both holidays.

I didn't even realize I was humming aloud until Truck asked, "What is that?"

"Um, 'Born in the U.S.A.'" I smirked, knowing I was pretty close to tone deaf, but not caring.

"I'm pretty sure that's not what it sounds like." Mac grinned at me, causing thunderbolts to jolt across my stomach.

I started humming "America," and Truck burst out laughing. "What the hell is that one?"

"Are you American at all?" I asked.

"I'm American enough to know that isn't any song our country wants to be known for."

Ava came to my rescue by singing the first verse in her beautiful voice.

"That wasn't what Georgie was singing," Truck laughed.

"It is too," I chuckled. "Ava knew exactly what it was."

"But you were doing it rather badly. It was only my keen ear that helped me figure it out," she teased.

I threw an ice cube at her. "Okay, how about this one?"

I started "The Star Spangled Banner," and they all groaned.

"And that is my cue to leave all you heathens and go shower." I tried to sound upset, but I couldn't. They were all too easy to be with.

I stood up and felt Mac's gaze over my bikini-clad body. I met his gaze with one of my own, staring until he finally looked away.

When I came out of the shower, I pulled on my red, white, and blue dress that I'd bought specifically for this occasion. It looked like a flag and glitter had thrown up on the material, but I loved it. Just like I loved our country. The halter top showed off the tan that coated my arms and back from sitting on the beach the last week, and the flounced layers on the bottom ended mid-thigh and were reminiscent of a ballerina. It really was too much, but I still adored it.

I finished my makeup and hair in the bedroom, hearing the shower in the adjacent bathroom kick on a couple times as everyone came back from the beach and got ready to head downtown to the bar.

When I came out of the bedroom, Truck teased. "You look like one of those ads where the mother and the daughter have on matching dresses."

"We don't get to celebrate our country enough," I said with a shrug.

"Not everyone believes we should celebrate these days. Most people feel like our country is slowly ripping itself apart," Mac said.

"Yeah, I know. And we are pretty messed up, but what other country on this planet allows people the freedoms and opportunities that ours does?" I asked.

"You've been hanging out with Mac too much," Truck retorted. "Maybe you should both run for office."

My jaw went slack. "Wait. Mac's a politician?"

"Not yet, but he'll be one soon enough. Four-year plan, right?" Truck asked.

Mac shrugged.

"How did you not know this about him?" Ava

asked with a smile. "Did you think he wore that pretty white Navy uniform for nothing? Now he just has to find the right wife to settle down with, pop out a few kids, and look like the true family man he wants to be. Isn't that right?"

My eyes met Mac's, and he looked away, coloring slightly. I suddenly realized why he thought kissing me was a bad idea: because I'd told him about my family. I'd had my fair share of people walk out of my life after learning about my dad or my stepdad or both, and I'd sort of built an immunity to it. I'd given the people judging me a one-fingered wave—even if it was an internal one—and moved on. But for some reason, Mac's rejection stung more than I expected.

I shrugged my armor back on—the one that normally said, *Go to hell*, to the people who couldn't take me and my family for who they were. By the time we got to the bar, I'd recovered enough of my good mood to be smiling. We all dove in to help with the ebb and flow of the crowd until close to nine thirty when Andy and Lacey shooed us out once more—this time to go watch the fireworks from the roof.

Ava protested leaving them, even for a few minutes, on such a busy night, but Lacey insisted. "Go. Andy can't make it up that rickety ladder anymore. It'll be calm down here while they're going off."

We made our way to the storeroom where a ladder swung down from the ceiling that led to the roof where a couple of battered wooden picnic benches and twisted metal lounge chairs sat near the brick edge of the building. The furniture wasn't fancy, and the rooftop wasn't an oasis. It was just a roof of a strip mall, but it was enough for us to huddle with our drinks. We were close enough to the marina that we could hear the music that was playing over the outdoor speakers. Ben, the leader of the house band, and his bandmates had taken a break and joined us as we waited like expectant children for the show to begin.

Somehow, I ended up next to Mac, as if our bodies had found a way to each other without us even knowing it. I sat down, the rough wood scraping along the back of my thighs where my short dress had stopped.

The air was still humid even though the sky had all but faded to black when the first loud pop split the air around us. It startled me, and Mac laid his big hand on my knee as if in reassurance. I couldn't help smiling at him, the sting of earlier slipping away. I wasn't one to carry a grudge. And I'd known all along that Mac and I were all sorts of wrong. He returned my smile, drinking me in with a gaze that reflected in his eyes as the first sparks lit up the sky. I tugged my eyes away from his and back toward the night, the colors sparkling like rainbows with an extra brilliance of white, dangling jewels making my heart bounce with joy.

In New York City, you had to fight for hours for a place near the water to watch the fireworks unless you knew somebody who knew somebody. I'd been near the water, on the water, and on rooftops in the city watching those displays, too. But I'd always been socializing, because no one in my group of city friends ever stopped to just stare at the lights. It was more about the party than the fireworks.

Here, everyone was quiet, watching in an awed

respect. The men who sat with us had served our country, and I felt like they had a different perspective than those who had never put their lives on the line for us.

I risked another glance at Mac and realized he wasn't watching the dazzling lights popping and dropping and dripping in the sky at all. He was watching me. His gaze on my smile and on my eyes.

I forced my gaze back to the lights as the finale set off a gazillion fireworks at the same time. The crowd at the marina cheered and clapped, and I joined them. There was something hopeful about fireworks to me. Like the ball dropping on New Year's Eve, it always signaled the start of something new. Something filled with possibilities.

Eli was kissing Ava as the lights left the sky and turned it back to darkness. Truck jogged away, mumbling something about the bathroom. I turned to Mac, and he was still grinning at me.

"What?" I asked.

"You surprise me."

"Why?"

"Just…I'm sure this isn't your first fireworks show, and yet, you looked as excited as my niece and nephews watching them."

"With all the humming and talk about America, I would have thought you'd already have guessed that it's one of my favorite holidays. Plus, fireworks are just…breathtaking."

"I think you're—"

A commotion in the parking lot below us stopped him from finishing his sentence, but I had an idea of what he was going to say, and it made my heart pound furiously in my chest. I'd been called beautiful and gorgeous by my share of men. But Mac almost saying it felt different. Something I couldn't explain. Like maybe the ache I felt really could be filled.

We all jumped up from the benches to see the commotion, and the wood scraped at the back of my leg, making me wince, but I ignored it as we looked down to see Brady and several others disembarking from a couple dark SUVs and a van.

Ava and Eli headed for the ladder.

Mac and I watched for a moment as the people waiting to get into the bar burst into a chorus of voices calling Brady's name. Brady was still all blond-haired, casual grace just like he'd always been when he and Ava had played the open mic nights I'd hosted out of the salon. It had been a weird combination. Hair salon and open mic nights. But the coffee bar next door hadn't been big enough to house one all on their own, and we'd worked out a deal where I held the music, he did the food and drinks, and we shared the profits. It had worked. I missed it, but it had never been quite the same since Ava and Brady had stopped coming.

I leaned over the brick so I could watch Brady work the crowd. He smiled and waved and took pictures with them, signing things as he made his way toward the door with some of his own security surrounding him. Mac put a hand on my waist.

"Don't fall." His voice was deep, full of worry.

I turned, my smile reappearing. "Brady is in heaven."

He took my smile in, and his didn't appear as I

thought it would. But then, I realized that Mac didn't really know Brady. He only knew him in a roundabout way through Ava. Brady could seem like one big egotistical monster if you hadn't seen his passion and kindness at work.

We turned and headed toward the ladder.

Mac went down ahead of me, and as I started my way down, he stopped me with a hand on my leg, swiping at it. "You're bleeding."

Concern laced his voice. I looked backward and wobbled on the ladder, all but falling into him. He caught me, arms going around my waist and making me feel protected in a way that was foreign to me. His eyes drifted to my lips in the dim light of the storeroom. The noise from the bar seemed to increase along with my heartbeat. We lingered in the moment, both of us focused on the other's lips as our hearts pounded together.

Finally, I breathed out, "Is it a lot of blood? I can't even feel it."

"I can't tell. Hard to see in this lighting," Mac said, stepping away and turning me to look down at my leg below my short dress.

I pulled away from the hands that were burning through my skin like the lights had just burned through the sky. "It'll be fine. I need to go say hi to Brady."

When I hit the main room, the crowd was hyped to a level that was almost a scream as Brady made his way through the room. He patiently continued with signing bar napkins, papers, and chests while people took pictures with their phones. He had two bodyguards with him who were all muscle, even more than Mac, Truck, and Eli. The bodyguards eyed the crowd and the people who approached Brady like Secret Service agents. It made my grin return because Brady had really made it.

I waited until Brady got close to the stage, and then I threw myself into his arms. When one of his agents tried to pull me away, Mac immediately had his hand on the guy's arm, and we all would have been a heap of punches if Brady hadn't waved the guy off. "Georgie-Porgie, I missed you!"

Brady hugged me tightly before stepping back and eyeing Mac who was still waiting at my side, for some reason. Ava and Eli joined us, and Ava embraced Brady more fiercely than I had.

Eli shook Brady's hand. "Thanks for playing tonight."

"Well, it was on my way and gave me an excuse to say hi to everyone," Brady said with a shrug.

His crew from the van was setting up the stage with his equipment. Two women dressed in matching white summer dresses were helping the crew. Brady was in a red, white, and blue plaid shirt, a leather choker peeking out from the collar. His jeans were worn and ripped in all the right, rock-star ways even though he was a country singer and not rock at all.

Ava jumped on the stage and took the mic. "Hello, Salty Dog."

Everyone cheered.

"What do you think of our Fourth of July surprise?"

More hollering, louder.

"Are you ready for some Brady O'Neil music?"

The crowd pretty much blew my eardrums out as their cries bounced around the small room, feet stomping on the wood floors, hands clapping. Brady joined Ava, taking another mic that was handed to him. "Hello, Rockport!"

I had to put my hands to my ears because the screams were so loud. I turned to see Mac watching me, as if trying to figure out a puzzle. Eli and Truck had gone back to the bar where Andy, Lacey, and two more bartenders were trying to keep up with the orders.

"I should go help," I said as I swiped at the cut on my leg that had started to sting.

I was surprised when I came up with blood. Mac saw it and pulled me down the hall toward the office. He punched in the key code to get in and led me to the small private bath.

"I think I can get it," I told him as he futzed under the counter, coming up with a first aid kit.

"You can't even see it. Turn around." He was all calm. I kept forgetting he was a military man. That he'd seen and been in worse situations than a cut from an old wooden bench. He joked around so much that it was often hard to remember. Even when he was serious, he didn't have an aura to him that I'd encountered in other soldiers. He was calmer, lower key about it.

I turned, pulling my floaty dress to the front and holding it tight so he could see better. Mac cleared his throat and sat on the toilet lid before dragging me a little closer until I was almost between his spread legs. The music from the bar faded away as my body heated at his touch and the intimate position. Heart beating fast, face flushing, I thanked the Lord I wasn't facing him.

"I think there's a splinter in there in addition to the cut."

I risked looking over my shoulder at him just as he looked up. Our eyes locked, and his fingers on my non-injured leg caressed my skin.

"It's going to hurt like hel—heck if I take it out, but I don't think we can let it stay in there," he said quietly.

I gulped. "No. It isn't good to let things fester."

His fingers were still caressing my leg. My cheeks were flushed. I could feel them without looking in the mirror over the sink. It wasn't from the heat of the bar or the humidity from outside. It was from this man. The man who thought I was a bad idea—not because of me—but because of my family and his future plans. I needed to remember that. I turned back toward the wall, trying to get ahold of the emotions flowing through me.

He pulled his hands away, and my heart beat in that constant swell of relief and disappointment he was good at bringing out in me. He dug through the first aid case and came up with a pair of tweezers and an alcohol swab, opening it with his teeth and making me swallow hard at the image.

"Ready?" he asked.

No. "Yes," I whispered.

It stung, and I twisted my dress in my hands to keep from whimpering and embarrassing myself. It was just a stupid scrape. I'd had worse in the salon from burns and scissor cuts.

"Okay, I'm going to try to get it out," he warned just as he stuck the tweezers in, and I did let out a little whimper. "Sorry," he said. I clenched my hands tighter, biting my lip, and gritting my teeth.

"There. Done. Out. Gone. Let me put some Neosporin and a Band-Aid on it."

His hands were gentle as he rubbed the ointment on. And then he blew on it, cool air that made my whole body burst into one big flame.

"Oh…hell…sorry."

I jumped, and Mac's hand went up my dress, and we both muttered something as we turned to look out the open door to where Truck stood, hands in his pockets, grinning.

I let my dress go, and it swooshed over Mac's face. He laughed and pushed himself out from under it.

"I have a cut. A splinter." The words came out of me in a tumble as I started to move out of the bathroom, but Mac placed a hand at my waist, halting me.

"Stop. I haven't put the Band-Aid on yet."

I looked down at him, and he was trying not to laugh. I looked back at Truck, and he was also holding in his laughter.

I waved a finger at both of them. "Get your minds out of the gutter, boys."

"I'll just go use the public restroom," Truck said. His laughter echoed through the room as he left.

I put my forehead in my hand. "This is awful."

Mac put the Band-Aid on my leg and then stood just as I turned, crowding me so my back was pushed into the towel rack that Ava always had real linens on since it was their private bathroom.

"Why?" Mac asked, eyes searching mine, smile disappearing.

"Why what?"

"Why is it awful?"

"That Truck thought that we were…you know…"

His hand went to my neck, caressing the back of it. "That sort of hurts," he said, voice low and guttural like it had been two days before on the boat before he'd asked to kiss me. His eyes made a journey to my lips, down to the lace of my dress that was heaving over my breasts like I was a sixteen-year-old girl waiting for her first kiss, and then back to my lips before stopping once more at my eyes.

I didn't know what to say. I hadn't meant it like it had sounded. Like I would be embarrassed to be caught being intimate with him. He was gorgeous and gentle, but as much as it stung, he was right that we couldn't be together, and it would be awful if the others thought we were together when we weren't.

My hand went to his arm, squeezing. "That isn't what I meant," I said quietly.

His head inclined ever so slightly, and I wasn't sure if it was in acknowledgement, or if he was heading toward my lips with his own.

The door to the office banged open again, and Ava came running in, pushing between us as she hurled herself at the toilet, throwing up. Mac's and my eyes went to her and then back to each other before he backed out of the tiny space.

"I'll go get Eli."

"No," Ava said before heaving again into the toilet.

I reached under the sink to the washcloths she kept there. The public was never allowed in this bathroom, and Ava treated it like it was one at the house, full of nice-smelling soaps and pretty towels. I wet the cloth and bent to place it on the back of her neck.

Once she'd emptied everything that she could have possibly had in her tiny body after days of hardly eating, she sat back on her haunches and leaned her face into my leg.

"Thanks," she said, taking the washcloth and rubbing it on her forehead, the makeup she'd worn rubbing off on it.

"What the hell, Ava?" Mac asked. "Should we take you to the doctor?"

She shook her head.

"No, it'll pass. In about three months." As soon as the words were out of her mouth, she pulled back in shock and frowned at both of us, hand to her mouth.

She was pregnant. Ava was pregnant. One of my very best friends was going to have a baby. With the man she loved. My heart jumped again, this time in joy, and I smiled. When I looked over at Mac, his face was going from shock to smiles as well.

"Oh my God. You can't say anything. I haven't told Eli," she said.

I sank down next to her and hugged her. "Congratulations."

"This is fu—frickin' awesome!" Mac said, and he came up and hugged us both in this awkward position with us all near the floor.

"Get off," Ava said, pushing us both away. "You're crushing me."

"And the baby!" I said, still smiling.

Ava put a hand to her forehead. "You two will never be able to keep this secret."

Mac shook his head. "I'm a great secret keeper."

"But not from Eli," Ava said.

She stood up, and I hugged her again, a full hug, and said, "I'm so happy for both of you. And I *can* keep a secret."

"We're so stupid," she said, but she was smiling. She was happy. "We didn't think it would happen the first time out the shoot."

"Wait! You were trying?" I asked.

She nodded with a blush that Ava rarely wore. "Well, the doctor said it could take three to six months for the pills to clear out of my system and for us to actually be able to conceive. I should have known better. Eli always has to be first at everything."

Mac and I burst into laughter.

Chapter Seven

Mac

CHANGE
Performed by Christina Aguilera

When we left the office and the bathroom, I couldn't help the grin I had on my face. For Eli. He was going to be a dad. He'd already acted like a dad since I'd known him, but now he was going to be a real one. With a real kid. He'd be awesome at it.

Ava frowned at my smile. "You're a shit," she said before heading to the stage where Brady was just finishing up a song and calling for her.

Ava still looked pale, but she climbed onto the stage and joined him while they sang the song that was about Eli and Ava when they'd first met and then left each other to follow their bigger dreams. I turned to watch Eli at the bar as Ava sang. He'd stopped to watch her like he had every time since I'd known them. He couldn't help himself. It was like the world drifted away when he was watching Ava sing. I had never really gotten it until I'd kissed Georgie. The whole world had receded when our lips had touched. Just like it had receded when we'd been squeezed into the bathroom together, a few moments before, with my hand on her leg.

When the song was over, Ava spoke into the mic.

"Fourth of July might not be the start of a new year. It might not be your typical resolution type of day, but it's certainly a day that began this amazing country of ours. And recently, I had some good news. News that will change things for me."

Eli was frowning and making his way from behind the bar toward the stage.

Ava was watching him. "I wasn't going to say anything today. I was going to wait, but then *someone* found out my secret, and he can't keep his mouth shut,"—she threw a glance my way—"so I better get it over with."

Eli stood on the floor in front of her while she looked down at him.

"Doodles, do you remember when we met, and I started calling you Dad?"

Eli's hands went to her bare legs, pulling her closer to the edge of the stage.

"Well, congratulations. You're going to be a real one."

It took a minute for him to get what she was saying. Then, his face broke into that huge smile that Eli rarely wore unless he was around Ava. He pulled her from the stage and was kissing her before anyone could have said two words.

Behind the bar, Lacey pulled out a mic they kept back there for just these sorts of occasions. "This round is on me! I'm gonna be a grandma again!"

Cheers for the free drinks. Cheers for Ava and Eli's parenthood. Cheers for Lacey saying she was a grandma when she really wasn't either of their parent. I couldn't help it. I turned to Georgie who'd been standing next to me the whole time and hugged her, picking her up off her toes and hugging tight.

It was such good news.

Georgie didn't even resist; she just hugged me back.

But then I realized whom I was hugging and set her back down. She brushed at her star-spangled dress and moved away toward Ava and Eli and the crowd who was clapping them on their backs and hugging them.

Ben and the band sang a cover of "Life Changes" by Thomas Rhett, which was such a perfect reflection of this moment, while Brady quietly disappeared down the hall to the back door and the dark SUVs, heading on to Phoenix.

The air felt jubilant, because it was.

♫ ♫ ♫

It was late, but everyone was still wired by the time we got back to the house after closing down the bar. We made our way down to the firepit with a bottle of champagne and the fixings for s'mores.

Truck raised his glass and said, "Here's to having a little Eli running around in less than a year. May he have all of his mother's spunk and none of his father's grumpiness."

"Asswipe," Eli griped, but he was grinning. He hadn't really stopped since Ava had broken the news at the bar.

"You aren't going to be able to continue to cuss like that anymore," I said, smiling. "You're going to be just like me, modifying your language."

"Why are you modifying your language?" Truck asked.

"Dude. Politics. Can't run my mouth on TV."

"I can't believe you actually think you're going to get elected," Truck said, picking up where he'd left off earlier in his harassment of my goals.

"I'd vote for him," Ava defended me.

"It's slightly frightening," Eli responded.

"It's frightening that I'd vote for your friend?"

Eli shook his head. "No. Yes. Just the thought of Macauley here running our country."

I stuck my hand to my chest. "That hurts."

"Convince us then," Georgie said, joining the conversation for the first time. "Tell us one thing you're going to do."

"Save the planet. World peace. Solve the hunger crisis."

Everyone laughed, but I didn't.

"You sound like you should be onstage at the Miss America competition," Georgie said.

It hurt just a bit, but it was true that my statements were simple. Maybe even bordering on the ridiculous. Preposterous. Immature. And that was all on me, because I'd always joked about it with my friends. I'd teased about my plans and about sowing my oats before becoming the family man who was needed to run for office. I hadn't meant it to sound so calculating. Yet, it was. There was more to it than just that. More to me. I didn't want to run for office for the power or the glory. I wanted to run for office to make a damn difference. I might not have had the full plan yet, but I knew we could get there as a nation.

Georgie seemed to sense my emotions, because she said, "Weren't you already out there saving the world in the Navy?"

"It isn't the same."

"Now wait a minute—" Truck said just as Eli added, "It is."

"Come on. You both know I don't mean to say that serving in the military isn't a great way to make a difference. I'm just saying we need more than that. We need someone in government who can pull everyone's heads out of their as—buttocks, so we can work together instead of separately."

"I can't believe you have that much faith in our country," Truck said.

"No politics," Eli chimed in before Truck or I could get riled up over anything. "You're never supposed to talk politics or religion with friends."

"That's going to pretty much be impossible to stick to if Dickwad runs for office," Truck griped.

I turned the conversation because Eli was right. We didn't need to go down this road tonight. I raised my glass and brought us back to the joy we were celebrating. I said, "To Ava and Eli and Baby Wyatt. May he be brought into a world that has righted itself from the cliff it's falling off of."

"May *she* have health and happiness on top of all the love that she'll have with you two as parents," Georgie said.

"To Baby Wyatt, whatever gender, and to Eli and Ava for bringing us all together," Truck added.

We clinked glasses, and Ava took a small sip before raising her glass. "To good friends, to Georgie's new chapter going back to school, and Mac's new chapter leaving the Navy."

"School?" I breathed out before I could help myself.

"Georgie's going to law school," Ava said for her. Georgie had told me her undergrad had been pre-law that first night on the beach, but she'd stopped me from asking more questions, and I hadn't pushed. I thought I'd learned everything I needed to know once she'd told me about her family.

"Nice! Congrats," Truck said, sticking up a hand that Georgie high-fived. "Now Mac will have someone to bail him out when he gets caught with his pants down with his campaign manager's wife."

I snorted. "So not going to happen."

"Why can't his campaign manager be a female? Couldn't he be caught with his pants down with her? Or maybe her husband? It would make the story just ever so slightly more modern," Georgie teased Truck.

He blushed. "True. That was very old-school, sexist of me. Who do we really want him to get caught with his pants down with?"

"No one!" I said with force. "No one. I'm clean as a whistle and am going to stay that way."

"I think Mindy from the DoD might not see it that way," Eli smirked at me.

Mindy had been, perhaps, my one mistake. I hadn't intended it to be anything more than the casual get-together that I'd had with all my other partners. But she'd stuck for about a month. It wasn't until we'd met up for our fourth Friday that I realized she already had wedding bells in mind. She was a civilian contractor I'd worked with, and she knew who my dad and my grandfather were. Knew that Dani was working for Guy. Knew that I was planning on working for him, too. She'd put three and three together and got five hundred million, somehow.

"Mindy has nothing to hold over me. Not one note."

"Because you're a jerk who doesn't write notes?" Truck teased.

I winced again. I had been careful over the years with anything I put in writing. Even when I'd been in college, I'd written every essay with the idea that it might, someday, come to light when I was running for office. It was the same with pictures I took with people. I was very cognizant that they wouldn't disappear and that, if I ever announced I was running, every a-hole who I'd ever been around would come running out of the anthill with their pictures of me.

Eli had never really given me a hard time about it. But Truck, the guys in my first unit, and the JSOC folks, like Nash and Darren, rode my ass every time I refused a group selfie when we were at a bar or drunk on the beach. Even when we'd had poker competitions on the USS *George Washington*, I'd carefully leaned back out of the picture when they were taken. Darren had told me I was like Michael J. Fox in the reruns of *Family Ties,* where he'd had a Ronald Reagan picture on the wall of his bedroom. And he was right. That had been me with presidents on my wall.

Ava said, "Don't bang on his dreams, Truck. Here's to Mac. I'm counting on you to fix our planet, create world peace, and solve the hunger problem, because I want our baby to live in that world."

Everyone clinked glasses again, but Ava's words settled into my heart. I had a niece and nephews from my two oldest sisters. I had cousins with kids. We were a big family. But not once had the thought of me handing over a world to those little ones hit me as hard as it did when Ava said those words. I'd wanted to make our world better. And now I had another, more important, reason to do that. For Baby Wyatt and all the other babies who might come our way.

I pulled the bag of marshmallows out, and everyone focused on toasting the little bits of heaven till they were the perfect color instead of being focused on me and my rose-colored wishes for our country. While the rest of them ate the marshmallows with chocolate and graham crackers, I ate them sugar for sugar, one after the other.

Georgie was watching me with a half-smile.

"Sweet tooth." I shrugged. I'd already told her that once, but it felt like it needed repeating.

"I think you just mean a sugar tooth, because chocolate and graham crackers are certainly sweet, but the syrup you doused your French toast in and the marshmallows you're pounding down are really just pure sugar," she said.

"Remember that time we came back to his dorm room and found him pouring the box of sugar straight into his mouth?" Truck smirked at Eli.

"God, yes. Or how about the time we had to literally pull the third box of Captain Crunch out of his hands so he wouldn't O.D. on the stuff," Eli replied.

"This is quite a serious problem," Georgie said to me, her smile easing into my soul and opening up all my nerve endings so I could feel the blood pounding through my veins way more than the sugar I'd inhaled. And I knew she was right. This was a serious problem, and it had nothing to do with sugar at all.

♪ ♪ ♪

I was groggy from alcohol and lack of sleep the next day when my alarm went off. It was early, but I wanted to be on the way and out to sea before the day got later. Before the sight and smell of Georgie had me deciding to stay another day…and another day after that.

The temptation of her was growing.

I hit the shower and then packed the few things I had. When I got to the kitchen, Truck groaned at me from the couch where he'd been sleeping.

"What the hell time is it?" he asked.

"About five thirty."

"And you're up because?"

I was running. I couldn't risk being around Georgie another day. She'd had this hypnotic pull on my soul since the first time I'd seen her standing above the crowd in her salon in New York.

If I stayed, I'd just want her more. Every moment I'd had with her since arriving in Rockport had my heart beating out a tune that talked of futures tangled together. It made me both a jackass and a chickenshit that I was choosing the life I'd always pictured for myself over that. Over the possibility of a future with someone I could love.

But if I wasn't going to give up my career plans for Nash—who'd been my brother in blood—I wasn't going to give them up for a woman I'd met three times in my life. I couldn't cross that bridge, because if I gave it up, all the years I'd spent working on those dreams would have been for nothing. A waste.

"I'm leaving," I told Truck.

"What? I just got here."

I nodded. "Dani needs me."

I knew he wouldn't argue with that. Truck understood siblings needing you. He'd do anything for his brother.

"You can come with me if you want," I told him.

"You making me choose between my two best friends?" Truck chided.

"We all know that I'm the favorite."

Truck snorted.

"Think of it this way," I added. "The two lovebirds are going to be even more lovey-dovey now that they know there's a little Wyatt on the way. You'll be stuck around that."

"I'll be stuck around Georgie."

I tried not to react. Tried not to let it show how much that one comment pissed me off and made me hate myself all at the same time.

"She just dumped some guy. Don't think she'll be ready for everything Travis Dayton has in store yet."

"Not because you want her for yourself?" he teased. I looked up and knew I hadn't been able to hide it from him. The desire. The emotions that rolled off of me when she was in the room. I looked down the hall, making sure the doors to the bedrooms were still shut.

"Can't happen."

"Why not?"

"She's one of Ava's best friends. I'm walking down the aisle with her in October. Shag-and-bag would just backfire." I shrugged.

"What if it wasn't a shag-and-bag?"

I groaned. "Are you coming or not?"

"You're leaving now?"

"As soon as I can say goodbye to the happy couple." And I inwardly hoped that would be before Georgie emerged from the room. I could escape fairly unscathed that way.

My phone pinged.

BRAT: Have you left yet?

ME: Shortly. Trying to convince Truck to come with me.

BRAT: The family would be happy to see him.

ME: But not me?

BRAT: We like him better than you. You didn't know that?

ME: This is why you don't have a boyfriend.

BRAT: Who has the time for a boyfriend?

This was so like Dani. She was the only single one of my three sisters. She was focused on her career, just like I was focused on mine.

ME: Is our roommate there yet?

BRAT: No, I told you, might not be till the end of the month.

ME: Right. I'll be home about the same time.

BRAT: Be safe out there on the high seas. Don't get abducted by pirates.

*ME: **muscled, shirtless pirate GIF***

*BRAT: **puke emoji***

ME: Again. Why you don't have a boyfriend. Pirates are supposed to be hot.

BRAT: Do we need a press release about you being gay?

ME: That's just rude to the gay community. They wouldn't want me.

BRAT: You're right.

ME: Love you.

BRAT: Love you, too. Be safe, for real.

I looked over at Truck. "Dani says the family would rather see you than me."

"Well, that's because they're smart."

The master bedroom door crept open, and Eli emerged. He looked like I felt. Tired and gritty.

"Hey, thought I heard your voices," he said.

"I'm just heading out. Truck here has decided to come with me because I'm the best friend," I teased.

"That's it. You're both out of the wedding." Eli pretended to growl.

"I hadn't agreed to go with the douchebag yet, but if I'm out of the wedding that easily, maybe I should," Truck said, getting up and shoving things into his bag.

"You want us at that wedding; you need us at that wedding," I teased, using my very best Jack Nicholson voice.

They both groaned.

"We use words like honor, code, loyalty…" I continued, and Truck threw a shoe at me.

"Just go with him. We both know we'll only hear whining for months if you don't," Eli said.

"I don't whine," I retorted.

Once Truck was packed, we hugged Eli and told him to give Ava a hug also.

"And Georgie? Should I be sharing the hugs with her as well?" Eli asked with a knowing look. Both my friends knew me better than I ever gave them credit for. They knew I was running with my tail between my legs. It killed me a little, knowing that I may very well look back on this moment someday and be filled with regret for what could have been.

But it wasn't enough to make me stay.

Chapter Eight

Georgie

Hushed voices brought me from my sleep, but when I emerged from the bedroom, it was to find only Ava sitting with a bag of candied ginger at the counter. I made my way to the coffeepot.

"Morning," I said. "Where is everyone?"

"Eli went into the office for a few hours. Mac and Truck headed back to D.C. on Mac's boat."

My hand stilled. "They left?"

She nodded. My heart constricted. Mac had left because of me. I knew he'd leave, but I hadn't expected him to go without saying goodbye. My heart didn't know if it should have been celebrating or wallowing.

"Is the coffee smell going to make you sick?" I asked.

"No. Just don't make me drink it," she laughed. "You know, it hit me after the guys left. You're going to law school in D.C."

"Yeah." I knew where she was headed and already

wanted to end the conversation.

"And Mac lives in D.C.," she continued.

"Don't even start."

"Why? You both seem to have a lot of…you know."

"Chemistry?" She nodded, and I continued. "There is, but I just want to concentrate on actually finishing law school this time. And it sounds like he needs to work on finding the perfect little wife for his political endeavors."

"You're saying you wouldn't be the perfect wife?"

My heart banged at her words. "Have you met me? No. I don't intend to be anyone's wife. Let alone some politician's."

I distracted Ava from talks of Mac and me with the wedding magazines that were sprawled out on the coffee table. Ava and Eli's wedding was in October, and she had her dress picked out, but we were still trying to settle on the bridesmaids' dresses. She'd said she didn't care what Jenna, her best friend from childhood, and I wore to the wedding, but Jenna and I had slowly ganged up on her to pick something.

"I kind of like this black halter with the A-line," I said, showing her the dress I'd sort of fallen in love with. It wasn't very formal, more like something you'd wear to a simple party, but it was also sophisticated enough for the beach wedding Ava and Eli were having.

"It would look beautiful on you. But I'm not sure black is really Jenna's color."

"She could do a red one, and I could do the black. Those are your colors, after all."

Ava took the magazine and looked at the dress.

"Why do I have to decide?"

"The wedding is only four months away, and if we have to order them, it could take that long to get them."

"Then, send it to Jenna. If she likes it, go for it. I told you, I don't care what you wear. I just want you there on the beach with me."

I took a photo and shot it off via text to Jenna whose number I now had because of all the wedding stuff we were planning with Ava. I realized that we'd have to make some changes to the bachelorette party, because Ava would be four months along by then.

"Does she know about the baby?" I asked before I hit send.

Ava shook her head. "No, she and Colby are coming to stay in a couple weeks, and I want to tell her in person."

"Phew. Good thing I asked."

Ava tossed a magazine at me. "Don't spill the beans. She's already going to be ticked when she finds out that you and Mac Truck knew before her."

I laughed, but my heart flipped at Mac's name.

"You have that look," Ava said.

"What look?"

"That wistful, 'if only' look."

I laughed. "I am never wistful."

"I wish I'd videoed it. You totally looked wistful."

"If I'm wistful, it's because I missed out on sweaty, vacation sex. Truck would have done as nicely as Mac."

Ava laughed. "I didn't say you were wistful over Mac, but now you've proven it to me."

I flushed. "Okay. It would have been nice to have sex with a ten."

"Why didn't you?"

"I told you. I don't want it to be awkward every time we're all together."

"I think it was more than that."

"Nope. Just that."

I could feel her eyes boring into me as I flipped through the magazine she'd tossed at me. I held up a picture of a cute guy in a tux. "Do you think you can find me one of these so I can have hot, wedding sex?"

"Think about what Mac will look like in a tux."

Holy hell, that made my fingers completely stop flipping through the pages. Mac would be beyond stunning in a tux. So stunning it made it hard to believe, even in my imagination.

Ava laughed, and I knew my face probably revealed the shell-shocked feeling I had.

"Yes…yes, he would," I breathed out.

"I need food." Ava left to go find something to munch on. Probably crackers. Or Cheerios. That had been her food of choice yesterday.

My phone buzzed.

RAISA: Malik says he is coming with me in September. HELP!

ME: Malik just wants to come to the States, period.

RAISA: But I do not want to be his excuse. In addition, he has been acting very strangely.

ME: More strange than normal?

RAISA: He is moody and silent.

ME: And that's different than normal, how?

RAISA: You will see when we meet up with you in New York.

ME: I won't be in New York, remember.

RAISA: Maybe this is good. He will not want to go to D.C. He likes New York better.

ME: He already asked to come see me in Washington.

RAISA: You have been no help.

ME: I want to see you both. I miss you.

RAISA: Fine. But you get to deal with his moods.

ME: I can do that.

RAISA: Love you, moy dorogoy.

ME: Love you more, malyshka.

I suddenly felt the need to get my new life settled. To move to the glamorous apartment with Daniella and her brother. To get my schedule and my textbooks. To research and discover my new city and my new campus. To have things ready for when my siblings came to see me. It meant that I needed to leave behind the little cloud I'd been living in with Eli and Ava.

When Ava came back to the couch, she had the Cheerios I'd expected, but she also handed me a bag of Skittles. They were my favorite. "I hid these from Mac because he would have eaten them in one sitting."

"Wow. He really does have a sweet tooth."

Ava smiled and nodded. "Obscene. It's going to catch up with him and that trim figure of his someday."

"I can't imagine him ever going all lumpy around the middle. Look at Eli; he's married with a baby on the way and no fat on him."

Ava's smile disappeared. "I'm going to have lots of fat."

"It won't be fat; it'll be baby. There's a difference."

"I know. But…it's going to be an adjustment. I've never really worried about my body or what I ate. It was just me, you know?"

"I don't think you have to worry now, either. Just be healthy, be balanced. That's the most important thing."

Ava waved a hand at my phone. "Who was bugging you?"

"Raisa. She and Malik want to come visit on her way to Stanford."

"Malik is coming with her?"

"Well, Mom can't step foot in the U.S., and as

much as I adore Petya, he's not exactly a welcome visitor here, either. I'm pretty sure every time he steps in the States, he's followed by half a dozen agencies that use up all the letters of the alphabet."

"I can never imagine that side of your life."

"I love them all. But in a lot of ways, they are like friends who come to stay or who I go and visit."

"Like me?"

I smiled at her. "Honestly, I'm closer to you than all of them. Raisa might be the exception."

Ava nodded. She understood not being close to family. There was no judgment in her eyes or her face. Her relationship with her father was nonexistent. He'd been a controlling, emotionally abusive bastard to her growing up, done some awful things to Eli and his friends, and basically walked out of her life once she got control of her trust fund.

"But at least you still talk to them. They're happy to hear from you," Ava said quietly, a hand to her flat belly. My heart panged for her, knowing that her father wouldn't know or care about his grandchild.

"I'm sorry."

"Don't be. I have Jenna's and Eli's families. I have Andy and Lacey. I have so many people who will care about this little critter that the one missing isn't a big deal."

She was confident in her words, but I knew there had to still be a very small part of her that ached for the loss of her parents. One by death, one by choice.

I still had my parents. I got a note and random calls from Dad in prison. I got a lot of texts and calls from Mom. I had people who would notice if I went missing. Before Eli had stepped into her life, Ava hadn't had many people who would have realized that something had happened to her. I was grateful to be one of them.

♫ ♫ ♫

Two days later, I boarded a plane back to New York and the storage locker that I'd placed the few belongings I'd kept after moving out of the apartment I'd lived in for over twenty years. It seemed strange that everything that mattered had fit into the smallest unit I could rent. My life with Grandma had been narrowed down to a few boxes.

After emptying the unit into the small truck I'd rented, I shut the door with a click that sounded harsh and final, as if it was confirming with noise what I knew in my heart to be true. Everything was going to be different now. My life was on a precipice. Like the ending of the first book in a duet. The crescendo high and yet so much still to come.

I was ready for my new life.

When I got to D.C., Daniella hugged me as if we'd been friends for a decade. If there was a poster child for professional D.C. staffers, she was it, in her pinstriped pencil skirt and matching jacket. She had on a lavender silk blouse that peeked from the suit and accented her gorgeous purple heels. Her hair was a shade darker than mine, and it made her blue eyes stand out. She had a smile that was wide and striking with full lips that tugged at a memory.

As if we were really lifelong friends, she insisted on helping me unload the truck after she'd changed, and to top it off, she followed me to the rental office to drop the truck off. After giving up the truck keys, I sank into her Mini Cooper, and she zipped through the D.C. traffic as if it was nothing. Between the help with the boxes and the way she drove, I was half in love with her.

"Keep spoiling me like this and I'll never move out," I told her.

She smiled at me. "I'm buttering you up so you don't move out when my obnoxious younger brother shows up."

I'd been worried about it before, but the way she teased about it, I had a feeling it was going to be okay. After we got back to the apartment, Daniella said she was heading to the gym but would be back for dinner, and then left me alone to unpack in the loft.

I'd fallen in love with the apartment back in June, and nothing had changed in the couple weeks I had been gone. It was modern, full of metal, glass, dark floors, white cabinets, and gray walls. The kitchen was to the right as we entered, and it opened up into the main living area full of windows that had a breathtaking view of the Capitol Building.

The apartment had a gray leather couch and black tables and shelves, but none of it appeared as cold as it could have because of the colorful blankets and pillows that were scattered across the furniture. What set the living area apart from anything I'd ever seen was the huge TV that had two smaller TVs on either side of it. It was disconcerting to see all three TVs on, even if only one had the volume up. When I'd first mentioned it upon seeing the apartment back in June, Daniella had said she used it to keep abreast of what was happening on the Hill after hours.

In the loft, I opened boxes, filling the wardrobe and the built-in bookshelves that lined either side of the queen-sized bed with my books, knick-knacks from my life with Grandma, and pictures of my friends and family. I softened the metal and black furniture with my own floral prints and the purples and teals I favored. Once I'd gotten through most of the boxes, I stood, arms wrapped around my middle, and stared out the wall of windows that let in the sunshine and held the same view of the Capitol Building as the windows downstairs.

I was finally here. An excitement that I'd been holding at bay filled me. It was like I had expected something to happen at the last minute that would have prevented my new life. But it hadn't.

I heard the apartment door click open, and Daniella hollered up the stairs that she was ordering Chinese, asking if I wanted some. I journeyed down the stairs with a smile on my face that I felt to my core.

While we waited for the food to arrive, Daniella made martinis as a way of welcoming me to the apartment and the city.

"If Robbie was here, he would be making fun of my martinis," she said.

"Why?"

"He's a beer drinker. I told him he's going to have to give it up and get used to the cocktails they serve at all the receptions we go to."

"My ex was all about wine and mixed drinks. The more expensive the better."

"Really?" she asked.

"He's a model."

She grinned at me. "I can see you with a model. I can see you being a model."

"I tried it out a couple times, but it wasn't for me."

"I knew it. The leather pants and peach top you were wearing the first time I met you looked like you'd stepped out of *Vogue*."

"I was jealous of your suit."

"You can have my suit. I'm so tired of wearing suits." She placed her empty glass on the coffee table and flung her head back against the couch, pulling a pillow to her stomach.

"How long have you worked on the Hill?"

"Nine years."

"You don't look old enough to have worked there that long."

She smiled at me, and her smile tugged at my memories again—so familiar and yet unplaceable. Like a dream that had flitted away before you woke.

"Thanks," she said. "I started on the Hill as a runner when I was in college. Then, I interned during the summers. Finally got a job there because of my grandfather. Washington is nothing more than one big nepotism cesspool."

I laughed. "Can't really be that different than corporate America."

"Getting your law degree, you'll fit right in here. Everybody's a lawyer."

When the food arrived, she turned on *The American President* and made fun of all the real and not real scenarios in the movie. She was funny, and it made me like her easy nature. There was no artifice that I could tell, just her being her. Like Ava, in many ways. I was glad I'd seen her ad and that she'd liked me enough to let me move in. I hoped the feelings between her brother and me would be the same, or at least that we'd be able to stand each other long enough for me to pass the bar.

Chapter Nine

Mac

HIGH HOPES
Performed by Panic! At the Disco

Truck and I spent a week out at sea together. We fished, swam, and pulled into ports to eat at dive bars. We just hung. Truck expanded on his desire to get out of Hawaii. I had a feeling there'd been a girl there who he'd been seeing and broken it off with, but he didn't want to elaborate. I didn't force it. If he wanted to talk, he would.

His baby brother had been in some trouble with the law in the small town in northern California that they'd grown up in, and Truck was in the middle of trying to get him straightened out. To get him on a course that didn't lead to serious jail time. Truck wanted to settle somewhere his brother could come stay for a while.

We didn't have that kind of trouble in our family, for whatever reason. Maybe because all of us kids had known exactly how it would impact our family if we'd messed up that badly. Our grandparents and parents were in the political and media's eye on a regular basis, and news of our screw-ups would have been plastered everywhere.

When Truck and I neared St. Petersburg, Florida, I sent a text to my buddies, Nash and Darren, to see if they wanted to meet up before Truck and I continued our journey down toward the Keys. Even though they were part of Joint Special Operations Command as members of a top secret S.E.A.L. Team Six squadron and would normally be stationed with the rest of the Naval Special Warfare Development Group out of Virginia Beach, they'd been stationed at MacDill due to classified Special Operations Command needs for the last two years. Long enough for Darren to bring his wife and baby down to Tampa.

> *NASH: Why would we want to meet up with you, traitor?*

> *DARREN: Traitor or not, we may need him when he's in office someday. We better schmooze him now while we have the chance.*

> *NASH: I don't schmooze.*

> *ME: Truck is with me.*

> *NASH: Well, hell, why didn't you say?*

We met at a restaurant that we often frequented whenever I was in town liaising between DoD Naval Intelligence and SOCOM. When Darren walked into the restaurant with his Captain America charm, eyes turned. His wife, Tristan, didn't even bat an eyelid at it. Maybe because she was equally blonde and beautiful on his arm. She had their newborn baby girl,

Hannah, swaddled up against her chest. They were the perfect, all-American family. Born in the heartland, serving their country. They were people country songs were written about.

Nash followed them in. He was the dark to their light with demons from his past that had followed him into his present. Demons that had him always picking the wrong women even when he craved what Darren had. Family. Love. Home.

"How are things?" I asked after we were all seated with drinks in front of us, except for Tristan who was still breastfeeding their little one.

"Shit. They're still trying to vet that op you've talked them out of twenty goddamn times," Nash said.

Darren cleared his throat. "It won't go through. The numbers are never in favor of it."

"The moneymen are drooling over it. They want the channels it will open." Nash glowered.

"It won't happen," I told them, taking a swig on my beer. "I've shown them the odds."

"Yeah, but you're not there anymore," Nash groused.

"If you really believe Mac had that much sway with the powers that be, then I have a bridge to sell you that goes all the way to Hawaii," Truck said.

It warmed my heart that Truck was really sticking up for me even when it sounded like he was putting me down. In his own way, he was telling Nash to back off. But my heart still clenched a little at the thought of letting Nash, Darren, and all the JSOC teams down. I'd left. It had been harder than I thought.

After dinner, Truck and I drove with Nash to

Darren's house where we were challenged to poker. Nash and Darren had been trying to beat me since I'd first been stationed on the USS *George Washington* and they'd been catching a ride. They'd already been S.E.A.L.s by the time I'd met them, and even though we'd only been on the ship together for a few months, we'd become friends—friends who cheated at poker in order to beat me, but still friends. Ever since I'd called them out on the "cheating scandal," they'd been determined to win on their own mettle. I was equally determined to not let it happen. Long after Tristan had put the baby down and gone to sleep herself, the four of us stayed up, trying to best each other in Texas Hold 'Em.

My phone buzzed.

BRAT: Where are you?

ME: At MacDill with Nash and Darren.

BRAT: Tell the otters I said hello.

Dani liked to bust their chops about being cute and cuddly sea creatures instead of hardened S.E.A.L.s.

"Dani says hi," I told them.

The men all grunted.

"Tell her she still owes me a beer," Nash said. And of course, I didn't, because there was always an undercurrent to Dani and Nash's conversations that I didn't encourage.

"What does Angie think about that?" I asked, referring to Nash's girlfriend of at least a year. Maybe more.

"I don't know, let me ask her," Nash said, waving his phone with a wicked grin that proved exactly why I didn't leave him alone with my sister.

ME: What's up?

BRAT: Roommate moved in.

ME: That sounds ominous.

BRAT: Only you would read dark and dreary into my words. Everything is good. You'll like her. She's got sass.

ME: Great. Just what I need. More women with sass in my life.

BRAT: You know you love us. When can we expect you to make an appearance?

ME: In another week or so. I'll stop in Wilmington to store the boat, and so everyone in the family can see Truck before he flies back to Hawaii.

BRAT: Okay.

ME: Do you miss me?

*BRAT: **puking GIF***

ME: So, you really, really miss me, huh?

BRAT: Just for that, I'm going to leave bugs in your bed.

ME: You wouldn't infest the apartment.

BRAT: Sigh. You're right.

I put my phone away.

"She still working for that senator?" Nash asked.

I nodded. "Yep. But only until I can snake her away to run my campaign."

"God help us all. Mac the politician." Darren grinned.

"Just for that, I'm taking all these chips," I told him as I turned over my winning hand. Everyone groaned. I swept the chips over to my pile and added, "Anyone think they can beat me yet?"

"One day, Macauley. One day." Darren smacked me on the shoulder.

♫ ♫ ♫

Early the next morning, Truck and I left Darren's house with a promise that we'd see each other again over Labor Day weekend. My family had a tradition of tennis and poker tournaments that were spread over the long weekend, and Tristan's family lived close enough to my family's homes in Greenville for them to stop by as long as their PTO held out. I hugged my friends goodbye and then was quiet while Truck and I put out to sea again.

"They're a good group," Truck said.

"Yep."

"Why the long face?"

"It's harder than I thought it would be. Leaving," I told him truthfully. "But I'm doing it for important reasons."

"For the Baby Wyatts and Baby Darrens of the world," Truck said softly.

I nodded. "Yep. They deserve a better country than the one we've deteriorated into. I want our nation to be worthy of them."

"If anyone can do it, it's you, Mac." That choked me up, and Truck saw it. He laughed and said, "Don't go all *Home Alone* and cry on me now, Macauley."

"You wish," I said.

"I wish that you'd cry? Only so I could rub it in when I see your sisters. That way, they would never let you live it down."

"They already have enough over my head."

"Siblings always do."

I sat, looking out at the ocean, the breeze in the sails sending me careening toward my new chapter. And for some reason, it made me think of Georgie and her own new chapter that she was starting. As if we had gotten to this juncture in both our lives, not by accident, but by fate. Yet, I'd left her behind, sailed away from her on purpose. Because it was obvious that politics and Russians didn't mix. That thought hurt almost as badly as leaving the Navy and my S.E.A.L. buddies. The thought that I couldn't have her and the life I wanted all at the same time.

Chapter Ten

Georgie

WHAT IF I NEVER GET OVER YOU
Performed by Lady Antebellum

A couple weeks went by with July slipping into the heat and humidity of early August. The air in D.C. was as humid as the air in New York had always been. I realized, as I settled into my new apartment, that D.C. had as much energy as the city I'd left behind, but it was an energy that held a different vibe. New York was contained chaos. D.C. was forceful control.

The planner in me required me to learn my new city—the facts, the directions, the streets. I needed to know it all. The places you didn't want to journey to on your own, as well as the places that were too rich for your blood. I'd chosen Georgetown after a significant amount of research, including the pros and cons of living in D.C., but now that I was here, I needed to experience it for real. To prove what I'd read.

The first couple days, I spent doing touristy things, like hitting up the memorials and the museums as well as learning my way around the city by foot and public transportation. Then, I wandered the campus so I knew exactly where everything was and how to traverse from one place to the next. I got my schedule and bought my books, and my excitement about going back to school slowly increased.

I found myself cracking the books open and even taking notes on the chapters. It felt good to be delving back into research and studies. The portion of my brain that I needed for papers and textbooks felt stale, and I wanted to kick the rust to the curb before the first day of school.

Once I'd started delving in, I couldn't stop. I journeyed to the law library almost daily, looking up abstracts and case law that applied. I was listening to the news Daniella had blaring from the three TVs and found new things to look up based on that news.

I was deep into my research at the library one day, typing furiously and highlighting lines in a newspaper article, when a man stopped at the table where I had my materials spread. He was in a suit and tie that seemed to have been crafted specifically for him, but what caught my attention was the look of curiosity he had on his face.

"Fourth Amendment?" he asked.

I nodded.

"Are you looking for something in particular?" he continued.

My cheeks flushed slightly. I wasn't exactly embarrassed by my uber enthusiasm, but I also wasn't sure why or if this man would really be interested in my recent obsession.

"I've been looking at varying case studies regarding search and seizure," I told him.

"Because you've been arrested?" he asked with a smile, leaning against my table in a way that put him in my personal space. I backed up at the same time I smiled.

"No, I haven't been arrested. I was just following a case on the news where a woman had told an officer she didn't consent to the search of her bag, and he did it anyway and then arrested her for the illegal drugs he found there."

The man, who still hadn't introduced himself, was slowly taking me in. "Did the officer have a warrant or cause?"

"No warrant. But the cause is the conflicting part, right? What exactly would deem a situation cause worthy?"

He looked down over my books. "Are you enrolled in summer classes or starting in the fall?"

"Starting in the fall."

He smiled. "Professor Collins on your schedule?"

I nodded.

"Well, now you've met me," he said. He stood from his lounged position. "I have to head out now, but if you stop by my office tomorrow around two, I can get you started on the case studies we'll be doing in the practicum course."

"Really? That would be great," I said, no longer caring if my enthusiasm topped the side of overly eager. "I'm Georgie, by the way."

"See you tomorrow, Georgie." He winked and left.

My stomach squished with ridiculous happiness followed by an audible growl that had me looking around to make sure no one had heard my hunger cry.

I didn't need to worry. The library was obnoxiously empty during the summer.

I packed up and headed back toward the apartment.

I stopped at a deli I'd been frequenting on my way and was waiting in line when a text from Raisa came in.

RAISA: Please put me out of my gloom.

ME: Do you mean, out of your misery?

RAISA: This is no time to correct my English.

ME: What's up?

RAISA: Father and Malik are at odds once more.

ME: Why now?

RAISA: They would not let me hear. They shut the door when I went by the study.

I often forgot about the dark side of Petya's business. Maybe it was on purpose. Maybe it was so I could have "plausible deniability." Raisa didn't have that option. She lived it. I'd joked with Ava about Petya being followed by multiple agencies when he came to the States, but I wondered now if that was also the case for my siblings. Would they have their own tails when they came? With a sort of shock to my system, I wondered if I'd been followed whenever Raisa had visited me in New York. I wondered if our conversations had been listened to.

The happiness that had filled me at the library

dimmed. Back in Rockport, I'd been hard on Mac for letting the idea of my family stop him from kissing me again. I'd pulled on my normal, to-hell-with-you attitude. But now it made me wonder if he'd been right to be wary. To step away from a woman with ties that could never mean anything good.

When I'd left Ava's, I'd also expected to leave behind Mac, our one stormy kiss, and the pull he'd had on me. Instead, he'd tormented my dreams in a way that left me aching in the morning like I hadn't ached before. As if I was suddenly missing something that had never been mine.

For the first time in a long time, my bitterness was directed at my parents instead of the person walking away from me. Would my family prevent me from more things in my life? Things other than kisses? Would I be admitted to the bar with their history sitting on my shoulders?

I returned to the last text from Raisa.

ME: It'll pass. It always does.

RAISA: It will not matter once I am at Stanford. I wish I were leaving tomorrow.

Suddenly, I feared that everything with Petya might actually matter, for both her and me, but I didn't want to be the one to darken her hopes.

ME: A few weeks more. September is right around the corner.

RAISA: Love you, moy dorogoy.

ME: Love you, malyshka.

Thoughts of my family and Mac followed me back to the apartment.

After eating a sandwich, I purposefully lost myself back in the Fourth Amendment with a podcast that I'd discovered on the topic. I allowed myself to geek out over the law and the facts that I could see in black-and-white instead of the what-ifs of my family.

When the last episode on the podcast ended, I took off my noise-cancelling headphones and heard the TV on downstairs. Daniella was home. I wondered if she'd want to catch up on the latest episode of *Fighting for the Stars*. I'd started watching the singing competition because Brady was going to be a guest host in a couple of weeks, but the show had slowly sucked me in—and Daniella along with me. It had been a good way to bond with my new roommate. We'd laughed, screamed, and thrown things at the TV over the judging.

Now, I could use the show and her company to continue distracting me from my thoughts.

I headed down the stairs, water bottle in hand. "Hey, Daniella…" I started, and I abruptly stopped when I realized that she wasn't alone on the couch. There were two dark heads tucked together—one decidedly male. "Oh. I'm sorry. I didn't realize your boyfriend was here."

The two bodies jumped apart. Daniella yelled, "Ew," at the same time that the male said, "What the fuck?"

My water bottle clattered to the floor as the male body that rose from the couch and turned to face me was the same one that had haunted my dreams. Now he was here...in sweats and a T-shirt that showed every part of him that I'd tried desperately to forget.

We all stood, staring at each other as if someone could find an explanation as to how—in all of D.C.—Mac had ended up in my apartment.

Chapter Eleven

Mac

WHY GEORGIA
Performed by John Mayer

I stood, staring at Georgie like she was a ghost. She felt like a ghost. A ghost in yoga pants and a Panic! At the Disco T-shirt that looked like it had seen one too many washings. Her hair was pulled back in a ponytail that hid her white stripe. I'd just spent weeks at sea with Truck in order to forget her. To put her behind me. And now she was in my apartment, looking better than any memory I'd had of her, even better than in that damn summer dress she wore the last night in Rockport. Because she was real. Flesh-and-blood real. Kissable-lips real. Body-that-fit-into-mine-perfectly real.

I could feel my sister staring at me like I'd lost my mind, but I didn't even turn to her. "What the fuck?" I repeated.

"Mac?" Georgie's voice was as surprised as I felt.

"Wait. You two know each other?" Dani asked.

Georgie turned to her. "You said your brother's name was Robbie."

"It is."

I groaned. "It's my middle name. Robert. I haven't gone by Robbie since high school."

"You were the one who hated Macauley," Dani teased.

"Just like you hated Daniella, and yet that's what you go by almost exclusively now."

"You still call me Dani."

"Well." I rubbed my hand through my hair and down my face that needed a shave. It was almost a full beard from the weeks on my sailboat. Dani was right. I was one of the last holdouts in our family, still calling her and all my sisters by their nicknames. Gabi. Bee. Dani. It was probably only fair that they still called me Robbie after years of hating the name Macauley with a passion.

Georgie was watching us, eyes ping-ponging back and forth, going wider and wider.

"You live here?" she finally breathed out, as if it was finally catching up with her.

I nodded.

She sat down on the bottom step. I didn't blame her for needing to sit. I felt like I might need to keel over myself. This was so screwed up that I didn't even know where to start. Dani had never told me the new roommate's name, I realized now. She'd just said she had brown hair and brown eyes. Georgie's hair was closer to black than brown, like my own, and her eyes changed color with her outfits, so it wasn't really Dani's fault that she'd told me she had brown ones.

Dani and I hadn't talked much while I'd been at sea. The cell signal was pretty much impossible unless

I was in port, and Truck and I hadn't spent much time in port.

Dani perched on the arm of the couch.

"How do you two know each other?"

"Ava," Georgie said just as I said, "Eli."

"Oohhhh," Dani said, and she gave me a wicked smile because I had told her about the dark-haired woman I'd kissed and left behind. Damn sisters. Nosing into everything. Dani started laughing. "This is really funny."

The more she laughed, the more it loosened the knots in my stomach. You couldn't not laugh with Dani. She had a great laugh. And she was laughing so hard that she had to wipe at her tears. I couldn't help the chuckle that escaped, and when I looked over at Georgie, she started to smile, too.

"Your smiles," Georgie finally said over all of our laughter.

"What?" Dani asked.

"Your smiles are so similar. I kept trying to figure out who your smile reminded me of. It's the same as Mac's."

"People used to think we were twins," Dani said. "And I'm not sure I can get used to you calling him Mac."

"I'm not sure I'll ever be able to consider him a Robbie."

I crossed my arms over my chest. "This is really preposterous."

"Preposterous or unbelievable?" Dani asked.

"Aren't they the same thing?"

Georgie finally rose from the seat she'd taken on the stairs, picked up her water bottle, and went to the kitchen where I could hear her filling it. Dani was watching me, and I pulled on my poker face—the one that had me earning lots of dollars against my academy and Navy buddies. It was harder to have a poker face with people who'd known you your whole life, but I tried.

I sat back down on the couch, and Dani joined me. This time, she left more space between us than had been there before. I could see how Georgie had mistaken me for a boyfriend, with Dani's head on my shoulder. I wasn't ashamed of being close with any of my family. Being a hugger was yet another thing, like my cussing, that I was going to have to filter out of my personality, though. I didn't want to be on the secret list women in the government passed around D.C. The list that said: "Stay away from that guy."

Georgie came back in and paused behind the couch, both hands surrounding her water bottle, squeezing. "What's this?" she asked, waving toward the TV.

"*Good Will Hunting*. You've never seen it?" Dani asked.

Georgie shook her head.

"That's almost a sin," I said.

"It's an incredibly romantic movie," Dani told her.

"It's not. It's an underdog story," I objected.

"With a great romance."

"And Robin Williams."

"Do you want to watch it with us?" Dani asked her. I could feel Georgie's eyes on the back of my head. I didn't want to chance looking at her, because Dani was still analyzing the air between us.

"Nah. I'm going to hit the hay. One of the professors caught me studying at the library, and he asked if I wanted to come by tomorrow and get a head start on some of the case studies."

I snorted. I bet he did.

"What?"

Now, I couldn't not look at her. I turned sideways, looking up. Her hands were still clutching the water bottle like it might be a lifeline, but her face was still. Her poker face was good but not quite as good as mine.

"You realize he was hitting on you, right?"

"No, he wasn't."

"Yes, he was," Dani agreed with me.

Georgie looked between us, her cheeks flushing slightly. "Why would he do that? I'm a student."

"Puh-lease. Guys in this city see a gorgeous woman, and they always hit on them. Sleep with them, too, if they find someone willing. Married or not. Welcome to D.C.," Dani explained.

"But it's against the code of conduct, I'm sure."

"Girl, you and I need to have a whole conversation about D.C. men if you're going to live here. I thought, with all the models and finance guys you dealt with in New York, you'd have a bit more of a 'sleaze-o-meter,'" Dani told her.

I was just watching. Georgie was flustered but trying not to be. It grabbed at my heart and yanked it up to my throat and then back down to my balls. It made me want to go with her to the professor's office so I could tell him to back the hell off. But I had no right to. I couldn't afford to want to.

"I can sense a sleazy finance guy a mile away, and an egotistical, self-centered model—because that's pretty much all of them. I guess I had hoped that was behind me in the academic world. I didn't have this problem when I was at school before."

"Probably because you were too young. Now, you're gorgeous, all grown up, and this professor thinks you'll be more up for it without the repercussions of a dramatic post-teen. It's like the officials who won't mess with the summer interns, but once you become permanent, you're fair game," Dani coached.

Georgie headed for the stairs to the loft. "You realize that, even if he was legitimately just wanting to help me out, I'll never be able to see it that way now."

Good, I thought to myself and took a swig of beer.

"You'll be fine. Do you want Mac to go with you just so he sees you have some oversized behemoth ready to go to battle for you?"

I choked on the beer. "What?"

Dani was smirking at me.

"No. I'm fine. I know how to handle myself. Pepper spray and all." Georgie continued up the stairs. "Goodnight."

"Goodnight," Dani said. When I said nothing, she smacked my chest.

"Goodnight, Georgie." Her name on my lips was like acid dissolving in my stomach, eruptions of thoughts that I shouldn't have tearing at the lining there and making me want to run into the loft after her and kiss her again.

I hit play on the movie, determined to put thoughts of Georgie sleeping in the bed upstairs out of my head.

After a few minutes, Dani whispered, "This is very interesting."

"It's the worst goddamn thing that could have happened," I whispered back.

"Maybe it's the universe telling you something?"

I already knew what the universe thought. I'd felt it in the kiss on my boat in Rockport. I'd felt it in every inch of my body every time I'd casually touched her. The problem was that the universe seemed to have forgotten she had a dad in jail, and a mom with a revoked visa, and that I planned on running for office.

"Whatever it's trying to say, the universe is wrong."

Dani laughed quietly. "I don't think that's the way it works."

After a few more minutes of the movie—of which I saw none, not that it mattered because Dani and I had seen this movie a thousand times at least—Dani added on, "Are you going to go with her tomorrow?"

"No."

"What if he's a real asshole who grabs her and then threatens to have her kicked out before she's even started? This is her second chance at law school. It would ruin it for her."

"You heard her. She can take care of herself, and I believe her."

"Did she pull a ninja move on you?"

"No. I never shove myself on anyone, you know that."

"Then, how do you know she can take care of herself?"

"Why are you pushing?" I asked.

Dani looked at me. "You like her."

"Dani, did she tell you about her family?"

Dani shook her head. I whispered to her about Georgie's dad and mom.

"Yikes."

"What would you tell some newbie who was trying to run for office with a wife who had a dad in jail for Ponzi schemes and a mother banned from entering the country?"

"I'd tell him to get a new wife or walk away."

"Exactly," I said.

"But you aren't trying to marry her, right? I mean, you obviously like her. There's no reason the two of you can't—"

"No," I said, shaking my head. "You don't understand. If I started something with her, I'd never be able to walk away."

"This is completely unlike you. You've never kept a girl for more than a month. Except that godawful Mindy who wasn't anyone that any of us wanted to see you with for the long haul."

I made a face at the mention of Mindy. I couldn't believe I hadn't seen that one coming. I didn't say anything; I just watched as Matt Damon blew off Minnie Driver on the screen, pushing her away with all his hateful words so she'd leave him alone. I couldn't be hateful to Georgie. Not ever. But I also couldn't let her under my skin or into my heart any more than she already was. The mark she'd left there would have to be a simple notch and not an entire tattoo.

Dani snuggled back down onto the couch, and I could practically hear her wheels turning from where I was, but there wasn't anything that could change the facts. And the facts were all that mattered in this case.

♫ ♫ ♫

When Dani and I left for the Capitol the next morning, Georgie hadn't appeared from the loft. I eyed it a couple times, wondering what she'd do about the professor. I hadn't been able to sleep a damn wink the night before. I'd tossed and turned, not only because she was under the same roof as me again, but because I'd worried about her.

Dani and I spent the morning getting me signed in with human resources and security at the Capitol. By the time we actually got to Guy Matherton's office, he and my grandfather were there and in the midst of some top-secret briefing. For a moment, I felt a brief pang at the loss of my old job. I'd always been in the know. It had been my job to be in the know. I probably had a clearance level higher than any of the people in this office, but that didn't change the fact I was the newbie on the block. Guy's assistant let him know we were there, and Granddad came out right away.

My grandfather was huge like me. Huge like my father. Tall and built. He'd kept his figure, even more so after the bypass surgery he'd had to have five years ago. He looked younger than he was, but he still looked like a speckle-haired, wrinkled version of me.

Granddad hugged me. "Robbie, I'm so glad you're finally here with us."

"He seems to be going by Macauley now," Dani teased just as Guy came out of his office to shake my hand.

"Nice to have you onboard, Macauley." The senator looked like a young Mark Harmon. He looked like someone you'd trust to go into battle with you. He was younger than my parents but still old enough to have teenage daughters. He was one of the up-and-coming on the Hill and not just because of his good looks. He was smart and seemed to always be on the right side of any legislation.

Out of the corner of my eye, I saw Dani smirk as he repeated my full name.

"Mac," I told him, returning his handshake with a firm grip.

"Daniella will get you up to speed, I'm sure. We have a whole pile of defense bills I'd like you to take a look through and give me your opinion on. Plus, there's a long list of things I need you to research for us. Isn't that right?"

Guy looked at Dani like she was a star. It threw me for a loop. It threw me right back to Dani saying she could sense the sleaze-o-meter a mile away. I hadn't ever thought of Guy as a sleaze. My grandfather wouldn't work for a sleazeball. I knew that. But Guy was married. Had two teen-aged kids. But he was smiling at my sister in a way I just didn't care for.

When we got to our desks, which were shoved together in a side room that felt smaller than the inside of a manned submersible vehicle, I confronted her.

"Has he ever made a pass at you?"

"What? No! Guy's one of the good ones."

"Then, how come he was looking at you like you were the best thing since the Bill of Rights?"

She grimaced. "It's like the way Dad used to look at you in your uniform. He's just proud of the success I've had. Success that's made him look better."

Out of all my sisters, Dani had the best track record with men. My middle sister, Bee, had a husband who we all still rolled our eyes at. And Gabi once had a boyfriend who was a drug dealer, and even though we'd confronted her about him using, she'd still been surprised when he'd been arrested. Dani had never had any bad men in her life. She'd always dated the clean-cut, wholesome type. But now, with the way Guy had looked at her, I was wondering if Dani was as oblivious as Georgie had been with her professor, which just made me worried all over again about Georgie.

"Do you want me to text her?" Dani asked.

"What?"

"Georgie."

"How did you— No."

"It's written all over your face. You really do have it bad for her."

"I left Rockport early on purpose so I wouldn't have it bad for her," I said with a sigh and picked up the first report I was supposed to review.

"And now she's living with you," Dani teased.

"Don't make it sound like that."

She grabbed my phone off my desk, typing into it.

"What are you doing?"

"Adding Georgie's number to your phone."

"Godda—dang it, Dani. Butt out."

"What are we, ten?" She smirked, handing the phone back to me. "Just tell her I wanted you to ask if she was okay."

I stared down at the open message box. At the top was the contact name Dani had entered. It read: "The One." My heart fell in on itself.

"She's not the one," I told her, putting the phone down. But I didn't change the contact name, and Dani noticed, smirking at me again.

"Working with you is going to be more fun than I expected," she said. I threw several paperclips at her. One hit her on the forehead, but she just laughed.

Coming back to D.C. had been what I wanted. Now, I was thinking I needed to be thousands of miles away again. I'd walked away from my naval career and my job at the DoD because I'd thought it was time, but maybe I needed to reconsider. Maybe I needed to get posted back on the USS *George Washington* until Georgie was done with law school. Then, I could come back, safely, to Washington. I was a chickenshit. She was just one woman. I'd resisted plenty of women before. I could do this, whether she was living with us or not.

Shit.

Chapter Twelve

Georgie

WALK ME HOME
Performed by P!nk

I was a little edgy by the time I got to Professor Collins' office door. Dani—because I couldn't think of her as Daniella now that I'd heard the nickname that suited her so much better—and Mac's warnings were playing around in my head. I wished I could have just forgotten the whole damn conversation. But wishing away things hadn't gone my way lately. If ever. I hadn't been able to wish away my father's arrest, my mother's departure, or my grandmother's death. I hadn't been able to wish away my body's reaction to Mac. Wishes and I were at an all-time low.

I knocked and opened the door when I heard, "Come in."

What I noticed now—that I hadn't the day before—was that Professor Collins was much younger than what had been stored in my memory. He couldn't have been more than forty. Young enough to be attracted to women on campus, old enough for me to say no way. My dad had been way older than my mom, and look how that had worked out.

"Hi," I said, drawing my bag to the front of me almost like a shield.

He looked up from his desk and smiled. It was an attractive smile. One I was sure got him a lot of crushes, especially from the younger students. He had a blond-haired, chiseled look that was probably drool-worthy if I wasn't already drooling in my dreams over a certain chiseled, dark-haired body. I had a flash of the scene from *Raiders of the Lost Ark* with the girl winking her "I love you" eyes at Harrison Ford. Professor Collins would have loved to be Harrison Ford.

"Georgie, is it?" He was nonchalant, as if he was trying to recall my name and the reason that brought me to his office. I couldn't tell if it was an act or real.

He came around the desk, leaning against it, legs out. I fidgeted by the door.

"Fourth Amendment, right?"

I nodded.

"Come on in. I'll dig up some case studies we're going to be going over, and you can get a head start."

He went to a shelf by the windows. Damn Mac and Dani. I pushed away my unease and sat down in one of the leather chairs in front of his desk. He came back with a binder in his hands and brushed against my legs with his, as if not paying attention, but returned to his position propped against the desk. I'd worn jeans even though it was too hot for them. I'd spent most of my time in Washington in a series of summer dresses, trying to keep cool. Not today. Not with the stupid conversation going through my head that I was thinking now wasn't so stupid.

He handed me the binder, our hands touching.

"Think that will get you started," he said, retracting his hands slowly, eyeing my left hand. My body and brain went on high alert. I would have been on alert by now even without Mac and Dani's voices in my head. "Where are you from?"

"New York," I said with a calm voice and straight face that I'd practiced for years.

"What brings you back to academia?"

"It was time to follow my own dreams again."

"That's a good reason," he said with a suave smile. A smile that I wondered if he practiced in the mirror. I looked at his left hand. No ring, but that didn't mean anything. "What made you give up your dreams before?"

"My grandmother passed away," I responded. I didn't know how much I wanted to share with him, because I didn't like the whole vibe that was in the air.

"You'll be older than most of the students, but don't let that put you off."

I bristled slightly. I was only twenty-eight. Some kids didn't even finish their bachelor's till they were twenty-four or more. I wasn't going to be ancient compared to them, but that was the way he wanted me to feel. I recognized it as an alienation tactic, and I had to stop myself from getting up and shoving the binder back into his chest with a few nasty words.

"If they make you uncomfortable," he continued, frowning as my phone buzzed and I had the audacity to look down at it. It was an unknown number, but I caught sight of Dani's name and scanned it quickly.

UNKNOWN: Dani wants me to ask if the meeting with Professor Sleaze went okay.

I smiled and looked up, realizing I hadn't heard what he'd said. "I'm sorry?"

"Phones won't be tolerated in class."

His easy nonchalance took on a bitter tone. I definitely didn't need to make enemies with one of my first professors. "Oh, absolutely. I know that."

"As I was saying, if the other students make you uncomfortable, you're welcome to let me know."

Building trust. Another tactic.

"Look…" I started to call him out on all his bullshit. To tell him that he wasn't going to be able to alienate me into sleeping with him. But then, I bit my tongue and looked away, because what if he had the ability and the ambition to stop my studies before they began? What if he said I made a pass at him? Would it matter?

I hated—with every inch of me—backing down from this jerk, and perhaps some of my feelings were floating on the air, because his eyes narrowed. Or maybe he was simply waiting for me to finish the sentence I'd started and had left hanging, which made me seem like an idiot who couldn't speak.

I swallowed my smart retort and stood, which unfortunately brought me much closer to him than I wanted to be. He stood, too, and we were almost nose-to-nose because I was so tall. I wasn't sure he'd really realized that before.

"I'm sure everything will be fine, but thanks for all this." I waved the binder at him, stepping backward. I kept my scathing words to myself because I wanted this more than anything else. More than putting an asshole in his place. I didn't want to put an end to everything I'd wanted before it had even started.

My phone buzzed again.

> *UNKNOWN: Dani is worried that you're lying in a gutter now.*

I couldn't help the smile. "Sorry. My boyfriend needs me to come get him. Car broke down."

"Boyfriend?"

"Yes. I moved to Washington to be with him. He works for Senator Matherton."

I was name-dropping and lying all at the same time. Things I normally hated, but things I knew would at least put some distance between me and a professor with predatory tendencies. He would be less apt to pursue me if I had important connections and a boyfriend to come storming down his door. It might, at the very least, not offend him so he wouldn't take the rejection out on me.

Professor Collins frowned again then turned back to his desk. "I'll need the binder back before the first week of school, so get what you need and then return it."

His smiles were no longer as wide. Shit. I had pissed him off.

I held back again, wanting to say, *Thanks but no thanks, dickhead,* and throw the binder into his office so it would spill open and rain papers all around. Instead, I said with a sweetness I didn't feel, "Absolutely. Thank you so much for the opportunity to get ahead on the course."

"You're welcome."

I rushed out of the office, fingers trembling with anger and bile. I'd handled way worse in New York. Finance guys who didn't know how to take no for an answer. Model friends of Jared's who thought that being in a relationship just meant there was more to go around. But what had my hands shaking this time was the possibility that this man was in a position to screw up my new life for me.

UNKNOWN: Dani is calling 911 as we speak.

ME: I'm fine. Sorry. Just walked out of the douchebag's office.

UNKNOWN: So, he was hitting on you?

ME: And is now completely pissed off and going to make my life hell.

UNKNOWN: Did you taser him or pepper spray him?

ME: Neither. I'm assuming this is Mac, BTW.

UNKNOWN: Yes, it's Mac, and do you need me to come take care of him?

I started to type, "No, I think it'll be fine. I told him that I had a boyfriend," and then backed it up. I'd used Mac and his position, and that wasn't normally me. I wasn't sure how he'd react to it. Then, I sighed and just typed the truth.

ME: I told him I had a boyfriend who needed me to come get him because his car broke down.

There was a long pause while the dots came and went, letting me know he was texting me.

UNKNOWN: So, I was the boyfriend?

ME: Don't go freaking out on me, Mac-Macauley. He didn't know it was you on the other end of my buzzing phone. It was just a buzzing phone to him.

UNKNOWN: If you need me, I'll always pretend to be your boyfriend to ensure the douche doesn't think he can take advantage of you.

My stupid heart went pitter-patter too fast. Ridiculous. I had to get a handle on this. It was exactly what Descartes warned of. Don't let the dream senses override the reality.

My pause had given Mac ammunition to use against me.

UNKNOWN: Don't freak out, Georgie-Girl. I would just be pretending to be your boyfriend.

*ME: ** Eyeroll GIF***

UNKNOWN: Dani and I are almost done here for the day. We're going to stop at Franklin's for happy hour. Do you want to join us?

Yes. No. Yes. No. That was the war that went on between my body and my brain.

> *ME: Thanks, but I'm going to take a look at this binder of case studies that I now have to give back to him next week.*

After way too much deliberation, I changed Mac's contact name simply to "The Guy." I'd no sooner done that than Dani was texting me.

> *DANIELLA: Come to happy hour.*

> *ME: Really, thanks, but no.*

> *DANIELLA: I swear my brother doesn't bite, no matter what your impression of him is.*

Jesus. The thought of Mac biting was enough to turn my body into a quivering mass of melted marshmallow. Biting…nibbling. The things that had me waking up from my dreams in sweats for weeks.

> *ME: I'm not afraid of Mac.*

> *DANIELLA: I think you're both afraid of each other.*

It was the frank way Dani had about her that I'd come to adore in the few short weeks that I'd known her. But it was also terrifying that she had read the situation between Mac and me so easily the night before. Unless Mac had talked to her about me, which just made me curious if he had and what he'd said.

ME: I'm going now. Have fun. I'll see you later.

♫ ♫ ♫

I was just heading downstairs to fill my water bottle, when I heard them come home. I sank back down on the bed. I had purposely turned off every light in the apartment, except the one over the stove, in order to make them think I'd gone to bed early. I was such a chicken. I was hiding, and I hated it. It wasn't my normal mode of operation at all. But I didn't want to talk with either of them, because they were both too good at reading what went on inside of me.

They were quiet, talking back and forth, but I couldn't make out what they were saying. I thought I heard my name but wasn't sure. Once the apartment got quiet, I went downstairs. I filled my bottle at the dispenser and then turned to find Mac standing there.

I gave a little yelp because he'd walked up so quietly. I placed my hand to my chest. It was pounding an erratic beat that had way more to do with his naked chest than the fact that he'd startled me. Below his naked torso, he had on a pair of pajama bottoms. They were slung low on his hips, perfect for tugging down; perfect for everything I knew I could have with him. Back in Rockport, I'd rated him as a ten, and now he looked all ten of those stars and more.

"Sorry," he said with a smirk that belied his words.

I made to move past him. "Well, goodnight."

He put a hand out and stopped me. His hand on my bare skin. He eyed me up and down, and I realized that I was in my sleep shorts and a tank and nothing else. It wasn't anything less than the bikini he'd seen me in earlier this summer, but somehow, this was more intimate—both of us in pajamas. It spoke of beds and kisses even more than swimwear did.

"Do you need me to come with you to see the professor next time?" he asked.

"No, he's not anything I can't handle." It was the truth. Even if it meant getting kicked out, I knew how to handle men like Professor Collins.

But there was something about his offer that tugged at the little girl in me. Ever since my grandma had died, I'd sort of handled everything in my life on my own. The burial. The estate. Mom and Petya had offered advice from Russia, Dad had been allowed a small visitation for the funeral, and the rest I'd done solo. I was used to it.

As if reading my mind, Mac said, "You don't have to handle it alone, though."

He hadn't removed his hand from my arm, and now his thumb was circling on the inside of my wrist, causing sensations that were like water running down a stream toward a lake, building up into something bigger as it rolled along.

"He's definitely a slime bucket, and I'll try to carefully warn the women in my class about him, but it's going to be fine."

We stared at each other, the space between us so small that, with a tiny step, I could have brushed my lips against his. Could have tested the results from our first go around. Would it feel like all the stars had lit me up like it did the first time? My eyes drifted to his lips, and when I looked back at his eyes, I expected to see him grinning at my slip, but instead, his eyes were dark pools in the ambient light of the apartment with the electronics and the lights of the city streaming in the windows.

"I feel like fate is trying to tell us something," Mac said quietly, the deepness of his voice accented by his attempt at a whisper.

"You're reading way too much into all of this."

"Am I? In a city of nearly eight hundred thousand people, you ended up in my apartment. I don't think enough can be read into it."

His hand had journeyed up from my wrist, skirting the inside of my elbow before continuing a slow dance up to my shoulder.

"Do you want me to move?" I asked, and his hand froze before he pulled it back to rest on the counter.

"No." It was guttural and chopped. "Why would you say that?"

"You ran from Rockport because of me. Now I'm here. I don't want to make you uncomfortable."

"Georgie, uncomfortable is the last thing you make me."

He didn't deny that he'd run away from Rockport because of me. That newfound bitterness crept into my heart, but I didn't know who I was directing it at. Him. My family. Me. I stepped around him, and this time, he let me go, but his words halted me as I started across the living space.

"Do I make you uncomfortable?"

Yes, I thought again. "No, Mac-Macauley. If you're good, I'm good."

I got to the stairs, and his voice halted me one more time. "Goodnight, Georgie-Girl."

I smiled and kept going. We'd both lied. We both made each other uncomfortable. But I loved the apartment and my loft with the view of the Hill. I loved how close it was to campus. I liked Dani and the camaraderie we'd built in just the few weeks I'd been here. I didn't want to lose any of that. If Mac and I stayed out of each other's hair, there wouldn't be a problem. We were adults, not teenagers in the throes of first lust.

I got upstairs and texted Ava.

ME: You awake?

It took her a few minutes to respond.

AVA: Of course, at the bar. What's up?

ME: My roommate's brother showed up.

AVA: This sounds ominous. Is he a wackadoodle?

I chuckled.

ME: Depends. Do you think Mac is a wackadoodle?

AVA: Wait. Your roommate is Dani? As in, Mac's sister, Dani? As in, you are now roommates with Mac?

ME: Bingo.

*AVA: **laughing emoji***

ME: This is hardly funny.

AVA: OMG. I can't breathe. This is hilarious.

ME: No. It's not. How can it possibly be that, in a city this large, I'd find a room with Mac?

AVA: Look at Eli and me. We found each other in a city of eight million. Fate has a funny way of playing its cards.

ME: Not you too.

AVA: Not me too, what?

ME: Talking about fate. There isn't such a thing.

AVA: Did Mac say that? That you were fated to find each other again? It doesn't sound like Mac. It sounds more like Eli. Or Truck.

ME: Maybe they've rubbed off on him.

*AVA: Maybe you've rubbed off on him. **eggplant emoji***

ME: Gross. No.

AVA: Says the woman who rated him a ten.

ME: This is just…weird.

AVA: Eli is going to smile so hard it will break his face when I tell him.

ME: I'm surprised he doesn't already know.

AVA: Me too.

ME: I'm off to bed, but make sure you send me lots of good vibes. I have a feeling I'm going to need them.

AVA: Am I sending vibes that you end up in his bed or vibes that you don't?

ME: You're impossible.

AVA: I just want you to be happy. Mac is a wonderful human being under all that bravado.

ME: I don't need a man to be happy.

AVA: Of course you don't, but take it from someone who thought she'd always be alone, having someone in your life who sees you for everything you are and loves you… There's nothing better. Nothing.

ME: Goodnight. I'm going before you get all sappy and write me a song while you're at it.

AVA: I may need to write a song about this

no matter what.

*ME: **eye roll emoji***

AVA: xoxoxo

Ava and Mac had both made comments about it being fated. I wasn't sure I believed in fate. I believed in working hard to make things happen. I believed in good karma, and bad karma, and that what you put out into the universe you got back, but I wasn't sure I believed in all things destined to be. Mac and I weren't fated to find each other. It was just a strange coincidence.

And no matter what Ava said, Mac certainly wasn't ready to see me for everything I—or my family—was and accept it anyway.

No. We were definitely not fated to be. But we could find a way to live together and not make it anything more.

At least, that was the lie I was going to tell myself in order to sleep.

Chapter Thirteen

Mac

DON'T GO CHANGING
Performed by Aly & AJ

I felt my eyes flutter shut in the middle of reading the report on my desk, and before I could encourage myself to open them, a paperclip hit me in the forehead. I jerked my eyes open to glare at Dani, sitting across from me with a smile on her face.

"This is war," I said, picking up the paperclip and aiming at her chest. She covered her breasts with her hands.

"Don't be juvenile." She said it with a stern voice, but she was smiling. "Why are you so tired? We got home early last night."

"I couldn't sleep."

"Couldn't or didn't?"

"What are you getting at?"

"Did you visit our new roommate in her loft?"

"No!" I said with too much intensity, and she caught on like only sisters can do.

"But you wanted to."

I rubbed my forehead and turned back to the report on the number of fishing boats in the state of Delaware and the impact on the local economy from their slow demise.

"She's pretty incredible. Almost too good for you, but not quite," Dani said, continuing to push the matter.

"Back off, Gooberpants." I looked up in time to see her stick her tongue out at me at the nickname I rarely called her anymore. "We already talked about this."

"Like I already said, she doesn't have to be the one you stick a ring on, Robbie. But I can see you having a good time together. You haven't really dated anyone except—"

"Don't!"

"Okay, I won't say it. I'm just saying, dating her would give you practice. Get you out of the single-man dance."

"You're telling me to date her, knowing I can't plan a future with her."

"It's just dating."

"I thought all women wanted was a potential forever from the men they dated."

"Maybe in the 1950s."

She went back to her report, and I tried to read mine, but all I could see was Georgie's pale, jade-colored eyes. Her real color. The way they'd clouded over with emotion when I'd rubbed her arm last night. The way she'd looked at my lips as if she'd wanted to kiss them. We were definitely battling an attraction stronger than I'd ever felt before.

I tossed the report on the desk.

"Some of this stuff seems so…"

"Mundane?"

"No. I mean, I know it's important to the people in our state. I'm just used to things that are…"

"More life and death?"

"Stop doing that."

"What?"

"Finishing my sentences. It's weird."

"It's the job."

"Finishing my sentences is the job?" I teased.

She rolled her eyes. "I know it's not the same as the stuff you did at the DoD, but this is also life and death for some people. Our state really needs a revitalization of the fishing industry."

I nodded. She was right on all counts. It did seem less critical in many ways, but I also understood that what I was reading about meant a lot to the families whose lives depended on fishing. It meant a house and food on the table. But it did seem less critical than the things I'd dealt with when planning black ops.

"I'm going to go get a coffee. Do you want anything?" I asked, standing.

"Chocolate."

"Any specific kind of chocolate?"

"You'll know it when you see it."

"That's trusting me with a lot. I remember bringing you back an Almond Joy one time, and you chucked it at me."

"Who wants coconut and nuts in their chocolate?" she said in disgust.

"See. Trusting me with a lot."

"Chocolate, Robbie. Chocolate. Not nuts. Not coconut. Chocolate."

"Okay, but when you hate it, I'm eating it."

And I walked out.

♪ ♪ ♪

That night, when we got home, Georgie was on the couch with some show on that had people singing. Dani flopped down on the couch next to her, instantly enthralled as they barreled into a debate that made me realize they'd been watching it while I'd been at sea.

I sat down on the other side of Georgie, putting my feet up on the coffee table, and our legs knocked together. She adjusted, pulling hers away from me.

The people on the stage were croaking out something in a godawful voice.

"What the hell is this?" I asked.

"*Fighting for the Stars*," they both said at the same time without looking at me once. Eyes glued to the TV.

"It's awful."

"Shh," Dani said.

"This duo is, but you should hear Kerri who is up next," Georgie said over the top of Dani's shushing.

The TV flashed to a row of people sitting at a table in front of the stage before returning to the couple onstage.

"Wait. Was that Brady?" I asked.

Georgie nodded. "Yep, he's one of the guest judges this week."

I couldn't help but feel that roll in my chest that I'd felt when Georgie had run into his arms at The Salty Dog back in July. It was unwarranted. Undeserved. I couldn't have her, but I didn't think Brady could either. She didn't seem the type to go flitting around the country after a musician.

I couldn't stomach the thoughts or the show, so I rose from the couch and headed to the kitchen. "I'm going to order from Bentley's. You ladies want something?"

"Of course. I'll have the lasagna tonight," Dani said without once having removed her eyes from the screen.

"What's Bentley's?" Georgie asked, looking at me.

"Only the best Italian outside of our grandma's," I retorted.

"Don't let Vinnie hear you say that," Dani said, laughing, turning to join our conversation as a commercial started.

"Who's Vinnie?" Georgie asked.

"Our brother-in-law. He's married to Gabi, our oldest sister. He owns an Italian restaurant in Wilmington. It's decent, but it's one step further removed from Grandma's than Bentley's, but we humor Vinnie and Gabi by saying it's the best," Dani explained.

I handed Georgie the menu we had hanging on the refrigerator because, as much as we loved Bentley's, we didn't have a standard order. It changed with our mood and often required a deep perusal of the options that we really had memorized.

"I'll have an order of the gnocchi," Georgie said.

"Good choice," I told her.

I called in the order, and she went to her purse, handing me some cash. "Nah, we take turns. This one is on me."

She looked to Dani, but Dani was back to staring at the singing on the TV now that the commercial was over.

"Honest. We take turns. Next meal can be on you."

"Okay, but if this is just a way to pay for the poor college student, I happen to know where you live and can gut you in your sleep." She winked.

I chuckled. "Said the lady to the spy."

She grinned. "I always forget that part about you."

Then, she returned to the sofa, and Dani, and the show they both were watching like it was the next coming of *M.A.S.H.*

As the night progressed, I observed with a strange sort of fascination as my sister and Georgie argued over the singers who came and went on the TV. They were so comfortable with each other that I was jealous, happy, and captivated all at the same time. Dani got along with everyone, for the most part, but she didn't let anyone get close. She'd had a hard time in high school in the shadow of our two perfect, gorgeous older sisters. She'd always felt like an ugly duckling. But she'd slowly come into her own beauty. Regardless, she made acquaintances easily, but friends not so much. It was refreshing to see her get along with Georgie.

When the show ended, Dani rose with a yawn. "I'm

turning in. I have a five a.m. spin class tomorrow."

"That seems obnoxiously early to have a spin class," Georgie said, and I snorted.

"What?" she asked me.

"That's exactly what I tell her every time she takes it. And then she'll be griping about how tired she is all day long," I responded.

"Well, tomorrow night, I have plans, so I can't do it at night."

"Like a date?" I asked.

"No. A work thing."

"How come I don't know about this work thing? Am I not invited?" I teased.

"Week one and you think you can just blow in and take over everything." She kicked my legs off the coffee table as she went by, and I kicked her in the butt. She flipped me off as she went around the corner.

"Classy, Daniella," I called after her.

She didn't respond.

I turned back to Georgie to see her smiling, and I couldn't help the smile that took over my face in response. "What?" I asked.

"The sibling thing. It's nice."

"She's a pain in the ass, but I love her. Are you close with your siblings?" I asked. I'd eased myself down onto the couch farther, my head resting along the back, and when I turned my head toward her, we were close. Almost as close as we'd been the night before when she'd looked like she wanted to kiss me.

The humor and lightness that I'd been teasing Dani with went whooshing out of me in one big breath.

"It's kind of hard to be really close when they live on another continent," she said quietly.

"I'm sorry," I said, feeling like a dick for having brought it up, for not thinking about the fact that her siblings were in Russia.

"It's okay. Raisa and I—that's my little sister—we're pretty close. She usually visits me during the summer, but she is starting at Stanford in the fall, and I don't think Petya and Mom wanted her to leave until she had to."

"Stanford, huh?" I repeated like a moron, but I just wanted to keep her talking to me. I wanted to keep her relaxed and sitting there where her smell could wash over me.

"Yep. She's one of the smartest people I know and all at the age of eighteen. She has this whole plan to create clean, renewable energy that she can offer to the world for free."

"Like in *The Saint*?"

"What?" she asked with a little frown.

"You know, the movie with Val Kilmer and Elisabeth Shue."

"Don't know it."

"I feel like your knowledge of American films is woefully lacking," I said as I grabbed the remote from her and did a search for the movie. When I found it, I hit play.

"Don't you have to go to sleep? You have work in the morning," she said.

"I haven't been sleeping anyway. Maybe I'll be exhausted after this."

She didn't move from her spot, and as the movie

progressed, she relaxed into the couch. Her legs that were tucked underneath her were touching my hips. I wasn't sure she was aware of it, but I was very highly aware of it. Bare legs that I wanted to run my hands on. I wanted to run my hands up them until they disappeared under the sundress she had on until I found her underwear that I could pull aside with the flick of a finger. She was watching the movie with fascinated eyes and smiles; I was watching her. I had to do something to put distance between us. Otherwise, I was definitely going to end up kissing her. Not just kissing her, but pulling her to me and devouring her. I hit pause.

"Why'd you stop it?" she asked, turning to me, her smile fading as she realized how close we still were on the couch. Her eyes flicked down to my lips and back up to my eyes as they had the night before.

I barely held back my groan and pushed myself up. "We need libations."

I went into the kitchen and took out the blender, a container of vanilla ice cream, and frozen fruit from the freezer. I'd made her curious enough that she followed along with me.

"Because all that sugar seems like a good idea when you can't sleep," she laughed.

I smiled at her. "Just wait."

I hit the mixer button then took the lid off, tasting it with a spoon, as if I had to check it. I never had to check it. Making milkshakes was second nature to me, but I was playing a ridiculous game that would probably cost me more than her. And yet, I couldn't help myself. "Here, taste it and tell me what you think it's missing."

I offered her a scoop on the spoon. She had to come close enough for me to put it in her mouth. It was torturing me, but I was hoping it was torturing her also. When I removed the spoon, she ran her tongue over her lips, and all I could think was how badly I wanted to taste her. Lips. Tongue. All of it. The sweet scent of vanilla and berries that was an addition to her normal cherry-blossom smell.

"I don't think it's missing anything," she said quietly, unable to meet my gaze.

"It is." I reached over her into the cabinet, my chest rubbing along hers for just a brief second, building the tension between us instead of removing it like I'd intended to do by leaving the couch. She didn't back away from me. I brought out a bottle of marshmallow vodka and waved it in front of her before going back to the mixer and adding it to the milkshake.

"A little nightcap for our sugar fest. Should counter the effects nicely."

She laughed. "You really do have a sugar tooth."

I just nodded. I did. I'd rather eat a brownie for breakfast than leftover pizza, but not many people knew that about me. I poured in a hefty dose of the flavored vodka, hit mix again, and then scooped more out with the spoon. I went to offer her a taste but didn't know she'd moved to watch me, the sound having been dulled by the noise of the mixer, so when I turned, the milkshake went flying off, hitting her in the face and hair.

We both stared for a stunned moment, and then I burst out laughing.

"Oh my God, you didn't just do that," she said, and I couldn't tell if there was anger or laughter or both in her voice.

She wiped at her face and then, before I'd even expected it, ran both her hands down the sides of mine, dragging across my five o'clock shadow, eyes full of humor. I was shocked into stillness that she'd retaliated so quickly. That her hands were on my face. That she was so close our bodies were bumping and speaking to each other again.

I grabbed her hands, turning my face so that I could lick one. The berries and vodka were all sticky sweet, and yet, they still didn't cover the taste of her skin. She didn't fight me. She didn't pull away.

"I think I'd like to kiss you again," I told her, the desire that was burning inside me echoing in my voice. I felt her pulse increase beneath my fingertips, rising to a crescendo, just like my own.

"It isn't any better of an idea now than it was then," she said, but her breathing was coming in gentle puffs. "Actually…it would probably be worse."

"That kiss was the best damn kiss either of us have ever had," I argued.

"We were just taken in by the sea, and the day, and the turtles."

I couldn't help a slow smile. "The turtles?"

She pulled away, flicking on the faucet. "They were pretty amazing."

I could only see the side of her face now, but I could see her lips quirking. The tease mixed in with her truth.

"You think our kiss was perfect because of the sea turtles?" I asked, knowing she was just trying to remove the sexual tension that was building between us. Knowing she didn't believe it any more than I did.

"*I* never said it was perfect. That was all you. But I do believe we were just caught up in…the whole adventure," she said, drying her hands and then placing the counter between us.

"That wasn't why it was perfect," I pushed. It wasn't. It was perfect because she'd fit into me like no woman that I'd ever kissed. Except she didn't fit…did she? Could I just date her like Dani had suggested? Could I date her and have her in my arms only to let her go?

I wasn't sure I could. I was pretty sure that I'd want to keep her just like I'd thought before I'd learned anything about her past and her family. It irked me that it mattered…that I was ready to let go of the chance at something beautiful because of what others would say.

"You keep using that word, perfect, Mac-Macauley. I knew you had an ego, but really."

We stared at each other for a moment. Waiting. Who would break first? And would it be toward each other or away?

"Thank you," she said quietly, eyes still on mine. "But I think I'm going to skip the libations and head to bed."

"Georgie," I breathed out her name, remorse in my voice as she moved out of the kitchen. Remorse for more than ruining our night. Remorse because of the things that were holding me back from following her.

"It's okay, Mac."

It wasn't.

"Finish watching the movie," I said.

She shook her head, going toward the stairs to the loft.

"Another night," she replied, her voice emotionless.

I hated myself, and I didn't. Because I needed the space as much as she did. Tonight had proven one thing: there was no way that the energy that existed between us was going to allow us to just live together as friends. The pull was already too strong. I just had to figure out what exactly that meant for me before I could persuade her of anything else. Before I could pursue her in any way, shape, or form. So, I let her run…and I thought that even she knew it wouldn't be forever.

Chapter Fourteen

Georgie

HURT
Performed by Lady Antebellum

As August wafted by me, I did a good job of avoiding Mac. After our heated—or cooled—milkshake moment, I doubled my efforts to keep away. It was self-preservation as much as selfless denial because, in truth, I wanted to kiss him again. I wanted a repeat performance of every moment we'd spent tangled together on his boat, because Mac had been right. Our kiss had been perfect.

The problem was, *we* weren't perfect. And I didn't want either of us to be hurt by that when reality showed up, knocking on our door like Descartes said it would. I could spend days being bitter about it, or just resolve myself to move past it.

I continued to fill my days at the law library. I loved it there, surrounded by facts and justice all rolled into one. Research had always been my forte back when I'd been in school getting my bachelor's degree, and I was relieved at how easily it came back to me.

I'd moved on from my search and seizure pursuits

to cases related to the rights of immigrant children and their parents, especially detained illegals. In some ways, it was close to home even though my mom had never been illegal, and I'd never been an immigrant.

I was neck-deep in highlights and typing once more when another person stopped by my table. I was relieved to find it wasn't Professor Collins. I'd avoided him whenever I'd seen him appear in the library but watched from afar as he flirted suavely with the female student behind the help desk, and she blushed and stuttered over his attention. It had turned my stomach.

The person who stopped that day was an older woman in a suit that fit her as beautifully as Collins' and the Whittaker siblings' suits fit them. I was clearly going to need my own suits before long to blend in with the new crowd. My sundresses, leather pants, and ripped jeans screamed New York instead of D.C.

"You're a bit of a puzzle," the woman said. Her voice was full of a southern twang that instantly captivated me as much as her dark-red hair and warm, brown eyes.

"I'm sorry?" I questioned.

"Summer classes are over."

I shook my head. "I wasn't in them. I don't start till the fall term."

"What are you working on, then?"

Collins had seen my overeagerness and taken advantage of it, but this woman seemed genuinely interested. I was determined not to be ashamed. I loved the law. Just like I loved America.

"It's…just things that interest me."

"Research interests you?"

My lips twitched at that. "If you're going to be a lawyer, research better fascinate you, isn't that true?"

She took me in, and again, it didn't feel predatory like Collins had. "You would be one of the first students to think so in a long time. Everyone wants the fancy opening and closing arguments to be the entirety of their time spent on a case."

I fidgeted slightly.

"Immigration law?" she asked, taking in my notes I had out on the table.

"Yes."

"Are you an immigrant?"

"No. My mother is Russian, though."

"She's an immigrant?"

"No. She still lives in Russia."

She considered me for a moment then snapped my book shut, waved a hand to all my belongings, and said, "Come with me."

"Excuse me?"

She laughed. "Sorry. Let me introduce myself. I'm Theresa Sedgewick. I'm a professor here and an attorney in the middle of a case that needs lots of research. Seeing as you don't have classes for another week, you might as well make yourself useful."

I sat for a moment, assessing her to see if she was being serious, the sting of Professor Collins's amorous ways still sitting in my heart.

"You don't know me at all," I protested.

"You're dedicated and engaged. That makes you perfect. It's practically all I need to know. But on our way back to my office, you can tell me the important bullet points you feel you need to tell me about your life."

She started to walk away, and I didn't let myself dwell on Collins any longer. I scrambled to shove all my work back into my bag and picked up the books I had out. "I just need to return these," I called after her.

She sighed, came back to me, took the books from my hand, and then walked to the front desk with me following her. She stopped and handed the books to the female behind the counter—the one that Collins came in to flirt with. She was younger than me by several years. "Aileen, be a dear and return these for us."

Then, she kept going toward the doors of the library, and I followed, feeling only slightly bad that Aileen was going to have to return my books for me.

Outside, I had to scamper to keep up with her. She wasn't quite as tall as me, but she was still tall for a female—and in a hurry. I had the feeling she was in a hurry all the time.

"Give me the bullet points," she said as we walked.

"Bullet points?"

"Parents. Bachelor's. Why you're here."

"Dad is Ian Astrella. Mom is Manya Leskov. They're divorced. My mother remarried a Russian businessman named Petya Leskov. I was raised by my grandmother and worked at her hair salon in New York City to put myself through Columbia's pre-law program. I originally was accepted into Harvard Law but had to return to New York to bury my grandmother and ended up taking over her business until the lease expired this year. I'm using the proceeds to help me pay for law school. I'm not sure that's bullet enough, but it's the basics."

She opened her office door with a key card, led the way inside, and then motioned toward a leather chair. It wasn't a whole lot different from Professor Collins' office, but I immediately felt more at ease here. I didn't feel like I was going to be the next example of faculty abuse. It felt very business-like.

"Let me get this straight. Your father is the same Ian Astrella who is serving time for his Ponzi scheme stealing thousands from people?" It was said without judgment. Just the facts.

I smiled. "Yes. But I really think it was millions."

"You are officially my most interesting student in years."

"You're not on my class schedule at all."

"A fact I'll be rectifying." She picked up her phone and buzzed some assistant who was sitting in some office somewhere that I hadn't seen yet. "Jean. I need you to get a student transferred into my practicum course for the fall term." A pause. She looked over at me. "I'm sorry. Your name is?"

I could hear the woman on the other side of the phone laugh, and I couldn't help but smile myself. That she didn't even know my name but was already taking a chance on me. "Georgie Astrella. Georgia. It'll be under Georgia."

"Did you get that, Jean?" Another pause. "Of course she does." Pause. "Fine. Georgia, do you want to be switched from Professor Collins' class into mine?"

Did I want to be switched out of Collins' class? Oh, yes. No doubt about it, and I was smiling and nodding all at the same time.

"She does." Pause. "Jean, she's sitting in front of me, nodding."

She handed me the phone. "She refuses to do it without speaking with you."

I laughed and took the phone. "Hello?"

"Young lady, my name is Jean, and I can absolutely, one hundred percent, switch your classes for you, but I want to make sure you are aware of what you are doing. Professor Sedgewick doesn't go easy on anyone. Her grades are usually abysmal with a few standouts, whereas Professor Collins is, well, let's just say that his classes usually do well. If you want me to switch you, I can, but it will likely cost you a few gray hairs and a few points on your G.P.A."

"Is she telling you I'm going to fail you?" Professor Sedgewick grimaced.

I couldn't help the smile that continued to grow on my face. "Thank you so much for the warning, Jean. But I think, after having met both the professors, I'd much rather take my chances with Professor Sedgewick than Professor Collins."

Jean, whoever she was, chuckled. "Smart girl. I'll email you a new schedule once I've handled it."

"Thank you so much."

"Don't thank me, but also don't come crying to me when she doesn't give you the grade you want."

My heart was happy as Jean hung up, and I put the receiver down.

"You've met Collins, then?" Professor Sedgewick

asked as she eyed me up and down. It wasn't uncomfortable but more assessing. "Did he give you the binder for his case work?"

I nodded.

"And what did you tell him?"

"That I had a boyfriend who needed me to pick him up because his car broke down."

She laughed. It was beautiful in her southern twang, and it instantly relaxed me.

"Do you have a boyfriend who needed picking up?"

I shook my head ruefully. "No, but Mac would have played along if I had needed to provide proof of one."

She assessed me again. "Mac?"

"He's my roommate. He and his sister, Dani, work for Senator Matherton."

"The Whittaker clan!" she said.

I looked at her in surprise. "You know them?"

"I know their father, the Vice Admiral, fairly well, and their grandfather, Robert, who is the chief of staff for Matherton."

I stared at her. "I'm not sure what to say. It seems very strange that a town this big would have me finding two people in a matter of days who know each other."

"Georgia, you'll see, this town is smaller than a five-hundred-person town in the middle of the Appalachian Mountains."

I laughed. "It's Georgie."

"Not anymore it isn't."

"Excuse me?"

"Georgie is a girl who works at a hair salon. Georgia is the lawyer everyone trusts."

"To be fair, everyone trusted Georgie to do their hair perfectly. No one left my salon unhappy."

"That is exactly what you'll want them to say when they leave your law office as well."

♫ ♫ ♫

By the time I got home, I was still smiling. Both excited and nervous. Theresa—because she'd insisted I call her Theresa—had given me a file with multiple cases to look up, all related to immigrant children. I'd happened to be in the right place, at the right time, with the right case law opened up today. It felt like my first truly lucky break in a while, and I thought maybe the universe wasn't playing with me as much as I'd thought.

When I entered the apartment, Mac was at the bar in the kitchen with a sandwich from the same deli down the street that I'd been frequenting since moving in. Congress was adjourned for the month of August, but Mac and Dani had been spending hours at the office anyway. I wasn't sure if that was because Mac was avoiding me like I'd been avoiding him, or if they really just had that much work to do while Matherton was on vacation with his family. Dani had mentioned something about several bills they were trying to get their arms around so Matherton could push them forward once Congress was back after Labor Day.

I couldn't avoid Mac now without being rude.

"Hey," I said, putting the volume of books and folders down on the side table in the entry.

"Wow. You really are taking this pre-studying studying serious."

I smiled. "Actually, I had a new professor take me under their wing today."

He grimaced. "More of them hitting on you?"

I shook my head. "No. This one was a woman, and before you say it, I know she could have hit on me too, but she wasn't interested in me for my looks, just my research skills."

I grabbed a mineral water and my leftover noodles from the fridge, nuking the noodles and then joining him at the bar, my happiness spilling over into my smile.

"Research makes you happy?"

I nodded. He sighed. "I'm not sure I'm cut out for it myself."

"But it's an important part of the legislative process."

"Yeah. I know. I guess I'm used to filtering through intel reports that are just…different."

He dropped his bag of chips, bent down to get them, and when he came back up, our legs got tangled together. He wasn't in a suit that had been his norm since coming back to D.C. Suits that fit him as if he'd been born wearing them and made him look even larger—if that was possible. Instead, he was in shorts and a T-shirt that stretched across the expanse of his chest. When my legs—that were also bare in a summer dress—touched his, it was skin to skin, jolting me back to our milkshake moment that had caused me to scurry and stay away.

Our touch was like every time we'd touched, thunderclouds rolling in and booming off my back and lightning going off in my eyes. I pulled my legs away and turned back to the noodles in my bowl, trying to remember what they tasted like, because the only taste I had now was of Mac and the salty sunshine of our kiss on a boat in Rockport.

He cleared his throat and opened the bag. "What's this professor's name?"

"Theresa Sedgewick."

Dani came down the hall to stand between us, an arm on each of our shoulders. "What about Theresa?"

"She said you knew her."

"Sure, she's one of Dad's friends. From college, I think. She helps us out at the senator's office once in a while when we need a third-party legal opinion."

I laughed. "This town really is small."

"Smaller than a submarine," Dani said. "What about her, though?"

"She saw me studying in the law library and asked me to help her with some research before classes start next week."

"Lucky for you! She's smart and talented." She stole one of Mac's chips, and he flicked at her wrist in a way that spoke to all their interactions that I'd seen—sibling harassment and love all rolled into one.

"Which of you is coming to the gym with me?" she asked.

"Not me," Mac said. "I'm going to watch the Redskins' pre-season game."

"Not me, either," I said. "I want to make some headway through the case so I know what I'm doing tomorrow."

"You two are no fun."

"Working out with you in the gym is no fun either." Mac guffawed.

"The Navy man can't keep up?"

"Who would want to keep up with you and the squats from hell?"

"You're not going to be able to fit in those new suits if you keep it up."

He groaned. "Fine," he said. "I'll go, but I'm not doing squats."

"Really?" Dani looked surprised, but I wasn't. He really was avoiding me like I had been avoiding him.

If Dani had noticed the increased disquiet between us over the last few weeks, she hadn't said anything. She still watched *Fighting for the Stars* with me and razzed Mac about being the newbie on the Hill. She acted like we were all exactly what we'd set out to be: roommates.

In the quiet that was left behind in their departure, I tried not to let the whole exchange dim the smile I'd felt when I'd walked into the apartment, but it had. Everything in my life was going better than I'd expected when I'd applied for law school and been accepted way back in January. Everything except this one thing. And I wished again that Mac and I would find a way past this. That the awkwardness would ease into the friendly banter that I had with any of my friends, male or not. Like the banter he had with Dani.

♫ ♫ ♫

Theresa wasn't kidding when she said she needed someone to do research. I wasn't sure if she was testing me, or just desperate, but she dragged me around with her for the next week like some combination of a personal assistant and a paralegal. I was neither, and she actually had both. She didn't have a law office. She told me she'd given it up when she'd taken on the full-time position at Georgetown, but she had a staff that worked part time out of her house on the outskirts of town.

Because she didn't have her own office, she rarely took on cases, but the ones she took were because she was passionate about them. Kacey, her paralegal, and Ryan, her personal assistant, were both enrolled in classes at Georgetown's main campus, not the law school. They came and went from her house with their own key, often ignoring the daggers Theresa threw out at them about not being there when she needed them. It wasn't true; they were highly efficient, and they also weren't afraid to tell her when she'd overstepped. It left me admiring all of them for their strength and outspokenness. It was the way I handled all my relationships.

*Except one…*my soul whispered to me. And I realized, with a shock, that it was true. I'd been avoiding a certain man with eyes the color of the sea and sky. I'd known that. I'd used my time with Theresa as an excuse to continue to ignore him and the issue, instead of just facing it head on—with facts, and truths, and proofs. But it was the complete opposite of how I'd handled everything else in my life, and I was sort of tired of it.

Theresa saying my name brought me back from my heart-to-heart with myself.

"Georgia is the only one who deserves to be paid, and she isn't even making any money," she threw at Kacey when she saw her heading toward the door on Friday.

"Georgia is going to learn soon enough that if she doesn't tell you no, you'll take until there's nothing left but a burnt stub," Kacey hollered back. "I'll see you next week."

"Next week?" Theresa groused.

"It's Friday. I have a boyfriend and a life waiting for me. If you had a relationship, other than one with the law, you'd understand."

Then, Kacey was gone.

I was smiling as I shut my computer.

"Are you leaving me, too?" she asked. "I suppose you have plans, also."

"No," I said, thinking about the apartment and the tension that was there now all the time because of Mac and me. I had a renewed desire to fix the situation, but I wasn't sure how.

"Oh Lord, there's that wistful look all you young people get."

I laughed. "I'm not wistful or young."

"What do you call that face?"

"Thoughtful."

She laughed.

"If that's thoughtful, I'm twenty-one again." She eyed me over the top of her steepled fingers. "Are you worried about classes starting?"

"No, not really."

"I won't hold back on you just because you're helping me, you know. Don't expect any freebies."

It was my turn to stare her down. "I don't expect handouts."

"Good."

My phone buzzed.

RAISA: They are at each other's throats again.

ME: You still don't know why?

RAISA: I have my...what is the word? Suspicions? But no facts.

ME: No proof, you mean.

RAISA: Yes. This. No proof.

ME: Just ask him about it.

I realized, after texting Raisa those words, that the solution was really that simple. I just needed to talk to Mac. Get things out in the open. Put everything on the table and move on so we didn't continue to dance around the apartment, avoiding each other.

RAISA: That is never easy with Malik.

ME: All you can do is try.

I put my phone back in my bag and picked up all

my belongings.

"One text conversation and everything is better?" Theresa smiled at me.

"What? No. That was my sister."

"But you've resolved whatever was making you squishy-faced?"

I laughed. "I'm not sure I'd say I was squishy-faced any more than I'd say I'd been wistful."

"Trust me. I've been reading people for years. You were squishy-faced and wistful. Now that you have that problem resolved," Theresa continued, "will you have time this weekend to spend on the case?"

"Sure," I told her, making my way to the door. "I'll be back in the morning."

"Bring more of that black-and-white coffee stuff."

I nodded and left. My brain was on Mac and the long overdue discussion we needed to have. But when I got back to the apartment, it was to find out that Mac had had very different ideas. Dani told me he had taken the train home to Delaware with his dad, which made me wonder if the only real solution to our situation was for me to just move out so he wouldn't have to run from his own home.

♫ ♫ ♫

My first day of classes came and went, leaving me exhausted and wired at the same time. The other students had been friendly, and, true to her word, Theresa hadn't given me an inch. If anything, she'd judged me harsher than the other students whenever

I'd made a comment.

When I made my way back to the apartment, it was late, and I was surprised to be the first one home. I felt like celebrating, and for the first time in a long time, I felt alone.

I pulled my phone out of my bag to text Raisa and realized I'd missed a text from Dani.

DANI: You've survived your first day! Congrats! We're bringing home Bentley's.

It filled my heart. I was just about to text back when the door opened and the siblings entered, in the midst of a heated discussion.

"He didn't mean that," Dani said.

"Of course, you'd think that," Mac was saying.

They both stopped when they saw me, but Mac seemed to take me in for longer, as if he was trying to assess if I'd changed from the last time I'd seen him.

"We didn't think you were home," Dani said.

I waved my phone. "I was just about to text you."

"Congrats on your first day! How was it?" Dani asked as Mac started to unload the bags, the smell of garlic and basil filling the apartment and making my stomach growl loudly.

"It was really good, but I didn't get a chance to eat," I answered over another loud grumble from my intestines.

"We can tell." Mac grinned, and my stomach flipped again but for a different reason. Because Mac's smile was gorgeous, and every time I thought I'd gotten used to it, I was proven wrong.

I pulled out plates from the cupboard, and we all dished up, sitting at the counter while I talked about my day, and they talked about theirs. It felt like, maybe, Mac and I were moving closer to the friendship that I was hoping we'd find.

We were almost done when Dani's phone buzzed. She looked down at the text before jumping off the barstool and heading down the hall.

"Who is he, Dani?" Mac tossed at her.

She just waved the phone at him and kept going.

He turned back to me.

"I'm glad you had a good first day," he said.

I nodded, picking up the plates, and he joined me. We cleaned the kitchen in silence. We both reached for the kitchen towel at the same moment, our hands tangling and then stilling. I pulled my hands away, crossed my arms over my chest, and swallowed. I wanted to have this talk. I wanted to move on, or move out, or just do something instead of hiding.

"You've been avoiding me," I said.

"Not so much avoiding as giving us some space," he said, but he moved closer to me as he said it, leaning on the counter next to me so our arms were almost touching.

"This is space," I teased, but he didn't smile in return. Instead, his eyes seemed to bore into mine, and I found my courage and resolve melting beneath the heat of his stare.

"Will you be honest if I ask you something?" he asked quietly.

That made me raise my chin in irritation. "I'm always honest."

"Is it just me, or is this," he waved a finger between us, "different for you, too?"

His words made me wish I hadn't said I was always honest. Because I wasn't sure I wanted to tell him how he made me feel. "Different how?" I asked, stalling.

His hand went to my hair, twirling fingers into my ponytail, tugging at the white stripe that had been there since that night my dad was arrested. He was too close for mere friends. For the mere roommates that I'd resolved we had to be.

"Different, as in, never had moments like these before. As in, I'm not sure I can stop touching you now that I've started. Different, as in, I feel like the pieces of us might just fit together better than any person has ever fit with me before."

The words made my heart soar and stop all at the same time, aches of regret filling me. "Except we don't, Mac. Not at all," I told him, being as truthful as he'd asked me to be.

"Forget everything about your family and my political goals. If we hadn't told each other any of that… If we'd just had that one incredible kiss and were here now, would you want me to take you out on a date? Would you be asking me, this very second, to kiss you again?"

He wanted to act like none of it existed. To pretend like we didn't know all the things about each other that would never work. And I wasn't sure if that hurt more or less than him not wanting to be with me at all, because I deserved to be with someone who chose me in spite of my family, not regardless of them.

"But I can't do that," I told him. "We *have* told each other those things. It's all twined together. Our families, our lives, and what we want for our futures. We barely know each other, but what we know is enough to know that our lives don't fit. Even in the short term."

I pulled my ponytail from his hands, smoothing it with my own.

"You're right that we barely know each other," he said. "You're right that, even in the short term, we seem like jagged edges instead of smooth curves. But all I know is that when I kissed you, I felt forever. Forever in one kiss."

I moved away from him and toward the loft because, suddenly, I wasn't ready for this conversation at all. I hadn't expected it to turn on me in this way. He'd taken everything I thought I was going to say and swallowed it up in talks of forever. And I was surprised and unprepared for the longing and bitterness that filled me at his words. I may have never longed for a happily ever after before, but I knew, if it wasn't for my family, I would have been caving. Giving in to him and the sweetest words that anyone had ever spoken to me…*forever in a kiss*. But I denied it all, instead. I spoke from the bitterness instead of the longing. "I don't want forever with you, Mac."

"No?" he responded, trailing after me, not at all put off by my words. Instead, he continued to push rather than walk away. "Because I think I sure as hell would like a chance to explore the idea of one with you."

Chapter Fifteen

Mac

MORE THAN FRIENDS

Performed by Jason Mraz & Meghan Trainor

I followed Georgie to the loft steps where she turned toward me at my words, smoothing her ponytail. I could see that my words had somehow penetrated the armor she'd drawn around herself, because I found a sea of conflicting emotions in her eyes that were a steely gray today.

So, I pushed because I had to. I had to know that I'd tried, or else the regret would have eaten at me for the rest of my life. "Tell me you feel nothing, and I'll leave you alone. But if you do feel something, then don't walk away without testing it. Without proving your own theories."

Back in Rockport, she'd disputed my instinct with some theory of René Descartes, and hell, maybe she was right. Maybe once we dated and spent time together, we wouldn't suit at all. Maybe instinct should have been left for military campaigns and not love. I wasn't standing before her, asking her to marry me, but I also didn't want to start something with her without the possibility that, someday, I might be putting a ring on her finger. That seemed like the worst way to start a relationship—with the knowledge of it ending instead of continuing.

She rubbed her forehead. "It's just…so impossible."

"Can you allow us, for a few minutes, to just be a law student and a senator's aide?"

"It isn't that simple."

She was right. It wasn't. But in the weeks that we'd been avoiding each other, I'd done nothing but think about this…us. About her. I hadn't been able to get her off my damn brain. She'd been with me in the dark of the night. She'd been with me in the shower. She'd been with me when I was supposed to be reading gun stats and modifying the bill Matherton was putting before Congress next month.

I hadn't been able to escape the thought of us even when I'd gone home for the weekend. Instead, my thoughts had run in circles about my career goals and her family. I thought about what Dani had said about just dating her with the thought of it ending someday, long before I ever announced an election campaign. I even thought about what it would be like to just assuage the physical need that was burning between us and leaving it at that. But at the end of every discussion I'd had with myself, I'd come back to the one thing I'd said to her that had been true.

That when I found the one I wanted to date, I'd be all in. That I would know, by instinct, that it was forever. I didn't think my instincts were that far off.

Regardless, what I did know, without one shred of doubt, was that I wanted more. More moments. More kisses. More her. More time to figure out if my gut was right, or wrong, or completely screwed.

"Dani and I are going home next Friday for Labor Day. We have a family tradition of ending summer with tennis and poker. Come with us. Get to know me. Allow us to spend time together before you write the idea of us off."

She turned away, looking out at the Washington skyline. The Capitol building was slowly coming alive with lights as the summer sun sank lower in the sky. I eased up behind her. I touched her shoulder and bent so my lips brushed slightly against her ear and the row of earrings that traveled their way up her skin.

"I want to know everything about you," I told her. "You're light and dark and hopes and fears all wrapped together. I need to know why. I need to know who Georgie is beneath the skin and the interchangeable contacts."

She shivered. I wasn't sure if it was at my words or the way my lips barely caressed her ear.

"A weekend," she breathed out, her voice quivering like my insides were.

"A weekend at least," I said with my breath still echoing across her skin.

"Okay," she breathed out, pulling away and disappearing up the stairs. I let her go because I couldn't believe I'd won. A smile filled my face and was reflected back at me in the window, joy surging through me that was quickly replaced with unease. Because what if she saw us all and ran for the hills instead of staying?

♪ ♪ ♪

Georgie and I didn't avoid each other the next couple days. In fact, we seemed to have reached a truce. A truce that when we were in the same room, we sat next to each other. But she was working after school with Theresa, and Dani and I were working late on the gun bill, so we didn't see each other except fleetingly. But knowing I was going to be around her for an entire weekend seemed to soften the knots that had worked themselves into all my muscles since I'd first gotten back to D.C. and found her ensconced in the apartment.

Thursday night, I was packing when I was interrupted by a text from Mom.

MOM: Dani says you're bringing a girl home.

My heart leaped at those words because they were and weren't true. Georgie had agreed to give me this weekend as a way to get to know each other, but I didn't want the family adding all sorts of pressure to that.

ME: We're both bringing our roommate with us. Just like we brought Stan and Mel. And she's hardly a girl.

MOM: You like her then, I see.

That I liked her was one way of saying it, but no way was I going to admit that to Mom at this point.

ME: I don't know what Dani told you. Georgie and I are just getting acquainted.

I'm not sure what I feel for her.

MOM: But you've never brought a woman home.

ME: Please don't read more into this than it is. Like I said, we're bringing our roommate with us, just like we have a gazillion times before.

MOM: So, don't bring out your baby albums yet?

*ME: ** Eye roll emoji ***

MOM: You know I can't tell which emoji means what.

ME: I'm rolling my eyes at you.

MOM: Just for that, I'm going to make sure the picture of you in the tutu is at the very front of the mantel.

ME: If she likes me after that, then it's meant to be.

MOM: It's texts like that which make me realize this is much more than bringing a roommate home.

I couldn't continue to deny it. It was more. Mom would know that as soon as she saw me mooning over her like I'd never mooned over anyone. So, instead of lying, I just ended the conversation.

ME: Love you. I'm going to go pack now.

MOM: Love you too, baby. See you tomorrow.

I knocked on Dani's half-open door. "Yep," she hollered.

I'd learned early in life that you never entered a sister's room without knocking first. Not if you didn't want to see things that would scar you for life. Almost worse than seeing your parents naked. Almost.

"What did you tell Mom?" I asked, leaning on the doorframe.

Dani didn't even look up from the suitcase she was packing with so many clothes I wasn't sure if we were going home for a long weekend or a month. "What did I tell Mom about what?"

"Georgie."

"Just that we were bringing her home with us."

"You had to have said more than that. I just got the third degree."

She smirked but didn't stop shoving things into her luggage. "I might have said something about her being stunning and you knowing it."

"I barely got Georgie to agree to come with us, so don't all of you start putting pressure on her for being there with me. She's not ready for that."

"Is this still about her family?"

I didn't say anything.

"I have to admit," Dani started. "It isn't ideal. It would definitely give your competition some fodder to burn, but if she's clean and you're clean, I don't think it's insurmountable."

"Really?"

"I think it matters more that you can show you love her. Real emotions. And like I said, that you're both clean. You're clean, right?"

"You know I am."

"I know nothing about my brother's dark side. I don't want to know."

"If you're going to be my campaign manager, you'll need to know."

"Who said I'm going to be your campaign manager?" she tossed back.

"You'd trust my political career to someone we don't know?"

"I may not be doing this that long."

This made me pause in my harassment of her. "What?"

She zipped up her suitcase and stuck it on the floor by her bed. "I'm just not sure I want to continue doing this."

"You're really good at it."

She nodded. "I am."

"Conceited."

"You said it; I just agreed."

I laughed. "Why do you want to leave, and what would you do instead?"

"I don't know. Maybe some brand imaging for a company or some celebrity."

It didn't escape me that she'd skipped answering my why, but sometimes with Dani, you had to give her time to tell you what she was thinking. She would, when she was ready, but if you kept demanding answers, she'd slam you back into oblivion—sort of like Georgie.

"Isn't that just the same game with a different face?" I asked.

"Without the ugly side if I work for the right person."

"Who would I have run my campaign?" I asked.

"Granddad."

"He's too old."

"He does a great job for Guy."

"But I need someone much more in touch with the millennials. You know they're the largest growing demographic."

"Are you planning a run for office sooner than I know about?" she asked, sitting on her bed.

"No. Not for at least two to four years."

"Then we have years to figure it out." She eyed me as I didn't respond. "You know, Rob—Mac, your whole life has been about your eventual run for office. I wonder how many things you missed out on because you were too afraid that what you did or said would someday come back to haunt you."

"This is about Georgie again."

"No. Maybe. Sometimes finding the person who completes you is more important than any job you might have."

"Is that really true, though, if you have a chance to change the world and don't?"

"After working with me for a month, you should

know that changing the world isn't going to be that easy. It isn't going to happen in a two-year Congress term. Or even a twenty-year Senate run."

"That's pretty pessimistic of you."

"Realistic. I've lived and breathed D.C. for nine years."

She'd been working on the Hill since she'd started college at Georgetown. She'd worked with our grandfather since she was a stick of a kid with barely any curves and braces on her teeth that she'd gotten, kicking and screaming, her senior year of high school.

"All I'm saying," she continued, "is that you being happy and fulfilled is just as important as anything you can do for the world."

I didn't agree, but I wasn't going to argue with her. Changing the world so future generations—so Baby Wyatt, Baby Hannah, and our niece and nephews—had a better world waiting for them…there wasn't much more important than that. I'd give up just about anything in order to make that happen.

♫ ♫ ♫

When Georgie got back to the apartment on Friday, Dani and I had already loaded the car and were antsy to leave the D.C. traffic behind us. Georgie said something about wanting to change, and I looked at her cotton sundress that showed off all her curves and told her the truth.

"You look gorgeous; you don't need to change."

She dragged her hand over her ponytail. It was still smooth and straight as always, but she seemed to waffle, and for a moment, I was afraid she wouldn't agree to go with us, so I just grabbed her suitcase and headed toward the door.

When we got down to the garage, I led the way to the black Cadillac SUV in the spot next to Dani's Mini.

"Whose car is this?" Georgie asked.

"Granddad's. He took the train when he went home. Said we could use it," I told her.

Dani, who'd been ahead of us, opened the back passenger door and climbed in.

"I can sit in the back," Georgie said.

"Nope. I'm planning on putting on the audiobook I've been waiting all summer to listen to. I have no desire to keep Mac company. I may even fall asleep."

I snorted, but I also wanted to hug my sister because she was giving Georgie and me exactly what we needed.

We were quiet, NPR on the radio, while I negotiated the streets of D.C. and got us onto the freeway. Dani, true to her word, had huge headphones on, with her seat tilted back, and looked to be almost asleep before we'd been on the road for more than twenty minutes.

"So…who all will be there this weekend?" Georgie asked, and I sensed not only curiosity but also nervousness in her voice.

"Lord. Pretty much everyone. There's an annual tennis tournament at the club, and our family has been playing and placing in it for as long as I can remember. We'll all play tomorrow at the house to see who gets to represent the Whittakers at the club on Sunday."

"You have tennis courts at your house?"

I nodded. "Do you play?"

She shook her head and teased. "No. There wasn't a tennis court in the building above the salon, sorry."

"You've never played at all?"

"Nope."

My brain went directly to thoughts of teaching her to play tennis. Of being able to touch her while I did. I couldn't let my body go very far down that road, though. Not while sitting in a car where she would be able to see, very clearly, where my brain and body had gone.

"Well, I can definitely teach you, but they won't let you near the courts on Sunday, then," I told her.

"Thank goodness."

We rode for a few minutes before she brought me back to her original question. "Who's everyone?"

"Right. Sorry. Granddad and Grandma will be at their place, which is just down the road, but they'll, more than likely, spend most of the day with us. My oldest sister, Gabi, lives in Wilmington with her husband, Vinnie, and their two rugrats, Troy and Sam. But even though that's hardly a fifteen-minute drive, they'll probably camp out in the guesthouse as long as Vinnie doesn't have to go back and take care of the restaurant."

"That's right. You mentioned they own a restaurant."

"Vinnie does. Gabi works at DuPont. She'll be at odds all weekend with Bee's husband, Thomas. Thomas is an environmental lawyer and acts like his job is the next coming of Jesus or something. The truth is, none of us like him."

She laughed. "You can't say that about your sister's husband."

I smiled. "Why not? It's the truth. There's something not right about the guy, and Bee knows how we feel. She ignored our opinion and mothered a child with him, anyway—that's Savanna-Rae—and she's the light of everybody's world. Frickin' cute as a kitten."

"That's a lot of people."

"That's pretty much all that will be staying at the house, but we'll have people in and out all weekend. Dad hosts a barbecue on Saturday, and that'll bring in a huge gathering. Sunday, after the tennis tournament, it'll be just the family again."

"Dani was right."

"About what?"

"I'm going to need a gazillion outfits. I'm not sure I brought enough."

She'd look gorgeous in a sheath dress twenty sizes too big, but I glanced over at her and said, "You look beautiful in whatever you put on."

She didn't respond, but I swore there was a flush to her cheeks. She turned to look out the window for a few minutes.

"Do you all have nicknames?" she asked finally.

"Huh?"

"Robbie, Dani, Gabi, Bee…" she trailed off. I laughed because I'd never really thought about what our nicknames might sound like to someone on the outside.

"None of us liked our full names, but Bee and I got it the worst."

"How's that?" she asked.

"Her real name is Phoebe, and I'm Macauley. Not exactly names you want to go to school with."

"I like Mac. And Phoebe is my favorite *Friends* character."

"Really?"

"Yeah, she's like me: quirky and true to herself."

"You're not quirky." Because she wasn't. She was unique. Spectacular. Elegant. I could think of a hundred more words that would have suited her, but quirky was not one of them.

"You say that now," she responded, "when you don't know me very well. I switch eye colors like jewelry. I think that's fairly quirky."

"How did that get started?" I asked, my own curiosity springing to life.

"After Grandma died and I went back to run the salon, my friend, Vicky, introduced me to a bunch of models. They got me a couple modeling gigs. The first one I went on wanted someone with blue eyes instead of my washed-out green, so they had me put in contacts. I liked how they went with the outfit I was wearing, and so, after that, it just became fun, changing colors with my mood, hair color, or outfit."

"Your eyes are not washed out. They're like jade."

"Jade is bright and vibrant. My eyes are pale and almost colorless."

"Not all jade is deep. Some are soft and brilliant."

I could feel her staring at me, but I didn't remove

my eyes from the road. I was trying not to play all my cards at once, trying to keep some compliments for later, so I turned the conversation. "You didn't want to keep the salon, so why did you after your grandma died?"

"The lease had this huge penalty clause. If I'd tried to get out of it, I would have pretty much lost everything she'd worked for. It didn't seem like the right way to honor her memory. Plus, I wasn't going to go into debt to pay off some douche who already had more money than God."

I'd been wrong about her so many times since I'd first seen her, but I realized, now, that I wasn't wrong about one thing: she was smart. Savvy in a way that was remarkable. Not many college students would have had the forethought to make such a wise business decision. Not many twenty-somethings would have had the bravery to stick their dreams on hold while they waited for the years to tick away on a lease they hadn't signed and didn't want.

We spent the entire two-hour drive from D.C. to Greenville sharing information about our lives, and our pasts, and how we'd gotten to where we were now. The conversation flowed back and forth between us effortlessly. As we got closer to Wilmington, she asked about my naval career.

"What did you do at the Pentagon?" she asked.

For the first time, I found myself shutting down a little. My time at the Pentagon was classified. Top-secret stuff that I could barely breathe a word about, and then, to only a handful of people who were already in the know. My dad was pretty much on that list with not many other people.

"I can't really talk about a lot of it," I told her truthfully.

"It really was spy stuff?" she asked, humor in her voice.

I chuckled. "Yes and no. I fielded a lot of intelligence reports and liaised with JSOC for S.E.A.L. team operations."

"Wow," she breathed out, and I didn't want her to get the wrong impression, so I added on quickly.

"Not really. The wow are the guys who put their life on the line to make the plans happen." Because it was true. The guys who were in the field were the impressive ones. Lives on the line day in and day out. I just sat back and helped decide which missions had the best chance of success. Which ones needed to be done. It was hardly glorious work.

"You never wanted to be a S.E.A.L. yourself?" she asked.

I thought about Darren and Nash and the lives they led. They were tough. Almost too tough. It was hard on Darren's wife—the things Darren saw and did that he couldn't talk about but came home with him anyway. Darren and Nash were both good men. I just didn't want their life. I wasn't afraid of giving my life for something I believed in as much as I believed in America—screwed up and all—but I didn't want a life spent away from those I loved either. I would dedicate my life to this country in a different way.

"No. S.E.A.L.s are almost always lifers, or at least until they can't make the physical requirements anymore. I knew from the time I was a kid that I wanted to go into politics," I said.

"Your dad's a lifer. Vice Admiral has to have come with a lot of sacrifices."

I nodded. It was part of the reason I hadn't wanted to try for S.E.A.L.s or any of the more coveted positions in the Navy. Dad's life had been a series of sacrifices. "He moved around a lot when we were younger."

"You didn't go with him?"

"He and Mom didn't want that for us. They wanted us to grow up in the same house, and at the same schools, and just be regular American kids." It was something my sisters and I were very grateful for, that our parents had given us a normal life instead of the life of military brats.

"Must have been really hard on their relationship," Georgie said.

I'd never really thought about what it must have been like for my parents, who I knew loved each other, to be away from each other for so long. Mom had been sad when he was gone but also busy with us kids and her life at the club and her social groups. "You know, I've never really thought of it that way. They still live apart a lot. Dad has an apartment near the Pentagon because he's there so much. Mostly home on the weekends."

"I'm not sure I could live that way with the person I'd agreed to marry," Georgie responded.

And before I could reconsider, I'd slipped out, "Good thing I've given it up then."

When she snorted, I winked to lessen the seriousness of my words.

"Don't get ahead of yourself, Mac-Macauley."

"Don't read too much into it, Georgie-Girl."

"You have to come up with better nicknames than that," Dani said from the backseat, and we both jumped, having forgotten she was even with us. It had been a little bubble of time that we'd shared, getting to know each other a little more. Like a first date, but with a history already tying us together.

Thinking about relationships and the toll the military took on them reminded me that Nash and Darren were coming to the house on Saturday. I turned to Georgie. "You'll get to meet a couple of my S.E.A.L. buddies this weekend. Darren's wife's family lives not far from us, and I invited them to the house for the barbecue. Nash is staying with them, so he'll be there, too."

"I'll finally get to see how the duo bested you at poker," Dani said from the backseat.

"They didn't best me. They cheated to win; there's a difference," I said.

"Is Georgie fully prepared for the competitive nature of our family and friends?"

I grinned at Georgie and shrugged. "I guess we'll have to see."

But I couldn't help a secret desire for her to love everything about our family as much as I did, because my family was everything to me.

Chapter Sixteen

Georgie

MAKE ME LIKE YOU
Performed by Gwen Stefani

I'd thought that the two-hour car ride with Mac and Dani would have allowed me a chance to study. My first week of classes had resulted in a workload that probably would have overwhelmed me if I hadn't started reading ahead of time. I had no intention of falling behind. But Dani had jumped in the back, leaving me to make conversation with Mac, who'd used the time to make good on the agreement of getting to know each other better.

During the week, I had considered telling Mac I couldn't go for a gazillion different reasons. But every time I thought about it, I'd remember his words about forever in a kiss, and I couldn't. Suddenly, the thought of getting to know Mac better was as tantalizing as the research I was doing for Theresa. Maybe more. Definitely more.

My head was still screaming at me about all the reasons a relationship between Mac and me would never work.

A relationship he'd never had.

A relationship I was fairly certain I didn't want.

But my heart was already speaking a different tune than my brain. My heart and mind were out of sync, harsh notes that were colliding against each other, and I wasn't sure how to bring them back into harmony again.

I'd packed the night before after asking Dani what I needed to bring with me. Her response had been, "Everything."

When I'd looked puzzled, she laughed. "We'll be in the pool, on the courts, in the sand, barbecuing, and at the country club, which means you'll need bathing suits, shorts, dresses, and everything in between."

I'd never put it together that Dani and Mac were from a wealthy family. They'd never acted snobby or entitled like many of the socialites I knew in New York or my mom's friends in Russia. Instead, the Whittaker siblings had always been real and down-to-earth with me. But then, Dani was talking about pools and courts and country clubs as if it was the norm, and it made me look around the apartment once more with new eyes. The decorations were understated but expensive. High-end quality. Dani had said the family owned the apartment with its view of the Capitol. But again, I hadn't really thought about what that meant. Money.

When I was in Russia, visiting Mom and Petya, I was used to being surrounded by obnoxious wealth. Petya's livelihood had Mom and my siblings living in a mansion that had once belonged to Russian royalty and was decked out in art and gold. Whenever I was there, Mom took me on shopping sprees that were paid for by Amex cards with limits that boggled the mind. But every time Petya had offered money to help with college or living expenses, I'd turned him down. I didn't want to owe Petya anything. Because, even in my teens, I'd understood that what he did wasn't on the up and up.

Needless to say, I wasn't unfamiliar with wealth. I wasn't even uncomfortable around it. I just hadn't really been prepared for it to be Mac's and Dani's life. It was the second or third time, at least, that I'd made assumptions about Mac that weren't true. I hadn't been dealing in facts with him at any time since first meeting him. Descartes would have lost hope in me by now.

At the end of our car ride, we pulled up to a black wrought-iron gate with a ginormous, cursive W welded into it. Dani said the Whittakers had resided in and around Greenville for generations. This seemed impossible to me. History that far back. Because even when visiting Russia, none of Petya's possessions had been his family's possessions. He'd garnered them all himself.

The wrought-iron gate hung between two brick columns. Mac hit a button in the car, and the gate swung open to reveal a driveway made out of cobblestones that curled away from the street. The landscape was green, and floral, and definitely manicured.

When we pulled up to the house, I stared at it in astonishment. It was like a combination of Mount Vernon and the White House rolled into one. It even had the same type of semi-circular, curved portico with columns that the south-facing view of the White House had. It was old-world charm dropped right in the middle of Delaware. And while it was smaller than the real White House, it was still a mansion by all terms.

The front door opened, and a woman who looked like Dani came out. It wasn't until I'd unbuckled and gotten out of the car that I realized it had to be their mother instead of their older sister. She was elegant with hardly any wrinkles, but as she got closer and her smile got wider, I could see the laugh lines that appeared on her face. It was the same smile Dani and Mac shared. The only difference between her and Dani was that her eyes were hazel instead of blue.

"Georgia, it is such a pleasure to meet you." She stuck out her hand, and I took it, but then she pulled me into a hug I hadn't expected because I was sure I'd crush her outfit. She didn't seem to care.

"It's so nice to meet you, too, Mrs. Whittaker," I responded with a smile after stepping out of her embrace.

"It's Clare, darling. We've never been a formal family."

I wanted to laugh because their house disagreed with her statement. Mac came around the car with my suitcase in one hand and his in the other. Dani was toting her own. I reached for mine, but he didn't let go.

Clare watched the exchange with a small smile before turning and heading back toward the door. I followed after Mac waved me ahead. When I entered, it was just what I'd expected, with a sweeping, colonial staircase, dark floors, and elegant chair rails. The kind of interior that never really went out of style. Beautiful and understated.

"Come on into the parlor. I have tea and lemonade waiting." She turned to Mac. "Georgia is in the blue room across from you because you insisted she needed her own room." Then, she looked at me and winked a wink that looked just like the one Mac had given me a few minutes before in the car. "I don't know why he thinks we're so old-fashioned. It's not like Gabi and Bee haven't been bringing their boyfriends home since their college days, and they never stayed in separate rooms."

Dani laughed, and Mac choked. "Mom. I told you. Georgie is our roommate, not my girlfriend."

She waved a hand at him. "Aren't you supposed to be bringing those upstairs?"

She took my arm, joining us together like we'd known each other forever, and led me into the parlor as Mac and Dani both headed up the stairs with the bags.

The parlor was definitely a room that was used often, because it looked well lived-in versus the museum I might have expected from the outside of the house. Books and picture frames were scattered everywhere, and the furniture was not worn but had the look of being broken in. There was even a basket of knitting sitting by an easy chair. The room didn't quite fit the elegance of the house, but it wasn't so overly out of place to be weird. The only thing that was out of place was the huge TV that sat over the mantel instead of the mirror or painting I might have expected.

On the coffee table, that I was sure was an antique, was a tray with glasses and pitchers.

Clare sat on the sofa and patted the spot next to her.

"Tea or lemonade?"

"Lemonade, please," I responded, sticking my bulging bag of books on the floor nearby.

She handed me a glass. "Georgia, Dani tells me your family is spread all over the place."

My turn to almost choke, and I did my best not to spray lemonade out of my lips. I swallowed hard before I responded. "If you count jail and Russia all over the place, then yes."

"Robert—that's Mac's granddad—followed your father's case closely when it first happened. Up in arms about what legislation needed to be written to prevent things like that happening in the future. He's still in prison, then?"

There was no aversion or judgment in her tone. Much like Dani and Mac, she was so factual that I felt comforted by it. It made my heart warm to the whole family even more that there was no dripping sarcasm or disgust in her voice. I'd gotten all ranges of it whenever I talked about my dad. The finance guys adored him like he was a saint, the models didn't know him so didn't care, but others were ready to condemn me along with him once they heard. It had never stopped me from being honest about my family. It was better to throw it all out there and know who was going to stick and who was going to skitter away into the sunset. The sunset I'd thought Mac had skittered into until he started whispering sweet words that I couldn't resist.

Facing his mom, I answered the question with the same truthfulness I always did. "Yes, he's still in prison. He had so many counts against him that it's not likely he'll be eligible for parole for another ten years, at least."

"Do you get to see him at all?"

I nodded. I hadn't made the trip in a very long time, though. Neither of us cared for me to see him that way. And the truth was—as much as I knew he loved me and had fought for me in the divorce—I didn't really know him. We wrote letters that were edited by prison officials and talked occasionally on the phone, but that was about it.

"And your mother? She's in Russia?"

"Mom," Mac said, coming into the room. "Do you really need to give Georgie the third degree as soon as she steps into the house?"

"If this is the third degree, I'll take it," I responded with a smile at his mom. "She's just trying to get to know me."

Mac poured a glass of sweet tea. "Who's coming for dinner?"

He was changing the subject because he didn't want his mom asking me about my mom. I wanted to believe it was because he was protecting me, but I also wondered if he was protecting himself.

"Gabi and Vinnie won't be here till the morning because Vinnie had too much to do at the restaurant, but Bee and Thomas should be arriving shortly. Your grandparents said they may or may not come, depending on how Gladys is feeling."

"What's wrong with Grandma?" he asked, frowning.

"Just getting over a summer cold," Clare responded. "Where's Dani?"

"Do I look like Dani's keeper?"

She laughed. "You've always been each other's keepers." And to me, she added, "Everyone used to think Dani and Robbie were twins."

"Apparently, he goes by Mac full time these days," Dani said, entering the room. She'd changed into a swimsuit and cover-up that were both sharp and eye-catching, just like Dani. The suit was cut everywhere so that there wasn't much material left showing underneath the almost transparent cover-up. It suited her.

"Really? I thought that was just with your military friends." Clare turned to her son with a questioning look.

"I've been informed that us pesky family members are the only ones who still call him Robbie. You should have seen the confusion it caused between these two." Dani waved her hand at Mac and me.

I couldn't help the small flush that covered my cheeks. It had been awkward finding out Mac was Dani's brother, Robbie, but I wouldn't have said it had confused us.

"You knew each other before you became roommates, then?" Clare asked, watching us carefully. I was suddenly aware that there wasn't much her kids ever got past her. Like I'd never been able to get anything past my grandma.

"We met through Ava and Eli," I told her. "When I saw Mac over the Fourth of July, I'd just rented the loft from Dani, but I had no idea that it was his apartment because I'd always known him as Mac and Dani had been calling him Robbie."

Clare laughed. "What a meet-cute."

Dani laughed, I swallowed, and Mac looked puzzled. "What?"

"You know, when the hero and heroine meet in a romance novel or movie. The meet-cute."

"Mom," Mac said, the warning back in his voice.

"Georgie, want to come swimming?" Dani asked, for once helping instead of adding to our discomfort.

"Sure," I replied.

Dani took me to my room, leaving Mac to bear the full weight of his mother's questions about us. The blue room was really the "Blue Room." It looked like the Blue Room at the White House—oval shape and all. Except, this room had a bed in the middle of it. The chandelier in the room was a smaller replica. The bed wasn't tucked up against any of the walls; it was freestanding under the chandelier with tall bedposts that reached almost to the crystals dropping from the light. The ceiling, unlike the one at the White House, was painted with clouds, cupids, and harps.

"This room is—"

"Obnoxious. But Mom always puts her favorite guests here. I think she's secretly hoping you spend more time in Mac's room than this one."

"I...I don't even know how to respond to that," I said, trying not to laugh.

"You have your own bath; it's through that door. The door on the left is a walk-in closet. Sometimes it houses the Christmas decorations, so you may be fighting for hanging space with Mom's angel collection."

I unzipped my suitcase. "I won't unpack now. I'll just change."

"I'll wait," Dani said.

I grabbed the suit that I hadn't used since being on the boat with Mac in Rockport, changed in the bathroom, and then came back to the bedroom where Dani had sprawled out on her back on the bed.

"Are you asleep?"

"No." Dani shook her head. "But I tell you, I probably will sleep in between rounds of tennis. Coming home is like taking a sleeping pill for me. Unwinding makes me lethargic."

I threw on a cover-up, and we made our way down a back stairway to a kitchen that would have made the guys on *The Property Brothers* jealous. The French doors led to a backyard paradise: beautiful patio furniture, a huge, sparkling pool, and a white gazebo.

The humidity had kicked in, and I was grateful for the cool water as we both dove in, swimming several laps before retiring to the chaise lounges on the side. I wasn't sure what had happened to Mac. I had expected he'd join us, and I didn't know if I was disappointed or relieved when he didn't. I needed time to compile some of the information I'd gathered from him in the car and since arriving at their home. I needed to realign the facts into the folders in my brain like all the other facts I gathered. Research. This time, research on Mac and his life.

When Dani and I finally went in to change for dinner, my slight unease about the whole weekend had returned. I'd just slipped back into my sundress, put my contacts back in, and swept my wet hair into a ponytail when there was a knock on the door.

I opened it to reveal Mac. He was still in the shorts and T-shirt that he'd arrived in, which made me feel better about my cotton sundress.

"I'm sorry I didn't make it out to the pool," he said.

"You don't need to babysit me," I responded, secretly glad he'd brought it up so I didn't seem like the insecure teenager I often felt like around him.

"After Mom cornered me, Dad came back from the club and started all over again. On the plus side, you won't have to revisit the whole 'who you are' thing again," he said, smiling. His eyes took in my wet hair and makeup-less face. I had my blue contacts in today. They were the same color as the flowers on my dress, and they seemed to blend in with Mac's and Dani's eyes.

"It's okay. I understand. Grandma used to give all my friends the same third degree, and after she died, Vicky kind of took up for her."

"Vicky worked in the salon?"

"Yep, she still does, just for the new owner."

"Was she upset that you sold it?"

I shook my head. "No, she understood why I did it. Is there a reason we are avoiding going downstairs?"

Mac was leaning against the doorframe, and I was still standing with the door halfway open. It brought us close enough that I could smell him. The salty smell that seemed to stick with him like a sea breeze. It made me want to taste his lips again, and my eyes drifted to them like they so often did. They were sexy, beautifully shaped lips and hard to look away from once I'd started.

"I just know that as soon as we go down, I'll lose you to the chaos."

"Chaos?"

"You'll see. Bodies everywhere. All the talking. And you'll get dragged into the card games whether you want to or not."

I smiled at him, resting my shoulder on the other side of the doorframe, which brought us even closer together. So close the hair on our arms was touching even though the skin was not. It was a weird sensation, heightening the roll of thunder that always existed between us.

"But you're a people guy."

He nodded. "I am. But people and family can be two very different animals."

I laughed. "Are you calling your family animals?"

He reached out a hand from where it had been crossed over his chest and touched the corner of my lips. "You have the most gorgeous smile I've ever seen."

He brushed the finger across my lips and heat shimmered its way down my body. Dense and intoxicating like that summer storm our first kiss had reminded me of. We were caught in that moment, particles drifting between us, and I wasn't sure I'd be able to move.

A door slamming downstairs and voices calling out broke us apart. He pulled his hand back slowly and said, "Come on, before Mom sends a search party."

We headed downstairs where I could hear the commotion before seeing it.

When we entered the huge kitchen, there were at least a dozen people milling around. Some were helping Clare with the food, some were gathered around a large oak table that looked like it had been standing in a farmhouse for centuries, and others were hollering back and forth from the adjoining, formal dining room.

A large man with white at his temples and Mac's blue eyes approached and reached out a hand. "Georgia, it's a pleasure. I'm Reggie, Mac's dad."

I shook his hand. "Thank you for letting me invade your weekend."

"Invade?" He laughed. "I actually feel like we're down a few this year."

Clare hollered for everyone to come eat, and I realized, even though their home was a mansion in Greenville, one of the richest cities in Delaware according to the internet, the Whittaker clan was very much a down-to-earth group. No sit-down, fancy meal. Just dish up from the pots and dishes on the counter and find a seat wherever there was room.

I found myself at the farmhouse table with Mac and two little boys of an indeterminate age—I was not up on kid-speak or ages. But it was clear they were related to Mac, because their smiles were all the same: wide with beautiful lips and almost dimples.

"Uncle Robbie, Mom says I can't play poker yet, so are you going to play Uno with us instead?" the oldest of the two asked.

Mac leaned over the table. "Shh. We'll tell your mom it's UNO, and we'll really play poker."

The boy made an excited yes motion with his fist.

"Can I play, too?" asked the younger one.

"You're too young," the older one said.

"Troy, if you get to play, then Sam does too," Mac informed him. The older one rolled his eyes.

"He'll just end up eating the cards again."

I couldn't help the laugh that escaped me at that. The boys turned their eyes to me. The older one had the blue eyes of Mac, but the younger one's were a deep brown.

"Who are you?"

"Sam, Troy, this is my friend, Georgie."

"Isn't George a boy name?" the younger one, who I'd put together as being Sam, said.

"It's really Georgia," I told him with a smile.

"Like the state?" Troy asked.

I nodded.

"Why would someone name you after a state?"

"I was really named after a character in a book." I smiled.

A woman joined us who didn't look like Mac or Dani. Instead, she had blonde hair and hazel eyes, but when she smiled, it was with Mac's and Dani's smile.

"Sam, Troy, don't bug Uncle Robbie and his date."

"Date. Ew. You said she was your friend," Troy said with a disgusted snarl at us both.

"Troy…" his mother warned. "I'm Gabi, and these two hooligans are my sons. I apologize in advance for everything they say or do."

"It's nice to meet you."

"I thought you weren't coming till tomorrow," Mac said to his sister as she sat down with us.

"Vinnie is coming tomorrow, but I decided to come get the guesthouse before Bee decided she was going to take it."

"Someday, you will not be quick enough." Another woman came up and flicked the blonde's shoulder. These two looked as much alike as Dani and Mac did. The only difference was that the shorter one had the blue eyes of the other siblings versus Gabi's hazel ones.

"I'm Bee," she said to me.

"It's nice to meet you," I responded.

"Moooooooommmmmyyyy," came a high-pitched squeal as a tiny person came running into the room and flung her arms around Bee.

Bee picked her up, and I could tell right away why Mac said Savanna-Rae was the light of everyone's world. She was like a doll come to life. Maybe Tinker Bell with a sweet side instead of a fiery side. Blue eyes, blonde hair, and skin so pale that she seemed ethereal.

The Whittaker family knew how to make beautiful people. The whole group was stunning. Like an Eddie Bauer ad without the outdoors. Or maybe one of the old family photos of the Kennedys. Glamorous and gorgeous. Not even a crooked nose amongst the bunch.

"Daddy won't let me have juice," Savanna-Rae pouted.

A man appeared behind them, slim, narrow, and dark-haired with a goatee that screamed hipster but an outfit that screamed hippie—tie-dye T-shirt and all. His eyes were small and dark. He stood out amongst the beautiful people as being slightly off. Like he didn't quite fit the mold they'd made. I realized this was the brother-in-law, Thomas, who Mac had said nobody liked. "It's too late for juice," he told his daughter.

I had to fight another laugh as I saw Gabi roll her eyes and Bee stick her tongue out. They were definitely siblings.

Bee took Thomas and Savanna-Rae off to the kitchen to get food and drinks.

"Ready to lose your shirt, Robbie?" Gabi asked.

"He goes by Mac full time now." Dani appeared behind us with a smirk on her face.

"What? Why?"

"I guess it's less confusing this way," Dani said as she, too, made her way toward the kitchen and the food.

"Less confusing for who?" Gabi hollered at her.

Dani waved her hand at me.

"But she's only one person; the rest of us all know him as Robbie," she said and then turned to look at Mac. "The kids will be thoroughly confused if you change your name now."

"Can I change my name?" Troy asked.

"No!" everyone hollered.

I smiled. It was light and fun and humorous. It was family in a way that you read about or watched in TV shows but never thought you'd actually see in real life. It filled my heart in a different way than my heart had been filled by Mac lately. I'd never really fit in with any of the cliques in school or college. I'd just done my thing. But this clique. This clan. They made me long to be accepted.

My phone on the table buzzed, but I didn't pick it up. Mac leaned in and said, "You don't have to avoid getting it on our account. There are too many of us with jobs that require us to pick up. No one would think to make a fuss."

"Are you sure?"

"Yep."

I flipped the phone over and saw it was from Raisa.

RAISA: We will be flying in to D.C. on the fifteenth.

ME: I can't wait to see you.

RAISA: I cannot wait to meet your sexy roommate.

I flushed, hoping Mac hadn't read the text. When I looked up, he had his eyes on Troy who had pulled his straw from his juice box and was trying to suck up peas through it.

ME: Don't plan on it.

RAISA: You just don't want us to tell him about your awkward stage.

ME: What awkward stage?

RAISA: When you cut off all your hair and looked like a boy.

I smiled.

ME: He met me for the first time when I had my hair cut off.

RAISA: No! And he still has the hots for you?

ME: No one says hots here.

RAISA: I will be the judge of that when I am at Stanford. You have been too old for too long to know.

ME: I'm only twenty-eight.

RAISA: It isn't an age, moy dorogoy.

ME: Gotta go. I'm with a group of people. But I can't wait to see you.

RAISA: Love you.

ME: Love you, too, malyshka.

I was excited to see my siblings. We didn't have the banter that Mac and his family did, but Raisa and I came close. We loved each other, and I wanted to believe that was all that mattered. But I wondered, for not the first time this summer, if my siblings would have any number of agencies following them once they arrived in the States, and that had me worrying about Mac and Dani and their family all over again. It renewed the sudden bitterness I'd been feeling toward my parents and the effect they had on my life, and it would have lodged into anger if I hadn't been surrounded by the laughter and charm of the Whittaker clan. Instead, I was dragged into games of poker where tales of Mac were flung about that could only bring smiles to my face.

Chapter Seventeen

Mac

After dinner, I played Uno with my nephews like I promised but was pleasantly surprised when Georgie sat down with us. I was relieved when that game lasted a whopping thirty minutes before they were taken to bed, because, while I loved my nephews, they were exhausting.

I turned to Georgie, rubbing my hands together, and said, "Ready for the real game now?"

She chuckled, having no idea how deadly serious I, or my family, would be about the game. I led her into the dining room where Mom had the poker chips out, and everyone was focusing way too somberly on their Texas Hold 'Em cards. We both bought into choruses of grumbling because we were joining late and would have more chips than those who had already been losing. I gave them all the stink eye.

"Be nice, we have a guest," Mom chided.

My family's obsession with their poker became increasingly obvious the more people lost their chips.

Their faces closed down until they were almost mannequins. After calling on one particularly long hand, I looked at Georgie only to find her hiding a smile behind her cards. I leaned close to her ear, hid my lips behind my cards, and said, "If you keep smiling, they'll know your tells instantly, and you'll be out before you've even started."

She chuckled, and Bee called out, "No cheating!"

"Let him woo the girl in peace," Dad said, and Dani snorted.

"Woo? Really, Dad? What are you, Grandma now?"

"Just for that, Gooberpants, I'm taking all your chips." Dad waved his cards in her face before pulling all the chips in the middle toward him while Dani groaned.

The sucky thing about playing poker with your family was that they knew all your tells. You had to get really, really good at covering them up, or they would eat you alive. I tried to explain this to Georgie, but she just laughed her way through the game, losing her twenty dollars without a care in the world. But she stuck around to watch as Dad and I battled it out, even when many of the others made their way back to the kitchen for dessert.

Dad started in on the stories about my younger days in an attempt to rattle me.

"So, Georgie, did Mac tell you about the Mercedes incident?"

"Oh, that's a good one," Dani said, coming back in with chocolate cake and offering a plate to Georgie.

"Mac was, what, in the third grade?" Dad looked

at me.

"Fifth, and you aren't getting away from this hand, Dad. I raise you five," I said, tossing more chips in the middle.

"He and this girl at school had decided they were a couple, 'going together,' whatever the term was, and had arranged a date night, dinner and all. When I told him he was too young to date, he snuck into the garage, started up Clare's Mercedes, and ended up crashing it into the gates."

Georgie turned to me, eyes big, smile glowing, and I must have let my guard down, because Dad folded instead of calling.

"What did the girl think when you didn't show?" Georgie wanted to know.

I scratched my chin. "You know, I don't remember."

"Liar," Bee said, coming into the room with her own piece of chocolate cake. "He was devastated because she broke up with him, saying if he didn't know how to drive, she couldn't possibly continue to date him. He cried for a week."

Everyone laughed, and Georgie tried to hold back her own laughter but failed. "I'm sorry," she said. "I shouldn't…but it's so sweet, and sad, and funny at the same time."

I stole her fork, taking a bite of her cake. She watched me eat it, and I lost my concentration again.

"Did you just steal my cake?" she asked.

"Oh my God, you can't leave anything sweet within ten feet of the man; it'll be gone in a flash," Gabi continued to torture me.

Georgie got up and returned shortly with a new piece of cake, and I was watching everything she did instead of paying attention to the game. Dad knew it as much as I did. For the first time in a really long time, my heart wasn't in the game. It was somewhere else. When I lost my final chips to him, my sisters all groaned.

"It's your fault," I said, waving at them. "You were distracting me with your stories."

"Yeah, it was us that was distracting you, um-hmm," Bee said with a pointed glance at Georgie who was talking to Dani.

"Someday, Robbie. Someday, you'll be able to beat the master." Gabi patted me on the shoulder.

"Never," Dad hissed playfully.

"Don't let Grandma hear you call Dad the master," I retorted.

There were mumbled agreements because we all knew Grandma was the real poker queen. Everyone slowly started meandering away to bed with yawns and talk of tennis. I walked with Georgie to the Blue Room and stopped her before she could go in.

"I'm really glad you came," I told her.

"I am, too."

"But don't believe everything they tell you."

"Why? It's sort of romantic that you tried to take your ten-year-old girlfriend on a drive."

I groaned, and she leaned up and kissed me on the cheek. My hand snaked out to stop her from moving away when she would have, the laughter from before disappearing as longing welled up inside me.

She pushed gently against my chest, and I let her

go.

"Goodnight, Mac-Macauley," she said quietly.

"See you first thing in the morning for tennis camp, Georgie-Girl."

She nodded and slipped inside the room, closing the door before I could change my mind, or her mind, about where we were sleeping.

I knew it was a good thing. We weren't there yet. We weren't at the part where I could lie down next to her and make her forget what was said about me and just believe what my hands and heart told her.

♫ ♫ ♫

The next morning, I was at her door at seven because the court was going to be taken up for the Whittaker Family Tournament as of ten. I knocked on her door lightly. I didn't want either Dani or Bee, whose rooms were just down the hall, to hear.

No answer.

I knocked again.

Still no answer.

I tried the doorknob and found it unlocked. I turned, looking both ways, and then entered. I certainly didn't mind being in a bedroom with Georgie, but I knew what I'd promised her about this weekend. And I knew just how much my family would never let either of us hear the end of it if someone saw us coming from each other's rooms.

The wooden shutters on the windows cut off almost every lick of light, even though the sun was already up, making it hard to see into the depths of the bedroom. I moved closer and caught my breath.

Georgie was curled on her side, one arm around a pillow, shoulder bare, hair flung out behind her on the white pillowcase, eyes closed. The bedding had slipped off, and her long legs were also bare. From the angle I was at, with the pillow hugged to her middle, she looked like she wasn't wearing anything.

My entire body reacted to that, my tennis shorts not hiding any of it.

I ached to climb in with her. To tuck that long-limbed body up against mine. And that did nothing for the hard-on I had. I tried to think of anything but the gorgeous creature lying in the bed.

I looked at the ceiling and the cupids that were making their way across it. Thought of Mom having them painted when I was a teen and how I had remarked that the ceiling didn't match the room. Thoughts of Mom helped. I slowly drew a breath and said quietly, "Georgie."

She screamed, throwing the pillow at me, hitting me in the face because I was too surprised to catch it.

"What the hell?" she said when she realized it was me.

And I was right back to having to think about the ceiling and the cupids, because she was wearing clothes, but not much. She had on a silk camisole with the strap sliding off her shoulder and the neckline hanging low enough that I could almost see the full curve of her breast and dark nipples. Below the top was a pair of silk pajama shorts that barely fit the curves of her. She was goddamn breathtaking.

"Tennis," I croaked out.

"Now?" She hadn't moved, but her breathing was fast, making the neckline dip farther.

"I told you early," I said with eyes back at the ceiling.

"Early isn't before the crack of dawn."

I went to the shutters and pulled them open a little so the sunlight started to peek in.

"It's seven," I told her.

"We barely went to bed at one."

I came back to the bed, which was a mistake because she was still showing me all her contours, and I was still having a hard time controlling my dick's reaction to it. I went to the door.

"You're acting weird," she said.

I waved at her. "You're practically naked."

She looked down at herself and then crossed her arms over her chest, which just pushed her cleavage up in a way that made me want to kiss it more.

"I'm not sure I'm ready to learn tennis at seven in the morning," she said.

"I promise you coffee and a homemade blueberry muffin first."

"You made muffins?"

I smiled. "No, I'm an awful baker, but Mom makes the best. Plenty of sugar-coated goodness on the top."

Her smile filled the room more than the sunlight. "Sugar."

I shrugged, knowing she was making fun of my sweet tooth and not caring.

"I'll meet you downstairs. But hurry, the court won't be available for long. Some of the others will want to warm up before the tournament begins."

Georgie snorted, but she didn't understand the driven nature of my family. If she'd thought poker last night was competitive, she was in for a real surprise over how cutthroat it got over tennis.

She stood up, and I had to combat my desire to close the distance and wrap myself around her. Instead, I opened the door without thinking and ran right into Bee.

"Morning, Robbie," she said with a smile.

"It isn't what you think," I said automatically.

She snorted. "Of course, it's not. You aren't coming out of the guest room after a night spent with Gorgeous-Georgie."

"We didn't—She isn't—Never mind." I gave up because anything I said would have just dug me in further with any of my sisters.

By the time Georgie came down, I had two cups of coffee sitting on the counter in travel mugs and two muffins I'd heated up. She went directly for the coffee.

She was in a pair of white shorts with buttons on both sides of her hips—like sailor pants of old—and they were tantalizing me to undo them. The shorts weren't much longer than her pajama had been, but they covered her butt, which at least helped my body's reaction, if only slightly. She had a red, white, and blue striped top on, and it made me think of Fourth of July, and the fireworks, and how she'd said she loved America.

She looked like America. Freedom and independence. Elegance and charm. At least, the America that I wanted for our world—that I wanted for my niece and nephews. Her hair was up in a ponytail, the way she wore it the most, but I liked how it showed off the graceful lines of her face with her high cheekbones and slender nose.

"Thank God for coffee," she said.

"We don't have much time. I reserved us until eight, but Bee and Thomas are after us, and they won't give us thirty seconds of extra time."

"Wow. First poker, and now tennis. This family does take its games seriously."

"You haven't even seen the worst of it yet."

After we finished the muffins, I led her out toward the court. It was hidden from the pool and patio area by trees and shrubs. I had never thought much of it growing up—having a tennis court in my backyard— but I realized, now, that it made a statement about us—about me. And I wasn't sure if Georgie would see the lifestyle of my family as a good thing or a bad thing.

I already had my custom racket in my hand. Even my nephews and little Savanna-Rae had their own, custom-made ones. We had a shed full of all our old castoffs that were for guests, and I helped Georgie pick out one from those.

Tennis was not only a big deal for my family; it was a big deal for the country club I'd grown up at. Competition was high, but our family had been one of the top three finishers every year going back to when Granddad was a teenager. We had a title and a streak to hold on to, so if you weren't good enough today, you would be cut with no qualms from anyone. No pouting to Mom or Dad would ever get you back in. No crying to the grandparents would help.

My time on the court this morning with Georgie was just for fun. I was planning on warming up a little while I showed her the basics before I got serious. There was no way I was letting Gooberpants win this year.

I explained the rules, what the lines were for, where she should serve, and the scoring process. Then, I served the ball into her court gently. She went to hit the ball, and the racket flew out of her hand. She turned as red as the stripes on her top, and it made me smile.

"It's okay. It happens."

"Has it ever happened to you?"

"Premature…racket…happens to him all the time," Thomas said from the sidelines. I hadn't heard him come into the court, but then again, I hadn't shut the door, either.

Georgie turned an even deeper shade of red, and that pissed me off. That he'd embarrassed her.

"We have the court until eight, Thomas," I told him with a glare.

"We know," Bee said, coming in and joining him. "Just wanted to watch you warm up, see where your latest weak points are."

"Honestly, Mac, let them play. Or warm up with them, because tennis and I aren't really going to happen."

"No. It's our court time."

"Don't be an ass, Robbie," Thomas said.

Thomas was never my favorite person, and calling me an ass when they were encroaching on my court time wasn't going to win him any points with me. I looked over at Bee, trying to tell her with my eyes what I was going to do with her husband if he didn't get off my court.

"Since when do you think you have a chance at a spot on the team, Thomas?" I asked with plenty of sarcasm.

Bee bristled. "We've been playing a lot this year. Wait till you see his serve."

"I'll see it after eight," I told Bee.

She rolled her eyes and dragged Thomas from the court. I made my way over to Georgie. "Don't worry about them."

"I see why you don't like him," she whispered to me, and I couldn't help but chuckle.

"Yep," I told her. "Here, let me show you how to hold it."

I wrapped my arms around her, grabbing her wrist that held the racket, and then swinging it with her. Having her body tucked up against mine was not any better than seeing her in the bed in the Blue Room. My hand tightened on hers, and I couldn't stop myself from placing a soft kiss on her jawline. She didn't stop me. I slowly kissed my way down until I reached the corner of her lips, and she turned ever so slightly as if she was going to meet my hungry mouth with her own. As if we'd finally be able to recreate the moment on my boat in July.

"Holy bejesus, Robbie. You just left her bedroom. We really need the court for practice; you two can do that anywhere," Bee hollered from the doorway to the courts.

Georgie pulled away, and I flipped Bee the bird. She just laughed, picked up the towel she'd left by the sidelines, and left again.

Georgie turned to me. "Really. I think…maybe this would be better another time."

"I told her it wasn't what she thought—me coming from your room. But older sisters never, ever believe you." I sighed.

She smiled. "It's okay."

"It is?" My eyes lit up at the thought of it being okay for me to be coming from her room.

"I didn't mean that as an invitation. I just meant I get it. But really, all I want to do is go finish my coffee, have another muffin, and break out my textbooks."

"I won't be able to visit with you until dinner," I told her.

"Perfect time for me to catch up on my classwork, then."

I left the court reluctantly, not wanting to let her out of my sight yet, wondering if this had been the right weekend to invite her home at all. It was going to be tournaments all day today and then all day tomorrow. It wasn't exactly the best time for her to get to know me.

Bee saw us leaving the court and raced toward it just as Gabi and Dani headed toward it. My three sisters collided at the doorway, but Bee had her foot inside. "Dibs!" she called out in celebration.

"Ugh! You cheat," Gabi threw out.

"You're getting slow in your old age, Cheetos Breath," Bee teased.

"Don't even start, Granola Fart," Gabi retorted.

"Wow," Georgie whispered with a smile on her lips.

"You're giving Georgie the complete wrong impression of our family," I hollered back at them.

"Don't start, Squirter," Dani tossed at me.

"Gooberpants, really, you had to go there?" I sighed and dragged Georgie away before it really got ugly.

"Do I even want to know?" she asked.

"You probably don't." I smiled at her as we made our way back inside. Mom was in the kitchen in her own tennis outfit, ready to go to battle on the courts.

"Didn't you have the court until eight?" she asked with a glance at the whiteboard leaned up against some of the kitchen cupboards.

"They started throwing names and euphemisms, and I called my training complete," Georgie told her, sitting at the counter.

"Starting early, are they? Did they call Robbie Squirter already?" Mom was smiling, and I groaned.

"Yes."

"Did he tell you why?"

"Mom!"

"When he was about twelve, he finally got serious about tennis and the tournament. He was so determined to win that he wouldn't leave the court even when he had diar—" I moved and covered her mouth.

"Mom."

"Your dad told the Mercedes story last night. Why can't I tell the Squirter story?" she asked as she pushed my hand away.

I knew I was probably the same shade of red that Georgie had been on the court.

Georgie was laughing—her laugh that always reached into my soul and grabbed my heart.

Mom patted me on the shoulder and went out into the backyard, probably to find a way to weasel in on someone else's practice time.

"I really like your family," Georgie said as I sat down next to her at the table.

"Yeah?"

"They're pretty amazing."

"Lunatics. All of them."

"But the love you all have for each other shows through."

I nodded. We did love each other. And we'd do anything for each other—even asshole Thomas. "You've heard some pretty scary things about me now. I feel like you need to tell me some things about you to even the field."

"Raisa said I didn't want you to find out about my awkward stage," she said, lips quirking.

"There is no way in hell I'll believe you ever had an awkward stage," I told her.

"Well, she said it was when I had my hair cut like a boy."

"You did?"

She laughed. "Yes, but you met me that way."

I thought back to the first time I'd met her in New York City. Her hair had been almost shaved on the sides with spikes and curls on the top and a purple tint that had matched her lilac contact lenses. She had the blue ones in again today.

"That wasn't a boy haircut."

"Raisa believes that if your hair isn't past your shoulders, it's a boy haircut."

I cast my eyes at her hair, the almost black strands pulled up into another ponytail, the white streak barely showing.

"You hardly ever wear your hair down," I said.

She ran her hand over the ponytail. "It's just easier up."

I didn't want to tell her about the dreams I'd had of taking it down. Of running my fingers through her hair and tugging it so she had to come closer to me and my lips. I cleared my throat.

"That's not enough beans, Miss Astrella. I need the good dirt. Like diarrhea kind of dirt."

She showed me her muffin. "Please, I'm eating."

"Eating isn't getting you out of this one. I need at least one thing to hold over you, as you've got about twenty on me now." I leaned closer to her, elbows touching, faces inches apart.

She sat there, thinking. She finally blew out a breath, and I could feel it over my skin and could almost taste the blueberries on my lips.

"I wet the bed until I was nine," she said quietly.

My eyes widened, because I hadn't expected her to disclose something that personal. And yet, she had. A dark secret that not many people would have shared unless they were being tortured to do so. My heart twisted with happiness that she had felt comfortable enough to tell me something so deeply private. To open herself up to me in a way she hadn't before.

I couldn't help myself anymore. I closed the tiny distance between us and kissed her. Soft. Trying to convey the emotion behind the kiss as much as the desire. To explain with my lips because the words were eluding me. At first, she didn't respond, but then her mouth pressed into mine. And it was just like when I'd kissed her in Rockport. Passion. Torrential seas. Waves of emotion that felt like they were pulling me under just as she saved me by bringing me back to the surface. My hand went to the back of her neck, and I was two seconds from pulling her onto my lap when a throat clearing stopped me.

I was still smiling as I pulled away from her and turned to see my grandmother standing in the kitchen archway. "Grandma!"

I was up out of the chair and hugging her in a flash.

"Mom said you've been sick?" I asked, eyeing her.

"Everyone worries too much. It was just a summer cold, but it's enough to put me on the sidelines today," she told me, hugging me tightly and then turning to the table and Georgie. "So, this is Georgia."

Georgie got up from the table and came over to shake her hand, but Grandma pulled her into a hug, saying, "We are so glad to finally have someone to tell Robbie stories to."

Georgie laughed as she hugged my grandmother back before stepping away. "I've already heard the diarrhea story this morning."

"Ooh, that is a doozy. How about the car stealing?"

"Heard that last night."

"Well, unless you are a world-class tennis pro, you can sit with me today, and I'm sure I'll be able to come up with some ones you haven't heard."

And I gave up. There wasn't going to be any more time for me to kiss Georgie or tell her how beautiful she was. Not until this clan had gotten out all their stories and thoroughly embarrassed me. I was okay with it, though. If she knew all these things about me and could still kiss me like she just had, everything was going to be okay.

Chapter Eighteen

Georgie

BUTTERFLIES
Performed by Kacey Musgraves

The competition on the courts was brutal, but Mac's grandma, Gladys, kept me thoroughly entertained with stories about all of them, even Mac's parents. There was no hiding anything in this family it seemed. You laid it out on the line, and they never let you forget it.

As people were ousted from the tournament, they drifted into and around the pool where Gladys and I were chatting. The noise level and energy increased as the number of people did. When Mac and his mom finally won, securing their spots in the tournament the next day, he dove into the pool, splashing and playing with his niece and nephews without a care—showing the side of Mac that I'd just discovered the night before—the big, goofy uncle who wasn't afraid to be silly.

As the afternoon turned into evening, dinner was delivered in white catering vans just as more people started to show up. The backyard lights were turned on, and it suddenly looked like a party instead of a family gathering. I'd been warned, but it still felt slightly overwhelming.

Dani introduced me to Stan, a skinny computer engineer who used to be Mac and Dani's roommate. He seemed completely out of place, and yet, everyone greeted him with the same welcome they'd greeted me. Open. Accepting. There were also friends of all the siblings, including a woman who Dani claimed was her best friend but seemed the snootiest of the entire bunch.

Mac tugged my hand toward the buffet line. I was surprised to find typical barbecue fare instead of something fancier. It hardly seemed worth catering, and when I said as much, Mac shrugged. "Mom and Dad want to make sure we have time to just be together without worrying about who's bringing what and having to spend time in the kitchen."

We'd just sat down next to each other at a picnic table when a large, heavily muscled arm wrapped around his neck and tugged. "Macauley!" a deep voice boomed.

Mac licked the arm, and the man laughed and pulled away. The man was all military. Muscles on muscles and tattoos on tattoos. Brown hair shaved to a stub. Dark eyes that were shadowed.

"Nash the Ass!" Mac returned.

"Robbie!" Bee hollered, waving her fork at the kids littered around the table.

Mac got up and hugged the man, and then turned to me. "Nash, this is Georgie, Georgie this is Nash."

Nash grabbed my hand and kissed the back of it, and Mac pulled it away with a roll of his eyes but was interrupted from saying anything by the arrival of another muscled man accompanied by a woman with a baby in a sling that hung from her body. Mac hugged them all, kissed the baby, and then turned to me.

"Georgie, this is Darren and Tristan and their adorable little girl, Hannah."

"It's a pleasure to meet you," I told them.

"Otters!" Dani said, coming up and giving both Darren and Nash a hug.

"Don't you look gorgeous," Nash said, slowly taking in Dani in her bathing suit and cover-up.

"Don't think you can get out of that beer you owe me with flattery." Dani waved a finger at him.

"Wait, I thought you owed him a beer?" Mac said.

"He wishes." Dani smiled and moved off. Nash went to follow her, but Mac shoved him toward the other side of the table where Darren and his wife had sat down.

"Go sit by Tristan; she knows how to control you," Mac growled, and I laughed because it was yet another interesting side of Mac. The protective brother. He had all these facets to him that were fascinating to see unwind like a multicolored thread, each layer making him more attractive to me when I hardly needed the additional push.

Dani returned with beers, handing one to both men and taking a pull on her own. "So, tell me, Otters, how exactly did you cheat at poker with my baby brother?" she asked.

Darren chuckled. "We rigged a camera behind a poster."

"Shh," Nash whispered. "Not so loud, we might

need that strategy tonight."

"No way. We're going to beat him for real this time," Darren responded.

"Good luck with that," Mac said, waving his fork at them. "You're at the Whittaker estate now, boys. We take no prisoners, and Dad has the place wired to explode at the mere sight of surveillance he hasn't approved."

I was smiling, and when Mac turned to me and saw my smile, his eyes journeyed to my lips and then back before winking. I turned to his friends. "What did Mac do when he found out you cheated?" I asked.

Mac groaned, shaking his head.

"Someone," Nash growled with a nod of his head toward Darren, "couldn't keep a fucking straight face, so he caught on as soon as I tried to reel in the winning hand."

"But you should have seen the look of pure shock on Macauley's face. It was—" Darren burst out into laughter—light, jovial, nothing I would have expected from a serious S.E.A.L. team leader.

It was all a little enthralling. Mac, his winks, his laughter. The easygoing attitude that flew from him and all of the family. My heart felt so full that it might have exploded. I hadn't ever had this. Ever. Not even when Raisa and Malik and I had played games, hiding from the bodyguards, or going skinny-dipping in the pond at the back of Petya's estate. Because our time apart had always been wider than our times together.

"You all going to sit out here, nipping at those beers, or can we count on winning your money?" Gladys called from the doorway.

"We're coming in, beautiful lady, but I want the spot next to you!" Nash called out.

"Watch it, Frog, I have friends in high places," Mac's granddad hollered back, but it was with a smile.

Tonight, there were several poker tables going with the winner from each table going on to the final game, much like a Vegas tournament. I was completely in awe of Gladys as she lost every ounce of friendly sheen she'd had all day and slowly thrashed her competitors.

I'd always considered myself to have a decent poker face, but I hadn't played much real poker, so just like the night before, I didn't last very long. Instead, I ended up with Tristan and Nash, watching as Darren, Stan, and the Whittaker family battled it out.

The baby was asleep again in the sling around Tristan, but she still swayed back and forth as she talked to me. "This is slightly more competitive than I expected," she said.

"I was warned, but it still surprised me. You should have seen them fighting on the tennis court this morning." I smiled back at her.

"How long have you and Mac been a couple?" Nash asked on my other side, sipping from a beer and eyeing me in a way that told me he was on the prowl. He was handsome—probably poster-boy-for-the-Navy-S.E.A.L.s kind of handsome—but he wasn't appealing to me like he would have been before I'd spent weeks with Mac. Nash seemed like a man with secrets while Mac was an open book.

"Don't even try it, Nash. You saw how Mac looked at her," Tristan scolded.

Nash smiled a wicked smile over the top of his beer. "He left her unguarded to compete with his family. It's his own fault."

"I'm right here, and Mac and I aren't really a thing," I said.

"Does Mac know that?" she asked, lips twitching.

I nodded. "He does."

"I know what?" Mac asked, coming up behind us with Darren in tow.

"Your lady friend has thrown you over for me already." Nash winked at me.

"I'm pretty sure that isn't what I said. Did all that S.E.A.L. training pound a few brain cells out of you?" I teased, and they all laughed.

An uproar from the dining room had us all making our way in to see what had happened. Gladys was triumphantly pulling all the poker chips from the middle of the table toward her, and the rest of the table was groaning.

"Did your grandmother just beat everyone?" I asked, because even though they'd all joked about it the night before, it was an entirely different thing to witness firsthand.

Mac grinned and nodded.

Nash made his way over to Gladys, kissed her on the cheek, and said, "Where you taking me on our date, Grams?"

"This one is claimed," Robert retorted, pulling his wife away from Nash.

"Man, all the good ones are taken." He pretended to sulk.

"What happened to Angie?" Mac asked Darren as they both watched Nash continue to talk with Mac's family.

"She left him. Said she couldn't handle the time he was gone," Darren spoke quietly.

"Were they married?" I asked and then cringed, the years of cutting hair popping in at unexpected moments, asking questions instead of staying quiet. "Sorry, not my business."

"No," Darren responded anyway. "But they'd been dating for about a year. It's tough to find someone who will put up with this career like this one does."

Darren pulled Tristan to him and kissed her forehead. And my heart tugged.

I hadn't thought I wanted that—a relationship or a baby. But I'd felt the same pull when I'd been around Ava and Eli this summer, and now, seeing Mac here, in his comfort zone, had me aching for things I'd never imagined. I was overwhelmed with an image of Mac pulling me to him just like Darren had Tristan. I needed air. Or space. Or both.

And thankfully, I got that, because on Sunday, Mac spent almost the entire day on the court at the club with his mom. I sat with the entire Whittaker clan, cheering them on, but it at least gave me a moment to stop and process all the multi-faceted aspects of Mac that I'd encountered.

Mac and his mom ended up taking second place, and it was late by the time we adjourned back to the Whittaker house for leftovers and one last round of poker. Mac watched me over his cards, and I was almost certain he threw in his hand about the same time I lost my chips, because the rest of the family seemed to gloat at what was, for him, an early departure from the game. He brought me a piece of pie, and we watched in a peaceful silence as Gladys easily eliminated everyone once again.

When Robert and Gladys went to leave, I was surprised to find her pulling me into a tight hug and whispering, "Next time you come, I'll tell you my secret to beating this bunch."

Mac overheard and said with mock horror, "Grandma, you can't tell a stranger your poker secrets. You need to pass those down to one of us."

"I have a feeling this young lady will be around for a while," she retorted and then departed with her husband for their house a few miles away.

My face flushed at her words and the implication behind them. Mac and I hadn't even had a real date, and yet, here she was, insinuating a future that he and I both knew was a rocky idea at best. I hid my embarrassment in a quickly whispered goodnight, and Mac looked like he was going to protest, but his dad called him into the kitchen, and I retreated to the Blue Room for one last night.

It was a sleepless one as I tossed in the sheets, thinking about Mac and me. Thinking about the kiss in his parents' kitchen. About how comfortable I'd felt at his side. The discord that had existed between my heart and my brain was slowly easing. I not only could see us together, I wanted us together. I wanted him to choose me, even knowing what he knew about me.

But after seeing him with his family, I worried I was being selfish. Because if we were together, I was asking Mac to do more than just accept me in spite of my family. I was asking him to risk everything he'd ever wanted. Tying himself, even in a short-term relationship, with the daughter of a Russian oligarch's wife and a Ponzi-scheming jailbird would always trail after him when he ran for office. There would always be a taint on him from his association with me.

Mac's grandfather rode back with us to D.C. the next day, so I took up residence in the backseat with Dani. The conversation in the car circulated around the gun bill and Guy Matherton's platform. While the three of them discussed politics, I opened my textbooks, but while I stared at the words, I was still trying to figure out the answer to the dilemma of us.

Mac and I didn't get a chance to talk once we arrived back in D.C. because Dani pulled me onto the couch to watch the latest episode of *Fighting for the Stars* that we'd missed. Mac did sit next to me, and I found myself tempted to lean against him and rest my head on his shoulder, but I held back, unsure with Dani in the room. Unsure because we hadn't had a moment to discuss what came next.

"Well, that just bites," Dani said after her favorite contestant got voted off at the end of the episode. She got up and headed toward the hallway. "I'm off to bed."

"Goodnight," Mac and I both said.

She'd gone two steps before she came back. "Before I forget, did you order a tux for Friday?"

"Yes, Mom. I have the tux reserved," Mac teased.

My heart flipped a little at the thought of Mac in a tux, remembering the conversation Ava and I had had this summer about how deadly Mac would look in one. I wasn't sure my poor heart and already weak resistance would be able to stand it.

"You should just buy one. You're going to be in one quite often now that we're back in full session." Dani leaned on the wall, and I had the odd sense she was leading up to something more than Mac ordering a tux. She seemed almost too nonchalant. The shoe finally dropped when she said, "Who are you bringing with you?"

I tried not to flush, because I finally saw where this was going, but it felt completely unfair for her to put us both on the spot like that. As if we hadn't just spent the weekend deflecting their entire family's veiled comments about us together.

"What?" Mac asked, frowning at her.

"You can't show up to a reception at the Chinese Embassy without a date."

"It's for work. Why would I have to have a date? I just assumed I'd be going with you."

"I'm not going as your plus one, Robbie. That's just gross. Besides, I have a date," she tossed out.

"You do?" More frowning from Mac.

"Yes. I'm taking Russell."

He snickered. "That's not a date; that's a trainwreck."

Dani didn't disagree with him, but she did say, "He and I have an arrangement. If neither of us is in a relationship, we go together. It's been our thing for four years."

"He's not for you, Dani."

"Why, because he has glasses and speaks five different languages?"

"He can barely converse in any of them."

"You're just whining because I won't let you go with me. But we can't show up together. People will start muttering things about incest on top of the nepotism we already encounter. Why don't you take Georgie?"

"What?" I choked out just as Mac said, "I'm not subjecting her to that."

Dani ignored both of our reactions and just looked at me as she said, "Mac needs a date for the reception. He's a stupid male and obviously left this until the last moment. Do you have plans for Friday?"

"Yes." I swallowed hard. It wasn't really true. But the stack of law books and folders by the door would be enough to keep me busy. Plus, Mac had just basically said he didn't want to take me. I was trying hard not to read anything into it at the same time I was trying to give him every out he wanted. This was asking him to put me and my family ties on display on our very first date. It was too much. Too fast.

"Plans other than studying?" Dani pushed.

I avoided her eye contact but risked looking at Mac from under my lashes. He was staring at his sister, obviously trying to tell her something without words, but she just continued.

"Great, that's all settled then. You can go shopping for a dress with me on Wednesday if you'd like. I did leave my dress till the last minute in hopes that I'd somehow grow more boobs between the beginning of the month and now. But that dream will never come true unless I get a boob job, and the thought of them cutting these open just gives me the willies," Dani said, grasping her boobs.

"God, Dani. Keep it to yourself. I'm your brother,

not your girlfriend."

"Lighten up, Macauley," she said before disappearing toward her bedroom.

We were both staring after her. Like a tsunami called Dani, the air she'd left behind was full of unspoken words and friction.

"You don't have to go," he finally breathed out.

"Okay," I said, but it hurt just a little. I'd sort of fallen for him and his entire family over the weekend, and I wasn't sure now if he still felt the same way. I hated feeling like an insecure teenager, but he was good at bringing it out in me. I rose from the couch and headed toward the stairs.

I hadn't heard him get up, but suddenly, he was at my side, pulling me back from the steps and turning me toward him. His eyes took in every inch of my face, and I tried hard to not have any tells. To not let him see that I actually wanted this more than I'd wanted anything but law school in a really long time. That he and his family had wrapped themselves up into my soul, and I hadn't been prepared to let go so soon after discovering them.

"I didn't think it was going to be that kind of an event," he said. "I thought it was going to be all work. And I don't want you to feel like you have to go, because I'm sure it will be boring as hell. You don't have to go just because she's basically asked you to."

My hand went to my ponytail, smoothing it, a tell that I knew Mac's family had read while we played poker and that Mac could read now. He reached out and tugged at it too, pulling the white strands through his fingers.

"Have you always had the streak?" he asked.

"No," I replied, trying to step back but being stopped by the steps.

"When did you get it?"

"The night my dad was arrested."

"And it never went away?"

I shook my head, not wanting to talk about my dad because he was part of the balloon holding Mac and me apart.

"Mac…" I gulped, wanting to let him off the hook, wanting him to know he didn't need to feel like he had to do any of this. To date me at all. "You don't—"

"Don't you dare say it." When he spoke again, his voice had gone down a deeper notch so that it resonated across my chest and into my stomach and farther down to places that had been yearning for him for weeks.

"You have no idea what I was going to say," I said.

"I do. And I don't want off the hook, Georgie— from taking you to the reception, or from dating you, period. I can't imagine letting you go without having tried everything I could to make you mine."

My heart leaped into my throat, thudding, trying to escape this poor human frame that contained it. His words were powerful and yet frightening. I wasn't sure I'd ever belonged to anyone. Not truly. Not completely.

When I finally found my voice, I said quietly, "We're complicated."

He nodded. "I know. But I still can't walk away. I don't *want* to walk away."

We both looked down to where his hand was gently caressing the inside of my elbow.

"I feel like I'm asking my high school crush to the prom," he said, lips twitching. "Georgie, will you please go with me to the reception this weekend?"

The humor sparkling from his gorgeous blue eyes blew away any resistance I had left. "Yes, Mac. I'll go with you."

♫ ♫ ♫

I didn't see Mac on Tuesday because I stayed late working with Theresa, and by the time I came home, the apartment was dark. Mac and I had texted enough for him to know where I was at and for me to know he was heading to bed because they had a five o'clock call the next morning with Japan. I tried not to let his "I missed you today" text go to my head or my heart, but even Theresa commented on my goofy expression.

Wednesday, I got a text from Dani while I was at school.

DANI: You going to be free at around two?

ME: Why?

DANI: Dress shopping, remember?

I had forgotten. I was sure I had something in my wardrobe that would have been acceptable. I'd gone to enough black-tie events in New York with Jared and the model clan, but the thought of going in a dress that Jared had seen me in didn't settle well in my gut.

> *ME: I believe I can leave by then. Let me just*
> *make sure Theresa doesn't need me.*

> *DANI: I'll pick you up at the south entrance*
> *of campus, unless I hear otherwise.*

When I asked Theresa, she waved her hand at me before making sure I was going to make time for her the following day. I agreed and then headed toward the campus entrance where Dani was waiting. She was in her normal office wear of a pencil skirt and button-down blouse, looking like the epitome of a businesswoman—both classy and sexy, somehow. I hoped to get a few pointers from her eventually so when I started my law career, I'd have the same vibe.

"There's a dress shop just outside town I go to for these things. They're really good about doing any alterations on the fly, so if we need any, they can still have the dress ready for us by Friday," she said as I got into the car.

When we got to the shop, it was an exclusive boutique, and I was sure it came with a budget to match. It wasn't that I didn't have money in my bank account, but I was trying to be frugal these days. Trying to ensure the money lasted me through law school and any nonpaid internships I needed to get under my belt before being hired on somewhere after passing the bar.

Dani sensed my hesitation before I was able to disguise it with a smile.

"I'm sorry. I didn't even think to ask how much you wanted to spend."

I smiled. "It's okay. As long as the dress doesn't cost ten thousand dollars, I'll be fine."

"It's not that high class. I'm on an aide's budget, remember?"

But I had a feeling, after seeing them all in action this past weekend, that Mac's and Dani's incomes were assisted by trust funds.

We entered the store and were greeted by a salesclerk Dani knew. Dani introduced us, and they chatted about their lives and people I didn't know as she led us back to a fitting area. There had been a few artfully displayed dresses on the mannequins out front but no racks of dresses. This shop was all one-off styles by top-notch designers, like the ones I'd used when I'd been with Jared. It wasn't something I'd thought would come with me into my new life.

"I know what Dani's looking for because she texted me some details earlier, but maybe I can get a few ideas from you so I can bring out a few things for you to try?" the clerk asked.

"I'm not really sure," I told her honestly.

"Okay, long or short?"

"She has to go long. It's the Chinese Embassy; there are all these hidden rules."

"You have beautiful brown eyes. Should we go with something to make those pop?" the clerk asked.

Dani laughed. "It isn't her real color. I'm not sure what is."

They both looked at me expectantly.

"Green. Pale green."

"And you have the perfect runway figure. Let me get Dani started, and then I'll pull a few things for you."

She brought a handful of dresses from the back into the dressing room for Dani. They were in shades of blue and gray that I knew would look stunning on her with her dark hair and blue eyes.

Dani ducked into the cubicle and came back out a few minutes later in an elegant gray dress that fit her at the waist and then flared out from there. It was beautiful, but not really up to Dani's normal flair. I made a face.

"Thank God," she said. "I wasn't sure if you were going to be one of those people who said everything looks good, or if you were going to be honest."

"It's not terrible; it's just not exactly you."

She nodded. "It isn't a dress that screams 'Take me off.' I want Russell to be thinking that from the moment he sees me." When I laughed, she frowned at me—so uncharacteristic of her. "Don't you dare mention that to Rob—Mac," she said.

"I wouldn't think of it. So, this thing with you and Russell isn't new then?"

"This thing with me and Russell isn't really a thing."

"But you like him?"

"I like him enough to let him take me home."

She ducked back into the dressing room.

In the meantime, the clerk had come back into the room with a handful of dresses for me. They were in shades of greens and purples that tended to be my go-to. It made me think of Ava, because whenever we'd shopped together, we'd been drawn to the same colors, as opposed to Raisa and my mom who were always drawn to reds and blues.

"Thank you," I said and went into my own cubicle.

First, I tried on a purple dress that had a halter top and a slit up the side. Gauzy and almost sheer in places where the lining had been cut to emphasize the skin underneath. It made me feel glamorous, but I wasn't sure it was tasteful enough.

I came out to find Dani in a stunning sapphire-blue dress. It was strapless, tight on the top before floating to the ground in soft rows. It was fabulous on her. "It's perfect," I told her.

"I can't say the same about yours," she said, as honest with me as I'd been with her.

When I came back out in a teal dress, Dani was back in her own business attire, sitting on the soft sofa and drinking a glass of wine. She looked up and shook her head. I agreed. It wasn't perfect.

I went back in and tried on two more dresses, but neither was screaming at me, either.

"Hold on, I'll grab a couple more," the girl said, rushing to the back.

"I have a beautiful black dress I wore to a runway party. It'll do if I can't find anything today," I told Dani.

"No."

"What?"

"You have to have something new for your date with Mac," she said, her words mimicking my own thoughts from earlier.

"It isn't really a date," I tossed back, even though I knew it was.

"You two are ridiculous," she said.

"It's just…complicated."

"So your family sucks. It isn't the end of the world," she responded. I hadn't really told her much about my family, which meant Mac had. Siblings. Friends. They'd talked about me. It made my stomach lurch slightly, even though it wasn't unexpected.

"They don't really suck," I told her.

She looked slightly flustered, when Dani never looked flustered. "I'm sorry. That was rude. I didn't mean it that way. I just meant that your family background isn't ideal if Mac truly wants to run for office, but it's not like you're tying the knot or anything. It's just a date."

I went back into the fitting room with two more dresses. One was a deep forest green—so dark it could almost be black. The silk was so smooth that it could have almost been lingerie. I unzipped it and slipped it on. The neckline was heart-shaped, sweeping into cuff sleeves that sat just off the shoulder. It was beautiful, the back dropping even farther, showing off curves in a way that was decadent. It fit like it was made for me, running down my legs and pooling just enough that any heels would barely peek out from beneath it when I moved.

As soon as I looked in the mirror, Dani's words about Russell flew through my head, because all I could think of was Mac running his hands over the silky threads. Running his hands over me and over my exposed skin before unzipping the dress and removing it from my body. My heart sped up, and my body ached at the thought. Of him, and his hands, and this dress.

"Georgie, you alive in there?"

My face was flushed at where my thoughts had journeyed. I wasn't sure I could move yet.

"Yep," I croaked out.

Taking a deep breath, I calmed myself and then opened the door. I'd taken two steps when Dani smiled. "That! That is definitely the one."

I nodded and turned toward the three-way mirror. It was perfect. The best dress I'd bought in a really long time.

"If Mac doesn't make a move on you in that dress, my brother will be dead to me."

I laughed. "On our first date?"

She shrugged. "You never know, maybe that's all you need to get each other out of your systems."

Her biting words were just Dani's way. It was like she didn't know when to hold back. And maybe she was right. Maybe that was all Mac and I really needed. A night of bodies entwined so we could leave whatever it was that existed between us behind.

The salesclerk came back into the room and stopped dead. "That dress was meant to be taken off."

Dani and I shared a look before bursting out in laughter.

Dani finally said, "Yep. That's definitely the one."

Chapter Nineteen

Mac

IF OUR LOVE IS WRONG
Performed by Calum Scott

The week tugged by at a pace that drove me crazy. The Hill was slowly filling back up as people came back into town from their summer homes and vacations. And with them, came the waves of people in and out of the senator's office. People looking for handouts, people looking for his support, and people who were just downright awful. People threatening, and cajoling, and leaving behind what they intended to be political time bombs.

Granddad and the senator relied on Dani more than I'd ever expected to defuse the bombs and set things back on track. Whereas, before, we'd sat at our desks, reading reports and writing bill language, now we were hardly ever at our desks. Dani was constantly in and out of Guy's office as well as the other senators'. I tagged after her, feeling ridiculously more like a notetaker than an influencer. I gritted my teeth, trying not to let my ego take over.

At the Pentagon, I was known—not just because of my father—but because of my own achievements.

Because the work I'd done had made a difference to the success of our JSOC missions. It was harder than I had imagined it would be to take twenty steps back and be, once again, the person who had to earn their spot.

Dani, on the other hand, was a force to be reckoned with. She was doggedly persistent, knew exactly what pressure points to hit upon, and rarely left a room without getting what she wanted. She was professional and respected wherever she went. She reminded me of Téa Leoni in *Madam Secretary*. I would never want to be on Dani's wrong side when it came to politics.

On Thursday, we entered Senator Fenway's office to leave talking points on the Matherton's gun bill. The senator's secretary smiled at Dani as she made her way into his office without stopping. The senator was on the phone but smiled once he saw us, waving to come in. I think Dani would have approached regardless.

He hung up and came around the desk.

"Dani. Nice to see you. What has Guy got you pitching today?"

"Don't even start, Senator. You know perfectly well I'm dropping off the talking points on the gun bill."

"Just dropping off? Maybe we should discuss it over drinks," he said, and the way he took in my sister from head to toe had me clenching my fists.

"I'm sure Abigail will want you home long before I'm ready to leave the building," Dani smoothly deflected him, handing him the notes we'd brought with us.

"Abigail won't be back in D.C. for another week," he said, and I swore his fingers held onto her wrist way longer than necessary. I cleared my throat, and he looked toward me as if seeing me for the first time.

I wasn't naïve. I knew there were plenty of power-hungry, whore-mongering politicians in D.C. I just hadn't paid attention to which ones were which. I'd been focused, instead, on wanting to change it all, and now it felt ridiculous and childish. Exactly the emotions I'd started to feel on Eli's beach in Rockport. Had I really never thought further past my goals than an eight-year-old's determination to "be the difference we wanted in the world"? I thought of my journal at home, full of aspirations and very little reality. My disgust with myself and the man in front of me continued to bloom when he spoke with his own, barely veiled, derision.

"Who's your shadow?" he asked Dani.

"This is my brother, Macauley. He's come over from the Pentagon to work for Guy."

The senator extended his hand, and I shook it, even though I'd need an entire bottle of hand sanitizer afterward.

"What did you do at the Pentagon, Macauley?"

"Can't really talk about it," I answered with a shrug.

His eyes narrowed, and he looked back at Dani, fake smile disappearing. "Tell Guy if he wants my spot on the Intelligence Committee, he'll have to have me shot and hanged first."

Dani sighed. "You know that isn't what this is about."

"Do I?" He waved the notes Dani had handed him. "Gun bill. Pentagon spies. What the hell is next?"

I stepped between Dani and the man, the hairs on the back of my neck standing up for the first time in ages. Dani placed a hand on my arm, stopping me before I said something I shouldn't.

"You don't have anything to worry about from Mac or Guy unless you're the representative from the state of Delaware, because Mac's the only one gunning for anyone's spot," she said, heading toward the door, and I followed.

Senator Fenway barked out a laugh. "A politician, huh? I'll make sure Lester Coats knows he's coming."

We didn't respond as we left. I fought every instinct that told me to go back inside and give the man a black eye. We were twenty steps down the hallway before I breathed a word. "What the hell, Dani?"

She shrugged. "While Guy Matherton is one of the good ones, Todd Fenway is one of the sleaze buckets."

"He hits on you like that all the time?"

"Please. That was nothing."

My blood boiled further, but I was also pissed at more than just Senator Sleaze. "And Granddad just sends you to meet with him anyway?" I asked.

Dani stopped short, turning to look at me with her hand on her hip. "Granddad has more important things to worry about than whether some scumbag is hitting on me. Don't you dare say anything. I've taken care of myself for nine years without you here. I can certainly take care of myself now."

She kept going, and I dogged after her. "Shit. I

didn't mean anything by it, Dani. You're fricking incredible. I mean that. But why doesn't anybody do anything about it?"

"Like what? Tell his wife he sleeps with the staffers? You don't think she knows that?"

"Jesus Christ," I breathed out.

But inside, I was freaking out. Not only because of Dani and the situations my sister must have been in over the years that I'd never once heard about, but because I wasn't sure I could be in the same room with those kinds of men and not end up punching someone. I wasn't sure I was going to be able to do any of what Dani did with grace and ferocity. It had me wondering if maybe Dani should run for office, and I should be her campaign manager.

♩ ♩ ♩

By the time Friday finally hit, I was ready to forget everything I'd seen and heard all week. The dog-and-pony shows, the "What's in it for me?" discussions, and especially, the grubby men who hit on my sister. The number of those had grown substantially as the week went on. In fact, they'd outnumbered the ones that I put in Matherton's "good guy" category by about nine to one. Dani had ignored every single one of their looks and backhanded comments, simply going in for the kill every time she needed to. She knew exactly when to push and when to back off, and I continued to be amazed by her.

If it wasn't for the fact that I would have Georgie on my arm that night, I would have bailed out on the embassy reception so fast that I wouldn't have left any contrails behind. But Dani had plans for me that involved discussing a human rights bill with an embassy aide, and continuing the gun legislation discussion with another of Senator Fenway's schmucks after I'd made her promise she wouldn't confront Fenway himself.

She'd snorted, saying there was nothing to worry about when she had Russell with her. But somehow, I couldn't imagine Russell, who'd barely spoken ten words to Dani in my presence, standing up for her to anyone.

Which was what I was thinking when I opened the door to let him into our apartment while I waited for Dani and Georgie, who were getting ready in Dani's room. All I'd done was shower, shave, and put on the tux that had been delivered by courier that afternoon. The rented tux tugged at my shoulders a bit too snugly, but it would do for the night as long as I didn't do any calisthenics.

Russell looked—surprisingly—good in his own black tux that certainly wasn't a rental. It looked like it had been made to fit him and accented the muscles I hadn't known he had until that moment. He'd left his glasses behind, or maybe he was wearing contacts, which only made me wonder what color contacts Georgie would have in when she emerged from Dani's room.

"Russell," I said as I let him in.

He eyed me just as I eyed him. "Tantini's?" he asked, referring to my tux.

I nodded.

"Dani said I should give you the name of my tailor

so you can have your own made. You'll need one, at a minimum."

He handed me a card, and I took it, setting it on the counter. I was just going to give him my two cents on what I was now considering his protection duty when I heard the clatter of heels on the wood floor and heard his intake of breath. I turned to see Dani coming toward us.

She was in a sapphire-colored dress that suited her blue eyes and dark hair. She looked beautiful with her hair down in soft curls and diamonds around her neck that I recognized as having belonged to our grandmother.

"You look stunning," Russell said, lifting her hand to his lips, and I didn't know whether I wanted to strangle him or slap him on the back for being a gentleman with my sister.

"You do look pretty spiffy, Gooberpants," I teased. She smacked me across the chest with her handbag.

She turned to Russell. "Drink?"

He nodded, and Dani went to the makeshift bar we had in the corner of the room. She poured what looked like two whiskeys. Dani, the whiskey drinker. My sister continued to surprise me.

"Where's Georgie?" I asked, looking down at the watch my grandfather had given me the day I'd graduated from the Navy's Officer Candidate School.

"Putting on her dress," Dani responded.

My whole body tensed at the thought of Georgie in her bra and underwear in Dani's room. In the stiletto heels I'd seen in the box on the coffee table earlier today. It was too much to even process before she was there, in person, coming toward me and making me forget every single thought I'd had in my head all week.

Georgie was in a green dress so dark it barely escaped being black, and I knew, before she was even close enough for me to see, that her contacts would be green, too. The sleeves sat just off her shoulders flowing into a sweetheart neckline that barely covered the top of her breasts while the rest of the material molded to her, showing off every gorgeous hill and valley. As she walked, her whole body swayed, drawing attention to every curve beneath the silky surface. Her dark hair was twisted into a sleek and gorgeous updo that almost hid her white streak and put her sun-kissed skin on display.

All I could think was, "Holy hell." And I guess I'd whispered it out loud, because Dani laughed as she came to stand next to me, watching Georgie come down the hall.

As she got closer, I could see her eyes were green, but they weren't her apple green contacts. They were the pale, jade that was her real eye coloring. The way she rarely wore them, and the way that always stunned the breath from me when she did. Maybe because they were really her. Like she'd been the day on the boat when I'd first kissed her. And suddenly, I knew there was no way I was getting out of this night without kissing her. No way that I could just say goodnight when the evening chimed midnight, and we were supposed to scurry back to our real lives.

I held out my arm, and she took it with a gentle smile. "You clean up pretty good, Mac-Macauley."

"That I do."

"You're such a conceited jerk," Dani said, and Georgie smiled.

Dani's phone buzzed. "The limo is here."

"You rented a limo?" Georgie asked.

"Of course. No one can show up at a black-tie affair in a Mini Cooper. Maybe if you had a two-hundred-thousand-dollar Jaguar, you could arrive in it, but otherwise, you get a limo."

"I feel like I have more to learn about D.C. than I do about the law," Georgie commented as we headed down the hallway for the elevator.

We got in, and Georgie nudged my arm. I looked down into her soft-green eyes and barely held myself back from kissing her right then and there—Dani and her date be damned. Georgie inclined her head toward Russell, and I brought myself back to reality instead of the dream of Georgie.

"Sorry. Georgie, this is Russell Cooper. Russell, Georgie."

They shook hands. "Nice to meet you. I've heard a lot about you," Russell said.

"You have?" Georgie and I both said at the same time, looking at Dani.

Dani didn't even blush, but it made me realize that she was way more into Russell than she'd ever let on. I couldn't wait to tease her about it once we were alone.

"Dani says you're working with Theresa Sedgewick on her immigration case," Russell said.

"I am. She's pretty impressive."

"She was my favorite professor at Georgetown."

"You have a law degree?" Georgie asked.

He nodded.

"Russell has three bachelor's, two master's, and a PhD, in addition to having passed the bar," Dani said, looking into her bag as if she didn't have a care in the world. But I'd figured it out. Dani's nonchalance was her tell. She cared a lot about this man, and I could only hope he knew how to defend her.

"Wow," Georgie said next to me.

We stepped out of the elevator and into the limo, and I wondered if Georgie was truly impressed with his credentials. I wondered if she was the type of woman to go for an academic versus a military man. She was sexy and smart, and I bet she had men hanging on her every word no matter where she was, but I hadn't really thought about what her type might be before now. I guess I'd only thought about how she was my type.

When we arrived, the Chinese Embassy's ballroom was decorated to the hilt. All glitz and glamour. It was full of politicians and their spouses, circling the room waiting for the next carcass to fall. It was yet another thing I didn't like about politics. I'd wanted to change all of that. To make D.C. events less about a deck of cards that got passed around with the biggest hand winning and more about what our country and our world really needed. I had wanted to put aside partisan politics and truly make a difference.

But everything I'd seen this week with Dani and the senators had continued to bat at my idealistic thoughts on politics and change. For someone who prided himself on seeing things others couldn't, I really had been naïve, and that reflected in my unusual quietness in a setting where I normally was outgoing.

As Georgie and I moved around the room, greeting people, it was Georgie who did the most talking. When I introduced her, she cut me off before I said her last name, and I quickly realized she didn't want people to hear it, to know who her father was. And to anyone not familiar with her, it wouldn't even have been noticeable. Instead, she appeared graceful, confident, and informed on my arm, easily keeping up with almost every topic that came up. She effortlessly turned the conversation with as much ease as Dani. I stood, watching with awe, the two undeniably brilliant women who had entered the room with me.

At some point, the appetizers disappeared just as the cocktails got stronger, and people shifted to the dance floor. I watched as Russell pulled Dani gently away from a group they were talking to and wrapped her in his arms, moving across the dance floor in a waltz that was unexpected, like so many things tonight about him and Georgie and me.

Georgie put her hand over mine. "Are you okay?"

I looked down the inch or so into her eyes, her tall body in those sparkly stilettos almost matching my own height. "Do you want to dance?" I asked, deflecting.

"I'm not sure I could do that," she referred to Dani and Russell's movements across the dance floor.

"We don't have to waltz." I handed our glasses off to the waitstaff and then joined my fingers with hers, leading her onto the dance floor where I pulled her tight up against my body. I could feel her curves through her green satin dress, and my whole body burned at the thought of removing it. The dress. My tux. Just skin. Even more skin than had existed when we'd been in our swimsuits.

"Do you waltz?" she asked.

"I can, but I'm not as good at it as him," I said, referring to my sister's date.

"They look good together."

"I'm not sure if I should shoot him in a dark alley or ask him to put a ring on her finger."

Georgie laughed, and it brought me back to her and away from whatever was going on between my sister and Russell. It brought me back from my week full of doubts, to the woman in my arms with eyes that I wanted to stare at for days.

"I haven't said it. I wasn't sure I could without embarrassing myself earlier, but you look gorgeous. No. That isn't the right word. Maybe there isn't a right word. You look like the stars came down and kissed you with their sparkle. Shit. That's really bad. You look—"

Georgie put a finger on my lips and smiled. "Thank you."

"I don't have Eli's way with words."

"Good thing you'll have speechwriters, then."

It was yet another reason for me to wonder if I'd done the right thing, leaving my Navy career behind to join the ranks of the political masses. It made me wonder if what I thought I wanted was what I really wanted. If maybe my heart was telling me something my brain hadn't quite caught up to yet.

"What is it?" Georgie asked.

"What do you mean?" I asked as our bodies swayed together to a tune that was slow and sultry.

"You keep disappearing into your head tonight. You're usually all smiles and bravado. But tonight, you seem…pensive."

I shouldn't have been surprised that she caught on to my mood, but it still caught me off guard.

"You're good at that," I said.

"What?"

"Reading people. It'll make you a really good lawyer."

She flushed. "Thank you. That means more than you trying—and failing—to compliment my looks."

"I've always thought I was good at reading people. Situations. It's why I thought I'd be good at politics. That I'd be able to see past the bullsh—crud people were spouting."

"You don't feel that way anymore?"

"I'm not sure what I was expecting..." I trailed off, not only because I was unsure of what I was trying to say, but also because I was losing my way with her body brushing against mine.

"It's only been a few weeks. You have to give yourself time to adjust," she said.

As she spoke, she somehow moved closer in my arms, as if she was trying to soothe me. Her curves crushed tighter into my body, and I lost any train of thought except the wave of longing coursing over me. I brought the hand that I had on her waist up to caress her full lower lip that had lost most of its lipstick throughout the night. I wanted my lips to be the ones that made the color ebb away. I wanted my lips to give hers a new color. A deeper shade of red that came from kisses burned across them.

She turned her head slightly and pressed her lips against my palm. And I was done. I needed to get out of the ballroom before I lost myself like a teenage wet dream. I needed to take her with me. I needed to make love to her…her family be damned…my future be damned.

The song ended, and she pulled away from me, and I felt empty. Scattered. Like I needed an anchor to hold me down in the storm.

"I'm going to use the restroom. I'll be back."

I watched her move gracefully across the room, drawing eyes as she went. Tall and beautiful.

I turned back to where I'd last seen Dani and Russell, wanting to leave, wanting to forget everything but Georgie and the desire that flitted between us.

Dani was by herself at the edge of the dance floor, and I joined her.

"You ready to go?" I asked, surprised at the normalcy of my voice. I'd expected to squeak like the teenage boy I felt like tonight. Naïve. Full of longing for things and people I shouldn't want.

"I'm spending the night at Russell's," Dani said.

For a moment, I came back to my senses, my protectiveness rearing up once more.

"What?" I growled, and she laughed.

"We have some work to do in the morning."

"You don't need to spend the night at his house to do work in the morning."

Dani kissed my cheek. "Thanks for being all big brotherly, but I'm the older sibling. I can take care of myself."

"But it's Russell."

She smiled. "I know. Russell is very good at certain things."

I put my hands to my ears. "No. No. No. Do not say that. Do not tell me anything further. I don't want to know. It'll make me see things in my head that I do not ever want to see about you or Russell."

She laughed again. "Goodnight, Mac. Have fun yourself." She winked at me as Georgie made her way across the ballroom toward me. "Just don't make her leave, because I kind of like having her around."

Then, she moved away to join Russell as he appeared from nowhere with two glasses in his hands. I didn't want to think about it—Russell and her doing who knew what godawful things together. It made me want to puke up the champagne and appetizers.

Instead, I turned my attention back to the elegant woman who was smiling at me.

"Are we leaving?" she asked.

"Yes. I guess Dani is going back to Russell's." The growl was still evident in my voice.

Georgie laughed, tucking her arm into mine. "She knows what she's doing."

"What? Has she told you something she hasn't told me?"

Georgie shook her head. "I'm not going to tell you anything. She's my friend. If she wants her brother to know, she'll tell him."

I let it go because I didn't want to think about Dani anymore. I texted the limo, and Georgie and I were quiet while we waited.

When it arrived at the steps of the embassy, I

followed her into the back seat, and as she went to scoot farther into the car, I pulled her gently back toward me. My palm slid across the green silk covering her long legs.

"This does look beautiful on you."

"Thank you."

My hand moved up her thigh, edging toward the place I hoped craved me as much as I craved her. When I drifted over her core, I was rewarded with her breath hitching, and as much as I ached to stop there, I didn't. Instead, I slid up to her waist and pulled her tight against me.

I'd been watching the movement of my hands, but once I had her where I wanted, I raised my eyes to hers. My heart stopped at the emotions there—ones that mirrored my own. Desire. Longing.

I bent my head. "If I don't kiss you, my body will slowly dissolve into nothingness."

"I don't think you need a speechwriter, after all," she said quietly.

"What?"

"When you speak from your heart, your words are beautiful."

And that was all it took. I broke. I took her lips with mine. It was just like both times we'd kissed before. All stormy seas and wells of passion bubbling over into feelings I'd never had for another woman.

I wasn't going to survive this easily. It was going to take months to rebuild myself if and when we were done. But I couldn't duck under the bridge any longer. I wanted to stand in the eye of the storm. I wanted to succumb. To give in to the beauty and the depths of her. I just had to hope there would be an us left when the storm passed.

Chapter Twenty

Georgie

DRESS

Performed by Taylor Swift

Mac was kissing me as if there was nothing left in the world but us. As if the world had stopped. And it felt like it had. There was a deep pool of emotions between us now. It wasn't just lust. It wasn't just a kiss. It was life springing up anew. Passion and sin and hope all tangled together in a way that I knew wasn't going to last but to which I couldn't say no. I wanted this just like I'd wanted it each time he'd kissed me.

I'd thought that, like Descartes, the more he kissed me, the less impact it would have on me. The more reality would fly in between the dreamlike senses. But these kisses weren't less. They were more. Deeper. Those first kisses had brought our lives closer together, but this kiss was wrapping invisible strings around us. Strings that would be difficult to unbind. Strings that would find their way into my heart where I didn't want them but where I knew they would tear a hole if and when he pulled away.

It wasn't until the limo stopped that Mac withdrew

his lips from mine. He caressed the side of my face with a gentle hand and then twined our hands together as the driver opened our door. He stared at me for a minute. Trying to read me. Or maybe trying to read himself. The driver cleared his throat, and Mac turned away.

I felt like I'd just lost something. Opportunity. Hope. I didn't know what, but I followed as Mac helped me out of the vehicle. We were quiet on our way up to the apartment. There were things I wanted to say but didn't know how to start.

Mac opened the door, throwing keys and wallet and phone on the counter. I placed my evening bag there as well. When I did, he captured my hand with his and pulled me toward him. I collided against his chest. His wall of muscle.

"I'm not sure I can stop kissing you yet," he said quietly, his already deep voice going down several notches more and sending goosebumps across my flesh.

I said, "Dani thinks we should just do it and get it out of our system."

He looked at me, eyes hooded for a second, as he took in my words, then his lips quirked at the corners as he tried not to smile. "What are we, sixteen?"

I smiled weakly back at him. "I think she just meant that trying not to feel anything for each other is just enhancing the emotions. Like anticipation. Blowing it all out of proportion."

"Please don't use that word," he groaned.

"Blowing?" I teased, and his eyes sparkled at my dare. He ran a finger down my cheek, to my neck, over my shoulders, and then down my back where the dress dipped, leaving the skin bare. My flesh—that had already been on alert—ached everywhere he touched.

"Do you think she's right?" he asked.

My hand went from his chest, where I'd been balancing myself, to my hair that suddenly felt tight in the updo I'd swirled it into earlier as Dani had watched, amazed, until I'd reminded her that I'd been a hairdresser for more years than I'd been anything else.

"Maybe...I don't know," I answered, pulling the pins loose and watching with pleasure as Mac's eyes darkened when my hair spilled about my neck and breasts. His hand at the back of my waist tightened, and the other hand came up to tangle in my dark waves, wrapping them around his fingers and then pulling so that I was forced to inch my face toward his.

"Maybe we should find out? Dani is rarely wrong." He kissed my jawline, inching slowly down toward my neck, and I couldn't help but tilt my face upward, granting him better access. His breath and kisses in the little curve where my jaw met my ear were heated, melting my nerves and my knees.

"Rarely isn't never," I managed to say in a voice that wavered. I knew he'd heard the quivering, but he didn't stop his kisses. His attack on my senses. He moved lower down my neck until he was placing kisses at the juncture of my neck and my shoulder—another tender spot—filling my body with desire by a touch and a caress.

"What's the worst that could happen?" he murmured.

The worst would be that we would find out that we couldn't live without each other. That those strings tying our bodies together would be hard to sever without cutting holes in our hearts.

He licked my skin, and my knees completely buckled, and he caught me. "You taste like golden sunsets."

My heart skipped a beat.

His hand found the zipper on my dress and tugged at it.

"Tell me no, Georgie."

"I can't. I bought it imagining you doing just this."

He groaned, and I swallowed the groan with my mouth on his. Joining our lips as if they'd always been together.

As he pulled the zipper down, his hand caressed the skin underneath, making me ache with need. I pulled away enough to let the dress cascade around my hips and slip to the floor. Mac's eyes darkened as he took in my body with breasts bare and only a thin strip of black lace covering me.

"Georgie," he breathed out my name, saying it as if it was the word *stunning* or *beautiful* or *gorgeous*.

He pulled me back to him, hand to my nipple, caressing. Then, his mouth took command of mine. Tongue and lips and teeth, teasing and pulling and twisting together. Hearts and pulses pounding.

He lifted me up, and my legs encircled his waist. While I was only in my heels and my black underwear, he had on too many clothes. They rubbed along all my sensitive parts as he carried me down the hall. We'd gone halfway when a tearing sound stopped us, pulling our lips apart with wide eyes.

He smiled at me. "Damn. Now I'm going to have to pay for this tux."

My hands flew to the back of the jacket and found where the arm and back seam had split apart, and I couldn't help the laugh that escaped me. "I guess this is the reason Russell buys his own tuxedos."

His smile faded. "I don't want to talk about Russell."

He finished the journey to his room before setting me down. I tugged at the buttons on the tux, pushing the jacket away while he pulled at the tie, our movements, which had been slow and heady, picking up pace as we tried to remove his clothes while still kissing. His chest was bare before the rest of him, and I kissed it slowly, moving down his abdomen until he was groaning again.

I undid the belt and the button on his pants, and he was tripping over them before he could remove his shoes. I sank down on the masculine, gray comforter that was on his bed. I pulled up one foot and removed the strap on my stilettos.

He stopped me once I had the shoe off, grabbing my foot and pulling it to his mouth, kissing the side and the sole, sending shivers down my whole body. He then pulled the other foot up and slowly undid the strap himself, the fast pace edging back toward the languorous one we'd had in the limo.

We were both in our underwear. His were tight, showing every part of him that wanted me, while mine were ready to slide from my body with desire. He put his hands down on either side of me on the mattress, leaning in to take my mouth in his. To take my breast in his hand.

We moved our way back on the bed, Mac trailing kisses up my leg, placing a hot kiss over the thin fabric of my underwear, making me moan. He journeyed up my stomach to each breast, giving them each their fair share of attention before trailing kisses up my neck and finally to my lips. My hand caressed his back and journeyed over the defined lines of his abdomen and down until a guttural groan escaped him when my hand touched him, making me shiver again, longing enveloping me.

"Mac," I whispered, having to say something before I couldn't.

"Don't," he said, kissing my neck, and my chin, and the corner of my lips.

"Don't what?"

"Don't say anything. Don't stop us. Just don't."

"Just need to set the ground rules." I gasped as his tongue returned to my breast, a hand journeying down and tugging at the fabric of my underwear.

"No rules," he said, switching to the other breast. My body burned, fighting to get the words out.

"Rules."

His tongue and mouth stopped the caress of my breast, and he looked up at me from his position there. The desire I saw in his eyes stopped my breath, made my words almost disappear.

"One night. When it's done, we don't have to continue. We can stop. No regrets. No feeling bad about calling it quits. No hard feelings," I said quietly, chest heaving. And I couldn't tell if he was disappointed or approving. Uncertainty wavered in his eyes. He nodded and moved as if to take me back in his mouth, but I pulled on his hair. "Say it."

"One night, Georgie. But I mean one full night. All night. Not just once. Not twice. I'm talking all night."

My body quivered as his hands moved across me. I smiled, moving my hand over his underwear again, and his eyes closed. I teased, "Just exactly how many times do you think we can get in?"

He groaned. "Stop talking, and we'll find out."

And we did, moving together as if our bodies knew exactly where to touch and kiss and suck and bite and surrender. As if we'd done this many times before. As if fate and the stars were laughing at our promise of one night. I tried to keep my heart tucked inside my body, but Mac's caresses slowly tugged my skin apart, leaving it open and raw.

When he finally reached for the bedside drawer and the condoms that were stored there, I felt like I was more exposed than I had ever been before. When he rolled the condom on, and my hands went there automatically, smoothing it on with him, pulling at him, eager to have him inside me, his moans were echoed across me. When I looked into his eyes, I saw nothing that spoke of the one night we'd agreed on. I saw, in his eyes, a future he wanted, and I still wasn't sure it could happen. I saw pain and the idea of love that might never come true.

But we continued, bodies pleasing each other, souls breathing into each other's hearts. Morning was going to be painful, but it would have to wait until we were done with the pieces of us that needed this. The touch that we'd feel for a long time after.

♫ ♫ ♫

I woke to a smell that was unfamiliar. Masculine. Salty. Like the sea. A scent as intoxicating as coffee, but this was full of promises I couldn't have. My body was wrapped in muscular arms that held me so tight I was afraid to breathe in case I woke him.

My heart leaped, and I told it to go away. To hide back in the cavity of my chest.

I opened my eyes, Mac's face inches from mine. He looked peaceful. Younger than the twenty-eight years we both showed on our driver's licenses. My body was sated and sore all at the same time. The challenge of one night that I'd laid down had been more than fulfilled as we'd savored each other over and over again.

But it was morning now. I could see the light beginning to filter in behind the gray blinds that covered the windows that I knew looked out toward Capitol Hill, because they faced the same direction as the windows in my loft.

Descartes was wrong. Dreams and reality could be the same thing. In this one brief moment, they were. They were a truth. The problem was, I couldn't make the moment last. The reality would drift apart from the dream. This was just a glimpse of a point where the x- and y-axis crossed briefly before journeying back along their own lines, the reality and dreams going their separate ways.

I moved slowly, testing to see if it would wake him. But it didn't. He was out cold. Our "night" had barely ended, but I was unaccustomed to being in someone's arms. Even when Jared and I had spent the night together, we'd always had our own sides of the bed. We'd never been so entangled—so exhausted from the passion—that we'd just fallen asleep where we'd stopped moving.

I continued my measured moves, not wanting to risk waking him.

Eventually, I'd removed all of my body from his, and I skirted to the edge of the bed, picking up my underwear and shoes. Then, I turned back for a last glance at him. His skin still bore the deep bronze of the ocean from his weeks of sailing just as his body still bore the mark of his military career. Toned and unforgiving in many ways. His dark hair was mussed from my hands. His blue eyes were hidden behind closed lids. He was more gorgeous than any man I'd ever shared a bed with. Jared may have been on magazine covers, but this man was built in a way that was both real and mesmerizing.

Last night hadn't felt like anything I'd experienced before now. It had felt like it was full of emotions that I'd never let out. Emotions that I'd always resisted. It felt like my life was now forever going to be known by a series of moments that included before and after. Like the lock sliding shut on my storage unit in July. Like the before and after that had defined my life from when my dad had been arrested. I would forever be looking at my life as before and after this night with Mac.

I tore myself away, walking out of the room.

I picked up the green dress from where it had pooled on the floor by the kitchen. I'd known when I bought it what I was doing. I'd known exactly where the dress would lead us. But I hadn't been able to get out of my head the idea of him unzipping it once I'd put it on.

I moved to the loft to retrieve clothes before going to my bathroom to shower. When I came out, the apartment was still quiet.

I grabbed the bag that held my research for Theresa and left the apartment, shutting the door quietly. I needed time and space because I didn't know if I'd be able to look him in the eyes and stick to what I'd said the night before. I'd said we could walk away with no regrets. That it was just one night. But the truth was, I wasn't ready for that. I wasn't anywhere near ready to walk away, and yet, I had to give him the chance to do so.

I spent the day at the law library, reading my textbooks, taking notes, and working on Theresa's research. I succeeded in keeping my mind off Mac as long as I didn't move, but once I did, the glorious aches from the night before would return, and my heart would speed up to a traitorous pace, reliving our moments…our kisses.

My phone vibrated on the table.

DANI: Mac is acting weird.

ME: Are you back from your night with Russell?

DANI: Yes. Why aren't you here?

ME: I'm at the law library. Like always.

DANI: Why aren't you here?

ME: I just told you.

DANI: This is why Mac is acting weird. You slept with him and left. Was he that awful? I mean, I don't really want to know. He's my kid brother. But I did have more faith in him than that.

ME: I'm not talking to you about this.

DANI: But you're not moving out, right?

ME: Why would I leave?

DANI: You're the best roommate we've had in ages.

ME: Puhlease.

DANI: Truth. You're family already.

ME: Trust me. You don't want me as family.

DANI: Too late. You already are.

This hit me in the heart. I hadn't been around them long enough to be family, but Dani had accepted me wholeheartedly, even knowing who my family was…maybe even more so than Mac had. I didn't know how to respond, so I didn't.

THE GUY: Dani says you're at the library.

ME: Yes.

THE GUY: Will you be home soon?

My heart stuttered again. Family. Home. It was just too much. I had a family I loved. That loved me back. But the only place that had ever felt like home was the apartment above the salon I'd grown up in that was now gone. I didn't really have a home anymore. Dani and Mac felt too much like home. Too much like things I could lose.

THE GUY: Do you want us to order from Bentley's for you?

ME: You're tempting me with gnocchi?

THE GUY: I'd love to tempt you with more than that.

I couldn't respond right away because my heart wanted to patter happily and hopefully at what he meant. Was he saying he wanted more than one night? I plunged forward, figuring it would be easier to read his answer than to have to look him in the eye. Chicken. I'd never played chicken until Mac.

ME: That would break our one-night rule.

THE GUY: You left before our night was over, so I feel like you broke it first.

ME: The sun was out when I left.

THE GUY: The end of a night is not the sun rising. It's being able to kiss the woman you were with as you wake up. To maybe have breakfast with roaming hands. To savor that moment together.

ME: I think we savored the heck out of it.

THE GUY: That wasn't anything. I could have gone a few more rounds.

ME: Liar.

THE GUY: I don't lie.

My body turned slowly into bubbling liquid covered in goosebumps at the thought of Mac having more in him. Of him being able to touch and fill me a few more times before I'd left.

THE GUY: So, gnocchi?

ME: No.

THE GUY: Too late, Dani already ordered it.

ME: Then, why did you even bother asking?

THE GUY: Come home. We need to talk.

ME: We already talked.

THE GUY: Come home, Georgie.

The demand and the plea were written in the text. Or maybe I just wanted to believe it was there, and my heart hurt from it all. From wanting to be wanted. From wanting to be a part of their family. From the guilt of knowing what my addition would do to them.

But I also knew I wouldn't be able to resist. That I would go home, drawn like a bat to the darkness of its cave as the dawn approached, hoping I wouldn't be trailing with me any blood-borne pathogens.

Chapter Twenty-one

Mac

SAVE ROOM
Performed by John Legend

I'd woken to her gone. The scent of her all over my body and my sheets, but not her. I'd wanted to wake up with the warmth of her in my arms. That was different than I'd ever felt after sex with a woman. Normally, I wanted to be gone before the look in their eyes changed from lust to love. I hadn't been prepared for love.

I hadn't been prepared until Georgie.

I pulled on a pair of sweats and a T-shirt and left my room.

"Georgie?"

Nothing. Silence. But she'd showered. I could smell the steam and the cherry-blossom scent that was in her shampoo or soap or just her. I looked toward the entryway where we all tended to throw our bags and keys. Her bag was gone. She'd left.

It hurt. It lodged a deep, bitter mark inside me.

One night she'd said.

I'd agreed.

Why had I agreed when I'd known all along that I didn't want just one night?

I'd agreed because I was selfish. I'd agreed because I hadn't wanted her to stop what we'd started. I'd agreed because I'd known she was still thinking about her family, and my plans, and the reason I'd run from her in Rockport. I still hadn't been able to convince her of the possibility of forever, but I'd stupidly thought that I could show her, with my hands and my mouth, what I felt, and that she'd know the truth without words.

I didn't want to shower. I wanted to keep the scent of us—of her—all over my skin for as long as possible. So instead, I made coffee and sank down on the couch, turning on all three TVs Dani usually had going whenever she was in the apartment, politics running across all of them. Some made my blood boil; some made me want to cheer; all of it made me want to stand up and shout that we could be better than this. Humanity. We didn't have to destroy each other and the planet as we fought for power.

I must have fallen asleep, because the front door clicking open had me jumping awake and barking, "Georgie," all at the same time. It was Dani. She looked at me like I had lost my mind.

She wasn't in her blue dress. She had on capris and a tank top.

"Where'd you get the change of clothes?"

She hadn't had a bag with her last night when we'd left for the reception.

"I have a few things at Russell's."

"So, this thing with Russell… It's more than

casual."

"No."

"You don't leave things at a guy's place if it's just casual, Dani."

She sank down onto the couch next to me, but she didn't respond. She watched the TV screens instead.

"Turner is such an idiot," she said, referring to the talk show on Fox with a senator from the Midwest.

I couldn't disagree. He was. They all were. Every fricking politician I'd met this week had been an idiot.

Dani made a disgusted sigh and then turned to me. "Where's Georgie?"

I shrugged.

"What happened with you two last night?" she asked.

What had happened? Everything. Nothing. The most amazing sex I'd ever had, which seemed stupid and cliché but true. We'd fit. Our movements never once awkward or out of place. It had been harmony.

"Why do you have clothes at Russell's?" I asked instead of answering her.

She stared at me.

"You don't want to talk about that," I said as she grimaced. "I don't want to talk about it either."

We assessed each other for a moment. Would we both give in and share, like we normally shared everything, or would we hold our nights close to our chests for the moment?

"What did Fenway's aide say about the gun bill?" She moved on to work.

"It's exhausting," I told her.

"What?"

"There's never a moment of just 'enjoy.' There's always something in the undertone or the subliminal message that I'm supposed to know the jargon for and don't."

"You'll get used to it. But what did he say?"

"That, while the current proposal was heavy on automatic weapons, it felt like it was missing a key component of licensing that his constituents might want to see in something so drastic."

"That little shit."

"Wait…what?"

"That's just code that Fenway is going to put together his own proposal. What an ass. After all we did last term to support their clean water bill."

"See. This is exactly what I mean. Why doesn't anyone just say what the fuck they mean?"

"Is this not about Fenway? Is this about Georgie?" Dani frowned.

"No, Georgie said exactly what she meant. I just don't agree with it."

"Ah-ha!" Dani looked pleased that she'd gotten me to say something about Georgie and me.

"I'm not cut out for this," I groaned, leaning my head back on the couch.

I could feel her watching me for a few moments before she spoke.

"Rob—Mac, I know I've been teasing, but I truly believe you could make a difference in this town. You have the whole package. It just takes some time to get used to it. You were in the military, where everything was pretty black and white, for years, and you've only been at this a few weeks. It'll come together for you."

I looked at her to make sure she wasn't yanking my chain in that typical way my sisters did, but she wasn't. She was serious. I just wasn't sure how I felt about any of it after the shitstorm this week had been. "Thanks. The military had lots of politics, too. I guess I was just used to the subtext that they had running beneath their conversations."

She nodded.

"I'm going to go shower," she said, rising from the couch. She sniffed in my general direction. "Maybe you should, too."

"Har-har," I said.

"Seriously, maybe Georgie left because you smell like garlic and stale alcohol."

I sniffed my shirt and my arms. "I don't stink."

"Made you sniff."

I threw a pillow at her. She chuckled and kept going.

I pulled myself up and went to my room. The tangled bedsheets brought me right back to the prior night. Georgie's and my skin molded together in ways that had my whole body going right back to where we'd left off. There was one truth that had come out of our hours together that I knew for sure... I didn't want it to be one night.

I brought up the search engine on my phone to look up Descartes. I needed ammunition.

♫ ♫ ♫

The TV was on with one of my favorites—*A Few Good Men*—playing, but I wasn't really paying attention. It was late enough for the sky to have dipped into shadows, but not late enough for me to start calling to check on her, when the door finally clicked open. I knew she was expecting that I'd gone to bed, or at least my bedroom, but I hadn't because we needed to talk. At least, I needed to talk, and I was hoping she did too.

I turned to watch her. She was in another damn sundress that made me immediately think of taking it off just like I'd taken off the green dress the night before. She placed her bag and a stack of books on the table by the door before glancing my way.

She stopped at the edge of the couch, looking down at me but not coming closer. No welcome home kiss. My eyes went to her lips and back up, her gaze locking on mine.

"You left."

"I had work to do," she said.

"You didn't leave because you had work to do."

She shrugged, running her fingers along the arm of the couch. Any minute now, her hand was going to go to her hair, which was down like it hardly ever was, cascading around her shoulders in perfectly tousled waves. Waves I'd gripped and held, bringing her closer to me as we'd made love.

My body reacted to those thoughts, and I was sure she could see the reaction through my sweats, but I didn't care. At the moment, all I really cared about was tasting her again. Golden cherries and sunshine.

Light and sweetness combined.

I patted the couch cushion next to me. "Come join me."

She shook her head, and there went the hand, running through the strands.

"I'm not going to bite." Her eyes flicked to my mouth, and I smiled, liking that she was thinking about kissing me. I added, "Not unless you want me to."

"Mac—"

"No."

"You do that a lot. Cut me off."

"Because you were going to say that we agreed to one night."

She pushed at her hair again, looking away.

I continued, "But I don't want just one night, Georgie. I told you that before we even went to Delaware. And I don't know how you could think, after what we shared last night, my opinion would have changed."

She looked back at me, and I could swear she was holding her breath, and that gave me hope.

"You know, in my humble opinion, I think Descartes would be proud of us."

Surprise registered across her face. "What?"

"Well, you say he wants us to test our perceptions. To validate that our senses aren't deceiving us." I sat up, arms leaning on my knees. I wasn't quite moving yet because I didn't want to give her a reason to disappear again. "And I would say we've tested ourselves several times. That what we feel…the chemistry we have when we're together…it's repeatable. Not a one-time thing."

She didn't deny it but watched me warily. I got up slowly, still trying to prevent her from skittering away. I eased my body next to hers.

"But he also said there wasn't really anything that could, for sure, separate the waking state from the dream state. That's what he meant by the whole, 'How can you be certain that your whole life is not a dream?' thing, right? So, I'm thinking that even if we're wrong, even if we're living some weird dream, does it matter?" I asked as I allowed myself to run a hand over her shoulder and slide it under the strap of her sundress. Gentle swirls.

"What happens when we wake?" she breathed out.

"There isn't a certainty that we will, is there? Couldn't we live our entire lives in this dream?"

"Morning always comes," she said, looking at me with eyes full of uncertainty but also desire.

"We fit, Georgie."

"I'd feel guilty if my life backfired on yours," she said.

"You're jumping like fifty-thousand steps ahead of where we're at. Right now, what we have, what we feel…it isn't anything I've ever felt. I want to explore it. I want to continue to explore you." I ran my hand along her cheek, and she slanted her face into the caress, chocolate-lensed eyes closing. "I want to explore what makes you the proud, independent woman you are, but also why you hide your white streak and why you're afraid to let anyone too close. I want to know what made you risk everything to follow a dream that you had when you could have just lived the comfortable life you had in New York. And yes, I want to explore more how you liked it when I kissed you right here."

I chanced bending slightly to kiss the spot where her ear and jaw met, and she shivered but didn't push me away.

"And I want to find more of those spots on your body."

"I think you found them all," she said, voice quivering.

I couldn't help the grin that appeared on my face. "Do you want to make a bet?

She smiled, her real, wide, gorgeous smile that hit me hard in the chest. It was her first one of the night. "You're saying that you can find an erogenous zone on my body that I don't already know about?"

"I'm saying there's a good chance I can find one, but that no matter what, it'll be a lot of fun to find out."

She considered me for a moment before moving my hand to her waist. My fingers dipped into her curves, and she adjusted so her body was tight against mine, our curves realigning again.

"What do I get if I win?" she asked.

"I think you should be hoping I win." I smiled, and she laughed softly, arms going around my neck.

"Maybe we should make the bet about who can find a new spot on each other's body first."

I grinned at her. "I like this bet."

"What do I get if I win?" she asked again.

"What do you want?" I asked huskily, her body

distracting me from much thought other than putting my lips and tongue on every single part of her.

"Hmm. A favor. Granted without question."

"What is this favor?"

"A future favor. One I don't know yet."

I let my hands journey from her waist up to the curve of her breasts, and her eyes fluttered closed and then opened.

"Why am I always having to agree to your terms before I can kiss you?" I asked and moved my hips slightly against hers, making her breath hitch.

"What do you want if you win?" she asked just as she put her lips at the corner of mine. The scent of her filled my nostrils, and my movements went from gentle caresses to demands fueled by aching need.

"A favor. Granted without question," I told her back, because I had a feeling I'd never be able to deny her anything but that her walls were going to have me finding ways to climb across them repeatedly.

"Fair enough. Erogenous zones for favors. Should we shake on it?"

"No, we'll kiss on it." I turned my lips to capture hers, the ache I felt requiring to be appeased. I forced her lips open, tongue taking control, not with a fevered pace but one that still commanded attention.

She returned the kiss. Her pace and ferocity matching my own as we made our way down the hallway to my bedroom. The bedroom I hoped she'd stay inside for more than just a night. That we would have many nights tangled up in my sheets. And my heart enlarged at that thought. A thought I'd never had for another woman. I wanted to keep her.

♫ ♫ ♫

Movement woke me, soft arms pulling away from me, and I muttered a protest, pulling her back. Our second night of lovemaking had been as long and as satisfying as the first. I was pretty sure I'd won our bet when I'd kissed the inside juncture of her thigh and pelvic bone before licking it and hearing her moan.

"No running," I told her.

"I have to use the bathroom," she said with laughter in her voice.

"Bathroom and then come back to bed," I said.

"Don't be bossy. I'll definitely leave," she tossed at me.

"You liked it when I was bossy last night," I told her, and even in the faint light of my room with the shutters closed, I could see her blush, and I kissed her. Unable to help myself. Not able to get enough of everything her soft lips and soft fingers offered me.

She pulled away from my kiss. "If you don't let me up, I'm going to pee in your bed."

I chuckled and let go. "I forgot I was talking to the bed wetter."

"Har-har. I shouldn't have told you that," she said. I watched as her naked, graceful body disappeared into my bathroom. I threw the covers off and found her dress, underwear, and bra that we'd discarded on the floor last night.

I looked around my room, trying to decide where would be the last place she would look for them. I opened my closet quietly, found my Navy uniform hanging there, tucked the items inside the pockets and jacket, and then returned to the bed just as the toilet flushed.

I was lying on my back, hands behind my head, when she emerged.

She stood, looking at me, unashamedly naked. I loved that she didn't hide her body from me. I loved that, unlike many women I'd been with, she didn't try to cover up immediately. She was beautiful—hair mussed, lips burned red from kisses—making my morning wood come to full attention.

"You look as if you've been up to mischief," she said.

"Who, me?" I asked, but I couldn't keep the humor out of my voice.

And just like I expected, she looked around for her clothes. On not finding them, her hands went to her hips. "Mac, what did you do with my clothes?"

"You said you were coming back to bed."

"You told me to come back to bed. I never agreed," she said, coming closer. I lunged and pulled her long limbs back onto the mattress with me. She squealed, laughing and gently fighting me all at the same time.

I had her pinned on the bed before she could blink. She was smiling up at me, my face inches from hers. "I won our bet," I said, and I kissed her jaw and her cheeks and then her lips. She kissed me back before pulling our mouths apart.

"Is this your favor?"

"Hardly," I told her. "This is me doing you more favors."

"Your sister is right; you're an egomaniac," she said, eyes full of joy. "Besides, I believe we agreed it was a tie. We both owe a favor."

"Most politicians are egomaniacs," I told her as my kisses journeyed to her neck and down so I could take a nipple into my mouth, and her body went limp.

"Don't say it," she said, voice raspy.

"What?" I mumbled, mouth full of her, journeying to the other nipple while my hand kept the first company.

"Pol-politician," she moaned. "God, Mac. Don't stop."

And I didn't, ignoring her warning about the word that scared her, and instead, paying attention to her body and every inch of it that I still couldn't get enough of. That I couldn't ever imagine getting tired of. I understood Eli for the first time in years. If he felt even a tenth of what I felt when I was with Georgie, I wouldn't blame him for giving up everything to live in a tiny town, working two jobs, because the woman he cherished owned a bar.

I didn't let that thought stop me. I didn't get hung up on it. Instead, I continued to worship the woman who was beneath me until I could make her say my name in that aching way she said it that was not only full of desire but also hopes and dreams.

Chapter Twenty-two

Georgie

HURTS 2B HUMAN
Performed by P!nk & Khalid

Mac and I spent Sunday in his room. He hadn't returned my clothes. I didn't complain. I knew that if I had, he would have given them back. There was not a threatening bone in Mac's body. Not when it was directed at me. If I'd wanted to leave the room, I could have wrapped a towel around my body and gone down the hall to the loft. If Dani was in the apartment, she would have given me hell, but I still could have done it.

Truth was, I didn't want to.

I liked that Mac ordered food on his phone and only left the room to answer the door when the delivery boy showed up. I liked that, as soon as he came back, he lost his sweats and joined me in my nakedness, wrapped in his sheets.

I'd never spent a day like that with a man. Lazily lounging in each other's arms until one or both of us found the need curling through our bellies again and then reaching out to languidly enjoy each other once more. The TV was on in the background, movies that

Mac or I chose when the name hit our fancy on the guide.

Our scents and bodies tangled together into something new. Something that belonged to both of us instead of just one of us. That thread that joined us pulling tauter. Harder to escape. Harder to cut without pain.

Mac never said the word politician again, and I pushed all the thoughts of his future aside, knowing the guilt would hit me eventually but being too selfish at the moment to care. Not when his thoughts and his words filled me up like a sponge that had sat too long, dry and hard. Now I was soft, bending to his curves, fitting us together.

He tugged gently at my hair, winding the white streak on his finger as *The Sting* played.

"Tell me about it."

"About what?"

His eyes drifted to my white streak. I looked away to the screen where a youngish Paul Newman was pulling a con—blue eyes, not unlike the blue eyes that were looking at me right then. I could still feel Mac's stare even though I'd looked away. I could tell he was trying to figure out all my puzzle pieces. He was worming his way into my heart, because he wanted to unwrap every layer of my skin and see what was left.

He'd acted like I'd had a choice the night before when he'd talked Descartes, reality, and dreams. But the truth was, there hadn't been a choice for me to make. I would be his if he'd have me, and when he couldn't or wouldn't, I'd try to live with what remained. I'd pick up the pieces and sew them together as best as I could, but it would be like the white streak in my hair—a mark that wouldn't go away.

"You said it happened the night your dad was arrested," he prodded, bringing me back to his current question, his current attack on the things I'd always kept inside me.

"I was only six. Dad wasn't there. They'd obviously waited until he left to raid the house. I was dead asleep, but the noise and the raised voices woke me. They weren't the normal lull of Mom and Dad's arguments. I'd already started to get up when my bedroom door burst open and men in SWAT gear burst in. They had face guards on—I don't know why. Like they expected smoke bombs to go off or something. But everyone was yelling, and there were scary men in my room, and my heart was about ready to explode from my chest."

"I can't imagine waking up like that as a child." Mac's voice was laced with concern and tenderness, as if he could protect that small child I'd been. My heart flipped.

"Anyway, they took Mom, and some social services lady stayed with me until Grandma could come get me."

"And the streak just appeared?"

I laughed. "This isn't cartoon land. No, we didn't realize anything about it until it started to grow out. But it's never gone back to being black."

"Your hair isn't really black. It's like a thousand different colors. Purples and blues and even reds."

"And white." I smiled up at him.

"And white." He kissed the strands and then kissed

me. Tenderly. "Thank you."

"For what?"

"For telling me."

I shrugged and turned back to the TV. "This movie isn't really that great."

Mac laughed. "But he had so much class. It's hard not to admire what he stood for."

"Wait, Paul Newman stood for something other than salad dressing?" I teased.

"Salad dressing whose profits go to charities."

This got me interested. "So, this is someone you really admire?"

He shrugged a little, embarrassed almost. It was kind of cute and sexy all at the same time. "Tell me," I repeated his words back to him.

"I've just read some articles about him. About how he saw the failings of our nation and that they were not because of leadership, necessarily, but because we'd lost our way as a community." Mac reached for the drawer by his bed where the condoms were kept. That we'd used repeatedly over the last two days.

Instead of pulling out a foiled wrapper, he pulled out a notebook. Masculine black leather with a gorgeous silver engraving of M.R.W. on the cover. He flipped through it and handed it to me. There were words written in writing that must have been his. It was bold, tall, and slightly slanted. Like Mac, in many ways. Bold with bends you didn't expect.

The page was entitled, "Quotes by Newman."

There were several on the page with a couple underlined. One of them read: "I'd like to be remembered as a guy who tried—tried to be part of his times, tried to help people communicate with one another, tried to find some decency in his own life, tried to extend himself as a human being. Someone who isn't complacent, who doesn't cop out. From *The Films of Paul Newman* by Lawrence J. Quirk.”

And a second one read: “It's kind of like those little electric bumper cars where you drive around and see if you can hit the other guy. That's exactly what the country is like now. You no longer have the sense of community. Of loyalty. It's lost its sense of group. It has nothing to do with leadership. Everybody's out there alone, getting his own whacks. Instead of deifying the community, they've deified the individual. Maybe that's necessary in principle. In the Bill of Rights. But… ‘What's good for the individual is good for the country’? It simply is not true. What is good for the community is good for the country. Once you put the individual on a pedestal, it's at the expense of everything else. From *The Stacks: The Eyes of Winter: Paul Newman at 70* by Peter Richmond.”

I flipped to other pages; there were quotes by other famous people. Some about leadership, some about government, some about community and country. His hand was running along my bare skin as he watched me read his notes. It was intoxicating, like everything about him.

“Wow,” I breathed out.

“You use that word a lot,” he said, hand still journeying over my skin.

“Wow?” I asked, and he nodded.

“Why do you have this?” I asked.

“When we first met Ava, all those years ago, in Rockport, she dropped quotes all the time. Some of them were said just to make us laugh, some to make a point, but I realized some of them were really good. Things that I'd want to be known for saying some day."

"So, you bought a journal and started writing?"

He chuckled. "You make me sound like a teenage girl, but yeah, I guess. At first, I was just writing them in this old-school notebook—a stupid, spiral-bound thing that kept coming apart. Dani bought me this as a birthday present, and I wrote down my favorites."

"It's pretty impressive."

Mac eased his body over mine, taking the notebook and throwing it to the side of the bed, his length and hardness making itself known. "I agree. Very impressive."

And he was devouring me again for what felt like the millionth time that weekend, and I let him because it felt incredible to be devoured by Mac.

♫ ♫ ♫

My alarm went off, and I groaned at the same time a male voice groaned next to me. It took all of two seconds for me to remember where I was. In Mac's room. In his bed. Where we'd spent all of Sunday learning more about each other than just the physical. Learning things that made him embed himself inside me in other ways.

I kissed the side of his cheek, rough with the scruff that had grown over his face in the course of the two days since he'd shaved. It was enticing, like every single thing about him.

"Clothes please," I said.

"Reality bites." His voice was as gruff as the beard on his chin.

I laughed, but I pulled myself from him, picked up his T-shirt from where it had fallen on one of his multiple trips to the kitchen the day before, and the rustle of clothes made him open his eyes and look at me.

"Clothes bite, too," he growled.

"I don't think you want me arrested for indecent exposure by walking to school naked."

He moved fast, coming from the bed and wrapping an arm around me, pulling my chin up so that our eyes met. "I don't want anyone seeing this body but me."

"There you go, being all bossy again."

I kissed his rough cheek and pulled away, but he caught my hand, pulling me back to his chest and his arms. "I sort of mean it, though. I don't want to share you. We're a thing now, right? You. Me. No one else."

I got what he was saying. Monogamous. Relationship. It was going to hurt when it ended.

"Yes. I agree. You. Me. No one else," I said. "So, that means you'll have to call off all the ladies on the Hill who are drooling after you and wanting to be Mrs. Next Senator from Delaware."

I'd brought up the politics this time. I hadn't meant to, but, in truth, it was part of him. Who he was. The notebook from last night showed that more than anything else.

"There are no droolers," he said with a smirk.

"Puhlease. You can't walk into a room without drool being left behind."

"Are you saying I'm sexy, Georgie-Girl?"

I flicked his chest like I'd seen Dani do. A familiar move. "Don't let it go to your head, Mac-Macauley."

"Too late."

I kissed him. A gentle kiss. A kiss that was not goodbye but maybe goodnight, even though it was morning. "I gotta go shower."

"We can shower in here," he said, arms still around me.

"No. That will take way too much time."

His smile was still there. "I'm just as good at the quickies as I am at the all-day thing."

"I'm not sure my body can handle more. Quickie or not."

That wiped the smile from his face. "Did I hurt you?"

My turn to laugh. "No. I'm just sore. Let's just say that I haven't done that kind of marathon in a long time."

"A long time?" His voice lowered, and I could hear the jealousy as well as the tease in it.

"Okay, ever."

His smile returned. "Good."

I pushed out of his arms. "I'll see you tonight."

"I'll be out of the shower before you will. I'll have coffee ready."

"I usually grab a latte on the way to class."

"Fine. I'll still be out to kiss you goodbye."

My turn to smile as happiness filled me again. When was the last time someone waited to say goodbye to me? To kiss me goodbye? Not since Grandma, probably.

I left to shower, my body sore in ways I couldn't ever remember except maybe the first time I'd ever had sex in my life. It had been with my lab partner in high school, in his room, hurrying before his parents came home, the forbiddenness of it more enthralling than the act itself.

Maybe that was what was calling to me with Mac. It should have been forbidden. He should have been off limits to me. Yet he was mesmerizing. Everything about him…including his family.

When I came out, he was showered, shaved, and in his suit, looking strikingly handsome and just like the man he wanted to be. A young politician. A dynamo in the making.

He smiled when he saw me, and my heart jumped back into my throat.

I grabbed my bag, shouldering it, and then met him at the door, the clean scent of his soap and shaving cream barely masking the heady, salty sea smell of him that had permeated the room all weekend.

"I'm going to miss you," he said.

I chuckled. "I'll be back tonight. You're kind of stuck with me, seeing as I live here. No escape for the weary."

"Thank God." He kissed my lips—a kiss that spoke of us being apart for days instead of hours.

I pulled away and left before I couldn't help but throw my book bag on the ground and stay.

♫ ♫ ♫

I was walking out of my first class, heading to my second, when my phone vibrated.

THE GUY: Dinner tonight? Anywhere you want to go.

ME: Better be careful, I might ask to be flown to Paris for dinner.

THE GUY: I may not be able to swing that tonight, but I damn well would try if that's really what you wanted.

*ME: **laughing emoji***

THE GUY: Really. Where do you want to go?

ME: Honestly, I don't care. Take me somewhere you like.

THE GUY: Better be careful, I might take you to a bug bar.

ME: Bug bar?

THE GUY: Where they serve bugs.

ME: You don't seem like a bug-eating kind of guy. I'm not sure I have anything to worry about.

*THE GUY: You're right. The thought of eating an ant kind of makes me want to **puke emoji***

ME: Phew. Saved by the ant.

THE GUY: Will you be home by six?

ME: Yes. Will you?

THE GUY: Lions couldn't keep me away.

I was in my next class when my phone buzzed once more. I was just going to harass him about not working when he should be, but it was Raisa.

RAISA: God. I will be so glad to be away from here.

ME: What's up?

RAISA: Malik and Dad have been fighting even more. Mom has been trying to intervene. It is obnoxious. Stanford, here I come.

ME: I can't wait to see you.

RAISA: Malik the Moody will be with me, but I will get to lose him after he drops me in Palo Alto.

ME: You'll miss him as soon as he flies home.

RAISA: Not for at least a month.

*ME: **laughing emoji***

I smiled happily at the thought of seeing my siblings this weekend. Then, my smile disappeared as I thought of having to introduce them to Mac. If it had just been Raisa, it would have been easier. But trying to introduce him to both my siblings, especially if Malik was in one of his petulant moods, was not going to be easy. I wished they were as effortlessly acceptable as Mac's family had been—humor, a Kennedy-like grace, and charm ebbing through them.

My family had darkness and beauty with a side of humor thrown in. But they were mine. And for however long this lasted with Mac and me, they would be a part of his life, too.

It made me nervous, but I tried to put all thoughts of his family and my family aside so I could concentrate on the board in front of me.

Chapter Twenty-three

Mac

LAY IT ALL ON ME
Performed by Rudimental with Ed Sheeran

I took Georgie out to dinner, but when we got back to the apartment, she said she had to study. I got that. I had a stack of papers in my bag that needed reviewing as well, so we sat on the couch, side by side, knees touching, as we both did homework.

I was used to homework. I'd done a lot of it at the DoD. I just hadn't been allowed to take it home with me. I'd had to stay at the Pentagon until it was done. Being able to read the papers as I relaxed in my workout shorts and a T-shirt was much more satisfying. Especially when my legs and hands kept touching Georgie's skin in the sleep shorts and T-shirt she'd changed into once we'd gotten home.

This one act, the ability to take work home with me, was probably the only thing I'd found to like about being on the Hill since I'd started in August. That thought had me contemplating my life and my goals again in ways that gave me heartburn.

Dani came in from her workout and flopped down in the armchair.

"You two look cozy," she said with a smile.

"Don't start or I'll ask you why Russell looked so disheveled after meeting with you in the conference room today."

"Disheveled? Really? And if you're implying we were having sex in a conference room at the Capitol, you'd be all sorts of wrong. Do you know how many cameras are in those rooms?" She shivered.

"Maybe not sex," I said with a laugh.

She rolled her eyes. "Is that the Blythe study?"

I nodded.

"Good, you can catch me up on it tomorrow. I'm going to shower and hit the hay."

She left, and I felt slightly guilty. Like I was running my sister out of the room because of whatever was going on with Georgie, but then I reminded myself that Dani would never hold back. If she was uncomfortable, she'd say it.

"Are you almost done there?" I asked, setting my stack aside.

"No. I have another chapter to read."

"Come read it in bed," I said.

She looked up, holding her place with a finger that I wanted to put in my mouth and suck on until she quivered.

"No way. I know what you do in bed," she replied with an expression that said she was trying not to smile.

"I promise," I said, crossing my heart, "I will not try to have my way with you."

"That leaves a pretty wide set of options for you to

torment me with."

I pulled the book from her lap, and she protested.

"Come on, Georgie-Girl. I promise. No sex tonight."

I dragged her down the hall to my room.

I pulled off all my clothes, leaving me in my underwear. She eyeballed me as I got into bed. I patted the spot next to me.

"Don't you trust me to keep my word?" I asked.

"Maybe I don't trust myself."

"You said you were sore. I won't let you harm yourself," I said, smirking.

She crawled across the bed, making it hard for me to keep my promise as her T-shirt dipped, showing me a glimpse of tantalizing flesh at the top of her breasts. I swallowed.

"What's that look?" she asked.

I just shook my head, knowing it would kill me and my balls to keep the promise I'd given, but I'd do it anyway. I pounded the pillows and tucked her body next to mine, placing her book on her lap.

"You know, I don't expect to stay in here every night," she said casually, still looking at the words on the page.

"Why not?"

"We aren't moving in together, Mac-Macauley. We're dating."

"I see your point, but it seems absolutely insane for you to sleep in your own bed."

"That's just because you want to have sex daily to soften your morning wood."

I laughed. "I just told you, no sex."

"You said no sex tonight."

"Ah, the lawyer in you, looking for every little nuance," I teased. "I've taken care of my morning wood on my own for twenty-eight years. I don't have to have sex to help me."

She looked up, a soft blush spreading over her cheeks. "Did you just tell me you masturbate every day?"

I grinned at her. "Not every day."

"Wow."

"There's that word again."

"I don't even know how I'm supposed to read now."

I laughed and turned on the TV. "I'll put on something boring."

And that was how we fell asleep: with her book still on her chest, the TV turned to the American History Channel, and my body trying hard not to react to the gorgeous woman next to me.

♫ ♫ ♫

The week went by with us in this fashion: dinner together, study together, fall asleep together. I was loving the simplicity of it all. The chance to get to know her that didn't end after a normal date. We didn't eat out every night. Georgie cooked one night. I cooked another. But it was just time we got to spend learning the curves of each other's bodies and souls.

On Wednesday, she reminded me her brother and

sister were flying in the next day. She was nervous, running a hand over her ponytail, not quite meeting my eyes. I grabbed her hands and pulled her up next to me. "Georgie. Stop. It's going to be fine."

"Raisa says Malik has been in a mood."

"Do you think my sisters are never in moods? Didn't you see Dani come home on Tuesday? If she hadn't gone to work out, I might have thrown something heavy at her."

She picked at an invisible lint on my T-shirt and then smoothed it out.

"What's really bothering you?" I asked.

"It's just… I know how hard it is for you to be linked to someone who comes from my background. If you liked them, it would at least be an easier pill to swallow."

It weighed on her heavier than me these days. Her family. The jail sentence and the Russian "businessman." The drugs her mom had used when Georgie was younger. If Georgie and I made it past the dating phase, and I actually decided to stick to the plan of running for office, it would all come up— every last pea of their mixed goulash of a history. I'd sort of gotten used to the idea. I'd already started running scenarios in my head of ways that we could state the facts, repeatedly, if needed.

On the other hand, the truth was, every day I spent in Senator Matherton's office had me liking it less. I was trying to figure out if it was the sleazebags that I saw hitting on Dani, the jostling for position, the current political climate, or the idea of me having to sift through it all to win and make a difference on the Hill. I hadn't said any more to Dani about it, and I hadn't breathed a word to Georgie, because I didn't want her to think I was making my decision because of her. She felt guilty enough.

I ran my finger along her face to the tender spot by her ear that I couldn't seem to keep my hands or lips off of, playing with the row of earrings on her lobe. "If I don't like them, it isn't going to make me like you less."

She pushed her forehead into my chest, frustration entering her voice that wasn't directed at me but at herself. "I've never cared before. People either accepted my family and me for who we were, and they stayed in my life, or they didn't like them and they left. But the thought of you not liking them and leaving…it's different. It hurts in a way I've never had anything hurt. Not since…"

I rubbed her back. "Not since you lost your parents."

She looked back up at me, eyes wide. "I didn't really lose them."

"You did. You lost the child version of them. You didn't get to wake up with them there to greet you. They weren't there at the end of the day to ask about school. You suffered a loss. A huge one. Your world changed. Loss is loss, even if it doesn't come from death."

"You're really smart for a jockish military man."

"Jockish? That isn't even a word, is it?" I grinned.

Her lips twitched, and I wanted to continue to play the part I'd always played to get her beautiful lips turned up into a full smile.

"Eli was the brains of our group. I was the arm

candy."

She laughed, like I'd wanted her to, and I kissed her sensual, full lips. She kissed me back hard, as if she was trying to take the frustration and fear and guilt and work it out through her lips on mine. I was happy to let her, hoping I could find a way to bring her comfort. To smooth the flyaways bouncing around her inside just like she was always smoothing away the flyaways on her hair.

♫ ♫ ♫

It was close to seven when Georgie and I made our way to the five-star hotel on the pier where her siblings had a suite reserved. They were meeting us in the lobby, and we were going to walk down to the new restaurants on the revitalized wharf.

Georgie had given up her cotton summer dresses, which I'd come to think of as being the embodiment of her style, for an elegant halter top and slacks ironed to a crisp. She'd exchanged her flat sandals for wedges that brought her close to eye level with all six-foot-four of me. I'd dumped my suit jacket and tie but kept my slacks and button down.

As we walked, heads turned. I was used to women looking at me. All my friends had given me enough flack about it when I was with them, even when any and all of them drew eyes as well. But the looks Georgie and I incurred… It was like people were trying to figure out who we were. Were we someone important? I liked to think the woman next to me was very important, but not in the way the people watching us might have thought.

When we walked into the gilded lobby, a squeal caused me to turn just as a body crashed into Georgie. My hand tightened on hers until I saw her smile over the top of the head that was buried into her chest, and I relaxed.

When the girl pulled away, I saw lots of Georgie in her. But she was blonde and shorter than Georgie by about a good six inches, even in her own heels. She had brown eyes that weren't anywhere near as pretty as Georgie's contacts, but they were appealing, surrounded in dark lashes and liner.

"I can't believe you're here," Georgie said, her smile wide and happy, just the way I liked it.

"You look model perfect," Raisa said with her own smile. Her voice, with its accent, accompanied by her looks, was certainly going to make her a hit with the guys at Stanford.

"You look like you've grown up," Georgie said and tugged gently at the blonde curls. "Where's Malik?"

Raisa pouted, her red-lipsticked lips jutting out in a way that would also be appealing to the right partner. I'd never been one to go for a pout. "He said to text him the name of the restaurant because he has some people to meet with first."

Georgie's smile turned to a frown. "Did Petya send him on business?"

Raisa shook her head, eyes flitting to me and then back to Georgie, and I wanted to call bullshit, but wouldn't. Georgie was nervous enough about me meeting them. "No. Just some friends of his," she said before turning to me and sticking out a hand. "You must be Macauley. It is a pleasure to meet you."

I shook her hand. "The pleasure is mine."

She took me in from the top of my head to the bottom of my dress shoes before turning to Georgie with a wider smile. "He is very good match."

"Har-har," Georgie said, linking her arm through her sister's. "Don't go all Mom on me. Are you able to walk in those?"

Raisa's shoes were wobbly spikes versus Georgie's wedges. "Of course. Am I not Manya Leskov's daughter?"

Georgie laughed. "Come on. There's a place on the wharf that Mac assures me has good seafood."

"Hey. Have I steered you wrong once with food in D.C.?" I asked, picking up Georgie's free hand as the three of us left the hotel to walk down to the waterfront.

"You have not, but your winning streak has to give out at some point," Georgie teased.

On the way, I listened as Georgie and Raisa caught up on the trip, Raisa's roommate at Stanford, and how things were at home in Russia. The sisters were close in a way that I couldn't imagine being if you really grew up on different continents. But then, Georgie had said Raisa had been staying with her over the last few summers. Her parents saw it as a way to strengthen her English. Georgie and Raisa had just seen it as a way to build and keep a relationship.

We were seated at the bar, waiting for a table, when Raisa's phone started going off in a series of high-pitched chirps that would have driven me crazy if I'd had to listen to it every day. She responded to all the texts and then looked up.

"Mom does not believe you are here with Macauley. May I take a picture to send her?"

Georgie sighed but then pulled me close to her. I smiled for the camera before turning and kissing her cheek. I couldn't help it. I could tell that her nerves had turned to gentle swells, and I was happy she was relaxing. Raisa giggled and took another picture with my lips on Georgie's cheek.

It was a picture I would never have taken before Georgie. Lips on someone's skin.

Georgie grabbed Raisa's phone. "Do *not* send her that one. She'll expect me to have an engagement ring the next time I see her."

"I think that can be arranged," I said before I even thought about it. Both women turned to me with mouths agape, and I could feel my cheeks heat up. I rarely blushed. Growing up with a family like mine and then hanging with Eli, Truck, and a unit full of twenty-something men made me pretty immune to it. But this slip, even though I was surprised by it, didn't cause me to want to take it back like it should have. "I mean…if you need a ring to make her happy."

Georgie flicked my shoulder and then looked at Raisa. "He's just teasing. He isn't proposing. He knows I wouldn't say yes."

That comment, deflecting or not, hit me to the core. That she could so flippantly disregard the thought of marrying me. That she could so easily say she wouldn't accept my proposal. Because, Lord, I'd been right about keeping her. I didn't think I'd ever find anyone else who could fit into all my pieces as carefully and as closely as Georgie did.

If she noticed I got quiet after that, she didn't say anything. I hardly needed to be there for the conversation between the sisters to keep up. They didn't exclude me, though. They just had a rapid-fire pace of talking together that was fun to watch and listen to.

When we finally sat down at our table, Malik still hadn't shown up. The ladies decided to order without him, as if it was something they accepted as part of his normal behavior. I couldn't help it; it made me dislike him slightly without ever having met him. The fact that he would disregard a meeting with his family so easily. That he would disregard Georgie, who he hadn't seen in a couple years so easily.

When I'd been stationed on the USS *George Washington*, every single time I'd gotten on dry land, the first thing I'd wanted to do was see my family. All of the crazy bunch at once. I never would have blown them off for some meeting. It made me wonder if he really was here on business for Petya. I was pretty sure, even with no longer being at the DoD to look into it, that Petya's business was only partially on the up and up. It made me want to protect Georgie. To keep her from anything that might blow back on her and ruin her chances at the bar and a law career, regardless of my own career.

"So, Raisa, Georgie tells me you want to create a new, clean energy source."

Raisa nodded. She didn't look like a scientist. She definitely didn't look like a green scientist like Thomas was a green lawyer. He looked like a hippy child who came to live in the twenty-first century.

Raisa, like Georgie, looked like she should have been on a magazine cover. Beauty and brains rolled into an intoxicating combination.

"Yes. We cannot sustain our world this way."

"Wouldn't Petya want to sell it if you came up with something?" I asked, and Georgie frowned at me. I hadn't realized that Stepdad was off-limits.

Raisa grinned at me. "Father thinks I will find a good boy and settle down. He thinks my being in the sciences will give me opportunity to meet smart man. He does not truly believe I will do this on my own. What he does not know will not…what is the phrase? Will not stomp him?"

Georgie and I chuckled. "Hurt him. Will not hurt him," Georgie corrected.

Raisa then launched into a discussion about a bunch of scientific terms that had my head reeling in ten minutes. I wasn't missing any brain cells, but her level of science was enough for me to need the CliffsNotes version. Raisa didn't seem to notice, and when I looked at Georgie, she was smiling, but she winked at me and then reached under the table to squeeze my hand. I instantly felt better. She wasn't exactly keeping up with her sister, either.

After we walked Raisa back to her hotel and made arrangements to see her the next day, we caught a CarShare back to the apartment. Georgie snuggled up to me, and I wrapped my arm around her shoulder, pulling her tight up against me.

"She's pretty incredible," I said into her hair, kissing her head.

Georgie nodded against my shoulder. "She's going

to change the world, and I'm going to be lucky enough to call her my sister."

"I think she's already lucky to call you sister," I said.

"You're just saying that because you think you're going to get laid tonight."

I laughed. "I'd love to get laid tonight, but I'd say it regardless."

She looked up at me, eyes happy, face relaxed. She'd been nervous for no reason. Like the night of the embassy party, I couldn't resist kissing her, a gentle kiss that turned heated in seconds. My hand running along her bare back and tugging at the knot on her halter top that I wouldn't undo in the car but had every desire to undo once we were alone. The night wasn't young, and we had work and class the next day, but I didn't care. Embedding myself in Georgie's body and soul for a few hours would be worth any bit of tiredness in the morning.

♫ ♫ ♫

The next night, we met Raisa and Malik at the hotel for dinner. Malik wanted to go to a nightclub after. It wasn't a club I knew from the times Dani had dragged me out, but when I looked it up online, it was in a decent area and had good ratings. I didn't have a reason to say no.

As soon as I met Malik, I knew I had an issue with him. Not only because he'd stood up Georgie the night before, but because of the way he sniffed and kept squeezing his nose. He was a drug addict. My heart sank for Georgie, and her family, and the pain that was going to ensue from this at some point. But also because drug addicts were the worst thing to have in a campaign family. They were notoriously going off the rails and would sell their soul for drug money.

Not that Malik looked like he was hurting for money. The watch he wore on his wrist was worth more than my sailboat, and I was sure his shoes cost more than any of my suits, even when my suits had not come cheaply.

His hair was as dark as Georgie's, and his eyes were as brown as his sister's. He was almost as tall as me but lean, graceful in his movements that spoke of a dance career even though Georgie hadn't mentioned one. I was sure he had no issue attracting the women, or men, or whomever he was interested in.

Georgie was in a black slip dress that accentuated her curves and made it impossible for me to stop touching her. She wore her contacts that were so deep a blue that it was like looking into the abyss in the depths of the ocean.

Raisa was in a red dress, standing out in a way that teenage girls often wanted to stand out.

When you looked at them together, they were, all three, gorgeous with those high cheekbones and slender noses that marked their heritage. With a sudden stop and start of my heart, I realized it was quite possible the siblings had a CIA tail. Or NSA or FBI. You pick an agency. They all had to have had an interest in the siblings if Petya was anywhere near being the "businessman" Georgie made him out to be.

Suddenly, the drug use became a much higher problem.

Malik was smooth and gracious in his talk. Loving to his sisters. There was nothing on the surface that was to dislike. But I was on high alert for no reason other than his sniffing and fidgeting.

When we got to the club, dance music burst from the speakers like a rattle of gunfire, making me wish I had my earplugs. Not that I wasn't used to bars. Dance clubs full of people much younger than me just weren't my norm these days. I was too used to places like Ava and Eli's bar. A different clientele and a different pace. But I liked to dance. Maybe it was years of being pulled onto the dance floor by my sisters. Or years at college where I went from the bar, to the dance floor, to a dorm room with a woman tangled up against my body. All I knew was it didn't bother me to dance like it did for many of the men in my life.

Malik seemed to know the management, because we were ushered in and seated at a semi-private booth with red velvet seats and drinks already on the table. I ordered a beer, not liking the idea of drinking out of any open containers in a place like this.

As soon as we were situated, I pulled Georgie in the direction of the dance floor. She smiled and yelled, "I have to bring Raisa."

I just nodded as she grabbed her sister's wrist, and we all joined the mass of people wiggling their bodies around, the flickering lights and music making it feel oddly dreamlike, and I wondered if Georgie was thinking the same thing and chalking it up to Descartes and doubting the reality of it. What I knew to be true was that, as much as I liked Raisa and disliked Malik, I couldn't wait to get Georgie to myself when the night was done.

Chapter Twenty-four

Georgie

LOVE ME ANYWAY
Performed by P!nk with Chris Stapleton

Mac surprised me, yet again, by being a dancer. I didn't see him—the tough, military man—as being a dancer, but he was. We'd twirled around the dance floor at the Chinese Embassy reception, but that hadn't been nightclub dancing. Here, he moved around with my sister and me like he was completely comfortable doing so. No awkwardness. No hesitation like many men I knew. Even the models in Jared's circle weren't all comfortable on a dance floor. Mac seemed to own it like he owned everything else he did. Strong. Full on. No doubts.

We were hot and sweaty by the time a slow song hit. Raisa quickly abandoned us for drinks and the bathroom, but I knew it was just to give us a chance to dance by ourselves.

Mac didn't waste time. He pulled me close. "Alone at last," he murmured.

"We're hardly alone," I said, referring to the bodies pushing against us.

"Alone enough for me to do this." He kissed me

and ran a finger down along my collarbone, making me shiver even though the heat poured from me and around me with the crush of bodies surrounding us.

His phone vibrated in his pocket, surprising us both enough that we chuckled. He ignored it, but then it vibrated again and again. He sighed, resting his forehead on mine. "I think I better figure out who this is and why they keep texting."

I nodded. "I'm going to the restroom. I'll be right back," I hollered at him.

He reluctantly let me go.

When I came back to the table, he looked tense, upset.

"What is it?" I asked, trying to be heard but also not wanting to shout out his business to the world. He came close and talked into my ear.

"It's Dani. She's upset. I can barely understand her with all the noise, but she asked me to come get her."

We had Dani's car. She'd loaned it to us for the night as Mac didn't have his own. My brother had not liked squeezing into it, even though Raisa and I had crushed ourselves into the almost nonexistent backseat.

"Wasn't she meeting up with Russell?" I asked.

Mac nodded.

"Go," I said.

He looked at my brother and sister in the booth. "I don't want to leave you. Come with me," he said, eyes flicking to my brother again, and I wondered what that was about. He'd been perfectly fine with Raisa the night before. It had relaxed me in a way I hadn't been all week with thoughts of him meeting my siblings.

I'd thought that maybe, just maybe, we'd be able to get over the hump of my family for now—enough for a relationship, at least. Dating. Not marriage. He'd teased about a ring the night before, but I would never tie him down to me and my family.

"It's fine, Mac. We can't fit five in the Mini Cooper. I'll make sure to leave with Raisa when she's done here."

His phone vibrated again, and he frowned, looking down at the text.

"Really, please. Go get Dani."

He kissed me. "Please be safe."

Then he left. I could see his broad shoulders and dark hair as he made his way to the door because he stood taller than most people in the room. I missed him as soon as he was gone.

"Everything okay?" Raisa asked when I sat down and drank the water from the bottle I'd ordered from the waitress the last time she'd come around.

"He had to go get his sister."

"It is a job that we always get stuck with," Malik said, not looking up from his phone.

"What?" I snipped.

He didn't even look up. "Do not get upset, Georgia. It is a truth. I am always having to bring 'Isa with me or go pick her up from some place. I had to travel halfway around the world to bring her to college."

"You volunteered. Father would have brought me," Raisa said, her face flushing darkly—and not from the heat and sweat of the dance floor.

"Don't mind him. He's obviously in a mood," I said and then pulled Raisa back out to dance.

We danced several songs before Raisa asked to go back for more water. As soon as we sat down, Malik said he was going to the bathroom. I watched his back with a frown. He was almost at the hallway that led to the restrooms when he froze. He was looking toward the front of the club. He glanced back at us with fear skittering across his face.

I looked in the direction he'd glanced, and my heart thudded loudly as well. A group of cops—in SWAT gear—were slowly making their way through the club, obviously looking for someone. They deliberately took in each person they went by as the crowd parted around them. When I glanced back at Malik, he was gone.

My senses—that I hated to trust—were going haywire, heart pounding, body tightening, head swimming. The police were making their way nearer to where Raisa and I sat. And I knew, for some reason I couldn't quite explain, that they were looking for us. For Malik. His fear… Goddamn, what had he done?

When I glanced at Raisa, she'd gone so pale it was as if she was going to faint. I peeked back at the cops, and an entire fight-or-flight adrenaline rush hit me, flashing me back in time.

The noise of the club turned into the sound of my mom screaming at them.

Mom was being forcibly pulled from the doorway of my bedroom with words like warrant *and* arrest *flitting in the air. Mom screamed and scratched and hit, and they flung her against the wall, pulling her arms behind her.*

The fear hit me so hard I could smell it. And it smelled like pee because I'd wet the bed. I'd been scared. No, not just scared, terrified. There were guns and men in dark clothes and padded vests with some kind of face mask. And Mom was still screaming at them, now in Russian, as they yanked her viciously from the room. They filled my space. One of the men, a square black man, stepped toward me and my bed. And I wanted to cry, but I didn't. Not yet.

"It's okay," the man said in a smooth voice, as if I would trust him by just his tone. I was shaking now, not only because I was scared of him, but also because I was scared Mom was going to be angry when she saw I'd wet the bed again. I could see the disappointment on her face already, and my stomach lurched uncomfortably, vomit burning my throat, but I held it down, unwilling to add puke to the urine.

"Honey, your dad gave you a music box the other day," the man said, brushing a hand over my hair, causing me to jerk away.

My dad had given me a beautiful music box. How did the man know? *I'd wondered. It was a colorful music box with a black and a white swan dancing to a tune that had made Mom get all teary-eyed and say something about Russia and the ballet.*

"We need to borrow your music box. We'll get it back to you. But we need it for something really important," the man with the mask continued talking to me.

Dad had said to keep it safe. To not break it. And to not ever lose it, so I'd put it in my secret spot. The little cubby under my window seat.

"Do you know where it is?" the man asked.

I didn't move. It was impossible for me to do so, sitting in my own pee, but my eyes flitted to the window seat, and his eyes followed my look.

"Okay. I'll get it. Is it under the seat?"

I didn't say anything. I didn't move. I just sat, hugging the bear I'd had for as long as I could remember. It was tattered with the stuffing squeezed to weird angles from all the times I'd slept with him. My mom had threatened to throw him away if he got pee on him one more time. She was tired of washing him.

The man moved to the window seat while I listened to my mom sobbing in the other room. She was crying harder than I'd ever heard her cry before, even when Mom and Dad screamed at each other.

The man lifted the window seat, easily finding the music box. He removed it from the space and came back to me with a smile on his face. The smile made me angry. Angry that he was smiling while my mom was sobbing. All I was able to think was, "Where is Dad? Where?"

"You did good, kid."

My whole body shook as the man with the gun came closer to me. He reached out a hand like the bad man in the nightmares I'd had since I was little. And that was when I found my voice. I screamed. And screamed and screamed. And Mom called to me in Russian, and it made me remember what Mom would see if she came into the room.

I stopped screaming.

"It's okay," the man said as he backed away slowly. "I'm going to have one of my partners come in and help you. Okay?"

I just stared, the tears starting to roll down my face.

When a lady finally came into the room, I had my face buried in my bear with my arms wrapped around my knees of the soft velour nightgown Dad had bought me. Mom would be mad I'd ruined.

The lady touched my arm.

"Georgie." Raisa's gentle touch and panicked voice brought me abruptly back to the club. "Georgie. Shit, shit, shit. He left me holding his crap."

I shook myself out of my memories and turned to Raisa. "What? What are you talking about?"

Raisa whispered, hardly moving, but with fear on her face. "Malik. He gave me his goody bag because I had a purse, and he didn't have a place to keep it. He said he needed to give it to someone at the club."

Malik's sniffles and nose-pinching came rushing back to me. I'd thought it was odd. Out of character. Goddamn it. He'd been high. "Oh, hell," I breathed out.

I looked at my scared sister, sitting frozen like I'd sat frozen on my bed full of pee the night the cops had invaded our apartment in New York. I thought about her getting ready to start her academic career to change the world with the clean energy she wanted to develop. She wouldn't be able to do any of that if they arrested her for drugs. She'd be sent back to Russia—if they even let her go at all.

My brain flashed to Mac. To the last week we'd spent getting to know each other. Getting to know the visible curves of our bodies and the things inside of us that weren't so visible. The wants and desires. The way Mac had offered to get me a ring. His words about, whether or not he liked my siblings, he wouldn't like me less. But this just might make him like me less. Especially if I did what I thought I needed to do.

It would be over. All of it. The dream disappearing into a harsh reality.

Before I could stop myself, I leaned over to Raisa and whispered, "Have you touched it?"

Raisa shook her head.

"Okay. Slowly, use the napkin to put it in my bag," I told her.

"What? No. No. No. We will just dump it," Raisa said, shaking her head ever so slightly.

I risked looking back. The cops were close. Any minute, they'd be at the table. "With the cops heading toward us? That'll make us look more guilty. Put it in my bag."

"No." She pouted.

"Raisa. They'll send you home."

Raisa looked like she was going to vomit. Like I had twenty-two years ago when they'd searched our home for a music box that had held a thumb drive with all of Dad's business dealings.

"It's okay, *malyshka*. It will all be okay. Just do what I said."

Raisa's eyes were huge as she grabbed the cocktail napkin, bent, and pulled something from her bag, sliding it into mine.

I saw Mac's smiling face flicker before my eyes, and I wanted to scream and scream and scream like I had when I was six and they'd taken my parents, and my music box, and my life. Because I was giving everything up again. Political career or not, Mac couldn't be with me now. Not only because I was from a Russian gunrunner's family, not only because I was from a Ponzi-scheming jailbird's family, but now because I was from a drug family—with my own drug charge on my record. If I'd been worried about being admitted to the bar before, a drug charge was sure to prevent it. Drug charges didn't go away. How much drugs were there? Would I be charged with possession? Or distribution? I started sweating.

But I also started thinking, my research of the summer swimming in my head. Then, they were there. The cops were at the table and asking us to go with them. I didn't have a choice. I grabbed my sister's hand and followed the men from the building. My heart was still pounding as my future was swirling down a drain. There was a small…infinitesimally slim chance of being able to right it.

We weren't taken to a police station like I'd expected. Instead, we were taken to a nondescript building over the 14th Street Bridge where we were separated and led into different rooms. As they took my purse from my hand, I had the forethought to say, "I do not consent to the search of my bag."

The man taking it looked up at me with shock.

"Did you hear me?" I asked. "I am not consenting to the search."

He left me in the room at what could have almost been considered a cheap card table with a two-way mirror staring me in the face. I wished I had my old bear with me. A bear I could squeeze, push my head against its belly, and pretend that none of this was happening. I was angry and sad all at once. I wanted to kill Malik for leaving us at the club. For putting the drugs in Raisa's purse instead of keeping it himself and taking responsibility for his shit.

I wanted to cry because Mac and I had barely had a chance to be a couple. A week of tangled sheets and shared dinners.

Eventually, the door opened, and a man and a woman in suits entered. They weren't the beautifully tailored suits Dani and Mac wore. They were off-the-rack kind of suits. My heart hurt at thoughts of the Whittakers. At the thought of what was going to happen now.

"Can you tell me what this is all about?" I asked and was surprised my voice wasn't shaking.

The woman slid a picture across the table to me. It was of my purse and a plastic, brick-shaped bag that I'd never seen before. I assumed it was the drugs Raisa had put in it.

"You're in quite a lot of trouble, Ms. Astrella," the man said, sitting with his arms crossed, leaning back in the chair like the jocks in high school had.

I didn't say anything. I just sat there with my own hands on the table, crossed over each other so I wouldn't fidget with them or my hair, trying hard to model Mac's grandma's poker face.

"You do know you'll never be admitted to the bar with possession and distribution charges on your record?" he asked.

My stomach fell to my knees, Mac's gorgeous face and blue eyes winking before me again, disappearing like my career.

I wanted to repeat the fact that I hadn't consented to the search, and that if they didn't have a warrant, the charges wouldn't stick. But I also wasn't at a police station. I was at some unknown location. I wasn't sure if the normal rules applied. I was a U.S. citizen, but Raisa wasn't. I hoped beyond hope that she knew not to talk.

"I'd like to call my attorney," I said instead of all the other things that were going through my brain.

They exchanged a look.

"That's one way to play it. But we both know the drugs aren't yours. They're likely Malik Leskov's, or Raisa Leskov's, or both," the woman finally spoke, eyeing me like I was a yummy pizza she was ready to devour. I wasn't going to be her pizza.

I bit my tongue before I could spit out that Raisa didn't do drugs. Malik, I couldn't speak for anymore. The mood swings that Raisa had mentioned made sense now. His arguments with Petya, too. Because if Petya knew about the drugs, he'd be furious. He didn't want that kind of attention. Although, I had a feeling the people in front of me were hoping to use Malik's drugs as leverage to get him to turn on his dad.

"Sorry. I'm not sure I stuttered. Phone call. Lawyer," I told them again.

"That's all you have to say?"

"I will add this. I've never seen that plastic bag before." And I thanked God that I could say that truthfully. "We were at a club. We left our bags at the table."

"You left your bags unattended in a crowded nightclub?" the man scoffed.

I nodded. "Now, I'd like to speak with my lawyer."

"You're Ian Astrella's daughter, Petya Leskov's stepdaughter. You want us to believe that you didn't know anything about the cocaine?" The guy was almost snarling. The woman put a hand on his arm.

"All I have to say—and I'll spell it out so you don't have any doubts about it—is: L.A.W.Y.E.R."

The guy was pissed. I could see that he wanted to push me, but the lady stood, taking the picture with her. She got to the door, glancing back at the man who had leaned so far back in his chair that I hoped, ungraciously, that he fell over.

The woman said, "Let's go."

The guy eyed me, shoved off the table, and slammed his way out of the room.

A different woman brought me my phone and stood there, waiting for me to place my call. I looked down at it, debating with myself on which number to dial. Mac was the one I ached to see. But he'd gone to pick up an upset Dani, and I wasn't sure I was ready to see the disappointment in his eyes like the disappointment I'd seen in my mom's the day she and Dad had been arrested and I'd given up the music box.

With a sigh, I dialed a number I never thought I'd have to use for this reason. It rang several times before it was answered.

"Hello, Georgia?" the smooth female voice said groggily.

I looked at the clock on the wall above the mirror. One thirty in the morning.

"Theresa, I'm so sorry to call you like this. I need your help."

There was shuffling on the other end. "What's wrong?"

"My sister and I have been taken to the…" I looked

at the woman who'd brought me my phone. I had no idea where I was at. I didn't know which agency was holding me. "We need a lawyer."

"Where are you?" she asked, awake now. Her voice was sharp and crisp. I didn't want to see her disappointment any more than I wanted to see Mac's, but she was a good lawyer. She was known in D.C. I could only hope for the best.

"Excuse me, where should I have my lawyer come?" I asked the woman.

She waved her hand for the phone, and I reluctantly gave it. She gave Theresa the address and then hung up. She left without another word, taking my phone with her.

I wanted to lay my head down and forget the whole evening. I wanted to go back a day and refuse to go to the club with Malik. I wanted to just believe it was all a dream and nowhere near my reality. Descartes' words, that Mac had repeated just this week, rang in my head. "How can you be certain that your whole life is not a dream?" I definitely didn't want this to be my reality.

It was almost an hour later before the door opened again. Theresa entered first, in a suit, hair up, makeup on. She looked like she was ready to kill the day, and it was only two thirty in the morning. The man and woman duo followed her inside.

"Did you ask why you were being taken?" Theresa asked.

"Yes."

"And they told you what?"

"They said they had questions for me."

"And did they ask for your consent to search your bag?"

"No, but I told them I did *not* give them consent to search it," I told her.

Her eyes flashed at me. "Good girl."

She turned to the duo who had seated themselves across from me. Theresa wasn't sitting.

"We'll be leaving now," she told them.

"No, you won't. We have a brick of cocaine that was found in your client's purse. She's not leaving without telling us where she got it," the man spoke for the pair again.

"Did you have a warrant?"

They both shifted.

"No?" Theresa laughed. "Like I said, we'll be leaving."

"We'll have it tested. When it comes back with her prints on it, she'll be right back here," the woman spoke.

"*If* it comes back with my client's fingerprints, it will still have been obtained illegally, without cause, and will not be admissible in any proceedings you'd like to sling at her." She looked at me. "Stand up, Georgia, we're leaving."

She went to the door. I looked at the pair as I cautiously stood, uncertain whether they'd be hauling me back into the chair, or if I'd be free to go. I got to the door, and Theresa opened it. We walked out. The duo followed us but didn't make any attempt to stop us.

"Where's Raisa?" I asked to any and all of them at the same time.

"Raisa is your sister?" Theresa asked, and I nodded. She looked at the duo. "Did you have a warrant for the sister?"

They didn't speak.

"I didn't think so. We'll be taking her with us as well." Theresa eyed them like they were the lowest form of species on the planet. Worse than dung beetles.

"Wait right here," they said and disappeared down the hall—a nondescript hall in a nondescript building that made me feel like I was living in some spy novel.

"Theresa," I started, and she shushed me. "I was just going to say thank you for coming."

She nodded, but her eyes said *stop talking*, so I did.

When they came back, they had Raisa with them. She looked tired but calm, and a wave of pride surged over me. My eighteen-year-old sister had held herself together remarkably well for being taken away. I hugged her tightly to me, and she hugged me back.

"We're releasing both your clients, but we're asking them not to go anywhere," the woman said.

"My sister will be at Stanford. You can find her there," I told them and then grabbed Raisa's hand and started walking toward the doorway at the end of the hall. We left silently.

Outside, we got into Theresa's Jaguar. Theresa put her keys in the ignition and then looked at Raisa in the rearview mirror. "What did you tell them?"

"Nothing. I said nothing. I know better. When Father gets questioned, we all say nothing. I said I was at the club with Georgie and Malik. Malik did not feel well and left early. Georgie and I left our bags at the table, which was stupid, but we danced. We came back to the table as the cops came in and asked us to go with them. We know nothing."

"I'm your attorney. As of right now, you're both my clients, but I don't want you to tell me anything other than what you just told me. Do you understand?" Theresa asked, starting the car and backing out.

We both nodded.

We dropped Raisa off at the hotel first. I got out of the car and hugged her tightly again. "I'm so sorry, Georgie," she said quietly.

"This is not your fault," I told her, brushing her hair from her face.

"Malik is such an idiot. Father is going to be furious," Raisa said.

I nodded. Petya was going to bust a few things, maybe even something on Malik.

"You need to fly out to Stanford today. If you need me to take you to the airport, let me know."

"No, I will call the pilot tonight."

Petya's private jet had brought them to D.C. I was wondering if it was still at the airport, or if Malik was already winging his way back to Russia.

"I love you, *malyshka*," I said, my voice shaky with the emotions and tears I'd been holding back.

"Love you too, *moy dorogoy*," she said, squeezing me, wiping her eyes, and then leaving.

I got back into the car, gave Theresa my address, and then was silent while we drove. I sat, fidgeting, trying to work up the courage to speak.

"Theresa, I'm so sorry," I finally said, letting it out

with a heavy breath.

"You did the right thing calling me," she said, reaching over and patting me on the hand.

"I just…"

"Was it yours?"

I knew she was talking about the drugs, and I shook my head.

"You told me about your stepdad. I had fair warning," she said with a small smile.

"They weren't mine. But they aren't Petya's either. He doesn't deal in drugs. He has no respect for it," I told her honestly, and I could see that she saw the honesty, because she nodded.

"I don't want to know any more."

We were quiet.

"Do you want me to stop working for you?" I asked as we pulled up to the apartment.

"God, no. I told you that you've been my most interesting student in years. Maybe decades." She almost laughed, and that lightened my heart ever so slightly.

"You've had someone more interesting than this?" It was hard to believe.

"Yes. Remind me to tell you about Mario Baretta on Monday. Now, go try to get some rest. I'll give you one final piece of advice, though." I looked at her. "Don't talk about this on your phone with Raisa. Don't talk about this in your apartment. Try not to talk about it at all. But if you do, do it in public, with lots of noise, and somewhere you've never been. Do you understand what I'm saying?"

I nodded. She thought we'd be bugged. My phone probably already had been. The apartment, if it hadn't been already, would probably be bugged when we were all gone from it. I felt sick. Bringing this to Dani and Mac. To the ties they had to the senator and Capitol Hill. To Mac's future.

I leaned over and hugged her.

"I'll see you Monday."

"Good. Bring me one of those black-and-white coffee things again."

I smiled weakly, stepped out of the car, and she took off.

When I looked across the street, there was a plain, black sedan sitting there. It was empty. But I had a feeling it hadn't been when we'd arrived. I let the anger I felt at Malik flow through me again. Anger at his stupidity. Anger at how he'd risked everything Raisa had worked for. Anger that turned to a tiny bit of fear because I wasn't sure what Petya would do when he found out. Anger that turned into sorrow as I headed toward the doors of the apartment and wondered how to explain this all to Mac and Dani.

Chapter Twenty-five

Mac

IF YOU'RE GONE
Performed by Matchbox Twenty

It was close to four in the morning, and I was going nuts for more than one reason. My heart was twisted up with anger and worry. Fury curled through me as I looked at Dani, curled up on the couch, sleeping.

I looked down at the ice on my knuckles and swore silently.

I went to the kitchen, putting the ice pack back in the freezer, shaking my hand. My knuckles were going to be bruised…that I could handle. I just hoped Dani's face wouldn't have the same color on it come morning. When I'd found Dani, hiding in the bathroom at The Oriental, I'd completely lost it. Her dress was torn, and her makeup was trailing down her face to where a red handprint emblazoned her cheek. It was a Dani that I'd never seen. Ever.

When she'd collapsed into my arms, tears flowing, I'd been terrified. Dani didn't cry. She barely muttered Senator Fenway's name and something about a meeting in the Roosevelt room before I'd torn off down the hall. When I flung open the conference room door, the asshole senator and his cronies were sitting around a table, laughing, smoking cigars. I launched myself at him, busting his nose and smashing him against the wall with my hand spread across his windpipe. Dani had watched from the doorway, not saying a word. Not stopping me. And that had only filled me with more rage, because the Dani I knew would never have let me go at it like that. I'd hit him yet again before his security was on me, pulling me away.

"If you ever, ever even look at my sister again, you'll wish I'd killed you right here and now," I thundered, shaking off the security.

His equally slimy aide handed him a cloth napkin that he put to his bleeding nose.

"Macauley, right?" Fenway sneered. "Guess what, Macauley, not only did you just end any political career you ever thought you wanted, but you just got yourself an arrest charge."

"We'll see what the press thinks about a married senator who thinks it's his right to attack a female who's told him no," I said, brushing off the security guys.

He laughed. "Did she, though? Did she say no, or did she just feel guilty after the fact?"

Dani launched herself into the room, and I caught her around the waist. "Ever hear of the Me Too movement, jackass?" I said as I walked Dani toward the door.

Once we'd cleared the room, I looked down at her and wished I hadn't taken my suit jacket off and left it in the car. I wished I had it to cover Dani's torn dress, but I sheltered her the best I could as we made our way through the hotel lobby to her Mini that I'd left waiting for me at the valet stand with a hundred-dollar tip.

I took off down the street. "Do I need to take you to a hospital?" I asked, worry screaming through me.

She shook her head. "He didn't get that far."

I pounded the steering wheel. "Goddamn it, Dani. Why the hell were you meeting with him tonight?"

"Oh good, blame the victim," she snarked.

"For fuck's sake, you know that's not what I meant."

"I wasn't meeting with him. Remember, I was meeting with Russell."

"Well, where the hell is Russell?" I asked, my anger suddenly directed at another male body.

She shrugged. "I don't know. He never showed."

My left hand was going to be as bruised as my right when I was done with Russell.

"How the hell did you get in Fenway's company?"

"He stopped the elevator and got in before I even registered it was him."

The goddamn audacity of him. To take advantage of her in a fucking elevator.

"Good. We'll have it all on tape," I said.

She snorted. "You really think that his flunkies haven't already confiscated it?"

When we got back to the apartment, she went to her bathroom and closed the door, and I called Granddad first and then Dad. Asshole senator and his flunkies could fucking take a flying leap. They'd messed with the wrong goddamn family.

By the time I'd explained what had happened to Dad and Granddad, and they'd gone into kill-a-senator mode, Dani had emerged from her room in a layer of pajamas that made me want to scream again. She hadn't asked for this shit. My whip-smart sister needed to be flaunting her kickass body and taking names, not hiding.

"What do you need?" I asked.

"Nothing. I just don't want to be alone with my own thoughts. Are you going to ice that?" she asked, turning on the TV and mindlessly flipping through the channels.

I looked down at my raw knuckles, feeling them for the first time.

I grabbed an ice pack for me and another for her. I handed her one as I joined her on the couch, pulling her feet onto my lap. She hissed when she placed it on her face, and I wasn't sure if the tears that coated her lashes were because of the pain or the entire night.

Once she'd fallen asleep, I continued to field texts from my family. It was after two before I started to worry about another woman in my life, my thoughts drifting back to Malik's constant sniffs, and Georgie's and Raisa's bodies in dresses that showed more skin than they covered.

They shouldn't have to cover anything. Goddamn men in this world needed to learn to keep their penises to themselves. To not eye every woman as if they were theirs. To just show some freaking respect.

I texted Georgie first, and when I didn't get a response, I called. It went directly to voicemail, and I gave up being calm. I paced the apartment. Calling the cops was out of the question. They'd laugh at me. I was tempted to call in some more favors with Dad and the DoD, but I also tried not to overreact. There were multiple reasons why she might not be picking up.

It was a little after four before the door clicked open, and I turned, irritation ready to fly from me, and then I saw her face. She was full of her own emotions. Anger and tears and sadness. And for a moment, I thought maybe she'd already heard about Dani, but then I realized there was no possible way for her to know.

Georgie's emotions were from something entirely different.

I crossed the room and swept her into my arms and held on tight with my face pressed against her hair. "God, I've been worried sick."

She squeezed me back, hugging me as tightly as I was holding her. And then, she was crying. The second woman in my life to be in tears that night. Georgie's tears were quiet, wracking her body, and I had to swallow hard because I was so close to losing it myself. To shedding tears that I hadn't shed in a very long time.

I held on to her. Swimming in her emotions. Swimming in mine. Unable to soothe either of us.

"Are you hurt?" I finally asked.

"I'm not hurt," she said quietly.

I loosened my grip on her and pulled her chin so I could see her eyes and read the truth there. "I'm not hurt," she repeated, and she took in my own face and seemed to read the concern that lingered there.

"I'm so sorry I worried you. I…I couldn't call."

I went to drag her down the hall, but she resisted. "Can we step outside?" She nodded her head toward the balcony.

I looked at her, confused, and it seemed to make her sadder somehow.

She pulled me onto the deck, and the wind hit us. We both shivered. She was in her black slip dress still. I was in the T-shirt and shorts I'd changed into once Dani had fallen asleep.

I pulled her to me. "Tell me," I said. "What happened?"

"One of the agencies took Raisa and me tonight. They found a brick of cocaine in my purse."

"What the fuck?" I couldn't filter my words. I didn't have it in me after everything I'd already been through that night, and I knew it was a mistake as soon as it was out, because she stiffened in my arms.

"It was Malik's."

"What the hell was it doing in your purse?"

She pulled away from me, and even though I tried to stop her, she kept tugging until I had no choice but to let go. Tears poured down her face.

"I told Raisa to put it there when we saw the cops coming."

I stared at her. Was she telling me she was a drug dealer? That she sold drugs for her stepdad? It didn't make any sense. I was too punchy to keep up.

"It's not mine. It wasn't Raisa's either. It was Malik's."

"Then why didn't Malik have it?"

She looked away. "He left when he saw the cops coming. He left knowing it was in Raisa's bag."

"Fucker." I turned toward the door, unable to deal with another shitty male tonight. Georgie caught me, pulling my arm and tugging me back toward her. "Stop."

"Why? Why should I stop? He let you take the fall for him."

"There was no fall. They can't even press charges."

I stilled and just stared at her.

"Fourth Amendment. Illegal search and seizure. They didn't have a warrant or cause to search my bag, and I specifically told them I didn't consent to a search."

"That just makes you look guilty."

"Yes," she said and glanced away as if it was too hard to look at me. "But it also makes anything they find pretty much inadmissible in court."

I looked at the beautiful, smart woman in front of me and saw her pain as well as her courage. But the truth was, taking it for her sister had been the worst thing she could have done for herself. And then it hit me. She knew all that, and yet, she'd done it anyway. She'd sacrificed herself for her sister. She'd sacrificed her entire future for her family.

Dani and Georgie had both been braver than I'd ever had to be. They'd handled, with grace and fortitude, the shitty hands that had been handed to them by stupid-ass males. The disappointment in my species curled through my body, even as I knew we weren't all to be lumped together. There were good men. Men I grew up with. Men I served with.

It took me quite a few moments to gather myself, and when I looked down again, Georgie's expression was pained. As if my disappointment in my male gender was disappointment in her. I wasn't disappointed in her at all. I was in awe of what she had done. But I was still angry that it could ruin her. I didn't want anything to come between her and the future she wanted.

This just made me furious with Malik all over again. But what I said continued to come out all wrong. "But now they think you're a drug dealer."

"Possibly. I think they know it was Malik's."

"Who are they?"

"They never gave me their agency credentials. I'd guess NSA or CIA."

"Not on U.S. soil. FBI maybe."

"Does it matter?"

I stood there, staring at her. "Why are we out here?"

"They'll bug everything, Mac—the apartment, my school, everything. My phone is already bugged, I'm sure. It was in their possession."

Realization started to hit me. This wasn't really about Georgie, or Raisa, or even Malik. This was about her stepdad. "They want Petya."

She nodded. "I'm sure they do. But I don't know anything that they could use. I'm not sure what Raisa knows. I'm sure Malik knows more than his share because Petya has been grooming him for a while, but now, with the drugs… He's going to be so pissed."

"Like pissed enough to kill his own son?"

"No…" Georgie said, but I could see the doubt in

her eyes. "I don't think so."

I'd been saying all along that her family didn't matter. That it wasn't a big deal, but her words settled on me like gravity hitting you after you'd been on the moon. Her stepdad was a Russian oligarch dealing in who knew what. If not drugs, probably guns. Maybe other things. There might never be a happy ending to this…to us. And the thought of that tore at me.

I rubbed my hands over my face, trying to hold myself together.

"I'm so sorry," she said quietly, her voice full of anguish. Pain that echoed across my own like a shot in an empty garage. "I'm sorry you're angry and disappointed and…"

She trailed off. I pulled her to me. She rested her head on my chest, arms wrapped around my waist.

I told her, "It's been one hell of a shitty night. But I'm not disappointed in you. You… You're incredible. Brave and smart and—"

"Wanted by every enforcement agency that exists."

We stayed there, holding each other.

"What happened with Dani? Is she okay?" Georgie asked.

"She's okay. That asshole, Fenway, attacked her in an elevator." My voice cracked, and Georgie looked up at me, eyes wide.

"Oh, no, Mac…" She looked in the glass doors to where my sister was sleeping on the couch. "Did he… Is she…" Her voice trailed away.

"No. He didn't. But he's going to regret ever having touched her," I said, my tone ominous.

She looked at my hand and saw the cuts and

bruising. She pulled it to her and kissed it gently, the heat from her lips making me wince.

♫ ♫ ♫

My eyes were heavy as they drifted open. I wasn't sure what had woken me as I lay there with Georgie wrapped in my arms. We were both in the clothes we'd been in the night before. We'd lain down on the bed, holding each other, trying to breathe comfort into one another.

I heard Dani's soft voice from the door. "Mac?"

I slowly moved away, trying not to wake Georgie. I ran a hand through my hair and over my face, trying to circulate blood, trying to shake off the grogginess. I went to the door and opened it. "What can I do?"

"Mom and Dad are here," she said quietly.

I shut the door behind me and went down the hall. Dad was in his uniform, hat on the counter. Mom was in the kitchen, searching the refrigerator and coming up with eggs and bread. Leave it to Mom to want to feed us in the middle of a crisis.

Dani looked better than she had the night before. She had her game face back on. The one I'd seen on her every day on the Hill. While my hand was purple, Dani's face just bore a red mark, and I was glad that, for whatever reason, the hit Fenway had given her hadn't been a hard one.

"What's the plan?" I asked, pouring a cup of coffee and joining my sister at the counter.

"Your grandfather has a copy of the tape they tried—unsuccessfully, might I add—to confiscate.

355

Seems like somebody at The Oriental knows better than to listen to some shitty security team," Dad said. "I've got some folks editing it, and then he's going to send it to every news station who'll take it."

I glanced at Dani. "You okay with this?"

"They're editing her face out," Mom said for her, but I just continued to stare at my sister, waiting for her to say she was all-in or not.

"I told them not to even bother editing it. I'm not going to be quiet about this."

"Daniella, we know you want to go at this head-on, but we want to give you the chance at anonymity if you choose it," Dad said.

She didn't respond. I wondered how long her silence would last.

"Meanwhile, Mac and I are going to head down to the police station. See if anyone pressed any charges against him."

"I was going to make breakfast," Mom said, her hand halting as she was just about to crack an egg in a bowl.

"I don't think anyone is ready for food, Clare," Dad said with a weak smile.

"Robbie?" Mom looked at me.

I gave her a wry smile. "Sorry, Mom." I looked at Dad and said, "Let me throw some clothes on."

I wasn't sure if we were really going to a police station, or if we were going back to the DoD to put out a hit on one goddamn senator from Alabama.

I went back to my room and quietly dressed without waking Georgie up before returning to the kitchen.

Mom handed me a travel mug full of coffee. "Thanks," I muttered. I turned to Dani. "I need you to do me a favor."

She nodded.

"Georgie… She had a pretty shitty night, too. Make sure she's okay?"

"What happened?"

I shook my head. "Not here."

Her eyes widened, but she nodded. She knew the drill. You didn't talk about certain things in certain places. It was a well-known fact that we'd lived with not only on the Hill but our entire lives. I didn't need to say more, but it had her looking around the apartment as if she could see a bug hanging from the ceiling on a web like a real spider. I had a feeling she'd be calling for a sweep of our apartment. If she didn't, I would.

Our eyes met one more time before I followed Dad out of the apartment.

Chapter Twenty-six

Georgie

TRYING NOT TO LOVE YOU
Performed by Nickelback

I woke up in Mac's bed without him. The apartment was quiet. I looked down at my crumpled black dress and wiped at the makeup that was sticking to my face—a mess. It was a mess. Everything was a fucking mess.

I got up, planning to head directly to the shower, and was surprised to see Dani and her Mom on the couch, the three TVs on, volume low.

"You're awake," Dani said, stating the obvious.

I went to my friend and hugged her. Sorry for what she'd been through. Sorry for what I'd been through. And sorry that I was going to be dragging them through more crap.

"Are you okay?" I asked.

She nodded. "Just pissed now, but look." She waved toward the TV in the middle as Clare greeted me with her own hug that made me want to cry all over again. It had been so long since I'd had anything close to a motherly hug.

I turned to the TV in time to see Senator Fenway's face and then a cut to a videotape of the senator and a woman whose face was blurred in an elevator. I realized it was Dani. In the video, she was shaking her head no even as he was narrowing the gap between their bodies. He pulled her, and she pulled back, ripping her dress as they battled. He overpowered her, pulling her tight up against him and kissing her. Her knee came up and hit him in the groin. His face contorted in rage, and he hit her right across the face, and as she was pushed backward by the momentum of the hit, the elevator doors opened, and Dani ran.

I felt like I was watching a movie. Just like my life last night had felt. Unreal. Fake. Someone else's story.

When I turned back to the couch, Clare was sniffling into a tissue and pulling Dani to her, but Dani's face was all disdain. "Dumbshit thought he was going to be able to say that it was all my fault. His career is over."

I looked closer at Dani's face and saw a mark on her cheek where his hand had hit her, but I was in awe of the power and strength rolling off of her. Dani really was my new female superhero.

She pulled away from her mom, turned off the TV, and looked at me.

"What happened with you last night?"

I shook my head, unable to talk about it in the apartment. She nodded, as if understanding. "Mac mentioned we might not want to talk here. I have friends coming to do pest control later."

Pest control. My eyes widened at her as she stepped away. Bugs. They were going to sweep for bugs.

"I'm so sorry," I said, guilt coursing over me again. The fact that they were having to debug their home because of me. It was driving me slightly crazy that Petya's lifestyle and Malik's screw-up were causing the Whittakers more headaches than they needed right now.

"Honestly, I usually have it done once or twice a year," Dani told me.

My mouth dropped. "What?"

She smiled. "Working at the Capitol and the Pentagon has its downsides. You wouldn't believe what people will do to get ahead on a bill or in an election. Ask Mom. We kind of grew up with it. With Dad and Granddad being pretty high up the food chain, our cars, homes, offices, and phones usually get a regular cleanup."

Clare was nodding, but I didn't know what to say. I wasn't sure I was prepared for this kind of life—wiretaps, and secret agencies, and sedans parked down the street.

"Where's Mac?" I asked.

"He went with Dad to make more threats, I'm sure." She shrugged.

"That's not at all what they said they were doing," Clare responded.

"That's just because they didn't want me to know they were going all manly-man, protecting their weaker female family members."

I snorted, waving at the TV. "I guarantee you, that proves, without a doubt, that you are not the weaker family member."

Dani's face wavered for the first time that morning.

"But I had to call Mac to come get me."

"You did the right thing," Clare said.

"You called someone you cared about to come get you. That just happened to be your brother," I told her. She nodded. We all sat in silence for a few moments. So much that couldn't be said. So much that neither Dani nor I wanted to discuss. "I'm going to go shower. I'll be back out in a few minutes."

I stood in the shower for a long time, trying to wash away the stench that had attached to me from the night before. But I knew, without a doubt, what I'd faced was nothing compared to what Dani had faced.

When I came back out, Mac, his dad, and two strange men had joined Dani and her mom. Mac handed one of the men my phone, and he took it to the counter, opening it in less than two seconds. He looked it over, closed it back up, and gave it to Mac.

"Nothing there, but they really don't need it these days. Could be tapped through the cloud, and you'd never know. Get a burner if you're worried," he said. Then, the two strange men left.

Mac saw me for the first time. He crossed the room, pulled me into his arms, and said, "You're looking better this morning."

I nodded. "Do you really think I need a burner?"

Mac and his dad exchanged a look.

"What?" I asked.

"Only if you want to talk with your sister about what happened. If it's just your normal conversation, you shouldn't need it," his dad said.

My insides tightened. Mac had told his dad what had happened. And even though not a single one of them was treating me any different than they had from the moment they met me, I couldn't help the shame that welled up inside me. It made me angry. Angry at both the shame and my family. I'd always been determined not to feel embarrassed because of who my family was, and yet, standing in front of this man and his family that I ached to be a part of like I'd never ached for anything before, it hit me like it never had.

I rubbed my forehead; a headache was forming that I knew wasn't going to dislodge anytime soon. The truth filled me. I needed to get out of their apartment and their life. These beautiful people would never turn away from me. They would never walk out just because of my family, but I wouldn't let mine drag down theirs. I couldn't live with myself if I did.

♫ ♫ ♫

Mac and I didn't have much time alone the rest of the weekend. His family was in and out of the apartment. By the time Mac and his dad had gotten back to the apartment, Dani had made the decision to go to the D.C. police and lodge a formal complaint. After that, we all watched the fall of Senator Fenway's career on the TV as every station, political or not, was overflowing with it.

Dani was interviewed, handling it with a grace that reminded me of my sister in the backseat of Theresa's car, saying she knew not to talk. Raisa shouldn't have had to deal with that any more than Dani should have had to deal with talking about being attacked by a man, or I should have had to deal with invoking Fourth Amendment rights to ensure the safety of my sister and myself.

Raisa texted me from a new number that she was on her way to San Francisco. It was a burner phone. But I wondered if it really mattered. My number would lead any agency that wanted it to her new phone. Harder to trace, but not impossible. Mac's dad had handed me my own burner when he came back to the apartment.

I thanked him, turning a thousand shades of red.

And it hit me again, for the hundredth time that weekend and with the same ferocity it had hit me in the club when I'd told Raisa to put the drugs in my bag. I had to leave. I was losing all of them.

Raisa called me once she'd gotten to San Francisco. Her burner to my burner. She told me Malik had taken Petya's private jet and flown back to Russia, and that Petya was furious with him. Petya had had to charter a plane for Raisa. Mom was getting a rehab clinic set up for Malik, and Raisa was worried about what exactly Petya had in store for him other than rehab.

"He left us with the drugs, Raisa. He left you to get arrested."

She was quiet. "He has been different the last few years. He has always felt entitled to more than what Father gave him. He was unhappy."

"Don't make excuses. He did a crappy thing, brother or not."

"Yes. But I will forgive him. This once. You should too."

I wasn't sure I could. I wasn't normally one to hold a grudge, but I also wasn't one who kept people in my life who weren't healthy for me. This thought made me want to laugh because my entire family was not healthy for me. But the ties that bound me to them could not easily be severed. I loved them, but I didn't have to like them. I had a right to be angry, and so did she.

It was late on Sunday when Senator Matherton and their granddad showed up. They had a meeting in our living room about what the rest of the week was going to look like, Dani's and his press conference scheduled for the next day, and what Mac's role in it should be.

Mac watched me with hooded eyes as I said goodnight to everyone on Sunday and journeyed up to the loft. I knew he could read my withdrawal even though we hadn't spoken hardly two words about any of it, but every time he'd started to corner me, there'd been someone else at the door or on the phone.

In a strange way, I was grateful—not for what had happened to Dani, but for the chaos—because it allowed me to distance myself and to start thinking about what I needed to do to move out.

♪ ♪ ♪

When I came out of the bathroom Monday morning, Mac was waiting for me. He wrapped me in a hug, and I let him. I even hugged him back because he'd been through more than I had in many ways, because he'd had to deal not only with Dani's situation but my own.

"How are you doing?" he asked.

"I'm okay."

"I'm sorry we haven't been able to talk. That our lives were a circus this weekend," he said into my hair.

"You have nothing to apologize for."

"It's going to be that way all week, but I want to be here for you, too. Have you heard any more from your family?"

"No."

He pulled back and looked into my face, a frown appearing. "What is it?"

I ran my hand along my ponytail before I could stop myself, and he read the tell for exactly what it was. Nerves.

"Talk to me, Georgie."

"I just—"

"No," he inserted before I could finish, and it pissed me off. I pushed away from him, grabbing my bags and hefting them onto my shoulder.

"You owe me a favor," I told him.

His face shut down, emotion leaving it. "I do, but not this one."

His expectation that he knew what I wanted just continued to irritate me. "As soon as I find a new place, I'm moving out. And my favor is that you let me do this without trying to stop me. That you let me do this…for you."

My voice cracked on the last words, and I hated it. I wanted to sound as sure and strong as Dani had all weekend. As strong and beautiful as she'd sounded every time she'd repeated what had happened to her.

"How on earth can you think that it would be for me?" he asked, frustration entering his own voice.

"You all have enough to deal with. You don't need me bringing wiretaps and intercontinental agencies into your lives on top of it. It's only going to be worse now that they found the drugs," I said, and I raised my chin, putting on my own emotionless face. Straightening my back. I needed to do this.

"You've probably been bugged and followed off and on for years. You don't think I already knew that? You don't think I considered that already?" he protested.

"You promised me a favor, Mac. No questions. Just granted." I turned toward the door.

"I don't want to grant this one."

I didn't look back as I opened the door and said, "I'm moving. You can make it painless for both of us, or painful. That's your choice, I guess. But I'm asking you not to, and I hope you'll agree."

And then I left, because if I didn't, I would have let him talk me into staying. I would have let him reason away my fears. But I didn't want to do that. I wanted to take my miserable family and move them away from the Whittakers and everything they deserved to have. I wanted them far, far away from my beautiful Mac and his future.

Chapter Twenty-seven

Mac

HOLD ME WHILE WE WAIT
Performed by Lewis Capaldi.

I was in the middle of talking through another interview with some news station in the Midwest when I saw my dad walk into the office. Senator Matherton's office had been abuzz all day. It felt, in some ways, like what I'd experienced in the war room at the Pentagon when an op was going down.

It was where I thrived.

What I didn't thrive on was the sly remarks made about my sister and Guy after they'd stood on the Capitol steps and given a press conference. I didn't thrive on the well of politicians who were trying to distance themselves not only from Fenway but also from Matherton because he'd stood up for Dani. It made my stomach turn and made me want to pound something…anything…maybe even a person.

When I hung up, Dad was at my desk, hat in hand, flipping it around in circles—a tell of my father's that I hadn't seen in a long time. Not even this past weekend over everything that had gone down with

Dani. Then, he'd been all action and anger. Now, he seemed wary. Sad.

"What's up?" I asked.

"We've lost contact with a squad," he said quietly.

My heart stopped, Darren and Nash flashing before my eyes. Darren's hands around Tristan's waist, kissing his baby on the top of her head. Nash flirting with Georgie and my sister, all sly smiles. No. Not them.

I shook my head. "Not Silver Squadron—"

He nodded.

My mouth went dry, and my heart crushed into ash. "What happened?"

"An op in the South African Republic. Looks like they were ambushed. We know we lost their leader, but that's all we knew before they went completely dark." Dad's voice remained hushed, not only because he was riddled with his own distress and sadness, but also because he was telling me things in the middle of an unsecured office on Capitol Hill.

Bile filled my throat. Anguish. We lost their leader. Darren was their leader. We lost Darren. And the anguish was swirled with anger. The op. The goddamn op that I'd been opposing for months. The one Nash had told me they were trying to resurrect. The one I wasn't there to prevent. Now, Darren, and maybe more, had given their lives for a stranglehold in a place that I'd told them wouldn't work. That I'd told them was full of literal and figurative bombs.

They'd risked everything. They'd given everything. For nothing.

I closed my eyes as the tears threatened to spill.

Tears of loss and pain and anger. They'd sacrificed it all while I hadn't sacrificed shit. I'd gone straight for everything I'd ever wanted, leaving Darren, Nash, and the entire team exposed to the stupidity of those at the DoD.

I'd walked, and it had cost Darren his life. Maybe Nash, too. Maybe others.

I was just like every fucking politician who had sauntered into this office since I'd joined, asking "What's in it for me?" without a care in the world as to what it was costing everyone else. And it had cost Darren his entire world.

I got up, ready to go bruise my knuckles on some more faces. Ready to gut myself along the way.

"Robbie," Dad said, stopping me. He pulled me to him in an embrace I didn't deserve, and I had to fight harder against the tears. I had to fight against the knot that had built in my chest and my throat and was threatening to cut off my air.

I pushed him away, and he let me.

"I'm so sorry, Son," he said.

"What the fuck happened, Dad?" I asked. "I told them a goddamn hundred times that operation was fucking impossible without losing men. I told them…" My voice cracked, and I stopped, wiping my hand over my face.

"An IED followed by gunfire. They knew we were coming," he told me.

An IED had exploded a world away from me, but it was as if it was right here in the room with me. Taking everything. Changing my world in a way that I wasn't prepared for.

"I want to go to the Pentagon," I told him.

He hesitated and then nodded.

Dani came into the room, took one look at our faces, and dropped the papers that were in her hand. "What happened?"

"We've lost contact with a S.E.A.L. squad," Dad told her because I couldn't say the words. Wasn't sure I'd ever be able to say the words. We hadn't lost them. I had. I'd given up. Walked out. Run away. Chased dreams so stupid, naïve, and ridiculous that they weren't worth the clouds they rested on.

"Oh my God." Dani sat down, putting a hand on her stomach. "Nash? Darren?"

"The leader. The others we don't know yet," Dad told her. But I knew…Darren…maybe more. I walked out. I couldn't deal with Dani's emotions. I couldn't risk seeing her tears on top of everything else she'd dealt with over the last three days. It was too much. Too much at once. Too much pain and anguish. Too many times I hadn't been there in the moment that people needed me. Dani. Georgie. Darren. Nash. The faces flew across my mind.

I knew one thing for sure. I wanted someone to pay, even if that someone was me. I wanted to face the fucker who'd rubber-stamped the op after reading all my reasons for not doing so. I wanted to see his face when he shouldered the guilt with me.

♫ ♫ ♫

It was close to midnight when I entered the apartment. I expected it to be dark. Instead, the lights were ablaze, and there were boxes sitting in a pile at the foot of the loft stairs. Another goddamn loss that I didn't know if I could take. I wasn't sure it mattered now, anyway, if she moved out or if she stayed. I wouldn't be here to coax her back to me piece by piece, even if I'd been able to.

I wasn't sure I deserved for her to come back to me.

Dani looked up from her spot on the couch, throwing her hands in the air. "I tried. I've talked to her until I was blue from lack of air. She won't listen to me."

She moved toward me, and before I could stop her, she hugged me. "Have we heard anything more?" she asked.

I shook my head. "Still dark. I'm heading down to SOCOM tomorrow. Hopefully, we'll know more then."

"I wanted to tell her, but I didn't know what I could," she said. If I knew my sister at all, she'd wanted to use it as one of the reasons to get Georgie to stay, but I didn't want her to stay because she felt sorry for me. I wanted her to stay because she loved me. I wanted her to stay because we fit. God help me, I still wanted her. I wanted her even more than I ever had. I wanted to bury myself in her skin and lose my guilt and anger there.

Dani let me go. "I'm heading to bed now that you're home. But come get me if you need me. Or if you hear anything. I'd like to know."

I let her go, gathered myself, and then headed up the stairs.

Georgie heard me coming and stopped to stare at

me before returning to the box she was filling with books.

"Where are you going?" I asked, trying desperately to hold onto my emotions.

"To Theresa's. She has an apartment over her garage she said I could rent."

I just stood, hands in my pockets, watching her. And maybe she'd expected me to fight her more. Maybe she'd thought that, after my refusal to grant her favor this morning, she'd have to push me this evening. And she should have had to. She should have had to stop me from dumping her box out on the carpet and restocking the shelf she'd emptied. But instead, I stood there mute, watching as the woman I loved thought she was moving on without me. Maybe, because of all of that, it was my silence that stopped her more than my words and actions would have.

She looked up, taking me in. My face. My stance. My heartbreak. And her hands stilled.

"What is it? Is it Dani?"

"We lost contact with a S.E.A.L. squad today," my voice cracked.

"Oh, no, Mac…not…" At my curt nod, she gasped, rising from her feet and heading for me.

Tristan's smiling face and their tiny baby haunted me. Nash's and Darren's smiles and jokes. They were men I'd promised an oath to defend and hadn't. The guilt took my heart in its hands again, squeezing.

Georgie wrapped me in her arms, and I buried my head in her neck. Her hands were at my back, rubbing in soothing circles.

"Wh-what happened?"

"They were on an op that I'd repeatedly shot down," I mumbled, trying hard to breathe, to concentrate on her hands and her scent. "This time it got approved, anyway."

"That's hardly on you. You weren't there."

"That's just it," my voice broke as tears finally hit my cheeks. "I wasn't fucking there."

Both her hands came to my face, wiping the tears as I fought them again. "This isn't your fault."

"But it is. Darren died because I decided my dreams were bigger than his. Maybe Nash, too…" My throat clogged as I begged that it wouldn't be more. That it wasn't all of them. "He died because I wasn't there to fight for him. To remind the fuckers pushing it that it was a death sentence."

"Mac—"

I pulled away. "Don't. Don't defend me, or them, or any of it. Just like you can't defend Senator Fenway for trying to take what he wanted. Just like you can't defend Malik for being a weasel and leaving you to take the hit for him. I left my fucking unit. My brothers. And some or all of them have lost their lives because of it."

I moved away from her, picked up her desk chair, and shoved it with all my might at the wall where it clattered and broke. The noise and exertion were better than tears. But it didn't ease the fury pouring through my veins. It didn't even come close. Everything in my life had come apart in the last three days, like layers of strata being pulled apart by an earthquake. Dani. Georgie. The squad.

I put my hand in my hair and let out a deep howl of

grief. I turned to her windows. To the Capitol Building, lit up and sparkling as if nothing had changed, when really, everything had. I sank down onto the bed, head in my hands, and I felt her stop in front of me. She tentatively pulled me toward her so that my head was buried in her stomach, and the tears flowed, finally unstoppable. She brushed her hands through my hair.

I circled her waist with my hands, wishing I could just keep them there but knowing that I couldn't. Knowing I wasn't ready to walk away, because when I'd told her I couldn't imagine letting her go without having tried everything I could to make her mine, it had been the truth. But also knowing that I wasn't sure we could survive the things the last three days had thrown at us.

I'd already spoken to Dad and put into motion things that I couldn't back away from. Come hell or high water, I was going to be on a flight to Florida and the Special Operations Command the next day. I was putting my uniform back on, and I wouldn't be taking it back off. I wouldn't be the reason some other squad got lost to the moneymen. To the greedy politicians. This was how I was supposed to change the world and keep it safe. I just hadn't realized it until now, until it was too late for my friends.

So, even though I wanted the time to make her stay, I didn't have it. All I had was this moment to show her that I loved her before I left. I didn't deserve the moment. Tristan hadn't been able to kiss Darren one last goodbye. She hadn't been able to make love to him with sorrow and grief in her heart, but I couldn't stop myself. I needed Georgie's touch. I needed it more than I'd ever needed anything.

I placed my lips on her stomach. Kissing. Pulling up her shirt and touching my lips to her skin. At first, she resisted, as if the touch was too much to bear, but then she gave in, straddling me, and pulling my lips to hers, and kissing me with such fervor that I thought we'd somehow lose our individual souls to something bigger and brighter than either of us. Our hands weren't gentle. Our kisses were like brands—fire—marking us as we gave ourselves to the passion and the intensity that was begging for relief.

After, we lay tangled in a pile of arms and legs. It was hard to see where mine ended and hers began. Skin. Hearts. Souls. But not lives. Our lives were being pulled, layer by layer, into different directions. Her family. My guilt. I wanted to reject it all. To demand to the universe that it let us be together like I'd said we were fated to be.

I kissed the top of her head that lay on my chest, my hand pulling at the white streak, letting it filter through my fingers. I finally found my voice and said quietly, "I'm leaving."

My heart cracked at her stuttered breath and the word that came from her as if I'd stabbed her. "What?"

"I've reenlisted. I leave tomorrow for Florida."

She turned so I could see her face, and there was so much pain there as well as another emotion that I wanted to label as love. I wanted to name it that way so I didn't have to feel it alone. So it would make this time together more real.

"I have to figure out what the hell happened while we wait to see if any of them make contact."

She still didn't say anything. She just watched me

with those damn beautiful eyes of hers that were golden tonight. That, no matter what color she wore, showed her emotions more than any facial expression and more than any tell.

"I never wanted this," I said, my voice cracking again. "I never wanted to love someone and leave them like Dad always did."

She swallowed. "You love me?"

And I couldn't believe that she doubted it. That she hadn't taken every moment of the forevers I'd spoken, every moment my lips had been on her body, every moment my soul had sat next to hers, and just knew, but she didn't. I touched her lips and said, "It isn't the best time to tell you, as I'm leaving, but I also didn't want to leave without saying it."

"Mac—"

"Don't. Don't you dare say you don't love me. I know you do." The words were harsh coming out of my mouth. Harsh because I couldn't have stood it if she denied it. I couldn't have stood one more fucking heartbreak.

"Loving you doesn't fix everything. It doesn't magically wave away the things that aren't right about us," she said softly.

I nodded. "I'm just asking… I'm just hoping that you'll let me figure it out with you when I get back. I just don't know when that will be."

"Wouldn't it be better to just use this time for what it really should be? Time for us to move on, to walk away before we both are left so hurt that we can't recover?"

It was too late for that. I wouldn't recover if she left

me now or later. If I lost the one thing in this damn world that could still give me hope. "You'd give up on us that easily?" I asked.

"On an us that shouldn't have been. We were weak to give in to it to begin with. I should have moved out as soon as I knew you lived here."

"You asked me to grant you the favor I owed you earlier today. And now I'm asking you for mine. Don't give up on us yet. Don't walk away just as we're saying I love you. The story doesn't need to end here."

I wasn't sure I deserved for her to agree. I wasn't sure I deserved a happily ever after when I'd cost Darren his, but I also couldn't leave D.C. without at least asking. Without, in some way, tying her to me. It was cruel. But I'd given up on thinking I was a decent human being. I was selfish. And I'd be selfish one more time if it meant a chance at her not walking out of my life.

Chapter Twenty-eight

Georgie

Having Mac say he loved me and that he wanted me to wait for him to come back made me happy at the same time as it made me sad. The thought of never seeing him again, of walking out of his life and not looking back, was like a dagger to my ribcage, spinning and twisting until all I could feel was the jagged point. But I also still knew, as clearly as I had on the beach in Rockport, that we were an impossibility. A dream that could never come to fruition in reality. I'd just forgotten that. I'd let my senses sweep me away in the thunder and lightning of Mac. But our x- and y-graphs were splintering apart now, curving farther and farther apart. I wasn't sure there was much we could do to bring them back together.

The first thing I'd thought on seeing his face burdened with sadness and so much guilt when he'd reached the top of the stairs was that I loved him. That I would do almost anything if I could erase those emotions from his face. Then, I thought of my boxes and the fact that, if I stayed, I'd just be adding more breaks to his heart…to my heart.

It didn't matter that he told me he was reenlisting. It didn't matter if he stayed in the Navy or eventually resumed his political goals, because being attached to a Russian gun dealer and his drug-selling son wasn't any better for a career naval officer than it was for a career politician.

After our lovemaking, which had been fierce and wild and raw with emotions and loss, I stared into his blue eyes and could see all the truths. The love. It was the first time in my life I'd looked at a man and thought that…felt that…wanted that. It hurt so badly to know I couldn't have it. I wanted to pout the way Raisa was good at pouting, but I couldn't. Instead, I had to figure out a way to love him and leave him.

To not grant his favor, just as he hadn't granted mine. It was exactly why we couldn't continue this way, because granting each other these favors should have been easy. It should have been what we wanted to do…give in to the other person. But we couldn't.

So, when he asked me not to give up, I just closed my eyes against the onslaught of his hurt as I said the words, "We aren't a romance novel, Mac."

"Maybe we should be."

I turned so my back was against his front. I couldn't look at him, but I also couldn't walk away from his arms yet. He was in my bed. He'd have to be the one who walked away. But he didn't. And I had to give him this…this one last night so that maybe he could escape his own thoughts and his own grief before he put back on his uniform and went to Florida with the guilt weighing him down. Guilt he didn't deserve to wear but shouldered anyway.

I understood that. But I wouldn't continue to add to the guilt by staying and watching as my reality continued to tear holes in the fabric of his.

♫ ♫ ♫

I must have fallen asleep, because I woke to an empty bed just as the sun was barely brushing aside the night. I woke to Mac being gone, and the heaviness that overtook me made the tears come. Tears I hadn't wanted to shed when he was in my bed but that I couldn't stop now.

I heard footsteps on the steps and brushed the tears away. When I sat up, it was to see Mac in his Navy whites, approaching. I'd told Ava he was a ten. And I remembered her words about Eli being a twenty, and my disbelief. But I thought I understood her better now. Because loving Mac made him a gazillion in my eyes. And in his uniform, he was an infinite number of stars.

He stood far enough away that we couldn't touch each other, but close enough for me to see how exhausted he was. How sleep had probably eluded him. He was scouring my face, looking for something.

"You've been crying," he said.

I wiped at my eyes again.

"That at least gives me some hope," he continued.

I started to talk, and he waved a hand at me. "Wait…God. I'm sorry. I do that all the time. Cut you off. But it's because I'm always afraid of what you're going to say. I wanted to tell you that you're right, we need time."

Holy hell, did that hurt, and try as I may, I knew it showed, and his eyes glimmered with the possibilities that I didn't want to give him.

He continued before I could speak again. "I need time to figure out what the fuck happened and find my friends, and you need time to decide how much you're going to let your family screw with your life."

This spiked the automatic defense of my family I always felt whether they deserved it or not. "They're family, Mac. You know what that means."

He nodded. "I do, but I'm not sure you've ever really had one. Maybe with your grandma. But definitely not with the people who've pursued their lives at the cost of yours."

He swallowed hard, and I knew he was thinking his statement now reflected on him in some way. As if his pursuing his dreams had cost Darren his life.

"You leaving the Navy didn't cause this."

He looked out the window to where the Capitol Building lights were flickering off as the daylight grew.

"It's debatable. But what isn't debatable is that I love you. That isn't going to change tomorrow, or the next day, a year from now, or ten years from now. How many times did Darren get to say it to Tristan before he was gone? Life is so fucking short. Maybe we aren't perfect, but we fit. Our bodies. Our souls."

He shook his head and turned back to look at me on the bed, easing closer. "I don't have my head on straight right now. I don't have the ability to convince you because of all the other shit going on in here." He tapped his head. "But this knows the truth." He tapped his heart.

He closed the remaining distance between us so he could gently rap on my chest. "And this knows the truth. Everything else is the lie, Georgie. Everything else is the senses and the dreams that you can't believe in. We're the reality. And when I get back, we'll figure it out."

My heart leapt. My heart wanted to believe it. I just couldn't see the end zone from the fifty-yard line. I wasn't even sure it existed.

"I wish you were staying here with Dani. She needs someone."

More guilt washed over me. But I would keep in touch. I wasn't abandoning her completely. I just needed to remove my FBI or CIA or NSA tail out of their immediate world.

"I'll look in on her. I promise," I told him.

He went to the steps, and I couldn't help calling after him.

"Mac?"

He nodded at me.

"Be safe."

He nodded again and said, "Damn, you make it hard to walk away."

But then he did.

The heart that had been slowly splitting apart in my chest finally cracked open all the way, the pieces burning my insides. But I knew I'd survive it. Like I'd survived every other hurt that had come my way. I'd known ahead of time that I would have a scar left when everything with Mac ended. The white streak always reminded me of the losses of my childhood, and even though I didn't have a visible mark from this, I'd always be able to feel the wound in my heart that was from Mac.

♫ ♫ ♫

I moved into the apartment above Theresa's garage and threw myself into school and the research I was doing for her. It seemed almost impossible that it had only been weeks since I'd begun work on her immigration case when it felt like years had passed. I tried not to think about Mac. I tried not to think about his words about my family, because it came too close to the anger that I'd already been feeling toward them ever since I'd met Mac. Ever since I'd truly wanted something that they were preventing me from having.

The first day he'd left, Mac had texted me a few times on both my old phone and the burner phone, as if he wasn't sure which I'd respond to. At first, it was just to let me know he'd arrived, but shortly after that, a text had come in with a picture of Nash. A Nash with stitches above his dark brows and sorrow on his face, but a Nash who was alive. I would never know what happened on the mission or how he'd gotten out, but it didn't matter. What mattered was that Mac wouldn't feel the heavy burden of losing both his friends.

I'd picked up the phone and called him, unable to not share in this moment with him.

"I'm so happy he's with you," I'd croaked.

"He's messed up. Emotionally, physically. We lost Darren and two others, and he's dealing with more guilt than I am for surviving it. I'm not sure we're good for each other right now, but at the same time, we are—if that makes any sense," he'd said quietly.

"It does."

"I miss you," he'd said.

And I had missed him too, more than anyone I'd ever missed in my life, and he'd only been gone less than a day. I missed him maybe even more than my grandma. But just like time had eased the pain in my heart over her, I knew time would help us, too.

"I have to go," I'd told him, and I'd imagined the sadness in his eyes at my words. "I just wanted you to know that I was so very glad that you got one of your friends back."

"Georgie—"

"Don't. Really. I need to go. Be safe, Mac-Macauley." And I'd hung up before he could have said anything else. Before I could have said words that I would have regretted saying.

As time moved further away from the traumatic three days that we'd had, I felt some knots in my back and my stomach start to ease. I felt like maybe life could move forward.

I met up with Dani several times for dinner. Never at the apartment. Always at a different restaurant than the time before.

The storm of her terrible night with Fenway passed after he left office in a cloud of shame, and the next hot political topic arose. Some dirtbag in South Carolina had tried to fire a trans man, and the LGBTQIA community was calling for his removal from office.

"I'm glad things have settled down for you. It continues to appall me what goes on in our world," I told her.

Dani laughed over her whiskey. "Georgie-Girl, I've been around Washington way too long to be surprised much anymore. It's why I want out."

"What? You?"

Dani nodded. "Yep. I want to go work for some normal business tycoon. Or maybe a regular old celebrity. Someone with no ties to D.C."

"But what about Mac? He'll be out of the Navy eventually and want to run for office."

"He won't," she said with a surety that surprised me. She laughed at the look on my face. "My brother has always felt like it was his personal responsibility to not only keep the entire world safe but also make it better than it was yesterday. He's just realized he can do that in a different way than he expected."

"You think he's given up his dream for good, then?" I asked. Dani nodded. This made me hurt for him in a new way, even though I'd sensed it in him from the moment he'd told me about Darren and put his uniform back on. After a moment, I said, "I know how hard that can be. There was a time when I didn't think I could ever get back my dreams of the law."

Dani took me in for a moment and then asked, "Truth?"

"Always," I told her.

"I'm glad Mac gave it up. Everyone here skitters like toddlers determined to get the most candy out of a piñata. It would have made Mac into something he isn't. It would have eaten at his soul to compromise on things that he values most, and he wouldn't have been able to survive in Washington without doing that."

I sat quietly, trying to digest her words. A small piece of me knew she was right. The Mac I'd fallen in love with wouldn't have been able to sustain the hits that would come from those kinds of negotiations. Negotiations that would have made him feel dishonorable.

Dani twirled her drink.

"Have you talked to him?" she asked.

I had a feeling she already knew the answer to that. "We've texted. And I talked to him when he told me about Nash."

"God, that was such a…relief. To know Nash was…" Dani choked and looked away. I hadn't realized how close she was to the squad, but the relief in her voice spoke volumes. "The guilt of it is eating at both of them. And I think Mac needs someone to keep pulling him back from the edge."

I looked down at my food, the chicken twirling unhappily in my stomach because I was pretty sure that person couldn't be me. My ledge had completely fallen out from beneath me and taken them along for the ride. Mac needed to climb up on stable ground that wouldn't continue to shift out from under him.

Dani reached across and put her hand over mine. "You're both good at tormenting yourselves. Mac wants you to be that person. I hope you can be it for him."

"Dani… None of you need my shit in your lives."

"You make him happier than I've ever seen before.

He gets all goopy and smiley. That's never been him. I'm pretty sure he's in love with you."

I couldn't look at her. If he hadn't told her his feelings, I wouldn't be the one to do so.

"Look. So, you're the daughter of a Ponzi-schemer. So, your stepdad is some Russian businessman on all the agencies' watch lists. So, your brother was dealing drugs. You act like those things are a reflection of you, when they aren't. Sure, you have to deal with it, just like I had to deal with being on the losing end of a battle with an aggressive asshole."

"I don't think you lost that war." I smiled weakly at her.

"You don't have to, either. You don't have to let their choices make you live a half-life."

And that hit home more than anything Mac had ever said to me about my family. He'd hinted at it the day he left, but his words had just upset me, because it made me feel like I was having to let go of my family in order to have him. Dani could have let being a victim cause her to scurry away and hide. It would have been okay if she had. There were plenty of victims who needed that to heal. But it would have made Dani something she wasn't, and that would have allowed him to victimize her one more time.

I wasn't a victim, but maybe I was letting my family make me act like one. Maybe I was blaming them for things when, really, I was just afraid. Afraid of loving and losing. Afraid of having a life that might someday get ripped out from underneath me like had happened to me before.

♫ ♫ ♫

"So, you're going to see Mac again?" Theresa asked.

I looked away, uncomfortable with the entire idea. Mac had been gone over a month.

The ache in my heart that I thought would ease the longer he was gone had just continued to sit in my chest, worming into my veins so that there were days that I felt like my entire body was on fire from it. I missed him. I missed his blue eyes, and his laughter, and his self-deprecation. I missed how he made me feel like the most exotic being on the planet. I missed feeling like my life was a dream that had turned into reality.

"I'm not sure it will change anything," I told her as we sat in her home library, drinking wine the day before I was scheduled to fly out to Texas. She'd gone to bat for me with my other professors so I could spend the extra days with Ava before the wedding. It meant a lot of work ahead of time and catch-up work when I got back, but it would be worth it.

"You still feel guilty. Like your dark shadows would overtake his light," Theresa commented as she watched me.

"Yes."

"You know, you can't live in D.C. without being investigated and wire-tapped, especially if you make any sort of waves in the existing status quo. My bet is you aren't even close to being the biggest reason Mac and his family would have multiple agencies interested in them. Vice Admiral Whittaker has a penchant for ruffling feathers inside the DoD and out. Robert Whittaker and his boss, Senator Matherton, make enemies as often as happy hour serves chips and salsa."

"But I don't want them to use my family as additional fuel."

"Like they're colluding with Petya Leskov?" she chuckled. "Matherton is putting together a gun bill that's about to outlaw assault rifles. I don't think that is exactly what Petya would want. Seems like it makes them enemies."

I still didn't say anything, because she wasn't necessarily wrong, and I had slowly been getting used to the idea that maybe I'd just been using my family as an excuse—a shield of sorts.

"Look. D.C. families are always complicated. There are black sheep and white sheep and downright dirty sheep. Don't let families dissuade you from being with someone who loves you. Love… It doesn't come often. Sometimes, it only comes once in your life." Sadness crossed Theresa's face.

I'd wondered, many times, why Theresa—a successful, smart, caring woman—was alone. Why she didn't have a partner by her side. "Is that what happened to you?" I asked. "You let your family keep you from the person you loved?" Then I flushed, aware that my question was way too personal. "I'm sorry, you don't have to answer that."

Theresa took me in over her wine glass. "Her family was in politics at a time when being lesbian wasn't cool or a catch phrase. She couldn't handle the heat. Got married to an Ivy League businessman and had three children with him."

"I'm so sorry."

She waved her hand as if I was missing the point. "All I'm saying is, if I had the choice to love someone with all my heart or walk because of some family issues, I'd always choose love."

She closed the book she had opened, wished me goodnight, and left the room. I made my way to the apartment above the garage. Even though I had my own kitchen, Theresa and I often ate together. I hadn't known she was lesbian. I wondered if people who knew thought we were a couple because I was riding to the campus with her most days. I didn't care. In fact, I would have been honored to be Theresa's partner.

Just like I would have been honored to be Mac's. To be the person to show up at a reception with him, our fingers entwined, our bodies in sync. I could see that life. But what if the love in his eyes turned to disillusionment, and then disappointment, and then dislike because he was constantly being brought down because of me and my family.

And the greatest what-if… What if I lost him?

I picked up the music box my dad had given to me. The one the cops had taken away and then returned without the thumbnail drive that had incriminated him. The black and white swans had their heads twined together. Swans mated for life. Mourned the loss of their soul mate for life. Black and white. Pieces that looked like they didn't belong together but did.

There had been so many what-ifs in my life. I'd never thought I was the kind of person to care about them. I hadn't dwelled overly on the ones that had defined my life up until this point. What if Dad hadn't been arrested? What if Mom hadn't lived in Russia?

What if Grandma hadn't signed a new lease when I was eighteen? What if she hadn't died?

I'd always seen those what-ifs as a path down a one-way street to hating life.

But ever since meeting Mac, I'd done just that. Let all the what-ifs define my actions. I'd used my fear of ruining his life to hide the truth. I was afraid he'd look at me like others had in the past, with judgment and condescension, as they walked away. Yet, even when I'd taken the drugs and been "arrested," he hadn't.

Instead, he'd said he loved me.

He'd said he wanted to work things out.

It was me who had walked—no, run—in the other direction.

I'd lost my parents at six. Like Mac had said, it wasn't in the normal way you can lose people, to death or divorce. I'd lost the ability to grow up with either of them. And I'd lost my grandmother at twenty-two. I'd lost a lot of people in my life. But this… This was me using my family to shield me from the potential loss of Mac.

But what if, instead of loss, I only gained? What if I gave in to everything I felt, and in doing so, I gained not only Mac and his love, but I gained a family? Gained people who would surround me with love and acceptance as they had since our very first meeting. What if I gained a future I'd never seen for myself?

Reality or a dream.

Could it be both? Reality that was a dream?

Chapter Twenty-nine

Mac

BRUISES
Performed by Lewis Capaldi

I sat at a bar in Florida with Nash. We both had beers in front of us, but mine was hardly touched while he was on his second. I was leaving the next day for Rockport. For Eli and Ava's wedding. I should have been filled with happiness, and I might have been closer to feeling that way if it weren't for Nash. I wasn't sure I should leave him yet.

I'd been there the day he'd climbed out of the plane on the tarmac at SOCOM. Nash had been responsible for getting the team out from under gunfire and to their backup rendezvous spot, carrying what was left of Darren and two other team members' bodies with them. They'd come straight from Africa to Florida— no stopover in Germany for our covert ops teams—so I'd seen the blood on all of them. I'd witnessed the rough stitches that the medic on the plane had given Nash, the bloodied bandages on two others. The flag-draped bodies. I'd seen the look on Nash's face. If I was riddled with guilt, Nash was consumed with it. He'd lost not only his team leader but also his best friend. He might as well have lost a body part.

I hadn't left his side for several days after he'd landed. Not because I was afraid he'd take his own life, but afraid that he'd take someone else's. Afraid that he'd be the guy with a gun, shooting up the place. He'd been pissed at the fuckers who'd approved the op, and I think, deep inside, he'd been pissed at me, and I shouldered it, because I deserved it.

We'd both be testifying against the assholes in charge of the operation in a few weeks before a Senate committee. There were several careers ending because of this. I had made it my new mission to make it happen. It was too little, too late, but it was all I could do when faced with the reality I didn't want.

"I gotta get outta here," Nash said, and he waved his hand at the bartender. When the bill came, I swiped it out of his hands. I wasn't letting him pay. Never again. If I was there, I was paying. I didn't know how else to show my sorrow and regret.

We walked out of the bar, and the humidity instantly weighed me down. Florida in October might as well be October in June. At least it felt that way this year. I'd almost forgotten what it was like because it had been awhile since my last stint in Florida, but after this, I could easily say that it was nowhere I wanted to live long-term. I liked weather, but I wanted variety. I wanted snowstorms, and fall leaves, and spring blossoms. The humidity I could always do without, but I'd take it if I knew there would soon be the scent of fall on the wind.

"Let me drive you home," I said, waving my keys at the rental I'd had for a month.

He didn't say anything until we got in the car.

"Don't drop me at my place. Take me to Darren's."

I grimaced. I wasn't sure Tristan wanted his drunk ass showing up at nine o'clock at night. But I also knew arguing with him wasn't going to work. He'd just get out of the car, get in his own, and drive there anyway. He'd somehow convinced himself that it was now his responsibility to look after Tristan and baby Hannah. While I could understand where his feelings were coming from, I also knew Tristan wasn't going to let him get away with it for long. She had her own grief to deal with; she didn't need his as well.

Besides, Tristan's mom was there, helping her until the Navy packed their things and sent them to Delaware where Tristan would be moving in with her family. Nash would be here, trying to put his squad back together. If it was even possible. If the powers that be would even let them.

My worry for him grew.

"You sure you don't want to come with me?" I asked.

"To a wedding? Uninvited?" He grimaced at me.

"There would be lots of people there happy to see you."

"It's a goddamn celebration, Mac. Do I look like I'm ready to celebrate?" The anger in his voice bounced off the windows it was so strong.

We drove in silence as pain washed over us. Guilt. Anger. Neither of us had gone through all the stages of grief yet. I wasn't sure I was ready for a celebration, either. But I ached to see people I loved. I ached to show them I loved them before it was too late. I shoved aside the voice that tried to tell me I didn't deserve it. I knew the voice was wrong. I'd been talking with my dad a lot about the weight of the guilt. He'd experienced his own losses in his career—even this one he felt. He was good at reminding me that all of us left behind deserved a life that was full. We just had to learn from the godawful lessons we were dealt along the way.

When I parked in front of the darkened house, Nash got out. I turned off the car, got out, and called his name. He stopped, turning back to me, the moonlight making the hollows of his eyes look even darker than they were these days. I didn't have words, but I stepped up to him and pulled him into a hug. His body was stiff and tight. Unforgiving. I just held on, and eventually, he hugged me back. Then he pushed me away.

"Get off, man. I know you want me, but geez, don't you have a girl?" he teased in a tone that was almost his old self. Almost.

But his words hurt almost as much as Darren's death. I'd had a girl once. A woman. A lady who smelled like cherry blossoms. A woman who fit. But she'd cut and run, and even though I'd still been texting with her off and on over the course of the last month, she was still holding me just out of reach. A glass wall had come down between us that I hadn't been able to break.

Nash didn't know this because, crazy as it seemed, we hadn't talked about Georgie once since I'd been there. We'd been focused on recovering. We'd been focused on funerals and retaliations.

"I did, but I'm pretty sure she left me," I said with a wry, half-smile.

"Pretty sure? You don't even know?" He chuckled, and it felt good to be the reason he laughed. It was good to hear it escape his lips when he'd been nothing but sorrow for the month I'd been here. Darren's funeral had been the worst of it for me, but not Nash. He'd had to bury two more members of his squad, wishing they were there instead of him.

I shrugged.

"Didn't think you were a quitter, Mac."

That hit too close to home, and he knew it. Maybe it was why he'd said it, but he looked like he regretted the words as soon as they were out of his mouth. He looked away and then back. He hit me on the shoulder. "We just saw how quickly things can change. Don't let her get away that easy if you really love her."

Then he walked toward Tristan's darkened house.

My mind was whirling around his words when I got in the car, and my phone dinged: Eli.

CAPTAIN: On your way yet?

ME: Not till oh five hundred.

CAPTAIN: Ava is nervous because you aren't here yet.

ME: First of all, it'll only be Thursday tomorrow, and the wedding isn't until Saturday. Second of all, come hell or high water, I'll be there. I wouldn't be late for my best friend's wedding.

CAPTAIN: So, I get to tell Truck that I win? I'm the best friend?

ME: Don't be an asswipe. You know Truck wins in both our books. He's the better man.

CAPTAIN: True story.

My hand drifted over the text button. I wanted to ask if Georgie was there yet. I wanted to know if she looked as gorgeous as she did in my dreams, the ache to see her swelling into a full-blown heart attack. My dad was right. Nash was right. Life was over too fast to waste the moments we had. I'd never known that love could feel like this. So goddamn satisfying and so goddamn painful.

I wanted to know if she'd listened when I, and then my sister, had told her that her family wasn't anything to get worked up over, but I was also afraid to know the answer. To know if she was still running.

When I'd gotten down to SOCOM, my first order of business was to destroy the fuckers who'd approved the op that had killed Darren and his squad members. My anger and guilt had eased only slightly, knowing that their careers would be over. It wasn't enough for the three lives they'd cost, but if I held out for more, I'd have to drag myself down with them, and so I settled for seeing them discharged. I settled for the Senate committee disintegrating the little group of diplomats who'd been pushing it. I settled, promising myself to never let it happen again. To save lives instead of cost them.

After I'd filtered through the mission details and drunk myself into a stupor with Nash, I'd returned to SOCOM and quietly probed at Petya Leskov's file, hoping I wouldn't raise any red flags in doing it. I just needed to know what I was getting into, and even though I knew, with all of my heart, that Georgie wasn't tied up in the business; I needed to see what others thought. Fucking Descartes weighing on me just like he weighed on her. Proof.

What I could find out wasn't much, but it seemed everyone believed Petya Leskov was a gun dealer. They just hadn't been able to confirm it. Drugs were definitely not his thing. There were pictures of his home from above, a mansion that used to belong to Russian royalty, and there were pictures of his private security team that rivaled a Special Forces unit. From what people could tell, he seemed to love his wife, his children, and his stepdaughter. CIA and NSA had run several intelligence ops to gather more details but had come up short every time. Georgie, herself, had been a repeated dead end.

So, I was left with what I knew to be true: Malik was in rehab somewhere, Raisa was ensconced in her scientific studies at Stanford, and Georgie was pursuing her law degree without being hounded by the U.S. government. But she'd always have a target on her back. All of the agencies would eventually circle back around to her in another attempt to gather intel on Petya as long as he did business on the dark side of the law.

This pissed me off. It made me want to protect her. But it also meant if I was tied to her, I would always be subject to the same targeting. No matter how "clean" I lived my life, I'd be scrutinized. Because I'd decided I wouldn't be running for office, being followed or bugged wouldn't be a big deal. If my superiors called me out on it occasionally, so be it. Losing Darren had forced me to wake up to the truth I'd already been realizing in my time on the Hill.

Politics weren't for me. I wanted honor and loyalty in my life not half-truths and betrayals.

The only thing that really mattered was loving Georgie. Showing her that she was cherished regardless of her family.

She'd moved out of our apartment for the same reason she'd taken the drugs from Raisa. To protect the people she loved. To protect my dream. But it was one I no longer wanted. I just needed to convince her that it had nothing to do with who she was and everything to do with who I was.

It was time someone protected Georgie and her dreams, and I wanted that someone to be me. I hadn't been there for Darren, but I could be there for her. The only future I gave a daman about was the one with her at my side.

♫ ♫ ♫

On the flight to Corpus Christi, I was restless. Up and out of my seat so much the stewardess started to comment on it. She also eyed me up and down like a steak she wanted to sauté and eat, but I wasn't interested. I understood a little better how Eli could be oblivious to the females hitting on him at the bar on a regular basis. None of them really registered when you loved someone enough.

An old Paul Newman quote about marriage registered in my brain. He'd said, "I have steak at home. Why should I go out for hamburger?" That was how I felt. I wanted my steak. I wanted Georgie. I didn't want anything else.

We'd face the challenges of my Navy career, her law career, and her family as they came. Hell, I had Thomas the Weasel in my family, and I was sure he was going to get arrested for some kind of marijuana charge at some point, hemp being the new answer to every environmental problem that Thomas could think up.

When I got off the plane, I had a text from Dani.

BRAT: Did you tell her about one-eyed Whittaker?

I didn't have to ask who "her" was. Dani was flying in for the wedding tomorrow, and I knew my sister would be on my team. Maybe between the two of us, we could get Georgie to see the light.

ME: Why the hell would I have told her about him?

BRAT: He fought for the Confederacy. He wanted to keep slavery. We have our own skeletons.

ME: I don't think she's going to care about a relative who lived almost two centuries ago.

BRAT: Did you tell her about the time you got caught streaking?

ME: I've never been caught streaking.

BRAT: Oh. Right. That was Bee.

ME: WHAT?! Bee was caught streaking?

BRAT: Oops. I don't think I was supposed to tell you that.

*ME: ** laughing, falling off chair GIF***

ME: I can't wait to give her shit about that.

BRAT: You'd rat me out?

ME: Sister dear, you rat me out all the time.

BRAT: But I'm trying to help you win the love of your life back.

ME: True story. I apologize. Your secret is safe with me.

I hadn't checked my bag, and after grabbing my duffel from the overhead compartment, I almost sprinted off the plane, through the gate, and out of the terminal. I had more energy than I'd had in several weeks, the weight on my shoulders lifting slightly. Hope filling me for the first time in days. I texted Eli as I went, letting him know I was there.

He pulled up with Truck in the passenger seat. I flung my bag into the bed and crammed my large frame into the backseat. I punched each of them in the shoulder and kissed Truck on the side of his head.

"Gah, get off me," he said, wiping at his face with a smile.

"Is she here?" I asked as Eli took off.

"Hello. Nice to see you, too." Eli snorted.

"Hello, my douchebag friends. Is Georgie here?"

Truck smirked at me. "She arrived this morning, but the women aren't at the house. They're staying at the Lighthouse Hotel."

"Fuck," I said, falling back and strapping on my seat belt, which I'd almost forgotten in my desire to learn more about Georgie.

"Dude, you have it bad," Truck said, grinning.

I flicked the back of his head, and he flipped me off. I loved these two men almost as much as I loved my sisters. I thanked God that neither of them had been on the squad I'd lost. The Coast Guard had its own elite team, but Truck hadn't ever shown interest in it, and Eli was now out of the military all together.

"How was SOCOM?" Eli asked, reading my mind.

"Shitstorm. But I'm going back to D.C. now. I have to testify in front of Congress next month."

For a moment, we were all quiet, the loss of military men settling down between us. Respect. Sorrow. Eli was the first to break the silence.

"Truck's going to work at the academy in New London."

"No way!" I said, truly happy for him. "They're going to let you train future Coasties? Whose ass did you kiss for that job?"

"I can tell you're back in the Navy. All the swearing." Eli chuckled.

It was true. Being around SOCOM had made it even worse. The Special Forces teams swore so much it was like they'd challenged themselves to find a way to say whole sentences without anything but swear words.

"Did Georgie say anything about me?" I asked.

"I win," Eli said, and Truck groaned.

"What the hell?" I glared at them both.

"I bet you'd say her name at least two times within the first five minutes." Eli's grin was contagious. I needed this. After the heartache and the gloom that had settled over SOCOM since the incident, it was good to be surrounded by smiles and harassment.

I'd told them both snippets of the Georgie debacle over the last month as they'd tried to keep me from derailing after the screw-up that had caused Darren to lose his life. To cause Tristan to lose her husband, and Hannah to lose her dad. My smile disappeared.

"Will it help if I tell you I think she's purposely *not* saying your name?" Eli asked.

"Yes. Yes. It would," I told him back.

"I have a new bet," Truck said.

"Oh yeah, what?" Eli asked.

"I bet the douchebag won't make it through the wedding without kissing her."

"You think he'll make it all the way to the wedding without kissing her? You really have never been in love, *Travis*," Eli teased.

"First, I'm not sure I want you two betting on the outcome of my love life, and two, what's with the Travis?" I asked.

"Travis here thinks it's way more 'professional' for him to be known by his real name in New London," Eli informed me.

"Hell, Truck is a fucking kid nickname," Truck griped.

I understood what he meant. It was why I'd gotten rid of Robbie and balked at being stuck in a bro-ship name with him when I'd seen Georgie this summer, but I wasn't going to let him know any of that.

"Doesn't matter what you go by, the cadets will just come up with their own nickname for you," I said.

Eli smirked. "This is very true."

Truck glowered, and I smiled, but as we got closer to Rockport, my brain slid back to Georgie. I wanted to make Eli drive straight to the Lighthouse Hotel, storm the ladies' bachelorette gathering, and demand that Georgie see me. Because no matter the glass wall she'd surrounded herself with, no matter her family or my career choices, I knew I could convince her we belonged together. I knew that if I could just touch her, she'd feel the truth in her soul, just like I did.

Chapter Thirty

Georgie

LIKE I'M GONNA LOSE YOU
Performed by Meghan Trainor & John Legend

I'd flown to Texas with flutters in my stomach. Flutters at thoughts of seeing Mac. Flutters at thoughts of telling him that the only thing I was afraid of anymore was losing him, and that I hoped I hadn't.

When I got to the beach house early Thursday morning, Mac wasn't there. Ava told me he wasn't getting there until later that day, and I could tell she was nervous about it. Nervous about part of her wedding party not being there. Or maybe nervous for Eli not having one of his "brothers" there.

I didn't have time to dwell on it, though, as we removed ourselves to the hotel downtown, and Jenna and I went into party-planning mode. We held the bachelorette party that night at the bar, and I almost expected the men to show up. Almost hoped the men would show up, but Ava said she'd threatened Eli with a month without sex if he dared. She'd sent him a list of perfectly acceptable bars in Corpus Christi, but he'd insisted they'd just get drunk at the house.

On Friday, after Jenna and I drowned our hangovers with greasy food that Ava refused to eat, we set to decorating the suite at the hotel for her bridal shower. We were joined by Eli's mom and their family friend, Leena. Jenna's mom was there, and Lacey from the bar. Even Dani showed up, and she hugged me while purposefully dropping Mac's name a half a dozen times to the others in the room. It was a small shower, but it was the women who Ava loved most in the world.

Ava had a cute little baby bump that was hardly noticeable if you didn't know she was pregnant. I was sitting next to her as she unwrapped gifts, and she suddenly grabbed my hand and set it on her stomach where I felt the baby's tiny movements against my palm. I gasped and then smiled, but then I wondered what my baby would look like if Mac were the father. What if…

I got to see one of my closest friends turn to tears as her mother-in-law gave her a ring to wear on her right hand that had once been her ring when she married Eli's father. And I wondered what Mac's mom would say to me if we were getting married. What if…

On Saturday, I got to help Ava into her wedding dress, knowing she was anxious to see Eli again after two days apart. That she was dying to see his expression when she walked barefoot down the sand outside their house in a white dress that was elegant and graceful but all spunky Ava in the flips and curves. And I wondered what Mac's expression would be if I was walking down the aisle toward him in a white dress. What if…

But nothing mattered once I showed up with Ava in the limo at their house and saw Mac waiting there for us in another tux. He opened the limo door and helped Ava out, and then Jenna, and then I was touching him, and my body rejoiced. Happiness filled me as I looked up into his blue eyes and saw a curious mix of emotions in his, which had me hoping there could be more to us than a story of a man and a woman who'd met but had let the world tear them apart.

I hoped there would be no more what-ifs.

I hoped there would only be a reality that was a dream.

"Georgie," he breathed out in that deep voice of his that still sent waves down my spine, even more so because of the absence of it over the last few weeks.

"Mac-Macauley." I smiled, and I saw the emotions in his eyes change to hope, and my heart leaped.

The wedding planner came bustling up and shooed us down to the beach. But Mac hadn't let go of my hand as he led the way. We halted at the dunes. We could hear the music playing and the chatter of the people who were sitting in the chairs. It was a small wedding. Eli's tiny family and Ava's almost nonexistent one. Andy, who was more like a dad to Ava than her real dad, showed up in time to walk Ava down the aisle. Truck held out his arm for Jenna, and Mac twisted the hand he still held so it was laying on his arm.

Mac and I were the first to walk down the aisle.

"You're breathtaking," he said quietly, and I smiled up at him, unable to stop. Unsure if the smile would ever disappear from my face throughout the day. So many good things to celebrate. Hoping beyond hope that this all meant that Mac and I would be one of them.

"You clean up pretty nice yourself, Mac-Macauley."

We parted ways at the end of the red carpet, Mac going to stand behind his friend, and me going to the spot marked on the sand by the seashells the wedding planner had used instead of flowers. I looked at Eli, whose eyes were glued to the aisle. He didn't look nervous at all. He just looked joyful, and when he saw Ava on Andy's arm, his whole face broke into a euphoric smile. It made him more handsome than when he was serious, but when I looked behind him to Truck and then Mac, my entire body was caught up in a blue gaze that had locked onto me. The entire wedding disappeared until it was just Mac and me on the beach where we'd first started to get to know each other.

While Eli and Ava exchanged their vows and their rings with words that stole my breath at their sweetness, I was still watching Mac, and he was still watching me, his large, beautiful smile drowning me. He was gorgeous. A gazillion points of gorgeousness.

During the wedding pictures, we had moments when we almost got to touch and speak but not quite. It was tantalizing, the anticipation hanging in the air between us. We journeyed back to town to a reception at the bar with Truck, Jenna, her husband Colby, Andy, and Lacey. The bar was closed for our private party. The first time the bar had been closed on a Saturday evening ever.

Once we got to the bar, Brady cornered me for a while, catching up on his tour and the behind-the-scenes gossip from *Fighting for the Stars*. Dani appeared next to me, and I hugged her while she listened on as Brady talked. I watched Mac over Brady's head, half hearing what Brady was saying. Mac watched me, his smile from earlier starting to glower the longer I spent at Brady's side. I winked at Mac, and I swear his whole face tore at the grin that took over it.

Brady left to go sing a song he'd written for the bride and groom about love lasting longer than the tides. It was good, but it wasn't an Ava song.

And then, finally, Mac was at my side again, twining his fingers in mine and pulling me onto the dance floor. The song was slow and moody as he turned me into him. My entire body sighed. That's what it felt like. Relief to be in his arms again after the ache of not being there. Of being apart.

"I'm redeeming my favor," he said.

This caught me off guard. "I think you already did."

"But you never granted it," he said, all seriousness, but I could see the sparkle of mischief in his eyes.

"A dance is your favor?" I smiled up at him.

He chuckled. "Not hardly. I need you to hear me out. Can you do that here, or do we need to go somewhere else?"

I didn't respond. I put my forehead on his chest, afraid of what I would say or not say. Afraid I'd let the what-ifs burden me down again. My heart was pounding because I so desperately wanted to hear what he had to say. I wanted to believe that the look I'd seen in his eyes all day was the same look that had been in his eyes when he'd said he loved me.

He drew me from the dance floor, through the storage closet, and up the ladder to the roof. The sun had faded, turning the sky deep purple. The wind had picked up, and I shivered. Mac ran his fingers up and down my arms, but it made the goosebumps worse instead of better.

"Georgie, no job—political, military, or otherwise—is enough for me to give up you," he said, and my heart sped up, feeling like it was going to jump out of my chest. But it was hard to see his expression in the twilight.

"You've already reenlisted," I heard myself say when I really wanted to say, "Thank God."

"I can go down right now and have Eli and Truck break my leg for me. Get out just like Eli got out."

"You'd break your leg so we could be together?" I asked, my heart beating a new tune. A tune of "what is." A reality and a dream built together.

"If you want me out. If that's the condition upon which you'll take me back," he said quickly and honestly.

"Mac, I don't want you to give up your career—any of them—for me," I told him, but he misunderstood. He thought I was saying what I'd said back in D.C.—that we couldn't be together—when that wasn't what I meant. I really meant that if he'd have me, I'd take him no matter his career.

But when I went to talk, he put a finger on my lips and said, "I understand that. I know that you don't want me to, and that makes me love you even more. The fact that you want me to have the future I always envisioned. The thing is, once you walked into my life, the only future I could imagine was one with you in it. One where I get to wake up guessing what color your eyes will be when you come out of the bathroom. One where I get to kiss the place at the corner of your ear and your jaw that makes you shiver and moan."

His words were so sweet they brought tears to my eyes, and he continued to misread them and said, "Do you know what I can't envision? I can't imagine living with the idea that you're out there with some other man. Where some other man gets to hold you, and protect you, and make you his. I can't imagine any other woman coming into my life and fitting into the curves of my life and my body and my soul the way you do. I can't imagine any career that requires me to give up—"

I kissed him. I tangled my fingers in his hair and pulled his lips tight up against mine, and my body relaxed for the first time in over a month. I was where I belonged. In his arms. For as long as he'd have me. He didn't even hesitate before he was kissing me back. Fiercely. Like a man who was drowning and asking to be pulled ashore. Like a man who loved a woman who loved him back.

I pulled away, and he groaned in protest.

"I was right, and you were wrong," I told him, and he looked at me questioningly. "I told you that you have all the beautiful words when you speak from your heart."

"It's because you are my heart. All of it."

He went back to kissing me and found my favorite spot below my ear along my neck that had me saying his name in desperation. Forty days of longing. He picked me up, tongues and lips still locked in a battle to show who had missed who the most, and headed toward the picnic tables that were on the roof, and we'd almost gotten there when we heard a ripping sound.

I pulled back from his lips as we both burst into laughter. My hand found the torn sleeve of yet another rental tux. He set me down on the edge of the table, moving in between my legs, my short bridesmaid dress riding up my thighs.

"Why did you pick me up?" I grinned up at him.

His smile faded. "I didn't want to let you go in case you changed your mind."

We stared at each other for a long time, and then I put both my hands on his face before carefully and gently brushing my lips along his. "I'm not changing my mind. Why would I want hamburger when I can have steak?"

"You're quoting Newman to me?"

I smiled at him, and he devoured my lips in a kiss that took us both to a new dream realm where it was just us, his hardness rubbing up against my middle, making me wonder why I'd ever thought I could walk away from this. Why I'd ever thought I'd want to walk away from this. From a man who saw me for who I was and still loved me with all my pieces and parts strewn around the world.

Truck's laughter from the rooftop entrance brought us to our senses.

"I absolutely won the bet!" Truck hollered at us.

"What bet?" I asked, looking over Mac's shoulder at Truck's grinning face.

"The bet that said he'd be kissing you before the wedding was over."

"The ceremony ended hours ago," Mac said, but his lips were smiling against mine.

"I didn't say the ceremony, I said the wedding." Truck snorted.

"Potato, potahto," Mac responded.

"They're about to leave," Truck said and then disappeared back down the hatch.

"You bet on us?" I asked as he helped me down from the picnic table and entwined his hands back with mine.

"I'd bet on us a million times."

His words tore a new hole in my heart. A hole that was anchored with the string that bound me to him. That would forever bind me to this man who was willing to sacrifice everything for the ideals and the people he loved.

"I love you, Mac-Macauley."

"I love you right back, Georgie-Girl."

Epilogue

Mac

YOU ARE THE REASON
Performed by Calum Scott & Leona Lewis

The snow was falling, and Christmas lights sent sparkles across the wet surfaces as I headed toward the apartment where Georgie was waiting for me. It reminded me of Fourth of July and the drops that had dripped through the heavens while I'd watched her instead of the fireworks. I'd been fascinated by her then, and now, only five months later, I was equally fascinated. And grateful. Grateful that every day I got to wake up next to her. Tangled with her body that fit perfectly with mine.

We were leaving D.C. the next day for Delaware and the chaos of my family, so I wanted it to be just us tonight. Quiet before the storm. Quiet where I could ask her to be mine forever without everyone looking on.

I'd always thought I would know when the woman I was meant to be with had walked into my life. And even knowing that, I remember still thinking Eli was insane when he'd moved in with Ava after dating her for two months and proposing to her after only six. I'd wondered if it could last, the passion and intensity that you could see in them when they were together. I'd doubted it because I hadn't experienced love.

And now I was a believer. A believer in everything.

Love. Happiness. The ever after.

Life could fuck it up. We could lose each other because of illness, or I could be sent out on assignment and lose my life there. But maybe knowing all that made me love her more each moment I was with her. Made me want for her to be mine in every way possible for as long as we had.

I just hoped she'd agree.

I'd barely convinced her that dreams and reality could be one. I wasn't sure she'd gotten to the white wedding, happily ever after part yet.

When I walked in the door, it was quiet, but the tree was lit up, and holiday music was playing. Georgie loved Christmas as much as she'd loved Fourth of July. I thought maybe she was just a fan of holidays in general. She'd certainly gotten a kick out of Thanksgiving with the chaotic Whittaker clan. Even her sister, who'd joined us, had commented on her smiles.

"Georgie?" I hollered, dropping my wet gear by the door and heading down the hallway to the bedroom we shared.

"Up here," she hollered back, and I turned and headed back toward the loft she hardly ever spent time in anymore. The loft that hadn't been her bedroom since before Florida and the shitstorm we'd all survived.

I took the steps two at a time and then stopped near

the top to catch my breath. Not because the stairs had winded me, but because she did. She was standing in a white silk nightie that barely covered her butt cheeks, hair down just like I liked it most, and she was watching the city move below her.

She turned, and I realized she had my note in her hand. The note I'd written this morning and shoved into her textbook just where I knew she'd find it. Once upon a time, I'd been afraid to write anything down that I felt. Afraid that someday it would be used against me. Not anymore. Now I wrote Georgie notes all the time. Love notes. Sex notes. I miss you notes. Anything and everything that would make her smile like she was smiling at me now.

"What took you so long?" she asked.

I growled and was at her side in a bound, pulling her to me and kissing her like we'd spent days apart instead of a few hours. There was a smell of cinnamon twisted in with her normal cherry scent tonight. It was enough to make me feel like I'd had more than one beer with the clowns at the Christmas party.

"I had to make a stop," I told her, pulling away from her lips.

She had her fingers on the buttons of my uniform. The uniform I'd put back on this fall and had vowed not to take back off again. I wouldn't either. Not unless they forced me to. I stilled her hands. "Slow down, Georgie-Girl."

"What?" she laughed. "Aren't you usually the one saying to hurry up?"

I smiled and pulled her down the steps to the Christmas tree.

"I want you to open your Christmas present here," I told her.

She smiled. "I'm already in my lingerie, Mac-Macauley. You already get to have your way with me."

I kissed her.

"Shh. I don't want to get sidetracked."

She laughed, and I almost forgot what I was trying to do, because her laugh and her smile always made me feel like the world had stopped around me.

"Do you remember when we said we had a lot of chemistry?"

She nodded.

"And we do, right?"

She nodded again.

"And you kind of like me, just a wee bit?"

"I don't just like you. You know that. I love you. You're kind and smart and gentle—"

"I'm not always gentle," I cut her off, and I could see she was wondering where my rambling was going, but I couldn't help teasing her. "And I'm quite handsome, too."

"But the best part of you is your family," she teased back.

I tried to look offended but couldn't. "I can't really argue it. They're great. Except Thomas."

She laughed again, and I kissed her.

"You're distracting me," I told her.

"Sorry. Present. Right." She stuck her hand out.

"I forgot what I was supposed to say," I told her

with a laugh.

"What you were supposed to say?" Her brow furrowed, but she was still smiling.

"Eli had it all planned for me, him being the word guy and all."

I thought maybe she was getting a hint of what I was trying to do, because her smile slowly melted, being replaced with something in her eyes that wasn't just love. Something that looked like my future.

"You can't do this while I'm in my pajamas," she said with a laugh.

"You look sexy as hell just like that."

"Just propose already," she teased.

And I couldn't help but grin at her because she knew me well enough to know what I was doing from the moment I started. I pulled the velvet box out of my pocket and placed it between her hands, but covered them with my own so she couldn't open it yet.

"I told you on the roof above the bar that I couldn't imagine my future without you in it. And I mean that. But I've also seen how short a time that people can have together." My throat caught, thinking of Darren's wife spending her first Christmas without her husband. "And I've also seen how long they can have, like my grandparents. But because we don't know what the road ahead of us looks like, I want to make sure that you're on it with me every step of the way."

"I'm already on the road with you, Mac."

"You are, but I want it to be official. I want you to be mine in every way possible. If you'll have me for the rest of your life."

Her eyes glittered with tears, the pale green that was all her reflecting the lights from the tree. "I would be honored to be on any road with you for as long as you'll have me," she said.

"Forever it is, then." I smiled and leaned in to kiss her before removing my hand and helping her open the little black box.

It was a ring that had a diamond in the middle with a rainbow of colored stones on either side. Multiple colors just like her multiple lenses.

"I didn't want you to have to pick just one color," I said quietly.

"Mac…" she said, wiping tears from her eyes.

I took the ring and slipped it on her finger and then picked her up and carried her down the hall. We were about halfway when the shoulder of my uniform ripped with a great big, resounding tear.

"Goddamn it," I swore, and she laughed.

And I knew that I'd do whatever it took to keep her laughing for the next hundred years, and I wished on all the stars that shone out the window that we would have that long and more.

♫ ♫ ♫

Need a little more of Mac and Georgie? Catch them in a _BONUS EPILOGUE_ with a sneak peek of the next _Anchor Novel_, _AVENGED BY LOVE_. FREE with sign-up:

https://www.ljevansbooks.com/freeljbooks

Need more of the <u>Anchor Novel</u> gang? Keep reading to see how you can get more of Truck and

Dani PLUS A LITTLE TEASER FROM THEIR BOOKS!

Or check them out here:

Truck and Jersey's fake-marriage, forced-proximity romance, **_AVENGED BY LOVE_**, is a small-town, standalone that one 5-star reviewer calls, "The greatest love story adventure."

The man shut the bar, clicked the button next to him, and we swooshed backward while he loaded the next car. Our seat continued to sway, and I gripped the bar.

Jersey laughed next to me, and I turned my head from the ground disappearing beneath us to her. To the beauty that was the pale vision next to me. "This is funny to you?"

"It's just...you're this big, bad Coast Guard, all protective He-man action. So, it's strange to see you afraid of a simple machine."

"We aren't birds. We don't have wings. If we fall, there will be nothing to save us."

"We're not going to fall. Don't look at the ground, look out." She took my chin in her hand and drew it up from the ground so I was looking out at the ocean, and I realized, for the first time, that the skies weren't blue, and the sun wasn't shining. I hadn't really noticed it when I was spending time with someone who was as bright as the sun. And Jersey was exactly that when she let herself come out from behind her shield.

The ocean was rough, and the wind whipping around us was more from the ominous clouds than the ride. The air was hot and humid, but it was also charged with energy, and I regretted ever stepping foot on the ride.

"What the hell are we doing on this thing in a storm?" I croaked out.

She laughed again. "It's beautiful, right?"

The stormy seas were beautiful, like she'd said, especially with the clouds seeming to blur into the waves. But that beauty could turn deadly in a second. I knew it for a fact, because I lived on the sea for a good portion of my daily life.

She tucked her arm through mine. "I'll keep you safe."

And then it was my turn to laugh. This little tiny thing next to me, offering to keep me safe. As if she really did have her own superpowers. As if she was Cat Woman, or Black Widow, or that damned Glasswing she idolized and could deliver me from a fall, unscathed.

Except, I'd already fallen. Hard. For her. For my wife.

AVENGED BY LOVE is FREE in Kindle Unlimited

Need Dani Whittaker's HEA? She goes all-in with Navy SEAL, Nash Wellsley in _DAMAGED DESIRES_? It's a **frenemy, military romance** that reviewers say is, "Beautifully crafted with deep characters," and "I couldn't put this phenomenal story down."

"Kiss me," she said, another dare. Her eyes held mine. The challenge laid out.

I bit back another groan. Trying not to touch her. My fingers clenched into fists on either side of her on the table.

Not moving. I could sit in the same position for hours—days—if I needed to.

"No," I said, holding her gaze.

"No?" she breathed out. The shock on her face made my lips quirk, releasing some of the tension in my body.

"Has any guy ever said no to you, Athena?"

"Yes," she said quietly before her chin raised and her eyes flared back to life. "You want to."

I did. I wanted to bite that pink lip and punish her for punishing me. Torture her with kisses and fingers until she begged rather than dared.

"I do. But kissing you wouldn't stop at kissing."

She rolled her eyes. "That's kind of the point here." She waved a finger between us.

"I can't," I told her, my voice thick with desire and regret. "Because I can't offer you more than a night. An amazing, sweaty, gods screaming hot night, but still only one night. And Mac would kick my ass."

"My brother has nothing to do with this. I'm a grown woman. I know what I want, and it definitely isn't more than one night."

Refusing her felt like ringing the bell and walking away, and that wasn't me. But I also knew if I accepted her challenge, I'd end up exactly what they called me, Nash the Ass. Nasty Ass Shitty Human.

<u>DAMAGED DESIRES</u> is FREE in Kindle Unlimited

Did you know that you can get the 1st **THREE ANCHOR NOVELS** as an eBook box set with a bonus novella? Don't miss any of these **slow-burn, sizzling, military romances** about true friends, real "family", and the dreams we reshape as we go through this wild ride called life. It includes: ***GUARDED DREAMS, FORGED BY SACRIFICE, AVENGED BY LOVE***, and ***THE***

HURRICANE — a bonus novella with the entire gang.
https://geni.us/anchorset

If you want to keep tabs on LJ' stories as she writes them and get exclusive content, giveaways, and more, then you might want to join her weekly newsletter, http://bit.ly/LJEmoGive. You can get all these FREE Flash Fiction stories when you sign up: https://www.ljevansbooks.com/freeljbooks.

Message from the Author

Thanks again for reading *Forged by Sacrifice*. At the beginning of the book—if you even saw it—I told you I didn't want to fill your head with my social media sites and other books because I wanted you to read the story and then decide how you felt about me and my words. I hope you loved Georgie and Mac's story of sacrifice and love. I hope their strength and resiliency along with my mix of lyrics and story burned a memory into your soul that you will think of every time you hear one of the songs from now on.

We talk about music, books, and just what it takes to get us through this wild ride called life a lot in my Facebook reader's group, **LJ's Music & Stories**. If you do nothing else with the links here, I hope you join that group. I hope that we can help *YOU* through your life in some small way.

Regardless if you join or not, I'd love for you to tell me what you thought of Georgie and Mac's story by reaching out to me personally. I'd be honored if you took the time to leave a review on Amazon, Goodreads, or BookBub, but even more than that, I hope you enjoyed it enough to tell a friend about it.

If you still can't get enough (ha!), you could also sign up for my newsletter so that you'll be able to keep tabs on all my stories as I write them. Not only will you get the details on releases, but you'll be entered into a giveaway each month for a chance at a signed paperback by yours truly 😊.

Finally, I just wanted to say that my wish for you is a healthy and happy journey. May you live life resiliently. With hope and love. I truly hope to hear from you!

Acknowledgements

My first acknowledgement is to my husband, who I adore more than words, thank you for being the person to take me from my moments of seriousness and self-doubt to laughter. Thank you for not letting me give up on this dream of mine and for supporting it with your time, our money, and your own effort. I am so lucky to have you as my partner in this crazy thing called life. I love our life together. I promise I'll try to be back on my feet soon. I love you.

To Evyn, thank you for being the best critic and line editor I could have. Thank you for not only helping me craft my words but encouraging me, understanding my creative drive and allowing me to be a part of your own creative world as well. I am amazed every day by your strength, your love, and your own personal journey. You were the very best gift to have ever entered my world. I love you.

Thank you to my big sister who wouldn't let me quit till I published, for always being my first alpha reader, and for telling me when I'm being stupid. Isn't that what siblings are for, after all? Ego checks and ego lifts!

Thank you to my parents who have been so proud of me that they show my book off wherever they go. To my mom, thanks for loving all my words even when they were oh so bad when I was a kid. And to my dad, thanks for reading my books even when they're romances novel instead of westerns.

Thank you to Megan Keith at Designed with Grace cover designs for not only my beautiful cover, but understanding the creative need in all of us. For reading my words and sharing them with the world when that wasn't part of your job. I'm blessed to have found you.

To Jenn at Jenn Lockwood Editing Services, thank you for being a partner in my creative process and for showing your love and support for my books. I never thought I could find someone who would completely get what I was trying to say even as a I rambled. Thank you.

Thank you to Karen Hrdlicka for making sure the book was perfect before it went live.

To the bloggers who have shared my stories with the world

on your own time and your own dime, I cannot say enough. The independent book world would not be what it is today without you. An extra special thank you to these bloggers who helped me get this book out into the world: Rachel at NovelMomma, Launa at Energy Rae, Ashleigh at Page Once Turned, Candyce at The Book Dutchesses, Heather at Books and a Blanket, Stacie at Boren Books, and Korrie the Curlyhairlass, as well as a whole host of other bloggers. If I didn't name you, it isn't because I appreciate you less. Thank you also to the ladies at Give Me Book PR for helping me share this story with a new group of readers.

To the other independent authors who have helped keep me sane on this journey, including Hannah Blake, Jami Albright, Mia Kayla, Annie Dyer, Kelsey Kingsley, Amanda Johnson, and Jennifer Hanks, I have not enough words. Thank you for sharing and supporting each other in ways that I never thought possible…without jealousy and while truly holding each other's crowns up when they fall. Hugs to all of you.

Thank you to Amy Harmon for not only inspiring me with your words but with your kindness and generosity. Every time I read your words, I'm encouraged to make mine better. Your talent truly blows me away.

Finally, but certainly not least, thank you to *my readers*. To those of you that I've come to know personally and those that I have not. Michelle Fritz, you are selfless and beautiful in all you do for us authors. Dee Shelvey thank you for making me smile very day when I've been ill. Michelle Odland, you allow me to be weak and then show me how I am strong, thank you. To Lisa and Leisa, I'm so happy that Guarded Dreams brought us together, and I can't thank you enough for sharing my stories everywhere you go. To Misty and Melissa, thank you for being with me since the beginning and also sharing my words all over the place. To every one of you who have read even one of my stories, *THANK YOU!*

About the Author

Award-winning author, LJ Evans, lives in Northern California with her husband, child, and the three terrors called cats. She's been writing, almost as a compulsion, since she was a little girl and will often pull the car over to write when a song lyric strikes her. A former first-grade teacher, she now spends her free time reading and writing, as well as binge-watching original shows like *Ted Lasso, Wednesday, Veronica Mars,* and *Stranger Things*.

If you ask her the one thing she won't do, it's pretty much anything that involves dirt—sports, gardening, or otherwise. But she loves to write about all of those things, and her first published heroine was pretty much involved with dirt on a daily basis, which is exactly why LJ loves fiction novels—the characters can be everything you're not and still make their way into your heart.

Her novels have won multiple awards including ***CHARMING AND THE CHERRY BLOSSOM,*** which was *Writer's Digest's* Self-Published E-book Romance of the Year in 2021. For more information about LJ, check out any of these sites:

www.ljevansbooks.com

FaceBook Group: LJ's Music & Stories

LJ Evans on Amazon, Bookbub, and Goodreads

@ljevansbooks on Facebook, Instagram, TikTok, and Pinterest

Books by LJ

Standalone

The Last One You Loved

A single-dad, small-town romance

He's a small-town sheriff with a secret that can unravel their worlds. She's an ER resident running from a costly mistake. Coming home will only mean heartache…unless they let forgiveness heal them both.

Charming and the Cherry Blossom

A contemporary romance with hints of magical realism

Today was a fairy tale…I inherited a fortune from a dad I never knew, and a charming guy asked me out. But like all fairy tales, mine has a dark side...and my happily ever after may disappear with the truth.

My Life as an Album Series

My Life as a Country Album — Cam's Story

A boy-next-door, small-town romance

Spirited athlete's Cam's diary-style, coming-of-age story about growing up loving the football hero next door. She vowed to love him forever. But when fate comes calling, will she ever find a heart to call home? Warning: Tears may fall.

My Life as a Pop Album — Mia & Derek

A rock-star, road-trip romance

Bookworm Mia is trying to put behind years of guilt when soulful musician, Derek Waters, strolls into her life and turns it upside down. Once he's seen her, Derek can't walk away unless Mia comes with him. But what will happen when their short time together ends?

My Life as a Rock Album — Seth & PJ

A second-chance, antihero romance

Growly, trash artist Seth Carmen knows he's better off alone. But when he finds and loses the love of his life, he sends her a series of love letters to try and win her back. Can he prove broken is beautiful?

<u>**My Life as a Mixtape**</u> — Lonnie & Wynn

A single-dad, rock-star romance

Lonnie's always seen relationships as a burden instead of a gift, and picking up the pieces his sister leaves behind is just one of the reasons. When Wynn enters his life just as her world is disintegrating, their mixed-up pasts give way to new beginnings neither saw coming.

<u>**My Life as a Holiday Album**</u> – 2nd Generation

A small-town romance

Come home for the holidays with this heartwarming, full-length standalone full of hidden secrets, true love, and the real meaning of family. Perfect for lovers of *Love Actually* and Hallmark movies, this sexy story twines the lives of six couples as they find their way to their happily ever after with the help of family and friends.

<u>**My Life as an Album Series Box Set**</u>

The 1st four Album series books + an exclusive novella

In the exclusive novella, *This Life with Cam*, Blake Abbott writes to Cam about just what it was like to grow up in the shadow of her relationship with Jake and just when he first fell for the little girl with the popsicle-stained lips. Can he show Cam that she isn't broken?

The Anchor Novels

<u>**Guarded Dreams**</u> — Eli & Ava

A grumpy-sunshine, military romance

Eli's chasing a dream that he's determined to succeed at, no matter the consequences. He isn't looking for love, but when the free-spirited singer, Ava, breezes into his world, he finds himself changing his tune.

<u>**Forged by Sacrifice**</u> — Mac & Georgie

A roommates-to-lovers, military romance

Mac is determined to change the world. A life in politics is his future. The dream Georgie once gave up is finally in reach—a law degree. When her family's past makes his future an impossibility, they have to decide just how much they're willing to sacrifice for love.

<u>**Avenged by Love**</u> — Truck & Jersey

A fake-marriage, military romance

Travis's focus is on his Coast Guard career and his brother's future. But once beautiful, comic-loving Jersey crashes into his world in desperate need of medical care, he offers a marriage of convenience to help. But what happens when convenience turns to love?

Damaged Desires — Dani & Nash

A frenemy, military romance

Nash is all about honoring a promise to his dead brother, so accepting a challenge from the long-legged force of nature tempting him isn't in the cards. Not if he wants to keep his only remaining friend and stick to the code he grew up on. Several dares later, he has to decide whether to continue hiding in his past or face a new future.

Branded by a Song — Brady & Tristan

A single-mom, rock-star romance

Brady's come home to help the sister he left behind and find inspiration for a new album. What he doesn't expect is to discover his muse in a woman who's completely off limits and lost in the past. Can he help her find the strength to sing a brand-new love song?

Tripped by Love – Cassidy & Marco

A broody-bodyguard, single-mom romance

Cassidy is juggling her restaurant, a tiny human, and unrequited love. There's no time for her ex to try and derail her. Marco is determined to bury the feelings he has for his boss's sister, but that doesn't mean he's going to let the sniveling father of her child steamroll her. What happens when a little white lie changes everything?

The Anchor Novels: The Military Bros Box Set

The 1st three slow-burn romances + an exclusive novella

Guarded Dreams, Forged by Sacrifice, and *Avenged by Love* plus the novella, *The Hurricane*!

The Anchor Suspense Novels

Unmasked Dreams — Violet & Dawson

A second-chance, age-gap romance

Violet and Dawson had a heart-stopping attraction they were compelled to deny. When they're tossed together again, it proves nothing has changed—except the lab she's built in the garage and the secrets he's keeping. When she stumbles into his dark world, Dawson is forced to break old promises to keep her safe. But when the swells subside, will their hearts still be intact?

<u>Crossed by the Stars</u> — Jada & Dax

A second-chance, forced-proximity romance

Family secrets meant Dax and Jada's teenaged romance was an impossibility. A decade later, the scars still remain, so neither is willing to give in to their tantalizing chemistry. But when a shadow creeps out of Jada's past, seeking retribution, it's Dax who shows up to protect her. And suddenly, it's hard to see a way out without permanent damage to their bodies and souls.

<u>Disguised as Love</u> — Cruz & Raisa

A chemistry-filled, enemies-to-lovers romance

Surly FBI agent, Cruz Malone, is determined to bring down the Leskov clan for good. If that means he has to arrest or bed the sexy blonde scientist of the family, so be it. Too bad Raisa has other ideas. There's no way she's just going to sit back and let the infuriating agent dismantle her world…or her heart.

The Painted Daisies

Interconnected, slow-burn romances with an all-female rock band, the alpha heroes who steal their hearts, and suspense that'll leave you breathless. Each story has its own HEA.

<u>Sweet Memory</u>

An opposite-side-of-the-tracks, second-chance romance.

Trouble—that's what her sister calls him. But she can't resist, not even when his past threatens her world.

<u>Green Jewel</u>

An enemies-to-lovers, single-dad romance.

He did it. She'll prove it. Her body's reaction to him be damned.

<u>Cherry Brandy</u>

An opposites-attract, forbidden romance.

Being on the run with only one bed is no excuse to touch her…until touching is the only choice.

<u>Blue Marguerite</u>

A Hollywood-celebrity, frenemy romance.

She may have to work with him to save her sister, but he'll never have her body or heart again.

<u>**Royal Haze**</u>

An antihero, secret-society romance.

He was ready to torture, steal, and kill to defend the world he believed in. What he wasn't prepared for…was her.

Free Stories

https://www.ljevansbooks.com/freeljbooks

<u>**Perfectly Fine**</u> – FREE with newsletter signup

A Hollywood, second-chance romance

He's a charming, A-list actor at the top of his game. She's a determined, small-town screenwriter hoping for a deal. They form an unexpected connection until heartbreak ruins their future.

<u>**Rumor**</u> – FREE with newsletter signup

A small-town, rock-star romance

There's only one thing rock star Chase Legend needs to ring in the new year, and that's to know what Reyna Rossi tastes like. After ten years, there's no way he's letting her escape the night without their souls touching. Reyna has other plans. After all, she doesn't need the entire town wagging their tongues about her any more than they already do.

<u>**Love Ain't**</u> – FREE with newsletter signup

A friends-to-lovers, cowboy romance

Reese knows her best friend and rodeo king, Dalton Abbott, is never going to fall in love, get married, and have kids. He's left so many broken hearts behind there's gotta be a museum full of them somewhere. So, when he gives her a look from under the brim of his hat, promising both jagged relief and pain, she isn't giving in.

<u>**The Long Con**</u> – FREE with newsletter signup

A sexy, antihero romance

Adler is after one thing: the next big payday. Then, Brielle sways into his world with her own game in play, and those aquamarine-colored eyes almost make him forget his number-one rule. But she'll learn…love isn't a con he's interested in.

<u>**The Light Princess**</u> – FREE with newsletter signup

An old-fashioned fairy tale

A princess who glows with a magical light, a kingdom at war, and a kiss that changes the world.